The story of Josephine Cox is as extraordinary as anything in her novels. Born in a cotton-mill house in Blackburn, Lancashire, she was one of ten children. Her parents, she says, brought out the worst in each other, and life was full of tragedy and hardship – but not without love and laughter. At the age of sixteen, Josephine met and married 'a caring and wonderful man' and had two sons. When the boys started school, she decided to go to college and eventually gained a place at Cambridge University, though was unable to take this up as it would have meant living away from home. However, she did go into teaching, while at the same time helping to renovate the derelict council house that was their home, coping with the problems caused by her mother's unhappy home life – and writing her first full-length novel. Not surprisingly, she then won the 'Superwoman of Great Britain' Award, for which her family had secretly entered her, and this coincided with the acceptance of her novel for publication.

Jo has given up teaching in order to write full time, and her nine previous novels have been immensely popular:

'Tension and drama . . . a book to read at one sitting!' *Prima*

'A classic is born' *Lancashire Evening Telegraph*

Don't Cry Alone

Josephine Cox

HEADLINE

First published in 1992
by HEADLINE BOOK PUBLISHING PLC

First published in paperback in 1993
by HEADLINE BOOK PUBLISHING PLC

10 9 8 7 6 5 4 3 2 1

ISBN 0 7472 3945 2

Printed and bound in Great Britain by
HarperCollins Manufacturing, Glasgow

HEADLINE BOOK PUBLISHING PLC
Headline House
79 Great Titchfield Street
London W1P 7FN

Many years ago, through traumatic circumstances, two delightful little girls were lost to our family. There followed a great deal of longing and heartache, although the girls themselves were deeply loved and cared for by the special couple who raised them.

Now, after more than thirty-five years, Rosa and Anne have been reunited with us. They are delightful people with young families of their own, and so we are doubly blessed. Nothing can ever replace those lost years. But our happiness will come from looking forward, not backward.

The story of Rosa and Anne is truly remarkable. Perhaps one day, when the painful memories are dimmed enough, the story will be told – by my sister Winifred, or by one of my newly found nieces, or maybe even by me, if I am allowed.

I am very proud to dedicate this book to Rosa and Anne.

Welcome home. We love you.

TO MY READERS

Many of you have told me how much you look forward to my dedications and that through them you see a glimpse of my own life. Without betraying too much, I can tell you that these little messages do tell a story all of their own.

Like any family, ours has its ups and down, its joys and sorrows, but beneath all of that is a great reservoir of love, and we always watch out for each other.

In the dedications, I might ask forgiveness of someone or ask them to come home, or I am fortunate enough to welcome a newborn into the fold. Often I thank a brother or sister or another member of the family for some kind gesture which has meant a lot to me. Sometimes I say goodbye to a dear one, or I may send a special message to a friend.

In answer to your pleas that I should write my autobiography, I can only apologise and say that I daren't even think about it. Too many loved ones would be hurt and shocked. Maybe one day I will write it, but it would be many years before it could be published.

Meanwhile, all of my novels do reveal the 'truth' in varying degrees, through authentic settings and realistic characters.

I always look forward to your lovely letters and comments.

Thank you so much, and God bless,
Josephine Cox

Contents

Part One

1886

FAMILIES

Chapter One

'I must be mad! What in God's name was I thinking of bringing you to a place like this?' Ben Ward shifted uncomfortably in his seat and stared at his sister with a look of horror. 'Honestly, Beth, your infatuation with Tyler Blacklock will get us both hung.'

Returning his stare with fierce dark eyes and a resolute expression on her lovely face, Beth reprimanded him in a quiet voice. 'You have no call to say that, Ben.' Her voice trembled slightly and at once the young man was filled with remorse. 'You know it isn't infatuation I feel for Tyler. I *love him*! And he loves me.' A hard look came into her eyes as she continued, 'I won't let *her* break us up . . . however hard she tries, or whatever threats she might use against me.' She glanced beyond him to where the howling wind was driving the rain into the carriage window. For a long unsettling moment she seemed entranced by the viciousness of the elements outside their safe haven. When she looked back into his face her expression was darker than the night. In a low foreboding voice she murmured, 'God forgive me, but sometimes I hate her.'

'No, Beth. You don't mean that.' He shook his head from side to side as though to will her words away. When she remained silent he took her hand in his, squeezing it so hard that she actually winced. 'You are your own worst enemy,' he whispered, his alarm betrayed in his voice.

He thought how exquisitely lovely she was, yet how dangerously rebellious. All the same, in spite of her tempestuous nature and even his own secret envy, he adored her. There was something very special about his sister. As far back as he could remember, she had entranced him with her spirit of adventure and her forthright nature. Her sense of fun and mischief was a joy to behold. As children, with only two years between them, they had been close, revelling in each other's company. His own nature was not so bold, not so defiant as Beth's. Where she led he followed; where he hesitated, she encouraged; and when Beth was made to suffer long lonely periods of isolation by their mother, he was her knight in shining armour, raiding the larder in the small hours and braving the dark to creep down to the cellar with a hunk of cheese or a muffin, which he would then feed under the door in tiny pieces.

As the years passed and matters worsened between their parents, Ben and Elizabeth looked to each other for comfort. They confided their childish secrets in each other, always hoping desperately that things might come right between Richard Ward and his wife. But they only worsened. Over the years, Beth and her mother came actively to dislike each other. It was a sad thing but inevitable, and, as much as Ben loved his wayward sister, he loved his mother more, so he learned not to take sides. In many ways he was like his father, preferring wherever possible a life without upheaval. Physically, he bore an uncanny resemblance to Richard Ward, being of the same squarish build and with light brown hair, although his father's locks were now somewhat thinner and faintly marbled with grey and, where Ben was of average height, his father was a lumbering giant of a man.

Beth had seemed to inherit the best from each of her parents, with the same small shapely figure as her mother but with thickly lashed dark eyes that were reminiscent of her father's – although, whereas Richard Ward betrayed very little emotion in his, Beth's were alive and passionate. Her beauty was bewitching. She preferred to leave her long brown hair loose down her back, but more often than not was obliged to wear it in a plump soft halo around her head. Tonight, in her haste to recruit the reluctant Ben and whisk him out of the house before they might be discovered, her hair flowed like a shimmering mantle about her small straight shoulders.

The carriage had reached its destination and was drawing into the kerbside. Turning to gaze at his sister, Ben sighed aloud. He knew in his bones that tonight was a great mistake and cursed himself for his part in it.

Knowing how her dislike for their mother troubled him, Beth leaned forward to place an affectionate kiss on his forehead. 'Forgive me,' she said tenderly, 'I should not have said such a thing.' But I can think it, she told herself. There was no love lost between her and her mother. Beth knew also that her own opinion of Esther Ward was shared all over London – especially in the rundown tenements and neglected houses that were ruthlessly demolished in the name of progress and without thought for the unfortunate souls who lived there. 'Let's not talk about her,' she said now, 'but I mean what I told you, Ben . . . I won't let her come between me and Tyler.'

'Oh, Beth!' he groaned aloud. 'You're so young . . . so vulnerable. She's only trying to protect you.' But he knew it went deeper than that. Esther Ward was a formidable woman who excelled in getting her own way. Her daughter, although possessed of a strong and determined character, was everything lovely and gentle in a woman. She had a compassionate heart, and as a rule she was very forgiving, but where her mother was concerned Beth's heart was cold. Too many times as a child she had offered her devotion to Esther Ward, only to have it rejected. Her childhood memories were still too vivid, too painful. She had known the kind of sorrow that did not pass with the years; she had seen the dark and cruel side of Esther Ward, and she could not find it in her heart to love her in the way she loved her father. Ben had seen the strangeness between his mother and sister, and had never really understood it. There was something awful between these two . . . something frightening. But then how could he expect Beth to forgive a mother who would shut her in the cellar for days on end, a small frightened child whose every word, every action, was seen as being a wicked challenge to her mother's authority? During these long periods of punishment even Beth's beloved dolls, bought by her father, would be confiscated. Richard Ward rarely intervened, for if he did then he too would be subjected to an endless tirade on his failings both as father and husband. Now, predictably, he was little more than a figurehead – always ready to offer advice and encouragement, but devoid of spirit. All his business energies were channelled through his wife.

'I don't need protection from Tyler.' Beth's dark eyes burned with conviction. 'He's a good man. You know that, don't you, Ben?' Her voice fell to a whisper. 'Strong and forthright. A man like Father once was.'

'Well, yes . . .' Ben was obliged to tell the truth. 'I believe Tyler Blacklock is a good man. But like I said, you come of reputable stock while he's . . .' He paused, his face flushing with embarrassment when she sharply intervened to finish the sentence for him. 'He's merely a labourer working for my father!'

After a short poignant silence while each deliberated on this angry exchange, Beth revealed, 'Your argument is not much different from Tyler's. When I saw him last, he tried to convince me that I'd be better off without him. Like you, he doesn't think he's good enough for me . . . constantly reminding me how our family is on the up and up and one day I will come into a sizeable inheritance. Do you know, he blames himself for the rift between me and . . . *her*.' She bowed her head, remaining silent for a while, her memories too bitter for words. Presently, she looked up and smiled. It was a sad smile, one that touched Ben deeply. 'Oh, I do love him so. And I know we could be happy together.' For a moment, just one fleeting moment, she was tempted to confide her secret in him. Instead, her dark eyes blazed defiantly. 'I wouldn't care if he swept the roads for a living. He's a good and decent man, proud and industrious. He was fifteen years old when they threw him out of that orphanage, eleven years ago. . .penniless, without a friend in the world. And look how he's improved himself. Why! You know how the foreman expects Tyler to keep an eye on the site when he himself is called away, and every manjack in Father's employ looks on Tyler with respect.'

'He's ambitious, I'll give you that.' Ben's face relaxed into a smile at his sister's fierce defence of the man she loved. 'And I believe he worships the ground you walk on, otherwise I would never have agreed to take part in this little escapade tonight.' Releasing a long drawn out sigh, he leaned back in the hard leather seat and raised his troubled brown eyes to the roof of the carriage. What he was doing was wrong, he knew that. And he reminded himself that, if they were to be discovered, the consequences – particularly for Beth – would be very grave indeed.

'Please, Ben. I must talk with him,' she pleaded softly. Only today she had overheard her mother arranging for Tyler to be dismissed from the Ward Development

Company. Even now, Beth feared it might be too late. Perhaps he had already left the area.

Ben looked into his sister's forlorn face, and the love he saw there made him both envious and afraid. For some inexplicable reason, it made him angry too. He wanted to destroy what Beth had with Tyler Blacklock, but, at the same time, hated himself for entertaining such destructive thoughts. Without a word he flung open the door and climbed down into the dark streets of a rain-swept September night. From darkened doorways and shadowy corners narrowed shifty eyes watched his every movement. It was Friday, the day when most working men received their meagre pay packets. Whitechapel was a place where labourers gathered to talk and sup after a long hard week. But like all populous places, Whitechapel attracted other creatures, more scurrilous and lethal than the rats who scavenged the sewers beneath the city.

Glancing up at Beth, Ben's voice carried a warning as he murmured, 'I hope you know what you're doing.' When she gave no response other than to plead with him to hurry, he shook his head, closed the door with a thud and called up to the driver, 'Wait here. I won't be long. And if you value the skin on your back, you'll keep your eyes peeled. Guard her with your life!'

'Don't you worry, Guv, they'll have to get through me afore they get to the lady.' The driver of the carriage was a shrivelled old fellow, with leathery skin and a mouth full of crooked, decaying teeth. When he laughed, as he did now, it was a most unpleasant sight. He was still chuckling as the young man made his way over the cobbles and into the narrow alley where the flickering glow from the gas lamps threw sinister shapes before him. It was a haunted place, a place where it was impossible for the carriage to follow. At its farthest end the night was bathed in a yellowish glow by the light emanating from the windows of a public house. The misty evening air was filled with the sound of gruff male voices uplifted in a melodious rendering of the song 'Danny Boy'. Deeply moved, and suddenly nostalgic, the carriage driver joined his own tuneless voice to the heartfelt crooning. "'From glen to glen and down the mountainside . . . for I'll be here in sunshine or in shadow, oh, Danny Boy, oh, Danny Boy, I love you so."' Like many of these dockers and labourers, he too had long ago left his old mammy back home in the green hills of Ireland. For the briefest moment a kind of sadness settled on him, but then his heart was gladdened by the singing. Oblivious of all else and forgetting the young man's specific instructions, he was soon lost in the magic of it all, with his own comical discord soaring above the sound of voices issuing from the public house; all of this to the keen interest of two dubious-looking characters who ambled a little closer in order to peer into the carriage more easily.

Unaware that she was being observed, Beth closed her eyes and settled back in the seat, her mind heavy with thoughts of Tyler, and her troubled heart spilling over with love for him.

Was it really just a year since their first meeting? A smile played around the corners of her mouth as she recalled the incident in Regent Street. It was a few days before her twenty-third birthday – a day not unlike today, with the rain lashing down in a bitter cold wind that penetrated even the thickest layers of clothing. She remembered how desperately unhappy she had been, after fleeing from the house during a particularly harrowing scene between her mother and father. Listening from the hallway, she had desperately willed her father to assert his authority and for once – just once – win the argument. But as always he conceded to Esther Ward's domineering nature. As a consequence a whole terrace of houses and the families living there became innocent casualties of what was arrogantly termed 'progress', but what was in fact just another means of making money . . . a 'business transaction' that took no account of homelessness and broken hearts.

For a long time afterwards, Beth found it difficult, almost impossible, to forgive her father. But beneath her disgust and frustration, she could not help but love that gentle giant, believing him to be as much a victim as the people whose homes were swept away in the wake of her mother's relentless pursuit of power. Yet, in spite of her love for her father, Beth could not entirely rid herself of a deep sense of outrage at his weakness. This outrage found many outlets – not least of which was Beth's rebellious attitude to the position which her mother had arranged for her at the finest milliner's in London. Convinced that she could be more gainfully employed, Beth had appealed to her father. He in turn had appealed to Esther. The astonishing result was that Beth found herself installed as clerk in the family's land development business. It was during her work here that she discovered further details about her mother's malign influence.

On that day when she had fled from the house, when Tyler's swift and courageous action had saved her from being crushed beneath the wheels of a carriage and four, she had found him a wonderful friend and companion. It wasn't long before that friendship deepened into a strong abiding love.

Leaning forward to look out of the window in the expectation that her brother might be returning with Tyler, Beth did not see the two suspicious characters stealing up ever closer to the carriage. Even as she watched the alley intently, their outstretched grimy fingers were reaching towards her.

* * *

Inside the bar, the singing had reached a crescendo of such volume that nothing could be heard above it. Pushing his way through the surging bodies, Ben sighed with relief when at last he saw the familiar figure of Tyler Blacklock; his tall physique, broad shoulders, and mop of blue-black shoulder-length hair were unmistakable.

'Tyler! . . . Tyler Blacklock!' His voice was lost in the din. Undeterred and anxious that Beth should be returned home before she was missed, he thrust forward, hastily elbowing any obstacle out of the way, to numerous shouts of 'Hey! Steady on, mate' and 'What's yer bloody game?' Once or twice he was good-naturedly embraced and encouraged to 'Give us a song, yer bugger!' Explaining that he was in a hurry, his eyes smarting from the thick layers of pipe-smoke that swirled in the air like so much grey fog, he ploughed a way through to his quarry. The acrid stench of booze and sweat hung round him like a clinging vapour. Now, as he burst through the warm writhing barrier of bodies, he all but fell headlong into Tyler Blacklock.

Swinging round to face him, Tyler's exclamation was one of astonishment. 'Ben! What in God's name are you doing here?' His ebony-green eyes flicked over and beyond the young man's head, as though searching for something . . . someone. Mingled relief and disappointment momentarily showed on his handsome features before he returned his quizzical gaze to Ben.

'You might well ask,' he gasped. 'I've asked myself that more than once tonight. It's Beth. She intended to find you this evening – with or without my help. And I certainly wasn't going to let her roam the streets of Whitechapel on her own.'

'What!' Tyler was horrified. Grabbing the younger man by the shoulders he demanded, 'Are you telling me you've brought your sister here . . . to a place like

11

this? Good God, man! Have you lost your mind? Don't you know there's a murderer on the loose hereabouts?' His eyes widened with fear and his grip on the other man became so ferocious that Ben actually cried out.

When Tyler impatiently shoved him aside and pressed his way through the multitude of burly figures that barred his path, Ben careered after him, calling out, 'I've left her in the carriage, with strict instructions to the driver. She's safe enough from any "Ripper".' His loud and desperate statement brought a stunned hush to all who heard it. There had been murders hereabouts, savage unspeakable atrocities that chilled the blood of ordinary decent folk. The ensuing silence, and the fearful murmurings that followed, sent a rush of awful anticipation through the hastily departing men. However, the revellers' anxiety lasted only as long as they could see both the men who had so openly talked of the 'Ripper'. This was Friday night and their pockets were jangling with the weight of coins. Every manjack there was merry with the flush of booze, his loins warm in anticipation of lying between the soft white thighs of some fortunate woman. Whether she would be his own long-suffering wife or one of the many painted floozies who fell too easily into a man's arms, only the night, and the extent to which the flow of booze had dimmed the fellow's wits, would tell. For now the hour was young enough and the company not too demanding. Soon, their deep gruff voices were raised once more in song, and the doors swung to behind the departing men, shutting out both the night and the creeping shadows.

As they rushed out of the building and on to the dimly lit street, both men were instantly alerted to the scuffle taking place at the mouth of the alley. Dragged from his lofty place, the carriage driver was courageously grappling with one of the burly attackers, while inside the carriage an even fiercer struggle was going on. 'God

Almighty, she's in trouble! Beth's in trouble!' Ben's frantic cry soared above the din. Tyler was already running, but on hearing the shout, surged forward, his face set like granite and his powerful fists clenched in readiness. Leaving Ben to help fight off the rogue who was attacking the driver, he flung open the carriage door to launch himself on the dark bulky figure that was writhing with another on the floor of the carriage.

Tyler's intervention was not a moment too soon. When the intruder pounced, Beth soon found herself pressed between the two seats, bucking and fighting, her small sharp nails scoring the podgy flesh of her assailant's face and causing him to cry out. But he was not deterred by her spirited defence, seeming only to become even more excited. Thrusting his arms out to grasp her flailing fists into his own, he leaned into her, his putrid breath fanning her face. 'Feisty little bitch, ain't yer?' he growled, his tiny smiling eyes almost lost in the ugly rise of pock-marked flesh above each cheekbone. Pinning Beth in a twisted painful position where she found herself unable to move, he inched his grotesque body forward, rising and falling on her in anticipation of imminent pleasures.

His hopes were swiftly shattered when an iron grip locked itself round the scruff of his jacket and hoisted him effortlessly through the air. 'Hey! What the bleeding . . . ?' His shout became a muffled moan when Tyler's bunched knuckles caught him full force in the face. Reeling with pain he fell backwards, blood spurting from his nose. His instincts caused him to reach into his pocket. Tyler never saw the knife. He felt only the sharp searing pain as the blade sliced deep into his shoulder, then again into the soft flesh of his upper arm as the ruffian fell on him, drawing out the blade with the intention of sinking it deep into Tyler's heart. But he hadn't reckoned on the awesome strength of his opponent. During the ensuing bitter struggle, and though Tyler was badly injured, the ruffian was soon fighting for his own miserable life.

In desperation he pitched himself through the open carriage door to land with a muffled thud on the hard jutting cobbles below. Without pausing for a backward look, he seized his chance and fled down the narrow alley. Finding himself outnumbered, his accomplice soon followed suit, the sound of their retreating footsteps echoing into the night, and the old man's voice screaming after them, 'Garn, yer cowardly buggers! What kinda rascal sets on an old feller an' a helpless lady? Shame on yer! SHAME ON YER!'

'You did well, old man,' Ben reassured him, at the same time retrieving the old one's cap from the cobbles and handing it to him. For all his bravado, it was clear the old fellow was badly shaken.

Beth was even more so. When Tyler drew her out from the small space beneath the seat where she had been trapped, she felt mortally ashamed. The front of her blouse was ripped open, exposing the milk-white skin of her breasts; her hair was dishevelled and there were angry red scratches running down her neck. In the soft light from the street lamp, she saw the look of horror on Tyler's face as he lovingly folded her into his arms. His voice was low and trembling as he reassured her, 'You're all right, sweetheart. You're safe now.' When he felt her shiver against him, his voice became hard as he asked gently, 'Did he . . . did that swine . . . ?'

She raised her head. The look in his eyes was terrible to see. 'No,' she murmured.

One word, just one word. It was enough. Relief flooded his face. 'Thank God! I swear, Beth . . . there would have been no hiding place for him!' Now he turned his anger on her, 'What in God's name was so desperately important that you could even *think* of coming into Whitechapel . . . especially at this time of night?'

'I had to see you.' Her dark eyes were filled with pain. 'I know I promised to think about . . . our relationship . . . to give it a week before we saw each other. But, oh Tyler, I don't need to think about us. *I love you*. I was so afraid you planned to go away.'

'Without telling you?' Half smiling, he shook his head. Suddenly, the pain was like a tide inside him. His shoulder was on fire and he could feel both blood and strength ebbing away. Even as his eyes sought Beth's loveliness and his arms crushed her to him, his senses were dimming. When Ben poked his head into the carriage he was greeted with, 'You should never have brought her here! For God's sake, Ben, get her home.' Slipping out of his jacket, Tyler wrapped it about her naked shoulders. 'Take care of her, Ben.'

'I won't go until you agree to see me. Tomorrow!' She was adamant.

Gently pushing her into the seat, Tyler promised. 'We *will* talk, Beth. You have my word on it.'

'Tomorrow.'

'Soon.'

'*Tomorrow!*'

In the lamplight her dark eyes appraised him, boldly studying his features, the handsome strongly chiselled features, the thick wayward hair that fell over his forehead like dark splashes against a bronze canvas, and the eyes, darkly green, intense. Now, her gaze fell to his chin, square and determined, the broad muscular shoulders . . . a sense of fear flickered through her. *Something was wrong!* In an instant she was on her feet, her outstretched hands reaching towards the vivid ruddy stain that ran from his shoulder and was spreading even as she watched. 'BEN!' Her shrill cry echoed into the night. She glanced towards the doorway where her brother was already clambering into the carriage. 'He's badly hurt,' she said, her dark eyes frantic.

One look at the wound confirmed it. 'She's right,' Ben agreed. 'You've lost a deal of blood.' Ignoring the other man's protests, Ben eased him on to the seat. 'We've got to get you to the Infirmary . . . and quickly.'

'No Infirmary!'

'Don't be crazy, man. You're bleeding to death.'

'Just get Beth home.' Tyler's only thought was that she should be taken home as quickly as possible after her frightening ordeal. He suspected also that she had defied her parents in coming here. Tonight's experiences had only confirmed what he had always believed – that, in loving Beth, he would bring her nothing but trouble.

'*I'll* be the one to decide when I should go home,' Beth told him angrily. Turning to the driver, who was leaning in at the doorway, she ordered, 'The Infirmary . . . and for God's sake, hurry!' Alarmed, he nodded and began to scurry away.

'NO!' Tyler's harsh shout brought the driver back to the doorway. Realising that he was rapidly losing consciousness, and knowing how Beth would have insisted on accompanying him into the Infirmary, with all its consequences, Tyler appealed to her brother. 'No Infirmary, Ben,' he murmured. 'Send the carriage to my home, number twelve Lewisham Street.' In that moment before his senses slipped away, he saw the other man nod in agreement. Ben understood. He knew his sister better than most. All the same, the younger man was mortally afraid that, in complying with Tyler's instructions, he was condemning him to certain death.

Chapter Two

'If you don't mind my saying so, Miss Ward, you look as though you've got the weight of the world on your pretty little shoulders.' Tom Reynolds was a small shrewish man with silver hair and a disturbing habit of watching people with such intensity that often they were driven to take refuge out of his sight. It was well known that he suffered an intolerably lonely life, his only company being a mangy terrier who possessed a fierce and uncontrollable appetite for human flesh. On the one occasion when Tom had brought the animal to work with him, it had created such pandemonium that Richard Ward was obliged to send his chief clerk home with the unfortunate creature – offering him the choice of returning to the office alone, or not returning at all.

The remaining two office staff – an aged dogsbody by the unlikely name of Methias Worry, and a giggly young woman with a unique talent for soothing irate business clients – had each secretly hoped that the despicable little man might choose not to return. However, he did, and Richard Ward for one breathed a sigh of relief, for though Tom Reynolds was without doubt a born trouble maker, and somewhat evil in character, he was also extremely clever and meticulous in everything he did. Not one brass farthing escaped his eagle eye, not a single mistake was allowed to pass his scrutiny. Using his ill-gotten skills, he had slyly wormed his way into Esther Ward's personal favour when he discreetly brought it to her attention that a certain Tyler Blacklock – on the payroll of the Ward Development Company – had 'dared to set his cap at your daughter'. Then, not satisfied with causing enough mischief to rouse Esther Ward's darkest suspicions, he had gone on to point out how he felt it was his '. . . bounden duty to report how I saw the young man in question, in the company of your daughter, strolling through Regent's Park, with all the world looking on'. Later, when Richard Ward was in turn confronted by his wife, he felt obliged to question the source of her information. Realising that in Tom Reynolds she had discovered a snoop who might well be of use in the future, Esther Ward had refused to disclose the source. Consequently, Richard was obliged to demand an explanation from Beth herself – and so the truth was out.

Beth did not regret that. She regretted only that her love for Tyler had created an even deeper rift between her father and mother. She suspected that Tom Reynolds was at the root of it all and many was the time when she had been sorely tempted to accuse him outright, but she had no proof and knew how invaluable he was to her father's business. Reluctantly she had let the matter lie. But she made no secret of her dislike for the fellow. It was in her eyes as she glared at him now, and it was in her voice when she told him coolly, 'How kind of you to trouble yourself about me, Mr Reynolds, but, there is no need, I assure you.'

Leaning on the edge of the small mahogany desk, he continued to stare at her, his tiny pinkish eyes slitted in a half smile, his whole face slyly contorted. He thought her to be inordinately proud. Proud and bewitching. And desirable. Oh, yes! He thought that, in particular, Elizabeth Ward was desirable; the most desirable creature he had ever set eyes on. If he regretted anything at all in his life, it was that he had never had a woman;

that he did not yet know what it was to experience that certain power over women which most men enjoyed. He laughed inwardly. Most men maybe, but not his employer Richard Ward, because he was thumb-nailed, dictated to and manipulated, with the same ingenious skill with which that foolish man's own ledger-clerk manipulated the figures put before him. But then, what man could rise above a ruthless woman the likes of Esther Ward? Such a woman could suck a man dry, and was to be avoided at all costs; unless, of course, a body could make himself useful to her in a subtle way that might bring its own reward . . . Her daughter Elizabeth, though! Now, there was a different kettle of fish altogether. She was a woman to be watched, to be coolly desired at the busy time of day or craved in the dark solitude of a long lonely night. She was a woman of exceptional spirit and beauty. Oh, but what chance would a man like him have, especially with the Tyler Blacklocks of this world to sweep such a woman off her feet? No chance at all . . . *on the face of things*. But he was not a man of faint heart. On the contrary, he was most vigilant, alert to every opportunity that might fall his way; and though his hair was white, he was still a man only two and thirty years of age. Passion flowed through his loins in exactly the same way as it did through the loins of any man. Oh, but he was cunning too. More cunning, he'd be bound, than any other man on the face of the earth. Cunning in every way imaginable. And his cunning was never sharper than it was now, at the very moment when he found his gaze locked with the bold and beautiful dark eyes of Elizabeth Ward. Straightening his slight form he told her in a syrupy voice that sent a shiver down her back, 'I'm glad to hear that, Miss Ward. However, should you feel the need to confide in a fellow, or to seek comfort from anything that might be troubling you . . .' His smile broadened and he paused for a moment. Then, in a more intimate voice, he murmured, 'You only have to ask.' He reached out to touch her, but when she instinctively backed away his small eyes glittered angrily. 'There may come a day,' he told her in an unpleasant voice, 'when you will be glad of my friendship.' He knew of Beth's unhappy relationship with her mother and he had long sensed trouble brewing there.

The brief response Beth afforded him was half-heartedly to incline her head and tell him patiently, 'If you don't mind . . . I do have a great deal of work to do.'

'Of course! Of course!' He sensed her dislike, and it rankled with him. How he would have enjoyed turning her dislike around; perhaps even to admiration. He wondered whether such a thing could ever be, and not for the first time felt a pang of bitterness. But the feeling was short-lived. Almost at once his arrogance rose above it. Time and patience, he thought, and a deal of precious cunning; worthy virtues that had been known to work wonders – and in all truth, there was no man more aware of time than he was; no man more patient, no man more devious, and no man more ruthless when it came to the bare bones of an intriguing puzzle, especially when that certain 'puzzle' was a lady of exceptional loveliness. But of course, beauty was not Elizabeth Ward's only attribute, although he was not really one to dwell on such things as money and prospects; however he could not deny how gratifying it was to see the Ward Development Company gaining a very important footing and enviable reputation in its own particular market. He had always thought himself to be a man of simple tastes. But men changed, some-times out of all recognition. More often than not it was a woman who changed them – and since Elizabeth Ward had graced this small office with her exquisite presence, he found himself changing by the day. Now, when he turned away from Beth, he felt like the cat who had got the cream. Or a taste of it.

Inwardly relieved when the obnoxious little man moved away, she bent her head to her duties and, as always, her thoughts turned to the man she loved. So much had happened in the week following the attack in Whitechapel. One thing in particular, causing Beth many sleepless nights and making her fearful for the future. Even now she had not dared to breathe her awful secret to anyone; not even to the very person who could put her mind at rest.

'Penny for them, Miss Ward.' Methias Worry had stood in front of Beth for some minutes before he ventured to coax her from her deep reverie.

'Oh!' She glanced up, a look of guilt written on her face which the old man was quick to perceive. 'I'm sorry,' she said, a slight blush refreshing her unusually pale and pinched features.

The old fellow nodded his head. 'Daydreaming, was you?' He chuckled. 'And why not, eh? A young and pretty little thing such as yourself.'

Congenial and much respected, Methias Worry knew when to mind his own business. It was obvious that Richard Ward's delightful daughter had more on her mind than the requirements and problems of their many clients. Even a blind man could see that she had far greater problems of her own; problems that weighed heavy on her. The friction between Elizabeth Ward and her own mother was not a very well kept secret, and no doubt that state of affairs was as much a heartache to the young lady as it was to her father. All the same, Methias somehow felt that Beth's troubled mood had little to do with her mother. He believed it was something far closer to her heart.

There had been rumours concerning a certain young

man by the name of Tyler Blacklock, the very same who had not been seen at work for over a week now, the very same who, if he *had* returned to the site, would have found his marching orders waiting for him. Esther Ward had given the instructions herself. Tyler Blacklock was never again to be given work on any site associated with the Ward Development Company. That vindictive woman had also made it her business to warn other companies as to the young man's 'unreliable and suspect nature'. They had no real reason to doubt her word, for though she was known to be a ruthless and formidable creature, she had earned herself a greater reputation for being unusually knowledgeable in the field of land conveyancing, this being all the more astonishing since she was a woman. Good builders were hard to find and quite often the construction gangs were packed with rogues and ruffians. One bad word against a particular labourer and he would find himself frozen out of every working site in London. Esther Ward had put the word out on Tyler Blacklock. The name would be remembered. The man himself would be avoided at all costs.

Beth greeted the old fellow with a warm and genuine smile. 'What's that you've got there, Methias?' she asked, pointing to the sheaf of papers clutched in his gnarled fingers. 'More work for me, is it?'

'I'm afraid so, Miss,' he told her, his wide grin displaying a surprisingly good set of teeth. He was always most proud to boast that: 'Good teeth is a blessing that runs right through the generations. Good strong teeth that'll tek me to me grave an' last a blessed sight longer than old Methias hisself!' It was a pity his old bones did not serve him so well, because as he bent forward to place the documents on Beth's desk, his joints were heard to creak in protest. 'Your father requested a duplicate of these plans and the schedule of work so far carried out. I understand he's calling back to the office before he makes his way home. He wants the originals locked into the safe as always, but the others he wants to examine at leisure this evening.' He squinted at the clock high on the wall behind her. 'It's almost four-thirty now,' he told her, glancing around as though afraid to see Richard Ward walk into the office. Shaking his balding head he explained how his ordinary work had piled up because 'These papers were more complex than I realised', and that was the reason it had taken him most of the afternoon to go through the legalities. 'So, if you'd be so kind, Miss, I wonder if you might put aside whatever you're working on and prepare the duplicates.' He lapsed into an uncomfortable silence, as though suddenly realising that he was talking to the boss's daughter, but then he reminded himself that Elizabeth Ward carried no airs and graces. Indeed, she seemed like any one of them, always friendly and eager to do her share of the work. Her industrious attitude was most welcome because as yet this particular company was only just beginning to acquire major contracts. Even now it was early days, and Richard could not afford to take on the extra staff needed. 'I know I should have had them done an hour ago, and I know it doesn't give you much time, but I would be that grateful, Miss . . . seeing as how your father did say they were important.' A look of anxiety shaded his features and he began nodding nervously, the way he always did when he thought he was about to be reprimanded.

'That's all right, Methias,' she reassured him, thinking how insignificant the old fellow's problem seemed compared to hers. 'Leave the papers with me. I had intended leaving early today, but I promise I'll have them ready before I go.'

'Bless you, Miss.' He made a curious little bow and

deposited the papers with a flourish on her desk. 'I wouldn't want Mrs Ward to think I was not doing my duties in a proper fashion.'

'Nobody will think that of you,' Beth told him, at the same time making a point of collecting the documents and placing them immediately before her. She was not surprised that he had been more concerned about what her mother might think of him. The old man's instructions had come from Richard, but no doubt it was Esther who wanted to scrutinise the papers. A quick glance at the title page had told Beth that they referred to a new and important acquisition. It was her father who had skilfully beaten off other commercial rivals in order to secure the prestigious site. Thankfully, this time there were no evictions. The site was a disused brickfield covering three acres of prime land and situated close to New Road in Marylebone. It was one of the few remaining sites left in that particular area, and was keenly pursued by a number of large, lucrative companies. It said a lot for Richard Ward's business acumen that he had secured the site in the face of such fierce competition. Sadly, Inner London was now almost entirely built over, with only the odd site being offered for redevelopment. As a consequence, most landowners had long turned their attention to renewing and redeveloping properties on which leases were starting to fall due.

'Thank you again, Miss.' Inclining his head in a quaint manner, Methias shuffled away. He was an old man with no income other than the wages he was paid here. The thought of being thrown out of work made him tremble in his boots.

Realising that he had set her an arduous task, Beth got straight to work on duplicating the material, all the while acutely aware that Tom Reynolds was slyly observing her from the other side of the room.

Some time later she glanced up at the clock. It

was almost six – the hour when the office normally closed. The work for Methias had taken longer than she had anticipated. As yet, though, her father had not returned to the office. Beth was thankful for that. There had been so much friction at home this week, and though on lesser matters she might be tempted to confide in her father, she found that she was both afraid and ashamed to face him now. Yet mingled with her fear and shame was great pride and joy. All the same, it would have been wonderful to share her secret with someone; with her brother Ben perhaps, or with a friend. Ben, however, was already regretting his part in the conspiracy, and thanks to her strict and closeted upbringing Beth had never learned how to make friends. But she must share her 'secret' soon, and with the one person who mattered more to her than life itself. With this comforting thought in mind, she put on her coat, pulled the blue woollen beret over her thickly coiled hair, and calling out a cheery 'goodnight' to her colleagues, hurried across the small wood-panelled office and made her way towards the door.

'Surely you don't intend leaving just yet, Miss Ward?' Tom Reynolds had watched as Beth prepared to leave. Now he was blocking her way. 'The weather's atrocious,' he told her with a sweet and deadly smile, 'there won't be a cab to be had. Not anywhere. But, if you wouldn't mind waiting until everyone else has gone and I'm able to lock up, I'll make it my business to get you home safely.' His eyes devoured her. 'You would find me to be excellent company.' He smiled, and his meaning was unmistakable.

Beth's curt reply belied her feeling of revulsion. 'That's very kind of you, Mr Reynolds, but I'm sure I can manage.' A bubble of wickedness rose in her as she added with a delicious little smile, 'However, I'm quite sure my father will be very pleased to know how concerned you are for my welfare.' It was as she suspected. The colour drained from his face at the thought of Richard knowing how his clerk had made advances towards Beth. He did not delude himself that his employer had any fondness for him.

'Goodnight then,' he answered, his face set tight as he stepped aside. There was bitterness in him, and the longer he gazed on her lovely face, the desire to take her for himself grew all consuming.

Amused by his grim expression, Beth nodded gratefully. Then, without another word, she quickly opened the door and emerged on to the pavement, with the rain pouring down on her. Drawing up her collar and holding the tapestry bag above her head to keep off the downpour, she found herself smiling; he was right about one thing, she told herself – the weather really was atrocious.

A quick glance down Catherine Court told her she would need to hurry if she was to secure a cab. Already the black-hooded Hansom carriages could be seen vying for fares in Trinity Square. At this time of the evening many office workers deserted their dreary workrooms for the warmth and cheeriness of their own cosy hearthside, and on this wet and windy Friday a thin line of dark-clad figures could already be seen threading its way down to the square. Concerned that her father might show at any minute, and desperate to make her way as quickly as possible to Lewisham Street, Beth threw caution and decorum to the winds. Plucking the hem of her skirt from around her ankles, and bending her head low against the driving rain, she ran down Catherine Court in a most unlady-like fashion, gasping when the wind was knocked out of her as she collided with Martin Drury, a fat and miserable wine merchant. 'Really!' he snorted, glowering at her from beneath wet spidery eyebrows as he struggled to remain upright.

'Sorry, Mr Drury,' she called, skilfully wending her way in and out of the astonished figures, before halting breathlessly on the kerbside, soaked to the skin and waving her tapestry bag at the driver of an approaching Hansom. By the time the cab drew up alongside, the throng had caught up with Beth and there was a deal of pushing and shoving from behind – the biggest culprit being the fat wine merchant who took great delight in rudely wedging himself between Beth and the carriage door. But he hadn't reckoned on her determination. When the heel of her dainty boot ground itself into the toes of his black shiny shoes, his round face screwed into a grimace of pain, then fell open with astonishment as she pushed in front of him and clambered into the carriage.

Having witnessed the incident with some amusement, the carriage driver was still grinning when he asked 'Where to, Miss?' When he was given his destination, the smile slipped from his face. First he wiped his damp hand over his thin bony face, then gave in to a fit of coughing, then he took his top hat off and shook the rain from it. Then he stared intently at Beth through the spyhole in the roof. When he realised she was not about to change her instructions, he shrugged his narrow shoulders, coughed again, closed the spyhole and turned his attention to the restless beast between the shafts. It was a grey day and, like his master, the big piebald was not in the best of moods. 'As you say,' the driver grumbled resignedly. 'Number twelve Lewisham Street.' When he pulled away, the black carriages behind were soon filled with wet and weary passengers. Before long there was not a single soul left standing on the pavement. Not even the fat wine merchant.

* * *

Beth never tired of the sights and sounds of the old city. Rain, shine, wind or snow . . . the streets of London were always bustling and alive to the sounds of vendors calling out the virtues of their wares, and urging the milling crowds to 'Treat yerselves today' or 'Get yer 'ot chestnuts 'ere'. There were flower-sellers, old bent men walking the pavements with sandwich-boards strapped to their backs, dare-devils on penny-farthings diving in and out of the horse-drawn vehicles, and newspaper stalls fronted by large posters carrying scandalous and newsworthy stories in big bold letters. The huge undertaking to construct a tower bridge linking the two banks in the dockside area commanded much interest, as did the running saga of events stemming from the unrest long felt by the working class. A series of demonstrations and riots in Trafalgar Square had evoked political and public awareness, and all of this was much reported and commented upon.

As the carriage neared her destination, Beth prepared to alight. Lewisham Street was in a rundown part of London; an area of grim and pitiful dwellings that should have been razed to the ground years before. Inhabited by poor but proud people whose worldly possessions consisted mainly of children, the street was bedecked with a profusion of Creeping Jenny plants and other various blooms adorning every window sill; in amongst these trailing gardens were many tiny cages containing numerous singing birds, mainly thrushes and bullfinches, whose melodious voices filled the alley with song. The people here might be deprived and stricken with poverty of the worst kind, but they would not be depressed. Hardy and bold, they were filled with a special kind of hope, a breed to themselves, looking out for each other and making the best of what little they had.

'Are you sure you're gonna be all right, Miss?' The

driver peered at Beth as she reached up her gloved
hand to pass him the fare. He glanced nervously about,
acutely aware of many watchful eyes . . . some slyly
regarding him from behind discreetly moved curtains,
others openly observing him from grimy doorways. He
had been surprised when the young lady had instructed
him to take her to Lewisham Street – a place which he
had not encountered before in his short employment
with the cab firm, but an area which he was given to
understand did not enjoy many visitors . . . apart from
the landlord and the tally-man, the milkman and, on a
Sunday maybe, the winkle-man, who was not particular
where he plied his trade.

The rain had cleared now, and folk were beginning to venture outside. Nearby, an old woman with
weathered skin and a toothless smile manoeuvred her
three-legged stool on to the pavement, promptly seating
herself beside the front door of her little house with
its astonishingly sparkling windows and pretty floral
curtains – the latter no doubt cadged or 'borrowed'
from someone more fortunate than herself. Children
spilled on to the cobbled road, rolling hoops through
the puddles and chasing each other with much glee,
delighted to be outside where they could run wild
and make as much noise as they liked. All down the
street, doors began to open and chairs were fetched
out. Big black perambulators appeared, complete with
excited grubby little occupants. Women sat in small busy
groups, chatting and chuckling, and at once the street
was transformed – as bustling and vibrantly alive as any
market-place on a Saturday.

Smiling up at the driver, Beth assured him, 'I'll be
fine, thank you.' The thought of seeing Tyler filled her
heart with joy and all her earlier anxieties seemed to
melt away.

'As you say, Miss,' he conceded with a nod of his head.

'I'll be on my way then.' He raised his long leather whip and gently tickled the horse's rump with it. When the animal began moving forward at a leisurely pace, he made a loud clicking noise to send it on at a trot. As the big wooden wheels whipped up the rain from the gutter, Beth stepped smartly away, although the hem of her dress was already soaked and her cape sodden. Her hair was hanging damply in wisps round her face and shoulders. Now, as she made her way towards number twelve, she shivered openly. Already she felt a chill settling on her.

Number twelve was one of the larger terraced houses and, like many of the more enterprising tenants who were not encumbered by hordes of children, the lady of the house had turned a number of rooms over to boarders. Being governed by certain rules and regulations, she was careful not to broadcast her services too far and wide, although – provided they received the lion's share of any revenue – the owners pretty well turned a blind eye. But there were always more unscrupulous landlords willing to make capital out of other people's misfortunes. Consequently many of London's big houses were subdivided so drastically that often large families, mostly poor immigrants, were forced to live together in one or two pitifully small rooms.

Florence Ball, however, was as wily and cunning as the best of 'them toffee-nosed buggers who think they're one above the rest on us!' She was well practised in the art of shepherding her three boarders into a 'safe' place whenever the landlord arrived on her doorstep. Always suspicious, ever alert when the door knocker sounded like a death knell through the big old house, she would inch the door open and ask a body's business before either reluctantly admitting them, or advising them in loud and delightfully vulgar tones to 'Piss off!'

Never sure how her own arrival might be greeted,

Beth lifted the iron knocker and rapped it gingerly against the oak panel. She waited for what seemed a lifetime before slow shuffling footsteps could be heard making their way along the passage. When the footsteps came to a halt, Beth tapped on the door with her clenched knuckles. A moment, then the footsteps started again. They stopped immediately on the other side of the door. 'Who is it?' The voice was sharp and rasping, laden with fear and suspicion.

'It's me . . . Elizabeth Ward.' Beth leaned forward to speak through the letter-box. At once the metal flap was lifted and a pair of beady bloodshot eyes appeared out of the gloom. 'It's only me,' Beth said again. 'I've come to see Mr Blacklock.'

'Hmph!' The voice snorted, and the flap dropped with a clatter. There was a deal of muttering and a series of sounds that told Beth she was about to be admitted. When the door was flung open, it was to reveal a sight that had become all too familiar to her during this past week. A woman of some forty years, Florence Ball was neither handsome nor sociable; instead, she was a shock on first sight and a curiosity ever after; always dressed in the same shapeless frock beneath a grey pinny, and being curiously bloated and round. She was destined to keep her apt surname until the end of her days, for there had never been a man brave enough to give her his own. Her grey hair was wild and unusually thick, springing from her head to form an unbecoming halo round her wrinkled features. Numerous fine flyaway hairs poked from her cavernous nostrils and broad chin, giving her the frightful appearance of a walrus. The eyes were small, the nose too bulbous, and the loose mouth always hanging open – 'ready to catch a bluebottle', her daughter said with some cruelty.

Eyeing Beth with the same suspicion she might regard any stranger, the unfortunate woman told her with some indignation, 'I know very well who you've come to see . . . though I can't hardly fathom why a lady of your sort should hanker after the likes of Tyler Blacklock.' Amused by her own bold observation, and the obvious fact that these two were strongly drawn to each other, she softly chuckled, all manner of lewd thoughts stirring her vivid imagination. 'Ah, but then again,' she murmured beneath her breath, 'happen I can . . . happen I can. And who's to blame yer, eh? He's a fine figure of a man an' no mistake. An' I should know, seeing as how I've stripped him naked an' bathed him more often than I care to recall.' Disappointed that her words were not creating the shock she expected, the woman stepped aside, inclining her grey head towards the stairway at the far end of the passage. 'You'd best come in, then. Don't want yer standin' on the doorstep for all the bloody world to know us business. Lord knows there's enough nosy sods out there to put two an' two together an' come up wi' trouble!'

Hurrying past her into the dim interior of the hallway, Beth wisely ignored the crude and intimate comments. Instead she told her with genuine gratitude, 'I know how well you've looked after Mr Blacklock this past week, and I'm very grateful. Really.'

'Aye . . . well.' Florence Ball shut the door and led the way down the passage. 'Just so long as the pair on yer don't forget.' She groaned and clutched her back as though suddenly in agony. 'I ain't so young as I was, an' that Blacklock's a strapping big fella. I don't mind telling yer it ain't been easy lifting an' turning a big fella like that . . . keeping him alive and tendin' his wounds. Naw! It ain't been easy, ain't been easy at all. But I done what were asked of me, an' I done it well.'

'I won't argue with that, Mrs Ball,' Beth was quick to assure her. 'You'll be well rewarded, as I promised.'

'Too bloody right I will! Else I should never have

agreed to tend him in the first place. Yer tells me it weren't his fault. Well . . . if it weren't *his* fault, who the divil's fault *were* it, eh?' The woman glanced back as Beth followed her up the stairs. She wasn't finished yet. 'In my opinion, when a bloke gets hisself cut up like that . . . well, all I can say is, nine times outta ten the bugger were asking fer it!'

'Not this time, Mrs Ball.'

'Oh. Yer reckon, d'yer?'

'I promise you. What happened to Mr Blacklock was *not* his fault.'

'Aye? That's what they all say.' Her voice was oddly serious and her mood darkened. She had known more than enough trouble in her chequered lifetime – trouble and strife, and worse things even than that. Fearful things, things that concerned the authorities; and robbery and . . . murder! She shivered. Deep in thought, and with Beth silent behind her, she continued on up the stairs until they reached the first landing. 'I reckon you'll find him a good deal improved at any rate, though there's still a way to go afore he'll be fit to work agin.' She frowned, adding in a sly voice, 'Though I understand there's them as wouldn't *ever* want to see the poor sod work agin.' She waited, but was visibly disappointed when her remark brought no response from Beth. But the woman's observations had not gone unheard, and Beth was well aware of what was being hinted. Even in Lewisham Street, it was no secret how Esther Ward had put the word out on Tyler Blacklock.

Pausing outside the door to Tyler's room, Florence Ball swung round. Settling her thick neck into her round dumpy shoulders, she eyed Beth with a kind of arrogance, surveying her slim shapely form and envying her dark bold beauty. She thought about her own Toby jug appearance, and bitterness touched her deep inside. She had *never* been that lovely; never been lovely in any way. Even as a bairn she was always squat and ugly. There was only one fella who'd ever fancied her, and that was because he was too bloody drunk to see his hand afore his face. Now, envy caused her to reveal her deeper, more secret thoughts. 'I were never pretty, yer know. Never 'ad but one fella.' She laughed at the memory, but it was a sad forlorn little laugh. One fella in all her life! And God alone knew, the fella in question weren't no bleedin' catch neither. But she was forced to grasp whatever opportunity came her way, and seeing as it might be the only time when she could tempt a fella to lie atween her fat white thighs, she had made that night a night to remember.

'One good man is all a woman wants,' Beth reminded her.

The woman shook with laughter. 'Yer right! Only *this* bugger didn't stay long enough fer me to find out what he were med of, because the very next morning, the blighter took one look at what he'd crushed in his arms so willingly the night afore, and didn't stay a minute longer than it took for him to pull on his bleedin' pants.' She chuckled at the memory. 'I mustn't grumble though,' she said, 'because he did show his appreciation after all . . . two silver shillings on account, and a thank you that took nine months in the making . . . three long days of unforgettable pain to deliver, and the past sixteen years to mature. I called her by the name o' Fanny, cause it was "Fanny" that got her mammy in trouble. Although the little sod never was partial to the name I give her . . . soon as ever she were old enough to backchat she changed it ter "Annie". Meks no difference though, she'll allus be "Fanny" ter me, whether she likes it or whether she don't.' She sighed noisily. 'Naw, dearie, I ain't never been nothing but dowdy and unattractive,' she moaned; at the same time thinking how her one good feature had been her

thick dark hair. Although even that was an eyesore
these days. Looking longingly at Beth's luxurious hair,
still stunningly beautiful even though it was now limp
and bedraggled by the earlier downpour, Florence Ball
wondered why some folk got nothing outta life and
others got it all. But then she corrected herself. There
wasn't a soul on God's earth that didn't have a cross
to carry; not even the lovely Elizabeth Ward. *Her* cross
was her mother . . . the 'lady' who had come up from
nothing and was now more hated and feared than the
worst ruffians who stalked the streets of London. Esther
Ward was a curse! If she had her way, every house in the
East End would be ripped up by the roots and the poor
sods in 'em planted in the graveyard. This daughter of
hers though . . . now she was a different kettle o' fish
altogether. Be careful, Florence warned herself. There
was 'them' and there was 'us', and it were allus best to
be suspicious o' 'them' . . . however gentle and kindly
they might seem. Nor should she forget that she was
owed money. And she wouldn't be doing right by herself
if she didn't wring every penny she could out of this 'ere
'lady'. Conscience never filled a hungry belly, nor would
it keep a roof over a body. Poor folk such as herself
couldn't afford no conscience. Where there was hard
brass to be made, it paid to keep sharp – and that's
just what she intended to do . . . keep sharp until she
had a fistful o' money. Money that was hard earned.
Money that was honestly got by. Money of a kind that
she might never clap her old eyes on again. Oh, aye!
She'd make damned sure that she got her just rewards
. . . although somewhere in her old heart, she felt the
stirrings of sympathy for this particular young lady; for
she *was* a 'lady', unlike the other one who'd bred her.

'Thank you, Mrs Ball.' Beth's voice was warm and
sincere. She waited patiently for the woman to open
the door and admit her into the room.

'Hmph!' The woman's smile took the shape of a grimace. 'Thanks don't count fer nothing. But *money*, well now, that's a different matter agin. But there, go on in, dearie.' When Beth brushed past her, she added in a low intimate voice, 'I'll see you're not disturbed.' As she closed the door on Beth's slight figure, she clutched her two hands across her enormous hanging bosom, bent herself forward and quietly chuckled at her own mucky thoughts. Still chuckling, and with an agility that belied her round bulky form, she scurried away.

As the old woman disappeared down the stairs, a younger figure stepped from the shadows on the gloomy landing. Young, tall and far too shapely for her age, the girl had witnessed the whole scene between the two women. Leaning against the cold damp wall, she continued to stare at the door of Tyler Blacklock's room. In her mind's eye she could see the two of them in there; the man who had awakened such passion in her; and the woman . . . oh, the woman! A woman of stunning beauty. A woman of compassion and goodness. The kind of woman a man would follow to the ends of the earth. 'Not like me,' the girl murmured bitterly. 'A man might look at me and think of one night, maybe two. But not a lifetime. Never a lifetime!' Her small brown eyes glittered with a strange mixture of hatred and longing. Her finely chiselled features stiffened with resolve. Ever since Tyler Blacklock first came to this house, she had wanted him; wanted him like any woman might want a man. In a few days' time she would be sixteen. She smiled, her voice soft and passionate as she whispered, 'You might not think I'm woman enough for you, Tyler Blacklock, but I've been woman enough all along, if only you hadn't been blinded by *her*!'

The hatred deepened in the hard eyes. When he was brought home badly hurt and helpless as a babe, she had been secretly delighted, thinking that at long last this was her opportunity. Helping her mother to bathe that strong lean body, seeing his splendid nakedness, and being close to him during the long dark hours, had raised in her a great longing. When he grew stronger and more alert, she had loathed her mother for turning her away; warning her to keep quiet about her part in the nursing of Tyler Blacklock. 'There'd be 'ell to pay if either of 'em knew I'd let a filly like you loose on 'im!' Florence Ball's only concern was for her 'payment' and she didn't want it jeopardised in any way. She had seen the longing in her daughter's eyes and had been amused by it. She had not seen what lay beneath, though. She had not seen the envy and the obsession. She had not reckoned with her daughter's cruel and possessive nature.

All this time Florence Ball's daughter had skilfully disguised her deeper feelings; biding her time and waiting for the opportunity that must surely come. It was ironic that when the opportunity did come, it was in the form of Elizabeth Ward herself. A certain thought had quietly festered in the girl's devious mind, until it grew and blossomed into her every waking moment. A plan! A devious and spiteful plan, that was twofold. First, it was designed to separate Elizabeth from her man; and secondly, it could fetch a deal of money in its wake. Here the girl softly laughed. How could it fail? What! The daughter of Esther Ward coming into a place like Lewisham Street and visiting a fella in his own room. My! What would it be worth to keep *that* little scandal quiet, eh? But not yet. Not just yet. Not until she had a heart to heart with her old mammy. Florence Ball was not a born trouble maker and so she might take some persuading. Ah, but a drop o' the old stuff would do it. Oil her with a measure of whisky, and Florence would open up like a flower in spring. She quietly chuckled. It was a well-known fact that if you gave folks enough rope, they would likely hang themselves.

As she strolled across the landing and passed within a few inches of Tyler's room, the girl paused, leaning into the door and listening intently. There was no sound from within. Her expression darkened. But then she remembered a saying of her mother's: 'Everything comes to he who waits'. Well, she did not intend waiting much longer. Patience was not one of her virtues. Now, as she anticipated imminent rewards, her devious expression changed to one of delight. She would have been even more delighted if she had known how, at that very moment, events were already underway which would pay her more handsomely than she had ever dreamed of . . .

Inside the room, Beth stood for a moment by the door, her dark eyes resting on the sleeping figure in the chair and her heart going out to him. This was the first time she had seen him out of bed since that night in Whitechapel when he was so viciously attacked. Those first few days when it seemed as though she might lose him had been a nightmare. Even in his pain he had insisted that Ben should: 'Take her away from here!' Yet in those desperate early hours she had defied him, staying by his side, until Ben persuaded her that her presence there could put both herself and Tyler in a deal of danger. For herself she was not concerned, but Tyler was helpless. Beth knew how Esther had hounded him; how she would go on hounding him. And if her mother ever discovered that she was still seeing Tyler, there would be no hiding place for him.

Ben had been a tower of strength. It was he who persuaded Florence to keep her tongue still about the affair, although it cost him dearly. But it was money well spent; particularly when that sly old woman produced a man of dubious character, but one blessed with detailed medical knowledge; a man with a dangerous thirst for the fiery liquid, and an appetite for young innocents that had brought him to the attention of the courts, and reduced his fortunes to the level of the poorest vagrant in Lewisham Street. The sight of the deep and ugly wounds had sobered him up long enough to stem the flow of blood and save Tyler's life. Afterwards he returned every day until the danger of infection had passed. Mrs Ball, who everyone knew was not a 'Mrs' at all but who enjoyed the title all the same, was a surprisingly capable nurse. Like the hapless doctor she was encouraged to give of her best by the promise of a weighty purse.

Moving quietly so as not to waken him, Beth ventured further into the room. It was a surprisingly spacious if gloomy place, the one small window overlooking the backyard, and beyond to where the belching chimneys of the adjoining houses coloured the skyline with a thick grey vapour. The room was sparsely furnished but clean. The double bed was topped and bottomed with brightly polished brass railings, and covered by a huge floral eiderdown. Above it, there was an oak-framed seascape nailed to the wall, the scene being somewhat obscured by the brown layers of tobacco smoke which, over the years, had firmly adhered itself to the glass. At the far end of the room, two dark panelled doors led into a walk-in wardrobe. Beneath the window was a long dressing table with curved front and large ornate mirror; close by was a wicker chair with a blue padded seat, and nearby stood a small oak set of drawers. Just visible in the gloomiest corner was a tiny handbasin with a mirror over, and a square patterned rug of indistinguishable colours covered most of the worn linoleum. In spite of the sparsity of its furnishings, the room was respectable and surprisingly welcoming. The one other chair, deeply padded with a high back, was the one in which Tyler was presently sleeping.

Laying down the tapestry bag, Beth tiptoed across the room, her gaze intent on the sleeping man. Pausing before him, she smiled, thinking how like a child he looked, with his mouth slightly open and his dark hair falling tousled across his face. There was colour in his face now, a faint blush that told her at long last he was on the way to recovery. Partially dressed, he made a pathetic and loveable sight that endeared him to her even more. His long legs were clad in familiar brown cords and stretched out towards the foot of the bed. He was barefoot, and wearing a dark check shirt with one sleeve rolled up to his elbow, and the other hanging unbuttoned over his lean strong hand. The shirt was open to the waist, revealing a broad expanse of chest covered with a carpet of dark hair from one nipple to the other, and showing part of the dressing that covered his wounds. He had lost a little weight, but his inherent stength betrayed itself in the thick muscular sinews of his neck and shoulders. As she gazed on him a while longer, Beth thought she would never love him more than she did at that moment.

Afraid to wake him, yet more afraid not to, she leaned towards him, her hand tenderly brushing his face. 'Tyler . . . it's Beth.' Her voice was incredibly gentle, betraying all the love she felt for him. When he stirred, she kept her gaze on his face, hungry to see her love returned in those dark green eyes that only had to look on her and she was lost.

In his troubled dreams, he felt her touch, heard her voice, and at once he needed her. Slowly, like a man emerging from suffocating blackness, he came to her. His eyes opened and she was there. 'Beth!' Joy flooded through him like a tidal wave, but then he remembered. He winced with pain as he struggled upright in the chair. 'For God's sake, Beth, you *know* you shouldn't come here!' Pressing down the pain that throbbed into his every nerve ending, he rose from the chair and clasped his hands over her small straight shoulders, looking down on her with eyes that were both angry and admiring, 'What am I going to do with you, eh?' he murmured through a half-smile. 'You're obstinate, disobedient, and downright determined to go against everything I say.'

'That's right.' Beth's eyes sparkled as she looked up at him. The touch of his hands on her shoulders created all kinds of turbulent emotions inside her. She could feel the strength in him, and knew that his love was every bit as powerful as hers.

'Oh, Beth! Beth! Don't you realise you could be making trouble for yourself by coming here?'

'You mean my mother?'

'Yes, I mean your mother, and your father . . . your way of life and the security you have.' He moaned deep inside himself, raising his face to the ceiling and staring hard at the flaking plaster, as though seeking an answer there.

'None of that means anything to me,' she told him softly. 'I love you, Tyler, and I want to be with you. Always.'

He looked at her now, at those glorious black eyes, at the strong and beautiful features which were so very determined, and he saw the frightening depths of her love for him; frightening only because he knew it could bring her great heartache. But how could he tell her? How in God's name could he tell her that there was no hope for them – and never could be? 'Oh, Beth! Beth!' The anguish was heavy in his voice as he tore himself away from her. From the window he stared unseeingly towards the skyline, the jutting roofs and clustered chimneys all merging with the greyness of another evening. 'Do you think I don't love you?' he asked bitterly, deliberately averting his gaze from hers.

'No, I don't think that.' Sensing his struggle, Beth kept her distance. Suddenly she was afraid.

'I love you more than life itself . . . more than I ever thought possible. I love you too much, Beth. Too much to risk your hatred. Too much to take you away from a life that's comfortable and safe. I'm nothing, Beth. I've *got* nothing, not even the dignity of work. Oh, I know I'll get work elsewhere, up north in the mills or the docks perhaps. But it's not enough, don't you see? I can't ask you to share a life that will bring you only hardship. I can't even be certain that I will get work, or even a place to live. I could be tramping the length and breadth of this country, the same as I've done before. Times are hard, and there are too many men chasing too few jobs.'

All of these things had long been a source of worry to him, and he used the arguments with conviction. Nothing destroyed love more surely than poverty and hardship, and he was not prepared to risk losing Beth in that way.

'*I* have money.'

'Never!' He swung round to face her, his eyes blazing, 'If a man can't support his woman, he doesn't deserve her!'

Beth would not be deterred. She came to stand by the window with him. 'Is that what I am?' she asked, forcing herself to look out where the guttering was spewing the rain on to the flagstones below. There was the whisper of a smile on her mouth. 'Your woman?' She liked the sound of it, and from Tyler's own lips it was the most wonderful sound on earth. Raising her head she looked at him boldly. 'Do you honestly think I care for what I have now?' she said, the smile slipping away and a serious expression shaping her lovely features. 'Like you, I have nothing. Nothing worthwhile at least.'

For a long poignant moment he continued to gaze

on her, wishing with all his heart that things could have been different. But they were not, and wishing would not make them so. In the hazy evening light that filtered in through the window, he saw the pain behind her smile. The dark eyes were soft and yielding, tearing at his heart like savage claws; the soft milk-white skin glistened like pearls, pale and smooth against the rich warm colour of her hair. Instinctively he reached out to entwine his fingers in the fine curling strands that fanned her face. When he saw the tears swim into her eyes, his resolve melted. With a moan he clasped her to him, bending his head and resting his face against her hair. She shivered in his arms. The dampness of her clothes and hair became obvious to him. Cursing himself for not realising earlier, he thrust her away at arm's length, glancing first at her coat and then at her wet, draggle-tailed hair. 'God Almighty, Beth . . . you're soaked!' With his good arm he tore the coat from her and flung it over the back of the chair. Propelling her across the room towards the crackling fire, he told her firmly, 'I'll fetch Florence. You must get these wet things off straight away or you'll catch pneumonia.' He turned away.

'No.' Winding her fingers in his, she kept him back. 'Stay here, with me,' she murmured. Her voice was soft, inviting.

'Beth, do you know what you're saying?' Her words had shocked and excited him. He saw the meaning in her eyes and he could hardly breathe.

'Love me,' she whispered. 'Like before.' Only 'before' had not been here in this room. Nor was it on a damp grey day. On that wonderful July evening a little more than two months ago, she and Tyler had travelled to Hampstead Heath, partly for the enjoyment of it, and partly out of curiosity. Her father had recently acquired a derelict gentleman's residence belonging to an old manorial estate there. The big house itself was not totally beyond restoration, but the project would demand more investment than could ever be recovered. Richard turned his attention instead to the three acres of grounds; prime development land. Hampstead was a most desirable area with many amenities, not least of which was the Heath itself. Besides which, it was easily accessible to central London. Intrigued by her father's vivid description of the once beautiful house and old rambling gardens, Beth wanted to see for herself. Against his better judgement, she persuaded Tyler to accompany her there on that glorious evening. It was the most memorable evening of her life, the sun was shining, the birds were singing and there was no one to spy on her and Tyler. Hand in hand they had wandered through the grounds, watched the creatures at play in the spinney, picked their way through the overgrown lawns and gardens, and been enchanted by the house itself, with its towering gables and sadly decaying structure which once had been so proud.

Later they had sat in the summer-house, a round, surprisingly well-preserved building where the sun poured in from all sides. Sitting in that small private place, surrounded only by God's wonderful nature and the sound of birds trilling out their joy, Beth had felt a great sense of peace. In that beautiful place, she and Tyler had made love for the first time – and for the rest of her life she would always remember that special evening, lying in his arms with the rest of the world a million miles away. On that evening a child had been created, a child of love, her child – and Tyler's. She had suspected for some weeks, but now she was sure. Oh, how she wanted to share her joy with him. But she was afraid. Already he believed he was ruining her life, coming between her and her family. Telling him about the child would only increase his feeling of guilt, and she did not want that. There was time enough for him to know. Beth felt instinctively that the time was not now.

She waited for his answer, her hands flattened against his chest and her eyes smiling into his. 'Love me, Tyler,' she urged softly. 'Here. Now.'

'You're a vixen,' he murmured, his green eyes darkening with passion, his hands stroking her hair. The struggle inside him was unbearable. He loved her so much, ached for her with his very being. But he was wrong for her, he knew that. Beth knew it too, only she wouldn't let herself believe it. This past week lying here, and when he had thought himself to be close to death, he had come to realise how much of a sacrifice Beth was prepared to make for him – and he could not let her do it. Yet he could not imagine life without her. He had come to the conclusion that his was a selfish love. Her brother Ben had said as much to him.

'She has an admirable suitor,' Ben had told him. 'Wilson Ryan, a man in his twenties, and who will one day come into a small fortune. His father owns a chain of milliners. He and Beth met when Mother craftily placed her in one of the Ryan shops, and he visits the house on every pretence. Beth likes him too, although I don't think she feels more than that. He adores her . . . worships the ground she walks on.' Tyler knew that Ben had not told him all this just to hurt him because, strangely enough, he and Ben liked and respected each other, although there were times when Tyler was discomfited by Ben's love for gambling and by his choice of friends. But what Ben did was not Tyler's business, and so it was difficult for him to offer advice. Yet, he was grateful for Ben's help where Beth was concerned, because, like Tyler, Ben knew that the love between Blacklock and his sister was an impossible love, a love that would bring unhappiness in its wake.

'No, Beth.' The touch of her fingers against his naked chest heightened his desire for her. It took all of his will-power to clasp his fingers over hers and to hold them still. But she only smiled, her dark eyes staring up at him, astonishingly beautiful, deep with love, drawing him in, mesmerising. She took her hands away and undid the small cameo brooch at the neck of her white blouse. After placing the brooch on the mantelpiece, she raised her hands to her hair, silently plucking at the mother-of-pearl clasp, until in a moment her long rich tresses spilled about her shoulders.

Her beauty made him gasp. Swept along on a tide of passion, he knew there was no going back. Quietly now, he went to the door and slipped the bolt across. He remained there a moment, his face turned away from her and his dark head bent. The struggle was still going on inside him; the fear and the love. But love was stronger; always stronger. Now, when he turned to see her standing there, the flickering firelight playing on her lovely features and her arms open to him, he knew he would never want any other woman. Slowly, he came towards her. There was no pain, no fear, only soaring exhilaration, and the thrill of knowing he would soon hold her as close as any man could ever hold the woman he loved.

When Tyler took her in his arms, Beth forgot all the bad things, all the things that sought to keep them apart. Here in the haven of his love, she felt safe, part of him. In her heart she truly believed that nothing on this earth could spoil their happiness. The warmth of his nakedness shocked through her, firing her desire. His hands were gentle, his mouth soft against her face, stroking her hair, caressing her breasts. His passion hardened and an agonised moan broke from him as he pushed into her. Clinging to him, sharing all the love she had to give, Beth knew above all else that here was the rest of her life; this man and their child. Until the end of her days she would want nothing more than that.

Downstairs in the kitchen the girl leaned back in the rocking chair and rolled her resentful brown eyes up to the ceiling. The thought of Tyler Blacklock and his visitor rankled in her like a festering sore. But she was not given the time to dwell on the images that were already rising in her mind. Instead her thoughts were rudely interrupted by Florence Ball's loud demand for, 'Another dram, darlin'. Just one more little drop fer yer ol' mammy, eh?' From the depths of the old leather chair, the drunken woman thrust out a dimpled arm to tap her whisky glass against the fender. When her pleading drew only a sullen silence, she jutted her head forward to peer at her daughter through bleary accusing eyes.

'Surely ter God yer ain't telling me there's none left!' she exclaimed with horror. 'Why, yer little sod! I'm buggered if yer ain't gone an' downed the bleedin' lot!' She began struggling from the armchair, but was roughly shoved back into its squashy depths. At first she was shocked, waggling her head from side to side in an effort to focus on the one who would do such a thing. When she saw it was only her daughter, she flung her arms up and waved them above her head, loudly chuckling and doing a little jig with her feet. 'Yer 'avin' me on, yer little monkey,' she laughed. 'I've a good mind ter tan yer bare arse . . . teasin' yer ol' mammy like that! Me as luvs yer an' who's allus been yer best friend.' Then the enormity of what the girl had done, trying to deprive her of what was rightfully hers, took the shine off her enjoyment. 'It ain't a nice thing to do to yer own mammy.' She made a face as though her feelings had been hurt.

'Is that right then?' The girl held the bottle up, ready to pour the golden liquid into her mother's tumbler, but then she paused, watching the other one's face as she said in a low cunning voice, 'So . . . you reckon you've allus been my best friend, do you?'

'Oh, I do. I most certainly do,' declared the inebriated Florence. 'Best friend . . . allus been yer best friend.' Her mood was suddenly made brighter by the sight of the bottle poised over her glass.

'Well now, that's strange.'

'Oh, aye? What's strange about it then?' She wasn't in the mood for riddles – and besides, her head felt like a bag o' fighting rats.

'It's just that . . . well, *I* always understood that best friends share all their deepest secrets.'

'And so they do! So they do!' She thrust her glass forward. 'The buggers allus share their drink an' all,' she said sulkily. 'Anyroad, what the 'ell are yer talking about . . . sharin' secrets? I ain't never kept anything from yer, 'ave I?' She smiled when the bottle was tipped forward and the smallest measure allowed to trickle out. 'You just tell me when I've ever kept anything from yer,' she snorted, 'an' we'll put the bugger right without any more to-do . . . else yer ol' mammy'll chop 'er tongue out an' no mistake.' She suddenly chuckled and winked knowingly. 'Oh, I get yer meaning, yer crafty little cow,' she whispered, with one eye glued to the door for fear it might come flying open. 'It ain't me that's got the "secret", is it, eh? It's *you*, ain't it?' She laughed louder. 'Silly fool! Don't yer think I ain't seen how yer pant after that feller upstairs?' She jerked her thumb upwards. 'He ain't fer you!' she snarled. 'So get him outta yer mind. What! Yer ain't got the bloody cradle marks off yer arse yet . . . and he's twenty-five if he's a day!'

The girl's smile was sweetness itself as she kept her mammy waiting for her precious 'ol stuff – and she would *keep* her waiting until the old slag saw different.

* * *

It was gone midnight when the knock came on the door. The muffled sound startled the girl from her deep reverie. There was no doubt in her mind now that her mammy would help. It was true, there were richer pickings to be had than Tyler, but he was what she wanted, and she meant to get him by hook or by crook. Men of Tyler Blacklock's quality were few and far between.

Curious and a little apprehensive, the girl made her way to the door. The house was quiet. Tyler had returned from taking the Ward woman home some time ago, Florence was still deeply under the influence, and the two remaining lodgers slept like dead men. Swearing beneath her breath, she inched open the front door.

The visitor was a gentleman, a stiff-faced little creature who declined to give his name but whose shock of startling white hair made him instantly conspicuous. 'I think it best if I come in off the street as quickly as possible,' he told her. When she hesitated, he reached inside the pocket of his jacket. 'It will be in your own best interest to hear what I have to say,' he suggested quietly, showing her the fattest wallet she had ever laid eyes on.

Within the space of a minute, she had opened the door and ushered him in. In another minute, they were seated opposite each other at the kitchen table as he explained the reason for his visit. As he spoke, her eyes grew wider with astonishment. Because here was the very opportunity she had long waited for.

'For God's sake, Beth!' Ben grabbed his sister roughly and pulled her to one side. 'Where the devil have you been 'til this time? Mother's in there.' He made an impatient gesture towards the sitting room which was situated a short distance along the hallway. 'Wilson

49

Ryan's in there as well. He's been here over two hours.'

'What does he want?' Beth spoke in a whisper. She had no intention of seeing either of them.

'You know very well what he wants!' Ben also spoke in a whisper, but it was a harsh accusing whisper. 'He came to see *you*. When Mother asked where you were, I told her you'd gone to bed with a severe headache, and had asked not to be disturbed.'

'Did she believe you?' Beth put her hand over her mouth to stifle the mischievous giggle. Whatever Ben told her now, he could not spoil the wonderful evening she and Tyler had spent together.

'I'm not sure. You know Mother has a naturally suspicious mind. But at least I managed to dissuade her from going to your room when Wilson arrived. Thanks to him she hasn't had time since.' He smiled at the thought of Wilson Ryan's serious and staid nature compared to Beth's natural exuberance. 'He does go on a bit, doesn't he?' Now, it was Ben who had to stifle his laughter, but then he added in a serious voice, 'He's a good man though, and he idolises you. He'd look after you, Beth . . . always. You would never want for anything.' This business with Tyler Blacklock was a great source of anxiety to him. He had hoped that she would make a richer match, though the reason for his hopes was more to do with his own pocket than with Beth's.

She shook her head. There was a strange sadness on her face as she told him, 'You're wrong, Ben. I would always want Tyler. I could never be content without him.'

He sighed noisily, his worried brown eyes meeting her determined stare with mingled affection and anger. 'I don't know why I bother with you!' he said hoarsely. When she smiled at his remark, he reluctantly returned her smile. 'All right,' he conceded, 'we can talk about this tomorrow.' Casting an anxious glance towards the half-open sitting-room door, he told her, 'Look, Beth . . . if you don't want to prove me a liar, you'd better go quickly to your room.' He crooked his hand beneath her elbow and began taking her at a fast pace across the spacious hallway, towards the foot of the wide curving staircase. 'Hurry! If she catches us here, there'll be Hell to pay.'

'I've a good mind to face her,' Beth whispered angrily, 'and tell her to go to Hell!' As the last word fell from her lips, she was struck by the venom in her statement, and was ashamed. Things like that were all right in the privacy of your own thoughts, but they should never be spoken aloud, especially not in front of Ben who had always enjoyed a much happier relationship with their mother. She looked at him now, and his harried expression caused her pain. 'Oh, Ben, I shouldn't have said that,' she murmured, squeezing his hand in hers, her dark eyes filled with remorse.

'Just go to your room, Beth . . . *please*.'

'Goodnight then.'

'For God's sake, Beth, just go.' He dropped his head to his chest in frustration.

Blowing him a kiss, she tiptoed up the stairs, her feet sinking silently into the blue patterned carpet, her small fists clutching the front of her skirt to raise the hem from round her ankles, and all the time she was acutely aware of the conversation taking place in the sitting room. From the low continuous droning she knew the discussion was intense. Occasionally she heard her own name mentioned, and her suspicions were confirmed. *They were discussing her*. Halfway up the stairs, much to the consternation of her brother who was still monitoring her progress, she paused to lean partway over the banister in order to hear the voices more clearly. The strong vibrant tones of Esther Ward were unmistakable, as was the quieter voice of Wilson Ryan, but despite almost tumbling into the hallway below, Beth was not able to distinguish the content of their conversation. Her father's voice was not very prominent. But then, it never was, she thought sadly as she continued on her way up the stairs.

At the top Beth turned to mouth goodnight to Ben. His answer was impatiently to flick his hand in the air in a gesture that warned her to get out of sight before she was discovered. When he saw her disappear into her room, which was almost opposite the staircase, he gave a quiet sigh of relief then strode swiftly along the hallway and towards the sitting room, anxious to return before his mother took it into her head to come and seek him out. Before long he too was adding his own voice to the deliberations, while at the same time making every effort to divert attention from the subject of his 'wayward sister' who, according to Esther, 'would greatly benefit from the discipline of marriage . . . and of course would make an excellent wife for a man such as yourself, Mr Ryan'. Wilson's unbridled enthusiasm brought a rare smile to her face as she mentally assessed the worth of his father's lucrative chain of shops. She had no love for Beth. No maternal instincts whatsoever. But she had no qualms about exploiting the girl in order to feather her own nest. No qualms at all!

Upstairs in her room Beth sat on the bed, absent-mindedly watching the shadows cast on the wall by the flickering light from her bedside lamp. In the dim glow she let her gaze drift lazily round the room. Strange how she had never really felt a sense of belonging to this house, or this room, or even to Esther. She had always loved her father, always thought him to be the most kind and gentle man on God's earth. Once upon a time he'd had strength too, and had dared to voice his own opinions; but Esther had robbed him of all that. She had sapped his dignity and enthusiasm for life, just as she would have done Beth's, if her daughter's will had not been stronger than her own. Beth still loved her father, although she could not help but feel deeply disappointed by the way he allowed his wife to domineer him. She loved Ben also, although she was anxious about his secret gambling and had pleaded with him on more than one occasion to stop. He had assured her that he was now on the 'straight and narrow', yet she suspected he might be lying. Whenever she broached the subject, he would turn it around and accuse her of 'deliberately antagonising Mother with your choice of suitor'. He meant well though, and of course it couldn't be easy being caught between two women whom he loved, when those two women disliked each other so intensely. Beth understood that, and all her life had tried hard not to cause him pain because of it.

Leaning back against the pillow she recalled her brother's words, when he had told her, 'You really are your own worst enemy.' In a way he was right. But she could never change the way she was. It was her nature to defend what she believed in her heart to be right, and her heart told her that the love she and Tyler shared was the most wonderful, natural thing in the world. Whenever she was in his arms or strolling beside him in the park, she was filled with a sense of peace and fulfilment. In Tyler, she had found everything she had always longed for. He was something precious. Something that money could not buy. She thought about him now, reliving events of the evening and letting his image fill her mind. The joy it brought moved her to tears. 'I'll always belong with him,' she murmured. 'Not here. Not in this place, where there are more bad memories than good ones. I don't belong here. I never did.'

The house on Bedford Square was a large solidly built terraced dwelling, with an imposing front entrance at the top of a wide flight of steps. There were fluted half-columns either side of the door, and an air of moderate grandeur about the house which told the visitor that here was a family who had risen from the ranks and would yet realise even greater achievements. Every room in the house was stamped with the same message; strong stalwart furniture in darkest oak, tall display cabinets filled with delicate china and the odd piece of best silver, carpets and rugs of best quality weave. There was even a housekeeper – although she was also cook, chambermaid, waitress and dogsbody all rolled into one. Esther had supplied the unfortunate creature with several different styles of caps and aprons to be worn over her basic black uniform, and expected the highest standards from her at all times. Coming from a lifetime in the workhouse, the servant was well versed in humility. She was given bread and board, and a liveable wage, and so made no complaints and gave no trouble. Surprisingly, Esther was quietly pleased with the woman, and had not yet made her a spectacle in front of guests. But then, she would have been hard pressed to find another such natural dogsbody and consequently was loath to do or say anything that might induce the woman to seek work elsewhere.

In spite of her mother's obvious disapproval, Beth had made a special effort to make her own room more cheerful. The floral curtains were sewn by her own hand, as were the pretty blue cushion covers and the small round doyly on the kidney-shaped dressing table. There was a red and blue peg rug beside the narrow bed, and two oblong framed prints hanging on the wall behind. The brown-painted window sill was brightened by a slim vase containing a colourful display of silk flowers, and the mantel cloth had long blue tassels that shivered and shimmered in the rising heat. The room was not too spacious. The bed, dressing table and matching wardrobe filled it to capacity.

In the quiet shadowy room, the booming tones of the grandfather clock in the downstairs hall sounded like a death knell. It had been a long day. Taking a clean towel from the drawer, Beth tipped a measure of cold water from the jug into the pink floral bowl on the dressing table; then she stripped off her clothes and washed herself all over. The cold water splashing against her bare skin made her shiver. After drying herself off, she slipped the cotton nightgown over her head, and sat before the dressing-table mirror to brush her long heavy hair until it shone like polished chestnuts. Then she climbed into bed and lay with her eyes open, staring at the extravagant patterns on the ceiling panels, and wondering why she suddenly felt strangely afraid.

Some time later she heard the front door close. 'Goodnight, Wilson,' she murmured, 'please stay away . . . you'll only make life difficult for me.' She had nothing against him, but whatever he and her mother might plan, Wilson Ryan was not for her. Not now. Not ever.

Chapter Three

With her head held high and a fiercely determined look on her weasel-sharp features, Esther Ward swept silently down the staircase. Dressed in a long straight skirt of richest burgundy, and a starched white blouse with dainty lace ruffles at the wrists and throat, she made a small but imposing figure. Her tiny feet were clad in expensive black leather ankle boots, which had a thick crossover strap that fastened with an elegant silver button. Her fine brown hair was scraped back from her high pale forehead with such severity that the skin at her temples was plucked up by the roots. The thin strands were drawn into a long twisted coil in the nape of her neck, and secured there by an unusually pretty tortoise-shell clip. A trim handsome woman with strong penetrating blue eyes, her authoritative demeanour and the inherent sourness of her expression made her seem much older than her forty-six years.

At the bottom of the stairs she paused, turning her head this way and that, her small bright eyes darting in every direction as though afraid someone might be watching her. But there was no one. The house remained eerily silent. Her attention was now drawn to the grandfather clock in the corner of the hallway. Seeing that it was not yet six a.m., she showed her satisfaction in that familiar way she had of pursing her small tight mouth into a wrinkled mass and smiling secretly with her eyes. Glancing along the passage once more, she directed her gaze towards the kitchen door, in her mind looking beyond to the small room where the dogsbody lived. Realising that the creature would be rising from her bed any minute to set about her many duties, and afraid of coming face to face with her, Esther hurried along the hallway. It would not do for the lady of the house to be seen sneaking out like any common thief. Going to the tall oak stand by the front door – and cursing when she accidentally kicked against it – she took her black coat from its peg, then the small round hat, with the dark gloves inside. One by one she put the garments on, with the same meticulous attention that always created the utmost irritation in those who were made to witness it. First the coat, and the fastening of that long thin line of tiny cloth-covered buttons; then the hat, with its feather which must sit just above the right ear and pointing towards her forehead; now the gloves . . . one finger at a time, each pressed home with firm deliberation, until the tip of every finger was tightly encased; then the glove itself, painstakingly smoothed free of all wrinkles and squeezed snugly about the wrist.

After a long moment when she fussily examined herself in the oval mirror, Esther was at last satisfied with her appearance. Straightening her narrow stiff shoulders, she peered once more into the mirror, her vivid blue eyes glittering triumphantly as she murmured, 'So you think you've got the better of me, do you, Elizabeth Ward?' She laughed, a low wicked sound that seemed to echo through the quietness of the house. 'Don't you ever think that, you little fool! Not ever.' She sighed, and all the while her piercing blue eyes studied the image in the mirror, head held high, expression uniquely arrogant. 'Better women than you have made the mistake of underestimating me, Elizabeth my dear,' she whispered hoarsely. 'Among them your own . . .' She paused, a devious smile lighting the whole of her face. Then, with incredible swiftness, the smile became a frown and the eyes glittered like hard bright jewels. 'Careful, Esther!' she warned the image in the mirror. 'After all these years there are things best not spoken aloud.'

She gasped when suddenly there was another image in the mirror, that of a woman taller than she, with long fair hair and homely features. She was staring at Esther with serious dark eyes, and the poker she held above her head was poised to come crashing down across Esther's shoulders. For one terrifying moment, she thought the past had returned to haunt her. With a cry, she swung round, arms raised ready to protect herself. But then she realised her mistake, relief surging into every corner of her being. It was quickly replaced with fury. 'Are you mad?' she hissed, forcing her voice low for fear of waking the family. Lunging forward she wrested the poker from the woman's nervous fingers and for one fearful second it seemed as though she might lay into the poor creature with a vengeance. But common sense prevailed, and she visibly relaxed.

'Oh! It's you, madam. I heard a noise and thought it was an intruder.' The maid was shocked to find that her 'intruder' was none other than her mistress.

'Idiot! Do I look like an intruder?' Of the two of them, Esther had suffered the greater shock. She was already made nervous by the reason for her early rising. Lately she had become increasingly anxious about the continuing relationship between Elizabeth and the Blacklock fellow; it seemed that nothing she could do or say would bring the unfortunate matter to an end. For a long time she had resisted resorting to 'unorthodox' methods, but on learning that Beth was still defying her, all kinds of plans had begun to germinate in her mind. In fact, she had been rather pleased and surprised by the extent of her own deviousness. She bitterly resented being taken for a fool! And last evening that was exactly what Elizabeth had done, even recruiting her brother to deceive his own mother. Did they really believe she had accepted Ben's story that his sister was asleep in her bedroom? Only Wilson Ryan's presence had prevented a dreadful scene.

But the incident had kept her awake for most of the night; this morning, as the dawn broke, she had suddenly realised what course to take. She had already learned that it was no use appealing to Elizabeth to see sense; nor did it presently serve any purpose to sully Blacklock's character further . . . that only made Elizabeth spring to his defence. No. The answer was for Elizabeth herself to break off the relationship. Wilson Ryan would marry her tomorrow, if only she was made to see sense; Agatha Ryan had passed away last year and Maurice Ryan's interest in the family business had diminished to the extent that much of the administration had fallen on the shoulders of his only son. One day in the not too distant future all of it would be his. . .and Elizabeth's, if only she would say the word. The Ryan interests amounted to a considerable fortune, and a merging of the two companies would make a formidable and powerful alliance. Excited by such a prospect, Esther would stop at nothing to see it accomplished.

At any rate, she was bent on imposing her own wishes above those of Elizabeth. It was more than a matter of good taste now. It was to do with bringing that impossible young woman down a peg or two! Impatient, and furious that she had been discovered leaving the house at such an unearthly hour, she glared at the servant, saying in a low threatening voice, 'You will say nothing about this to anyone. Do you understand?'

'Yes, madam. But what am I to reply if anyone should ask your whereabouts?' She was extremely anxious; it was unsettling to be part of such a conspiracy.

'You will say nothing. I shall be back in the house before the family come down to breakfast.'

'Very well, madam.'

'Now get dressed at once. I will not have a servant of mine wandering the house in her night attire.' She scrutinised the woman's long fair hair, mentally comparing the thick strong hanks with her own thin scrapings. Strange how the woman put her in mind of someone else . . . someone she had not seen for over twenty years. A good and gentle woman whom she had greatly wronged, yet whom she believed had wronged her more. The memories she had kept at bay for so long suddenly threatened to overwhelm her. 'Go away!' she snapped. 'And don't ever let me see you with your hair loose again or I shall have to arrange for it to be cropped short.'

For what seemed an age, the other woman gave no answer, her clear gaze meeting Esther's. Then, with a slight nod of the head, she murmured, 'I'm sorry, madam. It won't happen again.'

'I should hope not. Be off with you. And, remember – you saw nothing untoward this morning.' As the woman turned away to go on silent bare feet towards the kitchen, Esther felt unusually disturbed. With curious eyes she watched until the kitchen door closed on the departing figure. There would be nothing said about the incident, she was certain of that. Yet she felt curiously unsettled by the whole encounter. 'Fool!' she muttered beneath her breath. 'I'm surrounded by fools!' After one last lingering look at herself in the mirror, she went quietly from the house.

'You're a bad woman, Esther Ward.'

In her tiny sparsely furnished room behind the kitchen, the maid tied on her apron and folded her long fair hair into a frilly white cap. As she made her way into the kitchen, there was a thoughtful look in

61

her troubled eyes, a look of pain and regret. When she spoke again, it was in a soft sorrowful whisper. 'Such a bad woman. So much unhappiness.' Her eyes went up, towards the ceiling, and beyond to where Richard Ward lay sleeping in his bed. For a fleeting second her gaze grew softer, more loving. But then she looked away.

'For what you did a long time ago, and for what you're doing now, you'll be punished one day, Esther Ward,' she murmured, 'and it'll be the Lord who'll do the punishing, I dare say.' She glanced once more towards the ceiling, before straightening her back and telling herself briskly, 'Come on now, Tilly, there's a long day ahead of you, and no time for brooding.' With a quiet song on her lips she went into the kitchen and was soon busily sweeping up the dead ashes in the grate.

'There's no answer, Mrs.' The driver wrapped his thick knuckles over the edge of the carriage door and peered through the window at the small upright figure seated in the shadows. This was a curious to-do, he thought. What the devil was a fine-dressed lady doing out at this hour? And then to get him pounding on a door in Audley Street, while she skulked safely in the carriage? There was something very odd at work here, he thought nervously, something very odd. 'I reckon it might be better if we were to come back later, Mrs . . . when the folks inside are up and about.' When his passenger remained silent, he grew a little bolder. 'It wouldn't surprise me if a bobby was to come along, walking his beat down this very pavement,' he told her respectfully. 'And, begging yer pardon, Mrs, but I don't fancy explaining what I'm doing banging on this 'ere door, at a time when all honest folk should be abed . . . excepting carriage-drivers, o'course, who 'ave to trudge the cobbles at all hours in order to mek a living.' Encouraged by her continuing silence, when she appeared to be deep in thought, he took the liberty of telling her, 'That's it then? We'll come back at a more decent hour.' He began to turn away.

'We'll do no such thing!' Esther Ward's sharp voice sailed from the shadows and stopped him in his tracks. 'Knock on the door again. And *keep* knocking until somebody answers. But not too loud. We don't want the whole neighbourhood awake.'

Inside the house, the insistent thumping on the door reverberated along the narrow gloomy passage and up the stairs to the damp but respectable bedroom where Thomas Reynolds believed he was still in the throes of a terrible nightmare; a dark and awful experience that night after night haunted his sleeping hours until he thought he would go mad, and which always ended with him swinging from the end of a noose. The constant rhythm of the distant muffled knocking on the door sounded like the roll of a drum, while the executioner prepared the gallows.

'No! Go away and leave me be. I'm innocent I tell you!' His eyes popped open, staring into the gloomy atmosphere of his room. The knocking continued, and he realised it was not part of his nightmare. Flinging the eiderdown from over his face, he pushed his head up on the pillows and wiped the back of his hand over his sweating forehead. It took a moment to compose himself, another to swill his hands and face in the bowl on the stand, then another to open the window and call out angrily, 'Who is it wanting me at this Godforsaken hour?'

'It's a lady as wants yer,' returned the relieved carriage-driver. 'For Gawd's sake, open the door, will yer? Afore we're all arrested!'

'A lady?' Thomas Reynolds cast his bleary glance to where the carriage stood by the kerbside, its impatient occupant discreetly leaning out and looking up at him. On seeing that it was Esther, his mouth fell open and his eyes rounded like a fish's. In a minute he had withdrawn into the room and closed the window. In what seemed an incredibly short time he had hurried from his modest little house, closed the door behind him, and was seated in the carriage beside the irate Esther who quickly gave instructions for the driver to: 'Hurry away from here. Take the horse at a steady pace along the byways.'

No sooner had they left Audley Street behind than Thomas Reynolds had acquainted Esther with all the facts. 'The girl will play our game,' he said proudly. 'And I have all the information regarding your daughter,' he added slyly.

She was genuinely shocked by the revelations – that Beth should actually have gone into Tyler Blacklock's room, and on more than one occasion. She wondered for a moment how much of the tale had been fabricated from the vivid imagination of this girl who – if Thomas Reynolds was to be believed – had taken great delight in recounting Beth's visits in graphic detail. When in turn the information was relayed to Esther, she took a moment to reflect on it. Then, in a sombre voice, she asked, 'And the man . . . Tyler Blacklock. You say he's recovered?' She was disappointed that he had not died from his wounds.

'Afraid so. I'm sorry about that. I really thought those ruffians could do the job.'

'No matter. In fact, it might be as well, because I've come to realise that there is a better way. Less dangerous, but markedly more effective, I think.' And after she had explained it to him, he felt bound to agree. He would have stayed to discuss it at greater length, but, as always, when he had been given instructions and money had changed hands, he was quickly dismissed – with the reminder to: 'Guard your tongue. And remember . . .

if any of this should ever come out, I'll see you behind bars before I'll admit to it. You do understand what I'm saying?' He understood all right! He understood only too well. Before he could reply, he was ousted from the carriage near Hyde Park and left to find his own way home.

It was ten minutes past eight when Beth came down to the dining room. Both her parents were seated at the breakfast table. As she came through the door it was her father who looked up to say with a warm smile, 'Well now, you look bright and cheerful. Going somewhere special, are you?' Anticipating a long conversation, he rolled up his newspaper and placed it beside his plate. Leaning back in his chair, he seemed to grow in stature. With his broad shoulders, soft hazel eyes and greying brown hair that curled at the temples, Richard Ward was still a handsome man. He was forty-eight years old, but carried his age well and had a childish quality that gave him an appealing air of innocence. Yet, beneath all of that he had a shrewd mind and a certain ruthlessness in business that belied his submissive nature at home. Still smiling, he regarded Beth with approval, thinking how lovely she looked. Certainly she had taken great pains with her appearance this morning, dressing in her favourite dark blue skirt, worn with a cream-coloured silk blouse over it and a pretty blue bolero that nipped in at the waist. Her shining brown hair hung loose down her back and her whole countenance was one of glowing excitement.

'No, I'm not going anywhere special,' she replied, first kissing her father on the forehead then seating herself at the table and pouring a cup of tea from the white china teapot. 'Just to the market.' She carefully omitted to say she was meeting Tyler there.

'Oh, well, then.' Richard smiled and picked up his

paper. He could see she was not in a talkative mood. 'The stallholders are in for a treat, I reckon.' His smile crinkled into a laugh and, always infected by her father's rare displays of happiness, Beth also laughed. But then, acutely aware of Esther's disapproval, they quickly fell silent, with Beth concentrating on daintily sipping her tea, and her father enthusiastically scanning the newspaper before making the comment, 'The working class won't rest until it has a party of its own to vote for. It won't be long in coming either . . . there are already a growing number of "Lib-Labs" in Parliament.'

Ester looked up at his remark, her voice scathing as she declared, 'The working class has a great deal to learn about politics. It has the Conservatives and the Liberals to choose between. Heaven help us if it ever gets a political party of its own.' She waited for an argument, but when none was forthcoming turned on Beth. 'You're surely not going out with your hair loose like that?' Without waiting for an answer, she went on, 'And I think you had better change into a skirt that covers your ankles . . . you look like a woman of the streets!' Her piercing blue eyes raked Beth's face. 'Have you no shame?'

'Leave the girl alone, Esther.' Richard lowered his newspaper and peered over the top at Beth. 'Times are changing, and the young ladies are getting bolder. There are pretty ankles to be seen everywhere these days.' He smiled at Beth, and her heart went out to him. 'And our Beth could *never* look like a "woman of the streets".'

Incensed, his wife pushed back her chair and rose to her feet. 'I might have expected you to defend her. Kindly concentrate on your newspaper and your politics, Richard, and leave her to me.' Now she was addressing Beth. 'Go upstairs at once. Change into something plainer . . . and pin your hair up.'

Beth gave no reply, other than to come away from

the table and glance at her father, hoping he would once again intervene. But he had hidden himself behind his newspaper and deliberately shied away from meeting her gaze. A feeling of anger and frustration welled up inside her, as she realised the simple truth. He was afraid! Richard Ward, the man who was rapidly making a name for himself in the cut-throat world of property development, was afraid of his own wife. Suddenly, her anger was directed towards the woman who had brought him to this. 'I have no intention of changing my dress,' she said defiantly. 'Nor will I pin up my hair. I'm not a child, so please don't treat me like one.' Less than a year ago, she would not have been so bold as to defend herself in such a way; but love had made her bold. Love, and fear, because she knew that if her mother had her way, Tyler would be sent packing and she would be walking down the aisle with Wilson Ryan. No! Not with Wilson Ryan . . . but with a chain of hat shops and a stepping stone by which the name of Esther Ward might become one of even greater consequence.

'Not a child you say?' The older woman met Beth's anger with a coolness that surprised even herself. When she spoke, it was with astonishing restraint. 'And, at twenty-four years of age, neither are you a woman.' With a slow, cruel smile, she added quietly, 'Do as you will. The consequences of your wilful and defiant nature will fall on your shoulders, not mine.' She had not forgotten her meeting with Thomas Reynolds that very morning. The plan that was unfolding even now filled her with a sense of elation. Now, when Beth went from the room, she turned her head towards the departing figure, her whisper almost inaudible. 'You won't be so proud in a little while . . . either way I'll be rid of you.'

'What was that you said?' Richard had long learned not to come between his wife and daughter. There was much that Beth did not know . . . please God, would *never* know. And there was much that both he and Beth owed to Esther. He dreaded the animosity between these two women, and was powerless to do anything about it. Right from the start it had always been there, as though the child sensed something. But maybe he was imagining things. How *could* she know? It was all so long ago.

'I said nothing,' his wife replied now.

'Oh, then I must have been hearing things,' he said, putting down his paper and staring at her with suspicious eyes. 'But . . .'

'Yes?' Her direct stare unnerved him. She meant it to.

'Well, I thought . . . it's just . . .' He looked towards the door. 'Must you always antagonise her like that?'

'But it is she who "antagonises" me, dear.' Her smile was disarmingly sweet. 'I'm only thinking of Beth, you know that. We don't want her going astray, do we? We both know the consequences of such behaviour, don't we, dear?' The insinuation was unmistakable.

'No.' His answer was immediate. Her warning might have been prompted by the normal anxiety of a concerned mother, but its real meaning was not lost on him. He knew exactly what she meant. 'You're right, of course,' he conceded. 'As you say, it's best if I leave her to you.' He returned to the contents of his newspaper, but his thoughts remained with Beth. And his heart was heavy.

Beth saw Tyler before he saw her. As she clambered from the omnibus in Oxford Street, a distant clock was striking the hour of nine a.m., the time when she and Tyler had arranged to meet. It was a beautiful morning, and, being Saturday, the streets were already busy. Shoppers bedecked in fine gowns or pin-stripe suits, the men sporting tall black toppers and the women carrying their parasols, hurried on their way, attending to their

own business and seeming unperturbed by the hive of
activity all around. A milk-cart rattling with churns
trundled along the street, and an old man sauntered
by, carrying a wooden sandwich-board and humming
the music hall version of 'The Ratcatcher's Daughter'.
As Beth went to pass him, he doffed his round hat and
made her a cheery, 'Top o' the mornin' to yer, darlin'.'

'And top o' the mornin' to *you*,' she said, wondering
with amusement what her mother would say if she heard
her exchanging greetings with the old fellow.

Coming to the kerb edge, Beth waited patiently for
the line of carriages to pass by. As yet, Tyler had not
seen her. He was standing underneath the awning of
the Princess Theatre, anxiously glancing from left to
right then left again, and occasionally bowing his head
to stare at his polished black boots. He made a strikingly
handsome figure, with his tall lean physique. He was
dressed in his best brown cord trousers with a long dark
jacket, his thick shoulder-length black hair brushing the
collar of his white shirt. Now, when he looked up to
see her scurrying towards him, his strong white teeth
flashed in a wonderful smile. 'Beth! I was beginning to
give up on you,' he said, rushing forward and grasping
her hand in his.

'Shame on you then,' she chided good-humouredly,
her heart spilling over with happiness on seeing him. If
they hadn't been in the middle of a busy thoroughfare,
she would have thrown herself into his arms there and
then. Momentarily shocked by her own thoughts, she
saw her mother's face in her mind's eye, and for the
briefest moment her bubble of joy was burst.

'Where to then?' Tyler asked, holding out his arm
while she slid her hand through the crook of it. It felt
good to be linking her arm with his; to be just one of
the many couples, strolling the pavement for all the
world to see.

Glancing up to where his shirt was open at the neck and the bandage was clearly visible, Beth remembered how he might have been killed on that night. And, if he had been, it would have been her fault. But he was here, warm and alive, and somehow she felt everything would be all right. 'To the market,' she said, smiling up at him, her dark eyes sparkling.

'The market it is, then,' he declared. As they moved away, his mood grew serious. 'Let's make this a day to remember,' he told her quietly. He might have explained how he had made up his mind to go North and make good: and afterwards, when he felt he could keep her in the style of a lady, would come back to claim her as his wife. But he said nothing. There was time enough. The day was only just beginning, and they had to snatch what little happiness was left to them. He would tell her later, before it was ended.

Tyler could not know that Beth was also biding her time before confiding her own closely guarded secret to him. As they made their way out of Regent Street and on towards the market, she was both nervous and excited, as she wondered how he might receive the news that he was about to be a father.

'Oh, Tyler, it's been the most wonderful day of my life!' Swinging round in her seat, Beth kissed him full on the mouth, to the amusement of some onlookers and the indignation of others. But Beth saw none of them. She only knew that she was wonderfully, incredibly happy. All around her in the gallery people were laughing and shouting at the antics on stage. Down below the ladies in the stalls and boxes were a sight to behold in their silks and satins, fur capes and glittering jewellery. This was gala night, with pretty lights and colourful stage displays, and now the flowers were being handed up . . . row upon row of extravagant bouquets given by admiring gentlemen in appreciation of their favourite actresses; and maybe with the hope of a rendezvous after the show.

Sliding his arm round her, and much to her delight, Tyler whispered in her ear, 'I love you, Beth Ward.' All day he had watched her at the market; when she stopped at every stall, picking up this and that and being excited by the hustle and bustle; then in the park where they sat on the grass, talking and laughing and sharing the enjoyment of children at play. Later they found a lovely little tea shop that served tiny white scones heavy with currants and accompanied by two round dishes, one filled with jam, the other laden with cream; and all served on a round silver tray with blue china teapot, matching sugar bowl and milk jug, and the daintiest cups and saucers. It had been Tyler's intention to make this day a day for building memories . . . memories which would sustain him and Beth through the long weeks, maybe months, when they would be apart. Now, as he looked at her shining face, seeing how enthralled she was by the singer's sad and beautiful melody as it floated up from the stage, he was filled with a crippling sadness. How could he tell her he was going away? That his mind was made up and would not be changed? How would he begin to explain? He did not know. All he knew was that he could not ask her to marry him when he was down and out, when there was no prospect for the future. He loved her too much for that. Oh, he knew she would try to brush aside his fears, tell him that it didn't matter, that *nothing* mattered as long as they were together. But he knew better. For Beth's sake more than his own, he would have to be strong.

'Happy, are you?' In the carriage on the homeward journey, Tyler put his arm around her and drew her close, his lips touching her face and a weight of sadness on him as he realised the time was drawing close when he must tell her.

'I've never been happier in the whole of my life,' she murmured, tilting her face up to his and looking deep into those green eyes that held so many dark shadows. She would have spoken again but he lowered his head, his mouth covering hers, sending deep unbearable sensations through her whole being. His nearness intoxicated her – the strong manly smell, the clean sharp perfume of a freshly laundered shirt, the touch of his skin . . . warm and slightly rough against her face. Another lifelong memory; another precious day with her love.

For a while they stayed huddled together in the corner of the seat, content in each other's company, with the rest of the world outside and only the fleeting glimpses of street lamps through the fog to remind them that this could not last. Soon they must step out of the carriage and face the world that would drive them apart.

Presently he pulled away, holding her attention with his eyes and keeping his hands on her shoulders. 'There's something I have to tell you, Beth,' he said quietly, 'and I want you to hear me out before you say anything. Will you do that?'

'Not if you're going to tell me that we can't see each other . . . that loving you will only bring me heartache.'

'Please, Beth.' All of his anguish betrayed itself in his voice. Hearing it, she feared the worst. She opened her mouth to protest, but was silenced when he shook his head, saying, 'Hear me out, that's all I ask, sweetheart. Just hear me out.'

Even before he revealed his intention to leave London, the tears were coursing down Beth's face. Strange how she had known that the day had been too beautiful to last. In her heart she had sensed the unhappiness in him, and she was not surprised to hear the words issuing from his lips – gentle words, yet so harsh and cruel, tearing her apart, raising both anger and helplessness in her. 'I *have* to go, Beth. You must know. I'm finished here . . . your mother has seen to that. There isn't a company anywhere in London that will employ me now.'

'Then we'll move away!'

He shook his head. 'No, Beth. I won't ask that of you, and I won't argue the point any more. I've decided to leave, find a job, and get a home together.'

'You don't want me?' Her dark pain-filled eyes tore him apart.

'Oh, you little fool! You blind little fool!' With a heartfelt cry he crushed her to him, hiding his tears from her and cursing a cruel world. 'You think I don't want you!' His voice was bitter and accusing. 'I want nothing else on God's earth.' Angrily cupping her face between his hands, he looked at her a while, brushing away her tears with his thumbs and searching those uplifted dark eyes that he had filled with pain. 'Think, Beth,' he urged, 'think what would happen if I stayed here. Things would only go from bad to worse. You would get hurt in the process. Your family would shun you. I would blame myself, and sooner or later . . . sooner or later, you would also come to blame me.'

'No. You're wrong.' In that moment, Beth was tempted to tell him that she was carrying his child. She knew that Tyler was a man who would live up to his responsibilities, and would not turn away. With just a few words she could have him, hold him to her for ever. But at what cost? It would be tantamount to blackmail. She did not want that. Instead, she appealed to him. 'Take me with you, Tyler. If you go, there will be little point in life for me.'

Looking at her now, in the dim glow inside the carriage, with her eyes beseeching him, he was desperate. For one split second he almost relented. But then he envisaged the consequences of such weakness, and fear for her overrode his own emotions. 'And then what?' he asked her pointedly. 'Take you to some back street alley? Find us a room where the rats run free and the damp flows down the walls? Find us a place where drunken men roll home at all hours?' His voice rose with emotion. 'And should I leave you there on your own all day while I'm trudging the streets looking for work?' He had painted a black picture, but he knew from experience that the reality would be far worse. His resolve hardened. He shook his head. 'No, Beth, I won't take you with me. But I'll come back for you, I swear to God. I'll come back for you, as soon as ever I can.'

Seeing that he was determined, Beth shook his hands from her and faced him defiantly. 'I have money. Enough to get us started at least.'

'NO!' The word exploded from him.

Ignoring his protest, she went on, 'We'll search until we find a decent room. And I can get a job. I'm a trained clerk, and between us we know enough about the construction industry to place ourselves well.'

'Beth, there's a depression on. It may be weeks before I can find work at all. But two things you can rely on. First, what money you have won't last long. Secondly, employers who'll take on a woman are few and far between. In fact, I've never met one yet who would even *consider* it! Here, it's your own father who employs you . . . you won't have such an advantage elsewhere.' He bowed his head, spent of emotion, his voice softer than a whisper as he told her, 'I won't rest a day until you're with me, Beth. Trust me. For God's sake, sweetheart, trust me.'

She gave no answer, but turned away to stare out of the window, her sad dark eyes following the jagged skyline. Now and then a trail of grey smoke drifted into the air, making wavy lines across the moon and blotting out its silver light. When she spoke, her voice was that of a stranger. 'Is there no other way?' she said. And when his answer came, soft and loving, 'No, sweetheart. There is no other way,' she choked back the tears to tell him, 'Then I have to trust you, for I love you with all my heart.' His hands slid over her shoulders and she turned towards him, nestling into his arms.

For the remainder of the journey, not another word was spoken. But there was no need for words. It was all in their hearts: Tyler already regretting the loneliness without her; and Beth keeping the secret of his child and feeling closer to him because of it. She prayed he would return before the child was born, and feared the time when her parents would learn the truth.

The carriage trundled to a halt. She was relieved to see that the house was in darkness. At least tonight there would be no questions, no awful scenes. Only a quietness in its own way just as dreadful. And the knowledge that Tyler would soon be gone, taking with him her joy. But not her reason for living, she reminded herself, for she had his seed warm and alive inside her. Until he returned, she would live only for the future that Tyler had promised. And she would learn to face the consequences of carrying his child, without shame, and without fear.

Having helped her from the carriage, he bent his head and kissed her, a long lingering kiss that held too much sadness. After a moment he released her, but kept her small hands in his strong fingers, concerned eyes searching her face. She also regarded him for a moment before saying in a remarkably cool voice, 'Where will you go?'

'North . . . to the dockyards. Or maybe Southampton.' He smiled down on her, squeezing her hands then pulling her to him in one last embrace, gently rocking her as a mother might rock her child. 'You'll know where I am

soon enough, sweetheart. I'll make sure of it. Every step
I take . . . wherever I lay my head . . . you'll know.'
Loath to let her go, he held her a moment longer.

'When will you go?'

'In the morning. Perhaps even this very night. Now
that it's decided, there's no point in delaying.'

'God go with you,' she murmured, dark liquid eyes
staring up at him.

'Wait for me, Beth . . . I'll be back.'

Her quiet smile made his heart ache. 'I know,' she said
softly, 'I know you will. Just as you know I'll be here,
waiting.'

As they parted – Beth going into the house that would
seem like a prison for her for every moment he was gone,
and he climbing into the carriage that would take him
away from her – how could they possibly know that the
cruel hand of Fate would shatter the vows they had so
lovingly made?

Tyler could not sleep. Beth was still too warm in his arms,
too vivid in his memory. For what seemed an age, but
was in fact only minutes, he had lain on his bed, arms
folded beneath his head and his eyes closed against the
intrusive candlelight, his tortured mind reliving every
moment with his love.

Restless and uncertain, he swung himself from the bed
and went to the mantelpiece where he stretched out his
arms, gripping either end of the cold marble slab and
bending his head forward, groaning at the images that
would not leave him be. Dropping his troubled gaze to
the grey lifeless ashes in the grate, he suffered his first
real doubts. How could he leave her? The thought filled
him with such despair that it spilled from his lips in an
agonised prayer. 'Dear God! How can I leave her?' The
struggle within him was fierce, and yet he knew there was
only one answer. If there was ever to be a future for him

76

and Beth, then he had no choice. He *must* leave! A tide of anger rose in him.

But then he made himself look forward. He was young, not yet thirty, his back was broad and strong, and he had a mind that was quick to adapt. Since leaving the orphanage he had learned many things; not least of which was the art of survival. And, as Beth had so rightly pointed out, he knew the construction industry inside out. In his earlier days he had been blooded in the labour of a dockworker. He had been a mudlark, a street-trader, an undertaker's boy, and a thief. He knew all the tricks and had risen above his beggarly beginnings. He could do so again. For Beth's sake, he could do so again! In that moment, he saw the brooch glittering in the candlelight. Beth's brooch. He reached out and took it between his fingers, a smile lifting his features, and her love warming his heart. For a long poignant moment, he held the brooch close, his sea-green eyes dark and moist, 'I'll make well, Beth,' he murmured. 'And I'll be back for you. As God's my judge, I'll be back for you!'

The quiet knock on the door startled him. He glanced at the small clock by his bed. *It was gone midnight.* Disturbed, he went to the door. 'Who's there?' he said quietly.

'It's me . . . Annie.'

'Annie!' At once he remembered how she and her mother had brought him through the worst of his fever. 'What do you want?' he asked in a whisper. 'Is there trouble. Is it your mother?'

'No. But I must talk with you. Please, Tyler. I won't stay long. I know it's late.' Her voice rang with urgency.

'Ssh . . . you'll wake the whole house,' he warned. 'Can't it wait 'til morning?'

'NO! Please, open the door. I must talk with you.'

'Just a minute.' He glanced round the room. On coming in he had taken his valise from the wardrobe and placed it at the foot of the bed. He had actually begun to pack a few things, but then abandoned the idea. It seemed too final somehow. Now he went to the bed and grabbed the valise, hurriedly stuffing it back into the wardrobe. Explaining his departure was a matter best left for the morning.

On returning to the door, he opened it just wide enough to admit her. 'What's wrong, Annie?' he asked in a concerned voice, before softly closing the door as she came into the room. When he turned, he was astonished to see that she was wearing only a long cotton dressing-robe, the flimsy nightgown clearly visible beneath. And beneath that, her firm round breasts, the dark nipples pushing up beneath the soft material. Strolling to the fireplace, she stretched one long slim arm across the mantelpiece and draped herself seductively, letting her dressing-robe fall open to reveal every curve and shadow of her body. 'I saw you come in,' she said softly. 'You looked so lonely I thought you might be glad of some feminine company.'

At once, and realising what a bloody fool he'd been to let her in, Tyler strode across the room, his voice deliberately low as he told her, 'I think you'd best leave, Annie.' Her answer was to turn her head and gently laugh. It was then she saw the brooch. Her fingers closed over it. The smile fell from her face as she came towards him, one hand reaching out to where his chest was bared at the neck of his shirt. Slim groping fingers touched the frayed bandage there. 'Do you think I haven't seen you naked?' she asked with a meaningful look. 'My mother let me bathe you . . . touch you.' The last two words were murmured like a kiss, her eyes narrowed with passion. When she saw that he was unmoved, something snapped inside her. For too long she had dreamed of lying in his bed, enfolded in his strong arms, their nakedness merging. Tonight she had thought to try for his love, and if he had given

it, she would have let nothing come between them
. . . not even the silver-haired man who had promised
her a handsome reward for certain 'services rendered'.
Now though, seeing the disgust written on Tyler's face,
she knew that they had been only pipe-dreams. Tyler
Blacklock could never bring himself to take her in his
arms. Passion drained from her and in its place came
a black hatred. 'Ah. . .so I'm not as good as your
precious "lady", is that it, eh?' The sneer disfigured
her bold beauty. 'You think I'm not grand enough for
the likes of Tyler Blacklock, eh?'

Jerking her head back to laugh, she fell against him,
her breath fanning his face, the smell of whisky strong.
'Look at me!' she cried, fighting him like a wild tiger as
she tore away her dressing-robe and began ripping her
nightgown from the neck down. 'I've been with men
before . . . I know what's wanted. Don't you like what
you see? Don't you want to stroke me . . . do what you
like with me, I don't care! Elizabeth Ward would never
give herself to you like that, would she, eh?' she taunted.
When he flung open the door, she lashed out blindly,
her sharp nails scoring the side of his face and bringing
blood. When it trickled down his neck, she laughed
hysterically, reaching out to lick it with her tongue.

Incensed, he grabbed her arm, his face set like granite
as he propelled her roughly through the door. 'You've
said enough, you little fool!' His voice was low, yet laced
with fury. 'GET OUT OF HERE!'

As he thrust her on to the landing, he was shocked to
the core when she began screaming and crying, lashing
out at him and shredding the nightgown off her own
back, her shrill voice piercing the sleeping quiet of the
house. Suddenly, all hell was let loose. Doors banging,
people shouting, running footsteps converging from all
directions.

'You bastard!' Tom Singleton was a docker, a huge

ape of a man. From the first day he had arrived here, he'd set his cap at Annie, and she had never repulsed his advances. In fact, there was many a dark night when she had sneaked into his room and satisfied his every need. But then, when Tyler took her fancy, Tom Singleton was given the cold shoulder. He took it badly, and now he saw the reason . . . Tyler Blacklock! When he swung his fist, Tyler was ready. Blocking the oncoming punch with his forearm, he tried to reason. 'I've done nothing, you bloody fool!' he yelled. But there was no placating the man. Dismissing Tyler's protests, he launched into him, egged on by the shouts of the other lodger and Florence Ball, who was cradling the half-naked girl and screaming for Singleton to: 'Floor the bleeder!'

Realising that the man had no intention of hearing his side of it, intent instead on giving him a real hiding, Tyler saw that he had no choice but to defend himself. He took the man on, and in spite of his bad arm, gave as good as he got.

The fight was fierce, with blood flowing on both sides, the sound of crunching fists almost drowned by the shouts of those who watched, Florence having deserted the 'sobbing' girl to enact her own particular fight by flailing her fat bunched fists in the air, all the while yelling, 'Garn, yer bugger! Yer dirty sod . . . ain't one woman enough fer yer?' When Tyler rammed the big fellow against the door, she forgot whose side she was on, and began jumping up and down with glee. Her enthusiasm quickly subsided however when Singleton went down, with Tyler standing over him, bloody but triumphant.

It was then that the other lodger stepped forward. It seemed he had been ready for such an outcome, because now he raised his arm to show the glistening blade clutched in his thick grubby fingers. 'Come on then, matey,' he growled, spreading his legs and holding out both arms in a defensive stance. 'Show *me* what yer made of.'

He could see that Tyler was badly hurt. The blood was pouring from a gash on his forehead, and there was a crimson stain spreading through his shirt from the old wounds beneath; his face was bruised and he was unsteady on his legs. But he stood his ground and faced the man, at the same time ripping off his shirt and wrapping it thickly round his arm, which he then raised to his face as the man began to move in, jabbing the knife before him, a sadistic leer on his unshaven face.

'NO!' Florence lunged forward, grabbing the lodger's arm. 'There'll be no murder done 'ere. Don't want no bobbies knockin' on *my* door,' she screeched, pulling him away. Grudgingly, the man backed off. With a dark scowl at Tyler and the snarled threat: 'We ain't done yet, matey!' he tended to Singleton, who was led away groaning, his legs buckling beneath him.

'I want you out!' Florence turned on Tyler. 'Yer ain't worth the bleedin' trouble!' When he turned away, she swung round on the girl. 'And as fer you,' she shouted, slamming the flat of her hand into the girl's face, 'yer deserve all yer get. What the 'ell d'yer think yer doing . . . wanderin' 'alf naked round the bleedin' 'ouse at all hours o' the night?' As she pushed her away she could be heard threatening all manner of retribution. 'I named yer right, that's fer sure . . . "Fanny" got your old mammy in trouble, and it's "Fanny" that'll get *you* in trouble, or my name's not Florence bleedin' Ball!'

Every word was accompanied by the sound of a fresh slap and the occasional tearful protest. 'Leave me alone, you silly old cow! I tell you, it weren't *my* fault.' However, once inside the scullery the two women collapsed into each other's arms, shaking with laughter but checking the sound for fear they might be overheard.

Inside the privacy of his room, Tyler laid out the soap and towel, then filled the bowl with cold water from the jug. Next he stripped the bandage from his shoulder and chest, wincing with pain as the frayed cloth stuck to the newly opened wounds. Gently he dabbed cool soothing water over the erupted skin, until the flow of blood slowed to a trickle. When at length it began to congeal and seal the wound, he washed his upper body and splashed his face with the cold water; afterwards drying himself, combing his thick black hair into some semblance of order, and putting on a clean shirt. That done, he took his spare pair of trousers from the wardrobe and placed them in the valise; next came his socks, shirts, and toiletries. Looking around the room, he suddenly remembered Beth's brooch. After spending a while searching for it, he realised it was missing. Of course. Annie had stolen it.

Clipping his valise shut, he crossed to the door where he took his jacket from the nail there, and threw it over his arm. As he proceeded down to the kitchen where he suspected the girl and her mother to be, his thoughts flew to Beth. It occurred to him that he might somehow get a note to her. But he dismissed the idea. They had said their goodbyes earlier. It was best that he make tracks now; there was nothing to be gained by causing her more pain. The brooch, though. Beth's brooch would bring her closer to him in the long, lonely months to follow. He had no intention of leaving this house without it.

'What!' Florence blocked his entry into the kitchen. 'So, yer ain't satisfied with tekkin' advantage o' my poor gal . . . yer accusin' 'er o' being a bloody *thief* into the bargain?' She put her whole weight against the door in an effort to keep him out. 'Sod orf!' she told him. 'Unless yer want me to scream an' 'oller fer the blokes up top.'

'Just tell your daughter to hand over the brooch, then I'll be on my way,' he said in a quiet determined voice. He knew she had no intention of creating another rumpus, but called her bluff all the same. 'Shout them if you like, though, because I have no intention of leaving this house without the brooch.'

'Stay there,' she ordered, 'I'll get the bleedin' brooch. Sod and bugger me . . . anybody'd think it were worth a bloody fortune. I've seen it, and so far as I can tell, it ain't worth all that much at all.' She swung back into the kitchen to where the girl was seated at the table, the brooch clutched in her hand and a look of feigned resignation on her surly face. There followed a short and fierce argument before the disgruntled woman appeared again, to hold out her hand so Tyler could see the brooch lying there. When he stretched out to take it, she snatched it back. 'Yer owe me two weeks' rent,' she reminded him. 'It's that . . . or this 'ere brooch. Judging by the way you mean to get it back, I reckon it just might be worth some'at after all.'

Without a word he slipped his fingers into the breast pocket of his shirt to draw out the exact sum, which he had counted earlier. This he delivered into her outstretched palm. And, grunting with approval, she gave over the brooch, promptly slamming the door on his departing figure and telling her daughter, 'Good riddance to 'im,' when she heard the front door close. A moment later, something disturbed the two women. Going to the kitchen door, the girl gingerly opened it and peeped out. She was relieved to see the bruised and burly figure of Tom Singleton coming furtively down the stairs with his friend behind. When he stared at her with a meaningful expression, she quickly nodded, a wicked smile shaping her ruby red mouth. Joined now by her mother, she watched as the two men went softly down the passage and out of the front door. Realising the seriousness of their intent, and suddenly afraid, Florence ducked back into the kitchen, pushing the girl before her and firmly closing the door. 'We know nothing! Remember that,' she warned the girl. 'We know *nothing*!'

Outside, fog hung like a grey cloud over the darkness, and shadows lurked in every corner. The eerie echo of his footsteps against the pavement gave Tyler an unnerving sense of being the only man alive on God's earth. Somewhere ahead of him, the sinister lamentation of mating cats rose up like something out of Hell. He thought he heard a sound – behind him. Curious, and a little afraid, he stopped and glanced back, but there was nothing; only the light from the ground floor of the boarding house. He turned away, smiling at the thought of Florence and her daughter, no doubt still arguing and enjoying every minute of it.

There it was again! A familiar sound, like the brushing of a boot against the pavement. Convinced that he was being followed, he stopped and pressed himself flat against the wall. Silence descended. The darkness and the smog intermingled to make an impenetrable barrier. Holding his breath, he strained his eyes to pierce the gloom. The silence was unbearable. Rivulets of sweat began to meander down his back, welding his shirt to his skin and raising fire from the raw wounds in his chest and shoulder. He remained like this for what seemed a lifetime, listening and watching. The silence deepened, an awful death-like stillness that wrapped itself round him like a mantle. He waited a moment longer. Had he been imagining things? Maybe it was only the marauding cats or the many vagabonds who were known to frequent the alleys hereabouts. Taking a deep breath to still his pounding heart, he bent to collect the valise from the ground where he had softly dropped it.

'NOW!' The gruff cry was the last thing he heard before a blunt heavy object came out of the darkness, crunching against his temple and sending him reeling sideways. Struggling to right himself, he realised there was more than one attacker, but could not identify them, these large shadowy bulks with limbs flailing and a thirst for blood that was terrifying. With startling clarity he knew they meant to kill him. Blinded by the blood that ran down his head and into his eyes, Tyler launched into the thick-set ruffians, his tight-clenched fists slamming into jutting bone and yielding tissue. But the harder he went into the fray, the more punishment he received. The men were merciless in their onslaught. Weakened by the loss of blood and earlier injuries, Tyler was soon overcome; forced to the ground in a pool of blood, seemingly lifeless. And still they came at him . . . with their fists, with their boots, and swinging the cudgel again and again, until vengeance was satisfied. Next they searched his valise and emptied his pockets. Only then did they turn away. From the window of the boarding house, the woman and the girl were silent accomplices; but to the half-naked sweethearts who huddled in fear only a few yards away, the greatest nightmare was that the ruffians should catch sight of them.

Inside the kitchen, Florence Ball pulled the girl away from the window. Wide-eyed and frightened, they turned their attention to the door. When it slowly opened, the older woman gasped, clutching the girl and repeating a hoarse whisper, 'We know nothing. Remember . . . we know *nothing!*'

With a satisfied smile, Tom Singleton gave his land-lady a share of the money, together with the warning, 'Keep yer mouth shut, or we'll *all* be strung up!' When he pressed Beth's brooch into the girl's hand, he made no comment; but his smiling eyes flashed a warning, telling her that she was in his debt and would do well not to forget it.

* * *

85

'*Is he dead?*' The young woman stood trembling, while her sweetheart bent to examine the broken bleeding body.

'I think so.'

'We should have helped! I know we should have helped!' With every word her voice edged nearer to a scream. Realising it, she pressed both her hands to her mouth and began sobbing.

'They'd have killed *us* an' all, you idiot!' he whispered, glancing nervously about as though expecting the men to pounce on him from the darkness. He straightened up, keeping his eyes fixed on the sprawled figure. 'God Almighty!' He shook his head in disbelief. 'They've battered the poor bugger to a pulp.' He pointed down. 'Look at him . . . look at his legs. If he's not dead, he'll never walk again, that's for sure.' He shook his head again. 'Madmen,' he murmured, 'Bloody madmen!' When his horrified sweetheart began sobbing again, he gripped her to him. 'We'd best get help,' he said, glancing once more at the broken, lifeless form. 'That's the least we can do,' he told her, drawing away from the bloodied scene. But he saw no need to hurry.

Beth woke with a start. It was still dark in the room, but through the chink in the slightly parted curtains, she could see a glimmer of light. She did not know how long she had been asleep, only that her dreams had been greatly troubled. Turning in the bed, she stared trance-like at the incoming shaft of hazy light, her uneasy mind going over the events of last evening, the many treasured images flicking in and out of her consciousness and disturbing her even more. So much so that sleep was now impossible.

In a moment she got up from the bed and put on her dressing gown. The air struck cold as she went on bare feet to the window. Shivering, she drew the cord tighter around her waist, folding her arms against her body and hugging herself. Sliding back the curtains, she looked out over the familiar skyline; tall irregular chimneys and higgledy-piggledy roofs shrouded in a blanket of rising fog that floated upwards to the sky. Ambiguous, clearly visible one minute and lost to sight the next, the awkward buildings seemed without substance, somehow unreal, emerging and disappearing like ghosts in the mind. And yet, it was all so comforting to Beth; reassuringly friendly and familiar. Raising her dark eyes to the sky, she watched the far-off clouds playing hide and seek with the rising dawn. She thought about life . . . and death. About love and fear. Of all the emotions that murmured through her, 'fear' was paramount. Fear that even now Tyler was many miles away; fear that he might forget her; fear that he would stop loving her. And, above all, fear that they might never again be together.

The heartfelt prayer began deep inside her, spoken now with a passion that was bitter-sweet. 'Dear God, don't take him from me for ever. I love him so.' Without her realising it, the tears were coursing down her face, warm and surprising against the coolness of her skin. With a heavy, yet hopeful, heart, she gazed at the sky a while longer, until the clouds began to disperse and the sun brought his face over the distant horizon. She felt tired, incredibly weary. Yet she knew she would not be able to sleep. Not now. Not when Tyler was so alive in her mind. Going to the bedside, she slipped her feet into soft flat shoes. Then, after lighting the candle which stood in its shiny brass holder on the dresser, she held it before her and went on quiet footsteps out of the room; catching her breath and remaining motionless for a moment when the sound of the door closing seemed to echo through the house. Satisfied that she had not woken anyone, she continued on her way, along the landing and down the stairs into the kitchen.

'Ben!' On opening the kitchen door, she was startled

to see her brother seated at the big pine table. The only
light in the room was from the small window high up
in the wall above the sink. He had been huddled over
the table when she came through the door, but now he
swung round, his eyes puffed and tired. When he saw
that it was Beth, he seemed relieved. 'Oh, it's you,' he
said. 'You couldn't sleep either, eh?'

Placing the candle on the table between them, she
asked, 'What's wrong, Ben? You look awful.'

'Couldn't settle, that's all,' he told her, his smile uncon-
vincing. 'Too hot . . . uncomfortable.' He chose not to
burden her with the truth, that he had accumulated
heavy gambling debts and that he had only a short time
in which to find the money, or the organisation would
carry out their threat to approach his father. He would
do almost anything to avoid such a confrontation. Filled
with shame and regret, he had feverishly searched his
mind for a way out. But there was none. Trapped and
desperate, he had toyed with the idea of going to his
mother. She had forgiven him many things in the past
. . . but gambling? No. He knew in his heart that she
would never tolerate such weakness. Now, as he looked
at Beth, seeing her genuine concern for him and knowing
that above all people she would want to help him, he was
greatly tempted to confess everything to her. She had a
little money of her own, he knew, although he did not
know how much or whether it would be enough to satisfy
his debt. Suddenly, he was mortified with shame. Afraid
that she might somehow know the awful thoughts in his
mind, he turned away.

'You're worried about something, aren't you, Ben?'
Beth knew her brother too well not to realise when
something was wrong. 'Is it me? Are you worried about
me . . . and Tyler?' When he gave no answer she came
and stood beside him, running her fingers through his
wayward fair hair and telling him fondly, 'Oh, you

mustn't worry. Everything will be fine. I just know it will.'

When he looked up, his warm brown eyes were smiling. He clenched his fingers over her small hand. Reminding himself that he was not the only one with troubles, and knowing the awful upheaval that had been caused in this house because of Beth's relationship with Tyler Blacklock, he said, 'Are you sure everything'll be all right?' There was a momentary impulse of anger towards her, but he pushed it down.

She thought for a moment, unable to answer his question in all truthfulness. If wishing made things come right, then she and Tyler would not be apart for too long and would live out a full and wonderful life together; but wishes did not always come true, just as prayers were not always answered. And so she spoke from the heart when she replied, 'I believe everything will come right for us, Ben. I *must* believe that, or there will be nothing for me.' The strength and conviction in her voice made him afraid.

'Sit here, Beth . . . opposite me, where I can see you,' he murmured, gesturing to the seat at the other side of the table. When, after a moment, she did as he asked, he said quietly, 'I love you . . . you know that, don't you, Beth?'

'Yes, I know you do.'

'And it's because I love you that I have to say what I feel.' He reached out and placed his hand over hers, pressing it to the table. 'Are you so sure you're doing the right thing? This affair with Tyler. Look at the turmoil it's caused in this house. You know if you go on seeing him, Mother will do all she can to break you up . . . by fair means or foul.'

'What do you mean?'

'You know well enough what I mean, Beth. She's

89

made no secret of her opinions. And you know what she's capable of if she sets her mind to it.'

'I know better than anyone what she's "capable of", and am well aware of her opinions . . . that he's not good enough for me . . . that she would make sure Father cut me off without a penny if I married Tyler . . . that she'd enjoy seeing us live in poverty if I defied her. And it would serve me right for not having had the sense to marry the eligible and respectable Wilson Ryan . . . whose father just happens to be on his last legs, and about to turn his entire business over to his only son!'

In her anger she instinctively rose to her feet and thumped her two clenched fists on the table-top, demanding in a low fierce voice, 'Why should I care *what* she thinks? Did she care how *I* felt when she locked me away for days on end, cold and hungry, terrified of the dark, and afraid to sleep because of what she took great delight in telling me . . . that the rats *ate* naughty children like me?' Suddenly all the unbearable memories were back, as vivid and horrifying as if they had happened only yesterday. 'I was a child, Ben . . . just a child, who had done nothing to deserve such barbaric punishment.' She did not turn to look at him. Instead she dropped her head low and closed her eyes, but the memories would not be shut out. They were locked into her mind for all time.

'Can't you forget it, Beth? For your own sake, can't you leave it all in the past?' He knew what she was going through. He had tried so hard to share her dreadful periods of punishment when they were children; feeling guilty when he was always spared, even though he and Beth were partners in whatever innocent childish exploits had made Esther Ward lock the girl away.

'No.' She clung to his hand. 'I can't forget. Oh, I've tried. Believe me, I've tried. But it's *her* who won't let me forget, because she's still the same wicked person she always was. Everything she does, everything she say . . . the way she looks at me, keeps me remembering. She hates me. She's *always* hated me.' She swung round, her dark eyes alive with pain. 'Why?' She raised her hands and wiped away the tears; tears of anguish, tears of frustration. *'Why does she hate me so?'*

He shook his head. There was nothing he could say in answer to Beth's heartfelt question. All his life, he too had wondered, just as his sister had; although Ben would never have admitted it to anyone. But what he did know was that in defying her mother where Tyler Blacklock was concerned, Beth was isolating herself and making a deadly enemy. 'Are you sure you're not trying to punish her by taunting her with Tyler? Give him up, Beth,' he pleaded now. 'For God's sake, give him up.'

Shocked and amazed that he should say such a thing, Beth stared at him. In the flickering candlelight she saw that he looked ill, seeming suddenly older, as though he had aged years in a matter of days. When she spoke, it was with immense calm and pride. 'Tyler is my life,' she said simply. 'It isn't me taunting her. *It's her taunting me.* If you can't see that, Ben, then there's nothing else for me to say. It might interest you to know that she has won one little victory at least. Thanks to her, Tyler can't get work in these parts, and so he'll be leaving the area first thing in the morning . . . if he hasn't already gone. It might also interest you to know that I pleaded to go with him.' She saw the horror on his face and was quick to tell him, 'He would not hear of it. Instead, he persuaded me that he should go ahead to find work and a place for us to live. But, I mean to join him. As soon as he sends for me, I mean to join him.'

'Think what you're saying. He may never come back.'

'He'll be back. I know he will.'

'Oh, Beth, let him go! Use this chance to heal the rift in our family. For all her faults, Mother's right. Wilson Ryan is well placed to give you a good secure life. He may not be the man you want, but you'll have your own house and an army of servants, a new beginning, and a place in society that any woman would cherish.'

'And children . . . is Wilson Ryan a family man, do you think?' Her secret smile intrigued him. How was he to know she had conceived Tyler's child?

'I'm aware that he's an only child, but . . . yes, I do believe he would value children of his own.'

'I'm inclined to agree with you. I think he *would* like children of his own, but they will never be mine. Oh, don't get me wrong, Ben . . . I like Wilson, he's a good kind man. But I don't love him. I never could.' She smiled and he thought he had never seen his sister more beautiful. 'I wish you could think well of me and Tyler,' she said softly, her dark eyes lighting from within, 'because there will never be any other man for me. Especially now that I am carrying his child.'

She knew her confession would surprise him, but was not prepared for the abject shock that was written on his face as he recoiled from her, his eyes stretched wide and his mouth a grim tight line. He stared at her for what seemed an age, his head going slowly from side to side as though he was trying to ward off the awful truth. His whole body stiffened as he stepped away from her, his eyes regarding her as they might a stranger.

Beth met his stare with a quiet sadness; saw the shock visibly ebb from him . . . his eyes closed, his body relaxed, and his voice was so low she could hardly hear his anguished words. 'God help you, Beth,' he murmured. And though he was filled with disgust that she should have been so wanton, he might have said more. His love for her might even have demanded that he be a little more compassionate. But a certain instinct cautioned him. The atmosphere in the room was suddenly ominous. He saw that Beth had sensed it too, because she slowly drew her attention from him and turned her head sideways, dark frightened eyes looking towards the doorway. Mesmerised by the look on her face, he watched her eyes widen with horror; a horror that was already shivering through him. When she gasped, his heart seemed to turn over. Reluctantly he made himself look towards the door.

It was like looking into the jaws of Hell, and the keeper was the devil himself! The black upright silhouette was incredibly still; only the slight rise and fall of the shoulders and the soft rhythmic breathing gave it life. In the saffron glow from the candle clutched in her hand, Esther Ward's sharply etched features took on an eerie appearance, the jaw muscles clenching and unclenching as the small glittering eyes locked on to Beth. There was a long fearful moment before the brooding atmosphere was broken; then it was by one word, issued through clenched teeth in a hard, curiously restrained voice: 'Whore.' It was a word filled with repulsion and long felt hatred.

'No, Mother!' Ben protested, as he started towards her. He had felt the hatred, and it was a shocking thing.

'Leave her, Ben!' Grabbing his arm, Beth stopped him in his tracks. 'This is her chance, don't you see?' All the while she was speaking, Beth kept her eyes on that awesome figure.

Confused, he glanced at her, asking, 'What do you mean, Beth . . . "her chance"?' The low harsh laugh from the doorway made him jerk his head round. There was something unholy here. Something that made him tremble deep inside.

'Ask her,' Beth told him. 'She knows well enough.' All her life, Beth had known that her mother wanted rid of her, but until now Esther Ward had had no real opportunity to fulfil that craving. Now, though, she had every reason to turn Beth on to the streets. The very same thoughts that were running through Beth's mind now, were also running through her mother's. The ensuing satisfaction was evident in the half-smile that twisted her small narrow mouth, and in the beady eyes that continued to stare at Beth with such malevolence.

Suddenly there was another figure in the doorway. Disturbed by his wife's leaving their bedroom a short time earlier, Richard had been alarmed when she had not returned. He was even more alarmed by the scene that greeted him now. Puzzled, he stared into the room, looking first at Ben and then at the daughter he loved above all else. Because of the circumstances of her birth, Beth was very dear to him. Sadly, it was those same circumstances which kept them apart and made him the despicable coward he was. He deeply regretted the power that his wife had over Beth; but it was too late now, he told himself sadly. It was all too late.

In that moment, as he stared at his children, he wondered what he could have done all those years ago. He wondered what he could do *now*. There was trouble here; something very wrong. On his son's face he saw both confusion and resignation. In Beth's, he saw a strange mingling of pride and regret; and something else which had caused him a great deal of heartache over the years. He saw the unbending defiance and a darker emotion that was echoed even more markedly in his wife's face. The same dark emotion that had etched itself deep into Esther Ward's soul. All these years he had witnessed that crippling emotion, had seen it slowly manifest itself in many ways and on many occasions: in any room where Esther came unexpectedly upon the child; in any unguarded moment when she might watch Beth at play. Sometimes in the dead of night his wife had gone to the nursery, where she would stand over the crib and stare at the infant, silently thinking thoughts that made his blood run cold. He had seen that dark and

terrible emotion grow and fester, until now it was like a
presence in the house. So real, so intense, that a body
could feel it, almost taste it. Now, as always, he felt like
an outsider.

'What is it?' he asked quietly. 'What's wrong?' When
neither Beth nor his son answered him, he looked down
on the woman by his side. 'Esther?' His tone was more
forceful.

Her reply took him by surprise; and yet it should
not have done. 'I want her out of this house!' She
did not look up at him, but kept her attention on
Beth.

'You what?' He bent his head to stare at her face,
but she avoided his gaze, looking ahead and remaining
motionless. He appealed to Beth. 'What in God's name
has been going on here?'

'It's best if I leave right away, Father,' she told him
in a low dignified voice. If she was sorry for anything,
it was that he had come in on the scene. It was not
something he could easily cope with, and she did not
want to see his face when her mother revealed the
reason for this uproar. She was under no illusion that
he would be spared the 'sordid' details, but would
rather they were told after her departure. She glanced
at Ben, whispering, 'Watch out for him, won't you?'
When he gave no answer but dropped his gaze to the
floor as though in shame, she wondered with regret
whether she had lost his respect for ever. Sighing, she
turned away, going slowly across the kitchen, every
step taking her nearer to that small formidable figure
and the man beside it, his pained expression touching
Beth's heart and crumbling the inner dignity she had
salvaged. But she kept her head high and her steps firm,
trying not to look at him and praying that sometime
in the future, somehow, she and her father might be
reconciled. She made no such prayer for the mother

who had always loathed her and who had made no secret of it.

As she covered the short space between herself and the door, the distance seemed never ending. Outwardly, she appeared calm and defiant. Inwardly, her heart was beating furiously and the constriction in her throat was physically painful. As she drew nearer, a sense of impending danger reached her. Suddenly her mother darted forward, sharp nails slicing into Beth's arm and the searing candle flame thrust before her eyes. '*Tell him!*' the voice hissed. 'Tell your father what a whore you are!'

'Let her go, Mother. Let her leave quietly.' Ben rushed to Beth's aid, but all his strength could not prise his mother's fingers away. She clung to Beth like a leech. In the candlelight he was shocked to see the blood oozing from beneath her fingernails and leaving a thick crimson trail down Beth's arm. '*Let her go!*' he yelled, desperately trying to force himself between them. 'Christ! Look what you're doing to her!'

'*Tell your father!*' Esther was like a mad woman. '*Tell him how you've lain with Tyler Blacklock . . . lain with him and brought shame on yourself and on the name of this family.*' She was laughing now, stripped of all pretence, her eyes revealing the virulent hatred that had silently eaten away at her for too long.

'For God's sake . . . let her go, Mother!' Ben was amazed and terrified by his mother's determination. Suddenly he screamed aloud as she touched the burning candle to Beth's loose flowing locks, laughing insanely when Beth frantically snuffed out the sizzling flames that crept through her hair. Ben tried desperately to twist his mother away, but she clung all the harder. Summoning every ounce of strength, he slid both his arms over the small hard body, knocking the candle to the floor and pinning her against the dresser. She was sobbing now, trembling uncontrollably, and watching Beth's every move as she retrieved the candle and placed it on the dresser.

'Whore!' she yelled, turning her attention towards the door, where Richard Ward stood, whitefaced and visibly shocked. 'She won't tell you, so I will,' she screeched. 'Your precious Beth is carrying his bastard! Do you hear me? She's carrying Tyler Blacklock's bastard! Don't you think that's ironic?' Her laughter was chilling to hear.

But in a moment it had died away and in its place there came a look of shocked disbelief as she saw the big man spread his hands out against the door jamb and jerk his face upwards, his expression one of incredible pain. When in almost the same instant he bent forward, clutching at his chest and his legs buckling beneath him, Esther knew she had gone too far. 'Dear God, Ben! Your father!' She clasped her hands over her mouth, only her eyes visible in the small wicked face.

Beth had also seen her father go down, and was at his side even as her mother was crying out. Falling on her knees she cradled him to her, startled when he pushed against her, as though fighting her off, his eyes staring up, silently condemning. In all of her life she had never seen such a look in her father's eyes. It shook her to the core. He spoke only one word, but it was said with such vehemence that it struck her to the heart. 'NO!' He put both his hands against her and tried desperately to thrust her from him.

'Get your filthy hands off him, you trollop.' Esther raged at her. 'Can't you see, he doesn't want you touching him?' She forced Beth away. As she straightened up, Beth was horrified to see her father's body shudder uncontrollably, before becoming deathly still. It was Ben who voiced her innermost fears. 'God help us. It's too late . . . I think he's dead!'

Esther's trembling voice rent the air, as she screamed

97

at Beth, 'If your father's dead, it's you that's to blame!' Like a mad thing she launched herself at Beth, tearing at her hair, her face, all the while screaming how she had murdered her own father, how she was not fit to bear his name, and how: 'I knew all along it would come to this. I tried to warn him, but he wouldn't listen.'

'Get out, Beth!' Ben held his mother in an iron grip, his eyes bulbous with fear as he yelled at his sister: 'Get out! For God's sake . . . get out of here.' As she pulled away, bruised and bleeding, he gave her another order, one that was astonishing to Beth. 'Don't ever come back here,' he warned in sombre voice. 'Go to your man, and leave us alone.'

'Now!' Esther echoed, struggling from Ben's hold and dropping to her husband's side. 'Put her out *now*. Don't let her stay another moment in your father's house. She can send for her things later. I want her out now . . . this minute.' There was wildness in her eyes as she stared up. 'If I see you again, I swear I'll not be responsible for my actions!' The look she gave Beth was curiously triumphant. And when she glanced at her brother's hard-set face, Beth knew in her heart that he, too, blamed her for everything that had happened here. She knew also that she had no one left in the world. No one but Tyler, and the child she was carrying.

In that moment before she turned away, Beth glanced lovingly at her father's still body. His eyes were closed, but she could still see the unforgiving look in them – the terrible accusation. The pain was gone from his face, but it was not gone from her heart. She loved him. Nothing would ever change that. She had lost him. But Death had not taken him from her. No. It was nothing so simple as Death that had parted them. It was her love for Tyler. And it was something else also . . . the same mysterious thing that had caused her mother's hatred of her. Whatever it was, it belonged to a past that had nothing to do with her. It was a long-ago enigma, something between Richard and his wife. A profound yet ambiguous thing that could have been resolved only by the two people who had created it.

One more loving glance at her father and Beth turned away, the tears streaming down her face and her heart lying like a lead weight inside her. She was vaguely aware of Ben telling his mother, 'I must fetch help. Don't worry. I'll get Miss Mulliver to sit with you.' She felt like a stranger – unwanted, unimportant. Suddenly she felt the house closing in on her, and had to get away . . . get to Tyler. He would know what she must do. Wiping the tears from her eyes, she went quickly up the stairs and into her room.

A few moments later, Beth left the house. The air was shockingly cold. The bitter, stiff breeze was creating small isolated patches in the fog, and the morning sky was fast infiltrating the darkness. The streets were deserted, with only intermittent sounds penetrating the silence . . . the curdling mewl of marauding felines, and the merry ditty of a late night reveller. Beyond the square could be heard the rumbling wheels of passing carriages, and the clip-clop of horses' hooves. These familiar sounds were a comfort to Beth. She thought about the new life forming inside her, and suddenly felt a sense of purpose.

At the end of the square, she paused and looked back. She recalled the events of the night, and pain struck deep inside her. She thought about the manner in which her father had stared at her, as though he had never known her, as though she had betrayed his trust and brought him unbearable shame. And Ben? What of him, her life-long soulmate and friend? He, too, had shown revulsion towards her. She remembered the way she had found him in the kitchen – head bent into his hands, and the anguished look in his eyes when he raised his head as she came through the door. That puzzled her. It was almost as though he knew what terrible things were to follow. Was she to blame? Dear God above . . . had she really caused her father to collapse? She had a compulsion to go back; to look on his face just once more. It was so strong that she half-turned, her steps eager to carry her back. But a deeper, more urgent instinct warned her against it. In her mind's eye she could see inside that house; see Ben's forbidding face as he ordered her on to the streets; and the hatred in her mother's voice followed her even now. Her father's eyes though . . . the way he had looked at her. That was what hurt the most. *The way he had looked at her*. She would never forget.

Raising her face to the brightening sky, she murmured, 'Take care of him, Lord.' Then, changing the small portmanteau into her other hand, she braced her shoulders against the chilling wind and hurried her footsteps from the square. Somehow, she knew that she would never again set foot in this part of the world. The realisation did not sadden her. She was saddened only by the thought that she would not see her father again; saddened too by the knowledge that she had not been able to live up to his expectations. But then, he had never spoken of what these were exactly. Now, when she thought more deeply on it, she realised that she and her father had never really spoken on any serious issue. And so she recalled older, more cherished memories, of when she was very small, and her father was her greatest comfort. But that had not lasted too long. Esther had seen to that. Esther Ward. Her mother. The woman whose hostile face would ever darken Beth's heart.

Now, as she hurried to her man, she deliberately thrust the painful images from her mind. Tyler would have the answers. She would tell him of the child she was carrying.

They would be a family then, starting out together on a new life. In all her unhappiness, that thought alone brought her comfort. All the same, Beth's heart was sore at what had happened. There was little she could do just now, but in the not-too-distant future, she would contact old Methias. He would reply, she was certain. He would send news of her father.

'He's gone, I tell yer, an' bloody good riddance!' Florence Ball was not too happy at being got from her bed at this hour of the morning. Not when she had only just nodded off after the earlier fracas.

'Gone?' Beth's heart sank to her boots. 'When? Do you know where he's gone?'

'No, I bleedin' well don't.' The woman poked her round flabby face out of the half-open door. 'But I'll tell yer this much, lady . . . the bugger had better not show 'is face round these 'ere parts agin.' She made no mention of the fact that she had seen her two lodgers beat him to the ground and continue to beat him even while he lay there helpless. She made no mention of the fact that shortly before she returned to her bed, he had been scraped off the pavement and carted away by the authorities, no doubt to the mortuary. And above all she made no mention of her own daughter having been in Tyler Blacklock's room in the dead of night; because then she might have had to explain the events that followed. Oh, no! She'd been around long enough to know when to keep her mouth shut. She didn't want the authorities beating a path to her door. Once they got their teeth into you, they never let go.

Instead, she told Beth, 'The swine went off in the dark hours when we were all abed, an' there's still two weeks' rent owing.' A crafty thought suddenly occurred to her. ''Ere! You're 'is fancy bit, ain't yer? Happen *you* should settle 'is bill.'

Ignoring her suggestion, believing the woman to be an opportunist, Beth asked again: 'You've no idea at all where he might have gone? Did he leave a forwarding address . . . a note for me, perhaps?' She was desperate.

'A "forwarding address"?' the woman repeated in a shrill voice, pressing her fat head to the door frame and indulging in a screeching fit that rocked the mounds of flesh all over her body. 'Oh, la de dah!' she mocked. 'Since when did any lodger of old Ma Ball's leave a "forwarding address"?' She raised her head and tried to compose herself. 'There ain't no note neither,' she told Beth in between bursts of cruel laughter. 'So yer might as well piss orf out of it. Go on! Sod orf, I tell yer! Your sort don't fit well in this street, wi' yer posh frocks an' la de dah ways.'

She would have slammed shut the door, but it was wrenched from her grasp and flung open to reveal her daughter, clothed in a vivid purple dressing-robe, with an almost transparent flesh-coloured nightgown beneath. Florence Ball's shock at suddenly seeing the girl there was quickly replaced by indignation. 'What the 'ell d'yer think yer doing, yer silly little cow?' she demanded. 'Get back to yer bed. Ain't yer caused enough trouble ter be going on with?' She suddenly eyed Beth and stopped abruptly, before she might have spilled out the entire night's events.

'*You* go to bed, Ma,' the girl retorted. Unable to sleep, she had heard the knock on the door and feared it might be a constable. When she realised it was not, she had crept down the stairs and eavesdropped from behind the door. Still embittered by Tyler Blacklock's rejection of her, but compensated by the thought of her just 'reward', she did not want Elizabeth Ward to be sent away so easily. 'I'm ashamed that you'd leave the poor thing standing on the pavement in the cold and damp,' she said now, regarding her mother slyly. 'You get off to bed, Ma. Leave the lady to me, eh?' Dropping back into the shadows, she whispered 'You *do* want another two weeks' rent, don't you?'

The older woman's eyes glittered in the light from the candle she was holding. 'Aye, 'appen yer right,' she said loudly, in a tone of apology. 'I'm forgettin' me manners, I reckon.' She now addressed herself to Beth. 'Yer look starved wi' cold, dearie. An' o' course yer want ter know all about 'ow yer feller took 'is leave.' She opened the door wider. 'You come inside, dearie,' she said with a smile that lost her eyes in waves of fat, 'an' we'll 'ave a proper chat, eh?'

When Beth was seated at the kitchen table and the two candles on the mantelpiece were lit, Florence saw how the girl was slyly gesturing for her to be gone. Feigning a yawn, she told Beth, 'I'm that tired, I think I'll tek meself back ter me bed. My Fanny 'ere can tell yer what yer need to know.' At the door she cast a warning glance at the girl and put a stiff grubby finger to her mouth, effectively telling her to keep her mouth shut about the night's events. When the warning was acknowledged, she smiled a cunning tight-lipped smile, nodded her head, and ambled away – the anticipation of an extra two weeks' rent putting a song on her lips and a spring to her step.

'I'm sorry to have got you both from your beds,' Beth apologised, 'but it's important that I find Mr Blacklock.' She tried desperately not to betray her panic at finding that he had already gone.

'Want a drink, do you?' The girl had sensed that Beth was in some kind of trouble and it pleased her. She had the bitch at her mercy now, and she intended to make her suffer. But she had no intention of rushing it. Oh, dear me, no. The pleasure in killing a rat was to watch it squirm. And that's what she wanted to do with Tyler

Blacklock's woman before she dealt the final blow . . .
she wanted to watch her squirm.

'No, thank you all the same,' Beth replied. 'I just want
news of Tyler. When did he leave? Did he give you or
your mother any idea which way he was headed?' In her
mind she went over every word of their last conversation.
'North', he had said, or to 'the Southampton area'.

''Fraid not.' The girl went to the dresser and opened
the lower cupboard. Dipping into it, she raised a gin
bottle aloft. 'Sure you won't take a nip?' You'll need it,
she thought with cruel satisfaction. When Beth shook
her head, she shrugged her shoulders and poured herself
a healthy measure into a small tumbler. 'Suit yourself,'
she said, suddenly giggling. 'The old trout would skin me
alive if she knew I'd been at her tipple.' Fetching both
tumbler and bottle to the table, she seated herself in the
chair opposite Beth, quietly regarding her for a moment
before raising the tumbler to her mouth and swilling its
entire contents straight down. Coughing and spluttering,
she poured out another measure, holding the tumbler to
her face and rolling it from side to side while she again
quietly regarded Beth.

'Me mam's right,' she lied. 'Your precious Tyler still
owes her a fortnight's rent. But the bugger's gone – took
off like a thief in the night . . . lock, stock and barrel.'
Her eyes narrowed as she thought of the callous way
he had bundled her out of his room. She watched the
effect her words had on the woman opposite, and her
bitterness was pierced with delight. 'Handsome man,
ain't he?' she asked now, her devious plan unfolding
and the silver-haired fellow's promise uppermost in her
mind. 'One for the women, ain't he? You can never trust
a man like that.'

Already regretting having entered the house, and
seeing that the girl was tipsy, Beth chose not to dwell on
her insinuating remarks. Instead, she asked once more,

'You have no idea where he might have gone?' She stood up, preparing to leave. There were other questions she might have asked, but she felt it would be futile. Tyler had gone, just as he had said he would. But she had never believed he would go without somehow letting her know where and maybe indicating the general direction he would take. Dear God, where would she find him now? Panic began to take hold, but she forced herself to stay calm.

'Well now, I *am* surprised.' The girl swilled down a mouthful of gin. 'You mean to tell me you really don't know where he's gone? I would have thought he'd tell you. I mean, you're a good catch by any standard.' She eyed Beth up and down before laughing, a deep unpleasant laugh. 'But then, come to think of it, it isn't that surprising after all, because he was a secretive bugger, wasn't he, eh?'

'What do you mean?' There was something in the tone of the girl's voice that put Beth on her guard.

'I mean exactly what I say.' The girl swayed danger-ously as she pushed out of the chair to face Beth with a look of cunning. 'Don't think you were the only one who knew Tyler Blacklock,' she said meaningfully. 'You see, he didn't mind bandying his favours about . . . if you know what I mean.' She began giggling. But then her expression darkened as she went on, 'I wonder whether you'd be so eager to find the bugger if you knew what he's been up to. I wonder if you'd think him such a fine fellow if I told you that . . .' She paused, relishing the look on Beth's face, and wanting to prolong her pain a while.

'It's obvious I'm wasting my time here.' Angered by the girl's innuendos, Beth grabbed her portmanteau from the floor and turned away.

'We slept together . . . me and Tyler.' The words sailed through the air with venom. 'I've lost count of the times we made love,' she added quietly. When Beth paused, keeping her face to the door, she went on in a harder voice, 'It's best that you know. Tyler Blacklock is a rogue . . . a bad 'un.'

Beth turned now, her dark eyes intense as she warned the girl, 'If I were you, I'd be very careful.'

'Oh, well, now . . . you might just be right there, because you see – that's just what I *ought* to have been . . . "careful". The fact is, your wonderful Tyler has had his way with me once too often.' She laughed aloud, patting her stomach with the flat of her hand and saying in a quieter voice, 'He may have skulked off like the villain he is . . . owing me mam a two week rent and all . . . but worse than that, the bugger's left me with a belly full!' She flung open her dressing-robe and arched her stomach forward. The nightgown was so thin her navel was clearly visible.

'You liar!' Beth felt the blood drain from her face.

'It's true, I tell you!' The girl's thoughts ran ahead, recalling everything the silver-haired man told her, and adding to it all that she herself had learned while eavesdropping on Tyler and his woman. 'Do you honestly think he cared any more for you than he cared for me? He began to lose interest in you when it became clear that your family would stop you from marrying him. He saw his cushy life going out of the window, don't you see? Oh, he was a good actor. One of the best. All that talk of going away to find a job, then he'd come back to you . . . it was all part of the act. Everything you told him, everything the both of you talked about, it was all repeated to me . . . how much you loved him and how you would defy your family to be with him. You fool, you bloody fool! He didn't want you to defy them. He wanted his foot in the door . . . to stake his claim. He didn't want *you* on your own. He wanted to be welcomed into the family with open

arms, to be part of the Ward Development Company
. . . Richard Ward's son-in-law; working his way into
favour and seeing himself taking over the whole bloody
company one day.'

The sight of Beth's horror-stricken face drove her on
to merciless depths. 'You know it's true! Everything
I say is the truth. Tyler Blacklock has used you, just
like he's used me.' Unable to contain her fury that
Tyler had turned her away in favour of Elizabeth Ward
whose grace and beauty far surpassed her own, and
deeply affected by her feigned emotional portrayal of
the wronged woman, she was surprised to find real tears
flowing down her face.

'You don't believe me, do you?' she demanded. 'But
it's true! I swear to God every word is true.' Rushing to
the mantelpiece, she took down a floral vase, which she
tipped upside down on the table. 'I'll prove it to you,'
she cried, grabbing up a small shiny object. 'He gave
me this,' she said, 'Told me to keep it as a souvenir of
our good times together.' She held it out for Beth to see,
smiling inwardly when Beth gasped aloud. 'He told me
it were yours . . . said you wouldn't miss it . . . that you
had far too many trinkets already.'

All manner of emotions sped through Beth as she
stared at her own brooch. The last time she had seen
it was when she and Tyler made love. There was such
a pain in her that she could hardly speak, and yet she
could not bring herself to believe what the girl was
saying. 'You stole that brooch,' she accused. 'I don't
know why you're doing this, but I won't listen to any
more.' With a coolness that belied her inner confusion,
Beth started towards the door.

'I *didn't* steal it!' The girl's voice followed her. 'As
God is my judge, Tyler gave that brooch to me, and
then we made love. When he was still warm from you!'
She followed Beth to the front door, her voice low and

trembling, sincere to the last. 'He's gone,' she said, 'and I'm left with his bastard. I don't expect I'll ever see him again . . . and I don't want to. There's no reason for me to lie. What bloody reason would I have to lie?' she demanded, sounding mortally hurt.

Beth walked down the street, her shoulders straight and her head held high, but her heart was breaking. The girl's voice went down the street with her. 'He's two-timed you, Elizabeth. Took you for the fool you are. It weren't *you* he were after. All he wanted was a position, that's all . . . a position in society, and your old man's money. Think yourself lucky he ain't left *you* in the family way.'

Shivering from the cold, more lonely than she had ever been in her life, and with the girl's awful words echoing in her mind, Beth walked the dark quiet streets, always wary and keeping to the shadows, until a solitary Hansom cab came alongside.

'Where to, Miss?' the driver asked as she climbed in. He couldn't help but wonder why such an elegant young lady was out on the streets of London at such a Godforsaken hour.

'Please, just take me to the nearest mainline station.' Her head was pounding, echoing to the girl's words: 'We made love' . . . 'carrying his bastard'. 'He didn't want you on your own . . . it was a position in your father's company. You fool. You bloody fool!'

It was four o'clock in the morning when the train began its journey north. After a while, the tall grimy houses and myriads of chimneys gave way to broad rolling stretches of green meadows and the occasional winding brook. Daylight flooded the land and the whispering rhythm of the wheels against the track played on her senses. Somehow, in spite of all the turmoil inside her, she had slept a deep quiet sleep. She was calmer now, but saddened by the thoughts that would not leave her be . . . thoughts of her father, and Ben. Thoughts of the girl and what she had said. Thoughts of Tyler. 'Oh, Tyler,' she murmured through her tears, 'if only I could be certain.'

But she could never be certain again. In spite of herself, Beth was suffering terrible doubts. How had the girl known so much? At first it had occurred to Beth that the girl could have eavesdropped on her and Tyler. But then she could not recall a time when she and Tyler had discussed these things in any depth while in his room. Of course, it was common knowledge that her family was opposed to her relationship with Tyler. But somehow the girl seemed to know more than that. And why would she lie? What could be gained from it? Besides, there was no doubt that she was genuinely upset. The more Beth thought of what the girl had said, the more she came to believe that there must be some truth in it. Anger and regret seeped into her heart. She felt bitter, cheated. What if Tyler really had made a fool of her? What if he and the girl had slept together after all? Was she lying when she said she was carrying his 'bastard'? But then, why would she lie? What capital could she hope to gain by it?

The questions persisted. Doggedly, Beth thrust the doubts from her heart, but they lingered, eating at her, demanding to be answered. Why would the girl lie? She had no real reason that Beth could see. Curiously she cast her mind back to the last time she and Tyler had spoken. Had he seemed sincere? Of course! But then she reminded herself that no matter how she pleaded, he would not be persuaded to take her with him. On top of that was his constant regret that he should be the cause of separating her from her family. It was a painful thing for her too, yet she could never denounce her love for him. All that mattered to her was that she and Tyler should be together. Why had it been so difficult for him to accept that? Don't let your imagination run away with you, Beth, she told herself. He gave you his reasons, and they were sound enough. But had her family been right all along? she wondered.

And so she argued with herself, wanting more than anything else in the world to know that Tyler had not 'used' her for his own ambitious purposes. She tried so hard to make herself believe that the girl was a liar, but could not convince herself. The damage was done. The truth could not be denied. If the girl was with child, and that child was Tyler's, then Beth never wanted to see him again as long as she lived. There was no doubting the girl's sincerity. Nor could she dismiss the most damning evidence of all. *The brooch!* Suddenly, everything Tyler had ever told her seemed suspicious. In her mind, Beth went over and over those special moments when they had been together; examined his every word. And the only thing that was paramount was that he had been adamant she could not go with him. Was it because of the reasons he gave? Or was it – as the girl had claimed just now – that he was more in love with the idea of being Richard Ward's son-in-law than he was with Beth herself?

For many hours she tortured herself with questions. Had Tyler really taken that girl into his bed? The thought was unbearable. Had he left his seed inside the girl . . . just as he had done with Beth? Was he only a fortune-hunter and a 'woman's man' after all? How did the girl get the brooch? Certainly, it seemed that he must have given the trinket to her. What else was Beth to think? Why hadn't he left word where he had gone? Did he not want her to know? Her mind was in turmoil. She felt drained, uncertain, afraid. She loved him still. She would always love him. But now, she doubted whether she would ever see him again. And if she did, would her love turn to hate? Her head told her to believe the

110

girl. Her heart told her differently. All she knew was, at this moment, she could not forgive him. He should have stayed, or else have taken her with him. But . . . the brooch! Above all else, it was that which created the gravest doubts.

Beth had started out with a dream in her heart, and a desire to spend the rest of her life with the man she loved. Now the dream was tarnished, and her only desire was to get as far away from London as was humanly possible. Her family had disowned her, Tyler had deserted her – and maybe that was for the best after all. Somehow she had to rebuild her life. For the sake of her unborn infant, she must put the past behind her and start again. It would be hard. Dear God, it would be hard! But she had her health and strength, and she had a little money. Whatever obstacles life had in store, she would face them head on. Beth had never been North; she had no idea what to expect. She was friendless and a little scared, but she was strong of heart, possessed of a determined spirit, and had a deep abiding faith in the Lord. She called on that now as she closed her eyes and uttered a heartfelt prayer. 'I know I've sinned, and should be punished, but I'm asking your forgiveness, Lord. Help me. Please . . . help me.' A simple prayer, spoken from the heart. But somehow it seemed to lessen her fears. And the future did not seem so bleak.

It was near midday when Beth stepped out of the railway carriage at Blackburn Station, weary from her long journey and so hungry that her stomach was playing a tune inside her. She went steadily across the station. There was a tea-shop close by but though she was hungry, the very thought of swallowing anything made her nauseous. There was hustle and bustle all around; porters rushing to and fro; passengers coming and going; train whistles shrieking: and in the huge arches that fronted the station

111

a small girl and a woman were approaching every likely customer who might buy their flowers. Mindful of the fact that it was not flowers she needed but the name and address of a respectable boarding house, Beth directed her steps towards the Station Master. If anyone knew the district, he should. Blackburn was a strange land to her; but it was North, and in the back of her mind she remembered Tyler's words 'North . . . or Southampton' he had said. Blackburn seemed an industrious town and, as such, as good a place as any to make a new start.

Suddenly her father's face came into her mind, and a great sadness engulfed her. Like Ben, he had rejected her. She forced the images from her mind and, praying that her father was not dead as she had imagined, quickened her steps. The portmanteau weighed her arm down, and every bone in her body ached. It was a wet raw morning, and after the milder climate of the south, the air was sharp and cutting.

Outside the station, Beth glanced down at the address which the Station Master had given her, and then folded the paper into her pocket. Pausing a moment to gather her strength, she looked out across the open square: at the carts rumbling along; at the people going about their business; at the ruddy-faced men in their short jackets and flat caps or sober coats and toppers; at the women in their dark fringed shawls, children running beside them; other women, grander, dressed in broad-brimmed feathered hats and gowns that swept the cobbles. As she gazed at the scene before her, it became hazy. Fearing that her senses were slipping away, she put the portmanteau to the ground and leaned against the strut of the great arch, deliberately willing herself to be strong.

You mustn't go down, Beth. Not here, in front of all these people, she told herself. Even her own frantic whisper sounded strange and far-off to her ears. Raising

112

her face to the sky, she let her gaze rove the many landmarks . . . tall elegant church spires and cylindrical chimneys from the many cotton mills hereabouts. She wondered nervously what this town of Blackburn might have in store for her. One thing was certain. She must put Tyler out of her mind; out of her life. One day in the future their paths might cross again. Until that day, she must not think too harshly of him, nor too kindly. Her love for him was like a clenched fist inside her. But then, so were the doubts. If he wanted her, then it must be up to him to seek her out. Only then could she be certain that it was *her* he wanted, and not the comfortable life her family's wealth might have provided. If Tyler really loved her, he would move heaven and earth to find her.

'Heather for good luck, Miss?' The small voice startled her. Turning her gaze downwards she was intrigued to see a pair of wide-awake blue eyes looking up at her. 'Go on . . . treat yerself,' the voice urged; the grubby thin-faced waif held out a small sprig of dried heather. 'Have a sniff,' she said with a smile that lit up her surprisingly lovely features. 'Pretty, ain't it?' she asked. 'And it's only 'alfpenny.'

'Well now, that's very reasonable.' Beth returned the girl's smile; there was something infectious about it. But she was forced to hesitate, mentally assessing how long her money might have to last before she secured employment. The girl thrust the sprig forward, extending her other hand for payment.

'A 'alfpenny, you say?' The delicate fragrance of the heather floated up to her, filling her senses. Reaching her fingers into the pocket of her jacket, Beth withdrew her purse. In that moment, the girl's small face became like a speck on the distant horizon, her tiny figure swaying from side to side. The ground rose and fell, taking Beth with it. From a dark swirling void, the girl's voice came to her. "'Ere! Are you all right, lady?' It was the last thing Beth heard before her strength ebbed away and she crumpled to the ground.

Tilly Mulliver walked up the steps of the grand house in Berkeley Square. A few minutes later she came into the spacious drawing room, where the maid brought her a tray containing a silver tea-service, two china cups and saucers, and a plate of dainty ham sandwiches. 'Thank you,' said Tilly, waiting for her to depart the room. She turned her head and smiled at the woman who was seated in the plush high-backed armchair; a woman not long past her fortieth year, with pretty, delicate features and shining fair hair. She was painfully thin, but there was a sparkle in her expressive dark eyes as she returned Miss Mulliver's smile. For a moment, neither woman spoke, yet there was an understanding between them, a bond; a love so strong that it had endured many long frustrating years.

Refusing the refreshments offered her, the woman leaned forward in her chair, her eyes intent on her visitor, her hands twisting nervously about each other as she said in a pained voice, 'Will he live, Tilly? That's all I need to know. Will Richard live?'

'Yes, Elizabeth.' Miss Mulliver nodded her head, a warm reassuring smile on her face. 'He will live. The doctor says he must take things easy for a while. But he has great reserves of strength, and they will see him through.'

'Thank God!' murmured Elizabeth, her voice quivering. The dark eyes moistened and she visibly relaxed. After a moment when her troubled thoughts fled back over the years, bringing her both heartache and joy, she looked up to see the other woman watching her, waiting for the question that was spoken in anxious tones. 'And Beth? . . . What of Beth?'

Miss Mulliver shook her head. 'She did not come back. But then, she would only have been turned away again. They made it quite clear that she was not wanted.'

'Even Richard?'

'When Esther told him that Beth was carrying Tyler Blacklock's child, it was a terrible shock. Don't be too harsh on him. When he's well, I know he'll regret what he said.'

'Do you think I should intervene?'

'No. Beth has a strong forthright character. She'll be fine.'

'Where will she go?'

'To him . . . to the man she loves. He'll take care of her.'

'I've done her wrong. All these years, I've done her wrong.'

'No! You must never think that. What happened was forced on you. It was not altogether your fault.' Miss Mulliver stared at the woman, so pale and delicate, so riddled with guilt and regrets, and all her life tied up with the past, with her daughter Beth and with Beth's father whom she had loved for so long. Tilly's heart went out to her, 'Perhaps it's time for me to leave the Ward household . . . time for us to leave this area altogether?' She was uncomfortable with the present arrangement.

'Please don't say that.' The voice was frantic. The dark eyes pleaded. 'I can't be too far away from him . . . from her. You know that.' She pulled herself up, her eyes fixed on the other woman's, and her lips quivering with anxiety. 'I need you to be my eyes and ears. Please . . . don't deny me this.'

A moment's hesitation, then, 'Don't worry. I won't let you down.' Tilly came to stand by her friend, leaning to kiss the fair gossamer hair. 'Do you want me to trace Beth and the man?' She must never forget how much she owed this woman.

'No. As you say, he will take good care of her, I'm sure. It would do my heart good to see her own father go in search of her when he's well again.'

'Then we'll pray for that, shall we?'

'And for Richard's full and speedy recovery.' The dark eyes melted into a smile and her whole face lit up with a gentle beauty. 'I'll never forget what you're doing for me,' she whispered hoarsely.

'Ssh. You know I would do anything for you,' came the soft reply. The dark eyes closed, and Miss Mulliver went quietly away, returning to the Ward household, and her duties there.

When, a short time later, the maid returned for the tray, she was surprised to find that the visitor had gone. Her mistress was fast asleep in the chair, but in her restless slumbers she called out a name over and over. 'Richard . . . Richard!' So much pain in her voice. So much anguish. 'Shh, it's all right, ma'am,' the maid whispered, stooping to drape a blanket gently about the woman's legs. She was startled when long slender fingers touched her face. 'Beth . . . will you ever forgive me?' When she looked up it was to see that her mistress was still asleep. But she had grown restless, and the tears were flowing down her face. Unsure whether to call the nurse from the library, the maid found herself held back by a remarkably strong and determined grip. 'It's all right . . . you rest now,' the maid whispered. 'Beth will forgive you. I know she will.' The fingers relaxed and there was a look of peace on the woman's face. 'There now. Sleep quietly,' the maid said, moving away. She wondered who 'Beth' was, and 'Richard'. And why did these two cause her mistress so much pain?

Chapter Four

'Where the devil have you been?' Esther Ward was standing beside the fireplace in the drawing room, with her hand still clutching the bell-pull and her whole countenance one of extreme impatience. Fixing her beady eyes on Miss Mulliver, she told her in a scathing voice, 'I have been standing here five minutes . . . five minutes, I tell you!'

She angrily flicked the bell-pull away and strode across the room to where Richard was seated in a tall, stiff armchair, a blanket over his legs and his head leaning back into the chair; his eyes were closed, but he was not asleep. 'It's chilly in here,' she snapped at the maid. 'How many times must I tell you that the master must be kept warm?' She glanced down at her husband as though seeking his approval, quickly returning her attention to the dogsbody when he remained unmoving. 'Well! Don't stand there dithering, woman,' she growled. 'Put some coals on the fire.'

'Begging your pardon, ma'am.' Miss Mulliver hurried to carry out the instructed task. 'It's just that when you rang, I was taking a tray of bread from the oven, and I had to change my apron.'

'A likely tale.'

Having built up the fire, and thinking that the air in the room was stifling and most unhealthy, Miss Mulliver asked whether she should open the window.

'You'll do as you're asked, and no more,' came the reply.

'Very well, ma'am. Will that be all?'

Esther hesitated for a moment, all the while regarding the other woman with a curious expression. After a moment she said, 'No. Get about your work,' adding quietly as the woman was about to leave, 'Is my son home yet?'

'No, ma'am. At least, I haven't seen him. Would you like me to check his room?' She was well aware of Ben's comings and goings at all hours; on more than one occasion he had been hopelessly inebriated; on another he was accompanied by a woman of the streets. Since his father's attack the night Beth had been sent packing, that young man had gone from bad to worse, with his mother covering up his every misdemeanour.

'No. That will not be necessary.' Esther loathed the fact that this lowly woman had seen the disgraceful decline of her son. When the door was closed, she sighed with unusual weariness and went to the window where she gazed out at the January landscape. It had not stopped snowing for two days now, and still it fell from the sky with a vengeance, covering everything in a thick white layer that blinded the eye and merged with the horizon so there was no judging where land ended and sky began. At eight o'clock on a Sunday, Bedford Square was quiet as usual. A solitary wagon went by, the horse's hooves plunging silently into the snow and the driver huddled up front, his flat cap pulled low over his ears and his scarf wrapped high up round his face. Only his eyes showed, narrowed against the cold. The trees around the square looked like silver ghosts, their boughs weighed down by the weight of this relentless snowfall.

Turning away, Esther blamed the hard cold weather for her strange mood. 'Will it never end?' she murmured, as always her mind on her wayward son. The last time she had seen him was yesterday evening as he was going out of the house. When she had asked him to be home early, in order that they might talk, he had made the comment, 'We have nothing to talk about, Mother.' But on being pressed, he had promised to be home by midnight. Hoping that this time he would keep his word, Esther had waited in the drawing room, going to this very window so many times that she had lost count. She had watched every carriage that went by, jumping up from her chair at the slightest sound, thinking it might be him at the door. Midnight came and went. The grandfather clock had struck the half-hour, then it was morning; one o'clock, two-thirty. When it struck three times it woke her from an uneasy slumber. Greatly troubled, she had hurried upstairs to see whether he had come in and gone straight to his room. His bed was not slept in. It was then that she went to her own bed, angry, frustrated and desperately worried. With Richard ill, she had entrusted a greater responsibility to Ben. Now it seemed she might have made a grave mistake: only this week she had discovered that he had seriously jeopardised the completion of a most important deal.

'I know how worried you are, Esther, but it isn't fair that you should take it out on Miss Mulliver.' Richard Ward shifted in his chair, his soft hazel eyes quietly regarding his wife. He had heard the conversation between her and Tilly Mulliver, and though he had learned of old not to intervene, his sympathies lay with the servant. She was a good and kind soul. Indeed, he had often been cheered by her bright affectionate smile.

'Richard!' Esther Ward had been startled by his softly spoken voice. At once, she was on the defensive. She had gone to great pains to prevent him knowing about Ben's unpredictable and damaging behaviour. Her apprehension betrayed itself on her face as she

119

came across the room. 'What do you mean? Why should I be worried?' she asked, forcing a smile. Richard Ward had built up his business against all the odds. It would kill him if he thought his only son was driving it into the ground. If Beth had been the problem, she would not have hesitated in telling him, but she would never willingly condemn her son.

'I mean *you*, Esther, constantly worrying about me. There's no need. I'll be fine, you'll see. I'll be on my feet and at the helm in no time at all. So do try not to take your frustrations out on poor Miss Mulliver. She has enough to be going on with, I think.' He smiled as she came closer, but the smile did not reach his eyes.

'Oh, but of course I worry about you,' Esther retorted. She could barely hide her relief. If only he knew that it was Ben she was more concerned about, not her husband. 'No one will be more delighted than me when you're "back at the helm",' she admitted reluctantly.

'Nonsense, Esther. The company is in good hands with you and Ben. I've never fooled myself that I was indispensable.' He knew only too well that he was driven by his wife. It was not something he enjoyed, but neither was it something that could easily be rectified. Over the years he had come to accept it. And, sometimes, even to welcome it.

'I don't want to hear you talk like that,' she warned. She also had been taught a lesson these past months, and it was this . . . her active part in the company was no secret amongst Richard Ward's business colleagues; even the bank manager was quietly aware of it; but since her husband had been struck down and she had emerged as the figurehead, doors were beginning to close in her face. She was a woman in a man's world, and while they were prepared to tolerate it as long as Richard was in the foreground, it had proved to be a different matter altogether, now that they were asked to deal directly with his wife. In desperation, yet not without a certain amount of pride, she had pushed Ben to the forefront. It was clear now, that he was neither mature nor committed enough. The whole exercise had been a disastrous mistake, and one which threatened to be the ruination of all that Richard had worked so hard to achieve. In a moment of vulnerability, she reached out to take her husband's hand. The rare and impetuous fusing of their warm flesh was a shock to both of them. When he looked up, surprised and puzzled, she said quietly, 'I mean it, Richard. No one can take your place at the head of the Ward Development Company.' She continued to stare at him for a moment before turning away, suddenly afraid that the truth would show on her face and he might suspect the real reason for her remark.

As it was, he asked, 'Everything *is* all right, isn't it?'

'Of course!' she told him, beginning to walk away. 'Everything is fine.' Inwardly cursing herself for that one weak moment when she might have aroused his suspicions, she went quickly to the door. 'I'm tiring you,' she said, turning with a half-smile. 'I'll go and see what's keeping that wretched nurse.'

'Esther!' His voice was sharp with pain.

'Yes?' She remained motionless, her hand fidgeting on the door knob, and a look of irritation beneath her gaze. 'What now?'

For what seemed an age, he gave no answer. Then, in what was almost a whisper, he asked, 'Have you heard . . . from Beth?' He saw her bristle. Memories of that night sprang to his mind and the pain was unbearable. Even now, he could not find it in his heart to forgive the daughter he had idolised for so many reasons, and who was now carrying the bastard child of one of their labourers. It was happening again, *just like before*. Not for the first time he wondered whether all of this was sent to punish him. 'I'm sorry,' he murmured. He dropped his gaze to the floor, deliberately casting the memory of Beth from his mind.

'No!' Esther swung open the door, her face set stonily. 'I have not heard from her. And, even if I did, she would not be welcome in this house. Never again. Not while I am mistress of it.' Her voice took on a menacing tone. 'You do understand why I could never have her back, don't you?'

His answer was a slow, definite nod. But he did not look at her. He understood. Oh, yes, he understood only too well.

'Then let that be an end to it.' She looked at his bowed head, and she remembered also. There should have been compassion in her heart for the manner in which he had suffered all these years; a suffering which she herself had viciously prolonged. 'Elizabeth has shown her true character, and as far as I am concerned, she can rot in Hell.' Her voice was like the hard scrape of metal against metal.

He knew she was waiting, waiting for him to say the words that would not come. He remained silent. And still she waited, and still he did not look up. Even when he heard the door abruptly close, he kept his eyes cast downwards for a moment, before closing them against the tears. 'I can't forgive you, Beth,' he murmured brokenly. 'All these years . . . and you finally played right into her hands. God help me, but I can't forgive you.'

It was a week later, on a bitter cold afternoon towards the end of January, that Tyler Blacklock straightened his back from his labours, wiped the sweat from his brow and started his way towards the timber office, where most of the men were already waiting to collect their wage packets. As he picked his way over the trenched, uneven earth which would soon carry the railway lines far beyond London town, the legacy of his terrible beating was painfully obvious. The deep scar that ran from his temple to the base of his jaw would heal in time, as would the ones on his body – so the doctors told him. But the jagged breaks to his right leg, and the ensuing treatment, had left him with a degree of pain and a marked limp that could well plague him for the rest of his life.

'I ain't sorry to be finished here, I can tell yer!' The big ganger swung the pickaxe on to his shoulder and shivered. 'The gaffer an' me have never seen eye to eye. The day had to come when he handed me me cards. No matter. I'll find work. I ain't never been out on the streets yet,' he said, falling into step with Tyler. 'And I ain't sorry it's the end of the week neither . . . me throat feels as dry as a bleedin' desert.'

'Gerraway, Pickerton!' yelled a broad-chested fellow from somewhere behind. 'It ain't "cold" nor "thirst" yer thinking on . . . it's them painted floozies wi' their legs wide open that's calling yer.'

'Aye, that's right,' shouted another, 'but don't forget the buggers'll 'ave their *fists* open an' all . . . waiting ter rob yer of every soddin' penny yer've earned.'

'Mebbe! But it'll be worth it, I reckon,' laughed the big ganger, playfully pushing Tyler and urging him, 'Come with me, why don't yer? Them little cows'll fall over themselves to bed a big 'andsome bugger like you.' In the two months that Tyler Blacklock had laboured on this site, Abe Pickerton had come to respect and like him. In spite of his troublesome leg, Tyler had shown himself to be a strong and conscientious worker, although his quiet serious manner meant that he had become something of a loner.

Glancing at his companion, Tyler shook his head, saying in a firm friendly voice, 'Thanks all the same, but no.' His dark eyes were smiling yet intense. 'My wages are already spoke for.' He laughed, a low rich sound that reassured the other man. 'No doubt you'll manage to keep the ladies well satisfied.'

The big ganger laughed also, with a noise like the earth shaking. 'Too bloody right I will! What's the point of earning a wage if yer can't spread it about a bit?' he wanted to know.

'It's easy ter see yer ain't got no missus at 'ome!' came a shout from ahead. 'Else it'd be yer bloody *brains* that's "spread about a bit".'

There followed a chorus of like calls and laughter, which swelled to uproar when the big ganger yelled back, 'Oh, I've *had* a missus, don't think I ain't suffered wi' the rest of yer. But the bugger 'ad a tongue like the crack of a bleedin' whip, an' she were too fond o' showing other folks 'er arse . . . so I left 'er wi' me best friend who'd tekken a fancy to 'er. Poor sod! I'd bet me week's wage he rues the day . . . if he ain't long gone by now, that is.'

Some half an hour later, the men were dispersing in different directions, each to enjoy their respective weekends in their own particular way. 'Sure yer won't come along?' the big ganger asked once more. When Tyler politely declined, the fellow shrugged his shoulders, took off his cap and stuffed it into his pocket. Then he spat into the flat of his hand and smoothed it over his roughened fair hair until every strand was larded to his head like a second cap. 'Suit yerself,' he said. 'Though I can't see what's so important that yer should save every penny like a bloody miser.' He had long been curious about Tyler. He regarded him now, looking him up and down before saying, 'That gammy leg o' yours . . . how did it get damaged?'

Having learned how to avoid such questions, Tyler merely replied, 'It's a long story.'

'Yer a strange feller,' the ganger said, his inquisitive gaze following the scar on Tyler's face. 'Either you've been in some accident or other, or you've got some very bad enemies.' He waited, half-expecting a helpful response. When all he got was a wry smile, he laughed and nodded his head. 'All right, I'm a nosy bugger and should mind me own business,' he said, adding in a serious voice, 'but I've tekken a liking to yer, Blacklock. You've a good head on yer shoulders, an' yer ain't afraid of hard work.' He paused, biting his bottom lip and nodding his head as he struggled to find the right words. Presently he told Tyler, 'Tell me it ain't none o' my business if yer like. And you'd be right, I'm not denying that. But I'd like yer to know that . . . well, if there are them as mean yer harm . . .'

Anticipating his offer of help, Tyler was quick to assure him: 'If it was anything like that, you'd be a good man to have on my side. But, it's nothing. It's over and done with. An unfortunate incident best forgotten.' Those weeks when he had been at the lowest ebb in his life, the thought of revenge had sent him almost insane. Time and again he relived that night when the ruffians came at him out of the darkness. He suspected that Florence Ball might have sent her two lodgers after him, but he could never be sure. Their faces were hidden from him by the gloom, and not once had they spoken so he might recognise their voices. Then again, the bastards could have been any two rogues wandering the streets, looking for a likely victim. Even if they passed him face to face in broad daylight, he would not know who they were. He recalled only the blackness, the shuffling of feet, the ferocity of their attack, and his desperate struggle to fend them off. Beyond that there was merely pain, a dull invasive pain that had remained with him for many long weeks afterwards. Only the memory of Beth and his love for her dulled his thirst for revenge. After a while, he could think of nothing else but Beth. The longing to contact her was like a burning fever inside him, raging night and day. Scarred and broken, he was tormented by the fact that all his plans for their future had come to nothing. The doctors had warned him he could be crippled for life. What could he offer her now? What hope was there for a life together?

For a long time he had wandered the streets of London like a tramp; going from place to place looking for work, any kind of work that would bring him a decent wage and give him back his self-respect. But when people looked at him, they saw only a down-and-out with a scarred face, a cripple who would be of little use to them. 'Sorry,' they said, shaking their heads and frowning. 'We've no work here.' And so he moved on, snatching a day's work here, a few hours there, living from hand to mouth and lodging in the worst dives imaginable. Every minute of every day he had to fight the desperate need to contact Beth. Shame and pride kept him from doing so. But above all else, he resisted for her sake. How could he expect her to pick up where they left off? He would not ask that of her. But he loved her more than life itself. They would be together again, he never doubted that. But first, there was much to do. And anyway, Beth believed him to be in the North. Let her go on believing that, until he was a whole man again, one who could take care of her. One who would not go to her empty-handed.

Two months ago, Tyler had learned how the railway authorities were looking for gangers to lay a new line from London to the developing suburbs. The foreman had not looked at the scar on his face, nor at the curious dip in his stride. Instead, his observant eyes had taken the measure of the man . . . the broad straight shoulders, the capable height and the strength in his arms and back. 'Can you start right away?' he had asked.

Tyler started work within the hour. Before nightfall he had secured a room and lodgings in a decent boarding house on the outskirts of the city. Before the week was out he had shown himself to be worth every shilling paid him. Within a fortnight he had purchased a decent set of clothes and put a small sum of money to one side. He had a rage to save every farthing, to save and save until he had a sizeable sum. If he had learned one thing, it was that money was a powerful asset. It could open doors through which no poor man could ever enter. More than anything, money could make it easier for a man to take the woman he loved, and give her the life she deserved. Beth was his driving force. She alone was the reason for his existence. Every waking and sleeping moment, every minute of every hour, every hour of every day, week and month, it was Beth who kept him going. She burned inside him like a warm glowing light. She was his life. His love. Everything he did was for her. He had no idea how long it would take, or whether she would forgive him for staying away, but he knew in his heart that there would come a day when he would hold her close. The long painful days in between might seem like a lifetime, but it would be a small price to pay when he had his Beth at last.

'You won't forget our arrangement?' The big ganger's voice penetrated his thoughts. 'Tomorrow night, between nine and ten. He's always there, eager to part with his money at the gaming table. Bloody fool! At least for my money I get a pair o' warm arms round me, an' a night I'll not forget in a hurry. Still, each to his own, that's what I say.'

'You're sure he has the say as far as setting men on?'

'I've told you! He's one o' the top hirers at the docks.

If anybody can see us right, he can. An', like I say . . .
there's big money to be earned on the docks. Enough
to make *this* pay packet look sick.' He held up his
fist and crumpled the small buff envelope between
his thick work-worn fingers. 'That's what you want,
ain't it, Blacklock? More money to stash away for
whatever purpose seems to drive you?' He paused, again
wondering whether this quiet man might open up to him.
After a while, he shrugged his shoulders. 'All right,
matey. It's your business after all,' he said. 'But stay
in the saloon, and keep well away from that backroom.
What! The buggers'll have you gambling your money
away before you can turn round.' He slapped a friendly
hand across Tyler's back, before striding away with one
last reminder. 'Think on, Blacklock . . . the docks,
tomorrow night, between nine and ten', leaving Tyler
to make his way towards the train that would carry him
back to Battersea and his humble lodgings there.

At precisely nine-thirty that same evening, Tyler emerged
from the broad-fronted house in the heart of Battersea.
With his tall lean figure, strong classical features and
rich shoulder-length dark hair, he made a striking and
handsome sight. The recently purchased dark suit and
long overcoat, with a thin white scarf loose about his
neck, ensured that he was well wrapped up against the
biting cold that swept the night streets. Putting his head
down against the chilling wind, he pressed on with a
purpose. A deep angry purpose which, if all went well,
would change his station in life, and ensure that he and
Beth would never want again for as long as they lived.

The tavern was crowded. Working men like himself
propped up the bar, singing to the accordion and enjoying a well-earned jug of ale. Others were seated at the
small round tables – some accompanied by women, and
some obviously alone, solitary gaze roving the room,

envying others their companions. Now and again, a well-dressed gent would slip in through the door and sidle beyond a narrow dark recess, which was guarded by a formidable-looking fellow attired in a black suit and white shirt, his brown hair larded down and a wary look in his eyes.

The hands of the old clock above the bar seemed to move with incredible slowness. It had been five minutes to ten when Tyler came in. It was now only five minutes past, and still there was no sign of Abe Pickerton. During the next fifteen minutes, the ale flowed freely. Consequently the proceedings grew rowdier, with the odd skirmish erupting and being instantly suppressed by the landlord's threat to 'Throw the bloody lot of you out!'

'Want a good time, do you, darling?' The woman – a petite thing with a pretty overpainted face – thrust herself against Tyler with obvious intentions, backing off with a surly expression when he remained silent, but smiling gratefully when he slid a coin along the bar as a gesture of compensation.

It was creeping towards eleven o'clock, with still no sign of the big ganger. Revellers were beginning to thin out, and soon the place would be empty. Disappointed, but not too surprised, Tyler decided to call it a day.

Outside, the air was fresh and exhilarating after the fog and heat of the tavern. Leaning against the wall, Tyler reached into the hip pocket of his overcoat and drew out a leather pouch containing a pipe and a thick wad of tobacco. On the rare quiet occasion he enjoyed the soothing effects of a smoke. On this occasion, he had much to think about.

Tyler had idled there only a minute, when he heard the unmistakable sounds of scuffling emanating from the nearby alley. There followed a muffled thud, and a cry, as though someone was in pain. The cry brought back sorry memories to Tyler; memories of darkness and skulking figures, of utter helplessness and grinding agony. In a moment he was hurrying towards the alley, his lopsided footsteps deliberately soft, his approach growing stealthy as he neared the narrow dark opening. Staying close to the wall, he peered down the alley towards the half-light from the open doorway there. There were three of them. It was difficult to ascertain exactly what was taking place, but from what Tyler could make out, one of the men was pinned against the wall by the bigger of the other two men, while the third stood back, his head turning this way and that, obviously keeping watch.

'Twenty-four hours, you bastard!' the voice threatened. A shadowy arm was raised high in the air, then the sickening sound of bone against bone. 'After that . . . we'll come looking for you!' The arm was raised a second time. Taking a deep breath and praying that his leg would not let him down, Tyler tore off his overcoat and began running down the alley. As the dark fluttering images of a certain night skipped through his mind, a blind fury took hold of him and a surge of incredible strength lent wings to his feet.

'Let's even the odds, you bloody cowards!' he cried. The voice sounded strange, not like his at all. With a surprised shout, the third man sprang forward. Tyler braced himself. He wouldn't go down this time. *This time he was ready!* The blood raced hot inside him, and all the need for revenge he had buried rose to the fore.

But then there came another cry: 'Leave it! We know where to find him.' At once the two men vanished into the night.

When the agonised groans behind him forced him to abandon pursuit, Tyler cursed aloud. He felt cheated.

'Help me! For God's sake, help me!' The man was

slumped on the ground. In the semi-darkness he was a moving shadow, his cries pitiful to hear.

'All right, matey. You're safe enough.' With now-familiar difficulty, Tyler stooped to one knee, his hands reaching out to help the injured man. 'Whatever possessed you to get mixed up with the likes of them?' he asked. The man's head was bent low as he clawed at the wall and struggled upwards. 'Easy does it,' Tyler warned. He could see the dark streaks of blood running down the man's face. It was obvious by his pained movements that he had taken a bad beating. Suddenly, the man showed his face, sullen brown eyes staring angrily. 'Bugger off!' he snarled. 'I don't need your help. I don't need anybody's help.'

Tyler's stomach turned somersaults. He was shocked to see that the man was none other than Beth's brother. 'BEN?' His voice was incredulous. 'God Almighty. What the hell have you got yourself into?'

'Get away!' Thrusting Tyler from him, the other man stared hard for a moment, his vision blurred by an over indulgence in whisky and, on top of that, the beating he had taken. Pressing into the wall to steady himself, he focused harder on the concerned face before him, and when he saw that it was Tyler Blacklock, he was mortally ashamed. He was also bitter and full of resentment. 'Get away, I tell you!' he yelled, lashing out viciously and growing more violent when Tyler stopped him from falling over.

'It's Tyler. Let me get you a cab at least.'

'No. I can manage. Just leave me be.'

'If that's what you want.'

'It is!'

'Fair enough, matey.' Tyler stepped back, releasing his hold on the other man, who took one unsteady step forward before buckling at the knees. Without a word, Tyler slid one arm round his waist, and drew Ben's nearer arm round the back of his own neck, holding it there while the two of them went at a slow agonising pace out of the alley. 'You bloody fool,' he told Ben, whose only reply was a pitiful moan.

Having located a Hansom cab and settled Ben into the back of it, Tyler shook him hard. 'Don't tell Beth you've seen me,' he warned. 'Do you hear me, Ben? *Don't tell Beth you've seen me.*' He wasn't yet ready to face her. Not yet. Not until he was a man of consequence, when it wouldn't matter whether he had a crippled leg or not. 'Ben! Do you hear what I'm saying?' he repeated, turning Ben's face so he could not avoid looking at him.

'Don't worry, I won't tell her.' Beth's brother stared at Tyler, his blood-smeared face screwed into a warped smile. 'You're a bloody fool,' he whispered.

'What do you mean?'

Ben laughed and the blood trickled from the side of his mouth. 'It won't matter whether I tell Beth if I've seen you or not,' he answered with a snarl. There was so much hatred in him, so much shame and despair. He knew he was being sucked into a world that was already bringing ruin upon him, and still he could not give up the gambling. He was a coward of the worst order. Even now, when Tyler was offering friendship and trust, he wanted to hurt him for being the man he was . . . strong and loyal. Everything he himself was not. Some time back, he had learned what had happened to Tyler, and from that had deduced that Beth was not with him. In fact, he had often wondered whether Beth even *knew* of Tyler's predicament. Here was the answer then. 'Don't tell Beth you've seen me.' It was obvious that Tyler knew nothing of Beth's having been thrown out of the family home. And, if Beth had known that Tyler was close to death, nothing on God's earth would have kept these two apart. Somehow, Fate had driven them in separate directions, each ignorant of the other's circumstances. The irony of it appealed to him. It went a small way towards compensating him for the miserable cards Fate had dealt him. Groaning with pain, he raised his head and looked Tyler full in the eye. 'Forget her,' he said. 'She won't need you any more, Blacklock.' His laugh was cynical, spiteful to hear.

'What are you saying?' A strange and frightening feeling came over Tyler as the words began to sink in. When all Ben did was to laugh in his face, he took him by the collar and yanked him up in the seat. *'What are you saying?'* he demanded again, shaking the fellow until he cried out.

'She's married!' The awful words echoed through the stunned silence. Ben saw the anguish on the other man's face, and still he was not repentant; instead, it made him feel curiously satisfied. 'You remember we talked about the fellow . . . Wilson Ryan? She's happy, Blacklock. There's even a child on the way.' He choked on the last word as Tyler suddenly released him and he fell back with a jerk.

'When?' One word, but uttered from the depths of despair.

'I don't know.' His mind was slowed by the drink and the pain. When was Beth sent packing? Three months? Four months? His thoughts were a jumble. 'Six weeks maybe . . . two months,' he blurted out impatiently. 'How the hell do you expect me to remember!'

He saw Tyler reel back, as though punched in the face. For one fleeting moment, he almost confessed the truth . . . that Beth was carrying Tyler's child, and because of it she had been thrown out and it was assumed that she had gone to Tyler. He almost confessed how she would never have married Wilson Ryan even if her life depended on it . . . that there had only ever been one man for her, and that man was

Tyler himself. He *almost* confessed. But he was not man enough. Even that realisation filled him with bitterness. He saw himself as playing a part in Beth's being thrown out of the house, yet he blamed her, not himself. Beth was the root of all their trouble. He watched as Tyler climbed from the carriage, his face set hard, yet with the look of a haunted man.

Outside, Tyler dug into his jacket pocket, then handed the driver two coins with instructions to take his passenger to a certain house in Bedford Square. And all the while Ben's words screamed in his mind. 'Beth is married. She's happy . . . a child on the way.' Outwardly, he was deadly calm. Inwardly, he was falling apart. How long had she waited for him? he wondered. Weeks? Months? How could he blame her? He should have let her know. Somehow, he should have let her know! Wave after wave of desolation swept over him, taking him down to the depths. Was it really all gone? All the dreams? All the love and the planning? Gone for ever! Suddenly, there was no purpose. No point in going on. He watched as the carriage pulled away, his heart weighing like lead inside him, and the tears coursing down his face. 'Beth,' he cried, 'how will I ever stop loving you?' The wind tore his plea away, and only the silence remained.

Inside the carriage, Ben twisted himself up to peer through the back window at that lonely solitary figure. There was a moment's regret. But then his own desperate situation came back to him. Soon, Tyler and Beth were forgotten.

Part Two

1887

FRIENDS

Chapter Five

'One silver shilling and a few miserable coppers. It ain't much to take home from a Friday flea market, is it?' The girl fidgeted on the makeshift seat that was little more than an orange-box covered with a sack, then leaning back against the wall behind, she crossed her spindly legs and chuckled, looking for all the world like a little woman. 'Maybe I should have picked a few pockets instead, eh?' The smile fell away and was quickly replaced by a worried expression, her thin features pinched and white with cold as she raised her scruffy head to stare at Beth. 'It ain't funny though, Beth, 'cause that awful Mr Miller's coming for his rent tonight and he warned me mam last week that if she ain't got some money for him, he'll start proceedings to have us all chucked out on us arse!'

'I'm sure he never said any such thing.' Beth recalled David Miller's very words, and Cissie's were far more colourful; what David Miller had said was, 'I'm sorry, Mrs Armstrong, but I have my own problems to contend with. My father's aged now, and we depend on the income from our houses to make a living. If you can't pay the rent on time, then we'll have to get someone in who can.' David Miller was a mild-mannered and compassionate man, but his stepfather, Luther Reynolds, was renowned as a mean, miserly bugger. It was he who owned the properties, and he was the one who had the last say. The beleaguered David Miller was merely his stepfather's mouthpiece.

Beth suspected that the young man had pleaded with his father in the case of Maisie and her rent arrears, but to no avail. However kindly the warning was put, the implication was unmistakable. Maisie was being given one last chance to rectify the arrears; failure to do so would undoubtedly result in the whole family being evicted bag and baggage. And with countless folk in dire need of accommodation, there were any number of tenants to fill the miserable terraced houses on Larkhill. 'Right, Cissie,' Beth said now, 'pack up your things. We're going home. Your poor mother's been out of her mind with worry.' Maisie Armstrong had been frantic when the time rolled round to five o'clock on this Saturday afternoon and the girl had still not come home. Beth also was worried and had volunteered to go out in search of Maisie's daughter. Her search had taken her first to the railway station, then here to the market-square, where she had found Cissie, cross-legged on her orange-box, with her few bundles of kindling wood gone and the market-place all but deserted.

'Aw, Beth, I'm sorry if me mam were worried but I ain't stopped all day, honest to God!' Her blue eyes grew big and round when it suddenly occurred to her how Beth might think she had not put the day to good use; especially when there was precious little to show for it. 'First thing this morning, I cadged a ride on a barge that were going to Liverpool docks . . . I was sure there'd be some flowers coming in from one o' them far-off countries. But there weren't! At least, *I* never clapped eyes on 'em, that's for sure. Then I hid in a waggon coming back, and it went all the way round Lancashire afore ending up in Blackburn.' She grimaced, rubbing her buttocks with the flat of her

hand and groaning. 'Oh, I were that sore, Beth. Anyway
. . . after that, I scoured the market, nicking whatever
old crates were lying around, so I could break 'em up
for kindling wood. It weren't easy neither,' she declared,
showing the blisters on the palms of her hands. 'Honest,
Beth, I've worked real hard all day. All bloomin' day,
and only four measly coins to show for it.'

'I think it best if we don't tell your mother about your
escapades today.' Beth had been horrified listening to
the girl's account of what she'd been up to. 'What's
more, Cissie, I want you to promise me that you'll
never cadge a ride on any more barges. Have you any
idea what trouble you could have got yourself into?' she
demanded. 'You know how often you've been warned
about the docks,' she insisted. 'I mean it, Cissie! I want
you to promise me.'

The look on Beth's face told Cissie that she was in
the wrong. 'Oh, all right then,' she said quietly.

'All right then . . . *what*?' Beth softly insisted.

'I won't cadge no rides on no barges, and I won't go
to no docks.'

'Promise, Cissie!'

Slapping her two hands against her linen skirt and
puckering a weary little face, Cissie made a loud perform-
ance of drawing in her breath through her mouth and
blowing it out of her nose. 'Oh, all right then. *Promise*,'
she moaned.

'Then we'll say no more about it, eh?' In the months
that Beth had known Cissie, she had learned that the
girl did not give her promises readily. However, Beth
also knew that when Cissie did make a promise, neither
Hell nor high water would induce her to break it. Beth
too would keep her word, and never disclose to Maisie
that not only had Cissie gone away from Blackburn,
but had actually disobeyed Maisie's strict instructions
that under no circumstances should she ever be tempted

on to the many barges that travelled the Liverpool and Leeds waterways; especially since most of them went to the docks – which according to Maisie was a frightening place where a young lass could be lost for ever without trace!

'Do you reckon I could sell this 'ere box for kindling wood?' Cissie asked, clambering from the latticed orange-box and beginning to tear a strip from it.

'No,' Beth told her with a smile. 'And don't *you* think we should put your mother's mind at rest, Cissie? I promised Maisie I'd have you back home within the hour.' Stooping to collect the box, she painstakingly hooked it over her arm and rested it against the bulge beneath her long dark shawl. 'Come on, let's get away before it comes dark,' she warned.

'Oh, all right.' Cissie felt ashamed at having disobeyed her mam. Anyway, Beth was right, the market *was* almost empty, except for the few remaining stall holders who might suddenly take an unhealthy interest in her and her orange-box and a few similar that had gone missing from round the market-square today. On top of that, the man from the School Board had been wandering the market-place earlier, looking for children to march off to school. Always on the look-out for him, Cissie had managed to hide until he'd gone; but even now he might be hanging about, she thought, nervously glancing from side to side. 'Let's be off,' she said with a mischievous grin. Then, whistling through her teeth, she took up step beside Beth and the two of them headed away from the market, down Cort Street and on to Ainsworth Street, with Cissie excitedly chattering and Beth quietly listening, thinking what a delightful little creature her companion was.

'What shall we do if Mr Miller *does* throw us out on us arses though?' Cissie glanced up at Beth, quickly adding before Beth could correct her, 'All right. I know he never said it in them words exactly. But it all comes to the same thing, don't it? If me mam ain't got no rent for Mr Miller when he comes tonight, we'll get us marching orders, won't we, eh? Chucked out on the streets with nowhere to go!'

'Nobody is going to chuck us out on the streets, Cissie,' Beth promised her. 'You have my word on it.' The few guineas she had brought to Blackburn almost six months ago had slowly dwindled away until now there was barely enough to see her through another month, which was when the child was due to be born. But Maisie Armstrong's family had come to mean a great deal to Beth, and she would do whatever was in her power to keep a roof over their heads. After all, Beth owed Maisie and her daughter so very much. More than ever before, she had come to believe that it was the good Lord Himself who had delivered her to Maisie's door.

Cissie never tired of recounting the day when Beth arrived in Blackburn and had keeled over – 'Like you were blind drunk. Gawd, Beth! You frightened the life outta me and me mam. Somebody shouted that you were dead, and everybody started running round in a panic. But me mam showed 'em, didn't she, eh? Fetched you home with us to Larkhill where we could look after you, she did.' Cissie swelled with pride whenever she recounted the tale. Her great love and admiration for Maisie were wonderful to see. They shone in her big blue eyes and trembled in her voice whenever she spoke of her. 'My mam,' she would declare boldly to all who might listen, 'is my best friend in all the world!' Beth was her next best friend, and Matthew was the brother who was just like all other boys and 'don't know much worth knowing'. Cissie was only nine years of age, but she was old and wise beyond her years, and though she was painfully thin and in Maisie's own words 'couldn't be

141

fattened up nohow', she was wiry and strong, a character with a heart as big as wide-open arms, and a capacity for loving that was an example to all mankind. Beth adored her. Almost from the start she had felt naturally drawn to the Armstrong family. There was so much pain in her heart when she thought about her own family. As soon as she was able, Beth had contacted old Methias Worry, who had reassured her as to her father's recovering health – 'mending slowly', he had said. That was all Beth needed to know. Afterwards, she believed it best to leave well alone. Her father had probably hardened his heart against her, so there was no point in dwelling on the pain of that particular episode. And Tyler . . . his memory also brought its own kind of torment. After all this time, it was clear to Beth that he also had rejected her, and that maybe Annie Ball had not been lying after all. That was the most painful thing. It was not easy to forget what that girl had said about her and Tyler, and it was not an easy thing for Beth to believe. Yet, if it was not true, then where was he? Why hadn't he found out that she was no longer in London? – that she had been thrown out for bearing his child? That the most natural thing for her to have done was to go North in search of him? Surely to God it would not have been too difficult for him to have traced her. If he wanted to, that was!

Six long months had gone by, and with the passing of every one of them, Beth had grown more and more disillusioned. Until now, she had had no choice but to accept that she had only been fooling herself. Even now though, the heartache was always there, more so as the child grew impatient to be born. Yet she had much to be grateful for, though it was not full compensation for all she had lost. Here in Blackburn, with Maisie and her two children, she had found another kind of love, a deep sense of belonging, and though part of her would always be with her father and with Tyler, she was strong enough to face up to the truth: that she had no one else. It was a sobering thought, and one which gave her many sleepless nights.

Now, glancing down at the girl's anxious face, Beth told her firmly: 'You're not to worry, Cissie. Everything will come right, I'm sure of it.' Lately, she had racked her brains as to a solution with regard to the rent arrears, because even if she dug yet again into her meagre savings, it would not be a long-term solution, and what little money she had would be swallowed up like a teardrop in the ocean. In the back of her mind, she had one or two ideas ticking away, but they seemed always to be flawed. This past week she had been too tired to apply her thoughts for any length of time. In less than four weeks the baby was due. It had been a long difficult carrying, and now she was impatient for it to be over. There was no telling what would happen after that. Beth had no real plans. She dared not let herself think about the future. Not when the present was so fraught with problems.

'But how do you know that?' Cissie asked with her usual directness. 'Mr Miller's a rich man, ain't he? And he can throw us out if he wants to, can't he? And he won't take no notice of you or anybody else if he's a mind to be nasty, will he?' Each question made Cissie realise just how desperate their situation was. Now she stopped and eyed Beth with a curious expression. 'You ain't gonna *marry* him, are you?' she asked incredulously. 'I know he fancies you, 'cause I've seen him staring at you with a funny look on his face. Oh, Beth!' She wrinkled her nose in disgust. 'You *ain't* gonna marry Mr Miller just so he won't chuck us out, are you?' Hurriedly, she answered her own question. 'No, you ain't! 'Cause he ain't good enough for you!' The thought of Beth in Mr Miller's arms was so awful that for a moment Cissie could not speak; instead she stared up at Beth in disbelief, her mouth wide open and her head shaking slowly from side to side. Presently she blurted out, 'You ain't, are you? It don't matter if we're chucked out, honest to God, 'cause we'll find somewhere, we will . . . we will!'

'Well, I never!' Beth exclaimed with a look of horror. 'What a vivid imagination you've got, Cissie Armstrong.' She laughed. 'Me and Mr Miller . . . *married*. The very idea.' Whether it was caused by the grim prospect imagined by Cissie, or whether it was the result of trudging round the town looking for Maisie's girl, Beth didn't know, but she found herself suddenly gripped by a particularly vicious pain. Sucking her breath in and forcing herself to breathe easily the way Maisie had taught her to whenever she felt unwell, Beth took the orange-box from under her arm and placed it on the ground.

'What's the matter?' In spite of Beth's attempts to disguise her discomfort, Cissie was worriedly tugging at her. 'Is it the bairn? Are you all right, Beth? Will I fetch help?' Fear and concern betrayed itself in her grubby upturned face.

'It's all right, sweetheart,' Beth assured her, 'I'm out of breath, that's all.' Bowing her head, she leaned on the box, the ground rising and falling before her eyes. 'Give me a minute, and I'll be just fine.'

'It weren't what I said, was it?' Cissie desperately needed to know. 'It weren't what I said . . . about you an' Mr Miller?'

In spite of her discomfort, Beth laughed out loud. 'No, no.' Thankfully, the pain quickly passed, and so she went on to reassure Cissie, 'Like I said . . . I was out of breath, that's all. But speaking of Mr Miller . . . I hope you remember what you're supposed to say if he asks why I'm staying at the house?'

'I ain't forgot,' Cissie vigorously shook her head.

'Me mam's told me how Mr Miller said we weren't entitled to have no lodgers. And I'm to say you're just visiting, because you're a cousin from down South. Ain't that right?' She put her two skinny arms round the orange-box, discreetly drawing it away the moment Beth recovered from her attack. '*I'm* carrying this,' she said when it seemed Beth might insist on burdening herself with the cumbersome thing. 'It's my box after all,' she added with a sly little grin.

'We'll carry it between us,' Beth declared as her small companion struggled to lift the box on to her narrow shoulders. Without delay, Beth took hold of one end of the box and Cissie took hold of the other. 'You're a good girl, Cissie,' Beth told her. 'But if Mr Miller asks you any questions, just tell him to see me or your mam.' She didn't like the idea of a child telling lies on her behalf.

As they proceeded, a strange quietness descended between the two of them, each lost in her own thoughts, Cissie wondering when she'd be able to see her lovely flowers again, and Beth reflecting on Cissie's words. 'You ain't gonna *marry* Mr Miller, are you?' In that moment Beth was surprised to find herself thinking of David Miller in a new light. More than that, she was shocked by a cold determination that if danger threatened Maisie and her family, and it was in her hands to make life easier for that darling woman, she must be prepared to consider every possibility, however distasteful or unlikely.

Although it was not yet dark enough for the street lamps to be lit, the day was blending into twilight as Beth and the girl made their way along Penny Street, towards the long stretch of houses on Larkhill.

When Beth and the girl turned the corner, Maisie breathed a sigh of relief. There was a smile on her face as she came out of the doorway and down the meticulously white-stoned steps, to watch the sorry little procession coming towards her. There was young Cissie, bedraggled and dirty as always, thin as a whippet and chattering away, her face upturned to Beth, and the big awkward box strung between them making it difficult for either of them to walk an easy pace. Beth's step was slow and heavy. Now and then she paused to wipe the sweat from her face, and to laugh at something Cissie had said. There was a weariness about her though, and something else Maisie noticed as they came nearer, something that alarmed her. Beth was stooping forward as though in pain, thought Maisie with concern, and as they came even nearer, she saw how her friend's familiar face was flushed with an unusually high colour.

When only a couple of doors away, Beth paused again, leaning forward and clutching her stomach, Maisie rushed down the steps towards her, leaving her shawl on the ground where it fell. 'Jesus, Mary and Joseph!' she called out, grabbing the box and flinging it aside. 'Are you mad? Carting a bloody old orange-box along the streets, and you only weeks away from birthing! Have you taken leave of your senses? Two hours you've been gone. Two hours, when I didn't know what to do for the best; there's the lad inside full o' the fever, an' the pair o' you wandering the streets with a bloody old orange-box!' She took Beth by the arm and began gently propelling her down the street. 'Look at you! Just look at the state of you!' she told the bemused Beth. 'You're worn out, lass, fair worn out. Oh, I should never have let you go. It's my fault. God forgive me, it's all my fault.'

As she helped Beth up the steps, she turned her frustration on the girl, who was trailing along, dragging the box behind her. 'As for you, my girl,' she told her firmly, 'it seems to me you've got some explaining to do. Where've you been all day, eh? I know damned sure there ain't no flowers to sell. I told you to get yourself off to school, didn't I, eh? You want to think yourself lucky you've got a school to go to, my girl! There were never such a thing when *I* were a lass. An' I don't want yer growing up not knowing yer words.'

'I do know me words,' Cissie protested. 'And I can write me own name!' The teacher had told her she was quick. She had also told her she would 'never be any good to anyone if she didn't come to school' when she should, and 'pay more attention' to her learning. But school was awful . . . sitting in long rows in a dark, miserable place, chanting things and getting your knuckles rapped with a long cane whenever you asked to leave the room. No, that wasn't for Cissie Armstrong! She wanted to be out in the daylight, running about and free to do what she was best at – selling flowers. No School Board officer was going to drag her off to no dark unhappy place. Not if she saw him coming first, he wasn't.

'Never mind about that now,' Maisie told her, pushing the girl ahead up the stairs. 'Get the kettle on, lass. Lord knows what the pair of yer 'ave been up to, but it's plain to see that Beth's on her last legs, poor luv.' She made no mention of her deeper fears; that the birthing might be imminent, and that an eight month birthing was renowned for taking both mother and child to the grave. 'Go on! Hurry up, I tell yer,' she snapped when Cissie paused to look forlornly at Beth's high colour and weary countenance as she climbed the steps to the house.

'It ain't Beth's fault,' she cried, 'it's *my* fault . . . I shoulda come home when you told me.' Cissie's tears were bright in her large blue eyes as she took hold of Beth's hand and asked, 'You'll be all right, won't you? I ain't made you poorly, have I?' She saw the shake of

Beth's head, and felt the slight reassuring squeeze of her hand. The next thing she saw was Beth seeming to crumple, her face suddenly drained white, and her mam's eyes big and fearful as she fought to keep a grip on her.

'God Almighty! Don't let go, lass,' Maisie pleaded with Beth. 'Keep hold of me.' Stooping low, she slid her short chubby arms round Beth's swollen waist, begging her to: 'Lean on me hard, darlin' . . . yer mustn't go down. Whatever happens, yer mustn't go down.' When Beth's weight fell against her, she was frantic.

'Oh, Mam!' Cissie was beside herself. 'Is she gonna die? Is she, Mam? Is our Beth gonna die?'

Ignoring the girl's heartfelt plea, the very same that echoed within her own breast, Maisie told her in a sharp voice, 'Get a hold of yerself, our Cissie! Run down the road to Ellen's house as quick as yer can. Tell her she's to come right away. Go on! GO ON!' She watched as the girl made her way down the steps. 'Tell her it's Beth . . . an' she's to come right away.' She could feel the terrible struggle going on in Beth, and knew she would never be able to get her to the bedroom on her own.

Cissie suddenly remembered. 'Ellen ain't there, Mam!' She and Beth had seen the kindly neighbour boarding a tram, no doubt to visit her recently widowed sister in Manchester. She told her mam as much now, and Maisie was panic-stricken until Cissie called out, 'Look! It's Mr Miller . . . the rentman.' She pointed to the slim figure rapidly approaching from the direction of Penny Street.

'Fetch him, lass,' Maisie told her. 'Tell him yer mam has urgent need of his help.' As the girl ran full pelt down the street, Maisie glanced at Beth's chalk-white face leaning on her shoulder. It was covered in a film of sweat, and she was breathing erratically. Her eyes were closed, occasionally fluttering open as though she

had heeded Maisie's warning and was determined she
would not lose her senses altogether. 'Oh, bless yer
heart, darlin',' Maisie cried, the tears running down
her face. 'Hold on, lass, there's help coming. Hold on,
sweetheart.' She pressed Beth harder into her aching
arms, and found a strength she never knew she had.

Beth heard every word, yet she was powerless to
move. Every ounce of effort was drained from her.
Yet there was no pain now, not like before. There
was only a dull insistent throbbing all down one side,
and a terrible sense of emptiness inside her. She was
hot, then she was cold, and all the while she could feel
Maisie's loving arms round her. She wanted to go on,
up the steps and into the house to the bedroom where
she might lie down and recover her strength. But the
steps loomed before her like the side of a mountain,
and try as she might, she could not put one foot before
the other.

Through the swirling darkness she heard Maisie's
voice again, soft and encouraging. 'It's all right, lass.
You'll be all right now.' Then another voice, a man's,
but one she did not immediately recognise. 'Gently
now. Don't fight me.' A moment of struggle, then she
felt herself being lifted. Her head fell back, the weight
floated from her body, and her senses drifted away.

'Beth . . . are you awake, Beth?' Maisie whispered,
stirring her from a pleasant, light and easy slumber.
Opening her eyes, Beth craned her neck and looked
towards the door; and there was Maisie, head and
shoulders peeking into the room, and a warm broad
grin lighting her face when she saw that Beth was indeed
awake.

'Oh, lass! Lass!' she cried, rushing into the room and
coming forward to sit on the edge of the bed. 'Oh, lass!'
she said again, reaching out and stroking Beth's pale

forehead. 'Yer gave us a real fright, that yer did.' Then wagging her finger, she chided, 'Yer a bad 'un, that yer are, Beth Ward! Pushing yerself to the edge like that, an' you only weeks away from birthin'. I've a bloody good mind to tan yer arse, that I 'ave!' Instead, she leaned forward and threw her two fat arms round Beth's neck, hanging on and hugging her until Beth was forced to cry out.

'So that's how you intend to punish me, is it, Maisie . . . by *choking* me to death?' When Maisie fell back laughing, Beth laughed too. She knew instinctively that all was well. Thank God she had not lost the child, although when she woke earlier, it was to fear the worst.

For a long emotional moment, Beth kept hold of the little woman's hand. Then, in a low trembling voice, she asked, 'The baby's safe, isn't it, Maisie?' Beth vaguely recalled how she and Cissie were coming along Larkhill when she was overwhelmed with a series of painful contractions, and oh, how tired she had felt; a dragging tiredness deep within her like she had never known before.

'Aye, lass,' Maisie quickly reassured her. 'Your bonny babby's safe, don't fret now. I've just this minute shown the doctor out, an' he's told me the very same. Your babby's strong as a little ox, an' you're to be got outta bed on the morrow. But yer to take it easy, mind!' she warned. 'No gallivanting about. In fact, yer not even to set foot outside this house until he tells yer. An' if I have any say in it, my girl, you'll stay inside these four walls until that little soldier decides it's coming into this 'ere world.'

All the while Maisie had been ranting on, all manner of things were going through Beth's mind, making her increasingly anxious. She had no idea a doctor had been attending to her. What was more, she had no idea how this doctor would ever be paid. Turning her head away from Maisie's scrutinizing gaze, she looked towards the window. She was astonished to see that it was daylight. The sky was dull and speckled with dark drifting patches here and there. But . . . it was daylight! Beth was under the illusion that she had been in her bed for only a matter of hours, and she expected it still to be dark. 'How long have I been asleep?' she asked Maisie.

'Two days . . . on and off.'

'Two days!' Beth was horrified. Struggling to sit up in bed, she leaned into the bolster, her large dark eyes stretched wide and seeming like black pools against her white face. 'I've been laid up here for two days?' she asked incredulously.

'That's right, lass,' confirmed Maisie. 'You've been in yer bed since Sat'day afternoon, an' it's now four o'clock of a Monday. I'll tell yer some'at else an' all,' she went on with a wave of her chubby finger. 'You'll stay in yer bed *another* two days if needs be.' She passed her hand over Beth's pale forehead and gently lifted the long brown hair aside. 'Oh, lass . . . lass . . . lass,' she murmured. 'As God's my judge, I were afeared we'd lost you and the babby both.' A teardrop trickled from the corner of her eye, before she swiftly wiped it away and forced a smile to her podgy face. 'We've a lot to be thankful for though,' she said in a brighter voice. 'Yer fine an' dandy, both on yer.' She laughed aloud, hugging herself. 'Fine an' dandy, an' that's the way we're gonna keep it,' she said. 'The doctor reckons yer were dangerously exhausted, body and soul. An ain't I told yer afore about pushing yerself to the limit? Well, ain't I?' she demanded. 'Up at the crack o' dawn . . . bent over that bloody dolly-tub wi' yer arms up to their elbows in soap suds . . . sneaking down the stairs while I'm still asleep, an' beating the parlour mats 'til the swirls o' dust reach heavens high . . . on yer knees

151

scrubbing the scullery floor, and washing down the yard when there ain't no need of it.'

Pausing to take a breath, Maisie clicked her tongue and shook her head in exasperation. 'An' if that ain't enough, yer up 'til all hours, writing letters for folks as can't write 'em theirselves. An' *now* look what it's brought yer to, eh? To the end o' yer tether, that's what! Time and time again I've told yer, "Slow down, lass. Take it easy, for God's sake!" But do yer listen? No, yer bloody well don't! Yer like a thing demented; acting like there's no tomorrow. But you'll listen *now*, my girl, else I'll lock yer in this 'ere room 'til you've grown some sense.' She put her two chubby hands to her face, rolling her eyes. 'My God! I must have aged forty years since Sat'day,' she groaned.

'Oh, Maisie, I'm sorry to be such a worry to you.' Beth was shocked to learn that she had been in her bed for so long. The last thing she recalled was being gathered into someone's arms. Her heart skipped a beat and she caught her breath, a crimson blush darkening her face . . . someone's arms! At once she wanted to know. 'Maisie, who put me to bed?' In her mind she could hear the man's voice: 'Gently now. Don't fight me.'

'Why, Mr Miller the rentman, o' course,' Maisie chuckled at the naked horror on Beth's face. 'Oh, don't worry, child,' she said with a serious expression. 'It were *me* as put yer in yer bed. Yer surely don't think I'd let a fella . . . *any* fella . . . see yer in a state of undress? Well, with the exception of the good doctor, o' course,' she corrected herself. 'I'll tell yer some'at though, my girl, if it weren't fer that Mr Miller I don't know how I could ever have got you up the stairs an' into this 'ere bedroom. He were kindness itself, the feller were . . . laid yer on this 'ere eiderdown like yer were a china doll, he did.'

'Oh.' Beth was lost for words. The thought of Mr Miller actually carrying her all the way up the stairs and laying her on the bed made her feel deeply embarrassed. Apart from which, in her present condition she was no easy burden. 'The poor man,' she said now, a mischievous smile creeping into her lovely dark eyes. 'It's all *I* can do to carry this weight around,' she said, patting the great bulge beneath the eiderdown. 'It's a wonder he didn't do himself a damage.' She saw the twinkle in Maisie's eyes and tried desperately to stifle the giggle that was bubbling up inside her, but it was no good, because when Maisie suddenly erupted in a fit of laughter, she couldn't help herself either, and soon the two of them were hugging each other and giggling like two naughty children.

'Come to think on it, gal,' Maisie chuckled, 'his narrer legs did have a bandy look when he took his leave. With a bit o' luck he'll not bother coming fer the rent on Sat'day next,' she cried. 'Happen the poor bugger'll be laid up wi' a bad back.' Her last word ended in a whoop of delight, and the tears rolled down her face.

'Shame on you!' chastised Beth with her whole face creased in a grin as wide as Maisie's. 'Wishing the poor man ill, after he helped us like that.' All the same, she had a vision in her mind of Mr Miller struggling up the impossibly narrow stairs and his thin wiry figure buckling beneath her weight. And in spite of her deeper gratitude, it was a vision that appealed to her sense of humour. Now that her initial fear and panic had long subsided, Maisie too was relieved to dwell on the lighter side of the entire episode. She responded to Beth's ticking off with another fit of the giggles.

After a while, Beth felt the need to question Maisie further. The real issues had not gone away, but the laughing had done her good, even though her sides ached and she felt suddenly uncomfortable. Now, though, her thoughts ran deeper. 'Maisie?' she began.

'Yes, darlin'?' After drying the tears of laughter from her eyes, Maisie was busily plumping the bolster behind Beth.

'You said the doctor had been to see me?'

'That's right, lass . . . Dr Morgan. He were fetched straight away on Sat'day afternoon, an' he's been three times since. Now stop yer worrying, Beth. The good doctor found nothing untoward with the babby. He reckons the young 'un will go its full term . . . nigh on a month yet.' Maisie knew well enough what Beth was thinking, and she had no intention of giving her any more information than was absolutely necessary. At least, not until she was forced to. She had to feign deafness though when Beth put the question direct. 'What's that yer say, lass?' she muttered, hurrying from the bed and making for the door as quickly as she could.

'I said . . . who fetched the doctor?' Beth felt instinctively that Maisie was hiding something from her. 'And more importantly,' she insisted, 'how in God's name are we to pay him?'

'Look, lass, I've some broth simmering on the stove,' Maisie said, flinging open the door and rushing through it. 'I'll be back in a few minutes,' she called from the other side. 'Just you bide quietly 'til I get back.'

'Maisie!' Beth had no intention of biding quietly. Although she still felt as though she was carrying two bags of coal strapped to her middle, and her strength was not fully recovered, she was certainly not going to lie in bed like an invalid while poor Maisie waited on her hand and foot. All right, maybe she wasn't allowed outside. And to be truthful, she had neither the inclination nor the stamina to trudge the cobbles just yet. But there was no reason for her to stay cooped up in the bedroom either.

On an impulse Beth threw back the eiderdown and inched her legs across the mattress, until in a moment her feet were resting against the cold hard lino. Even that small achievement took its toll. Sitting on the edge of the bed, with her head bowed and her two hands spread behind her to support her weight, she took a moment to gather herself, wondering whether Maisie wasn't right after all to insist that she stay in her bed. But no, she couldn't do that. As long as she was able, Beth meant to keep mobile, and to be of help to Maisie wherever she could. And there was still this business of paying the doctor. He *would* have to be paid, there was no escaping that. Maisie had no money, bless her heart, and Beth's own little nest-egg was sadly depleted. She felt guilty and ashamed to have been such a trouble to this family, when all they had shown her was love and kindness. There was no doubt that she had created a problem here, and it was only fair that, somehow, she must be the one to deal with it. But how? How on earth could she pluck money out of thin air? And yet there must be a way, she reasoned.

For one brief painful second she thought of her brother. Could he perhaps help? More to the point, *would* he help? No, of course he wouldn't! Hadn't he shown his contempt for her? Hadn't he made his feelings plain enough? Rightly or wrongly, Ben had blamed her for their father's being struck down. He would not forgive her, of that Beth was certain. Now, when she thought of her father and that last terrible scene, it was inevitable that she also thought of Tyler. Bitter-sweet memories overwhelmed her and the prayer was on her lips before she could stop it. 'Dear God, will I never get him out of my heart?' And she knew she never would.

The room was stifling, claustrophobic. Determined, Beth reached out and collected her dressing-robe from the foot of the bed. The cream robe had been a present from her father; its silky texture was unashamedly luxurious, with a fringed tassel around the waist and the skirt falling in deep swirling folds to the hem. It was a lovely thing. For a long poignant moment, Beth held it against her face, deriving pleasure from caressing its smooth surface, and hurting inside from the memories it evoked. She had lost so very much . . . the love and respect of both Ben and her father. And Tyler. 'Oh, Tyler,' she moaned now, 'why did it all have to go wrong for us?' The tears rolled down her face. She paused to wipe them away, closing her eyes for a moment and wondering how she could ever justify the badness in her; for she *was* bad, or she would never have slept with a man outside marriage. She thought of Tyler, of the wonderful times they had enjoyed together, and recalled the night when this little being was conceived. All manner of emotions raged through her . . . pride, fear and shame. And rising above all of these was a love so great that it towered in her heart, diminishing all beside it.

After waiting these long agonising months, Beth had to believe now that Tyler was never going to find her; maybe didn't want to find her; perhaps had never intended to find her again. Oh, how she had fought against believing the terrible things that girl had told her. Fought and prayed, and hoped against all reason that one bright morning she would look up and there he would be. But he never was. And now she knew he never would be. And yet . . . and yet, she went on loving him. In that dark silent place where dreams were made, she went on loving him with all her heart. But not hoping. Not now. The hope was long gone, as were the dreams. Only the reality remained; a stark reality that left her without her man and with an empty future. All she could look forward to was her child. Tyler's child. The consequence of a love that she had dared to believe would last a lifetime.

Suddenly, she did not want to go on. 'What would it matter if I died?' she murmured. Yet even as the awful words disturbed the air, Beth was mortified. 'Shame on you, Beth Ward!' she told herself. 'How dare you talk like that, when you have a new life inside you?' When her thoughts encompassed Maisie, her shame was tenfold. The thought of her child heightened her shame and made her immensely proud at the same time. *The baby*. This tiny being that moved and fidgeted inside her. No one would ever know how much she was looking forward to holding this baby in her arms; sometimes in the dead of night when she couldn't sleep because of its frantic movements, Beth would imagine how it would be, this perfect being that was both her and Tyler. Would it be a girl with tawny-coloured hair and dark eyes? Or would it be a boy, with long, strong limbs, handsome features and striking green eyes that would remind her constantly of Tyler and tear her apart with every glance?

Tenderly, she placed the palm of her hand over the place where the baby lay. 'You can't know how I've prayed that he would be here to see you born,' she whispered softly. 'But he's not coming for us, little one. Your father isn't coming for us.' A warm sad smile shone from her eyes as she stared ahead, 'I have to let you go, Tyler,' she murmured brokenly. 'Or never know another moment's peace for as long as I live.'

Slipping her arms into the robe, Beth raised herself from the bed and stood unsteadily for a while before tying the belt around her, afterwards making her way carefully across the bedroom. It was little more than twelve feet square, with faded green walls and a tiny prettily tiled fireplace that was presently emitting a cheery warmth from the glowing coals in the grate. An old cracked mirror hung from the picture rail above the fireplace; Beth could see herself in it now, fragmented and distorted. She smiled at the weird image, thinking how aptly it reflected the way she felt. The one small wardrobe was of the same light brown wood as the little chest of drawers that stood beside the narrow dresser. There were two beds, each well used and sagging in the middle, with shiny brass knobs atop the corner struts of the iron frame; a hand-stitched eiderdown in coloured squares covered each bed, and a small crucifix hung on the wall between them. The bed nearest the window was Beth's, and the other was Cissie's; but since Beth was nearing her birthing, Maisie had swapped beds with her young daughter, dispatching the protesting Cissie into the next bedroom to share with her brother, who had protested even more vehemently: 'Don't want no girl in my room.' But Maisie had shouted down his objections. 'You'll do as yer told!' she had instructed them both. 'Else yer can bloody well sleep in the yard wi' the rats.'

After that, the complaints ended and the two young-sters made the best of the situation. Often they could be heard talking into the early hours, Cissie recounting her dreams of being 'rich and famous one day', and Matthew laughing good-naturedly. 'I'll be rich and famous afore you, Cissie Armstrong!' he told her with pride. After all, he was the man of the house now, wasn't he? And she was 'only a snotty-nosed girl'.

'Good Lord above, woman!' Maisie was just pour-ing the hot steaming broth into an earthenware bowl when she swung round to see Beth emerging from the stairway. 'Whatever do yer think yer doing?' Rushing forward she took Beth by the arm, intending to turn her gently about. 'You'll get right back to bed this very minute, my girl!' she ordered, her homely face creased in anxiety. 'Else I'll fetch the doctor an' no mistake!'

Stiffening herself, Beth pleaded: 'No, Maisie. Let me stay down here with you. I'll be fine, honestly.' When she felt the dear woman's hand relax on her, she looked straight into those concerned violet eyes, saying in a firm voice, 'I can't stand being cooped up there in the bedroom. And it makes me feel guilty, having you running about after me. There's nothing wrong with me, Maisie. I can't come to any harm sitting down here, now can I?'

Maisie wasn't too easily convinced. There were certain signs in Beth that had her worried. For a start her colour was too high, and the ankles that had been dainty and trim were slightly swollen. On top of all that, the baby seemed not to be lying as low as it should be at such a late stage. All the same, though, if Beth was getting agitated cooped up in the bedroom, happen it would be best if she did sit down here awhile. After all, she would be under Maisie's eagle eye the whole time, so like Beth rightly argued, what harm could she come to?

'All right then,' Maisie conceded, pointing to the big old rocking chair beside the fire-range. 'Sit yerself there, an' mind yer don't move, my girl! Else it's back up them stairs an' no mistake!'

With great fuss and deliberation she insisted on helping Beth across the room and into the chair, afterwards setting the bowl of hot broth and a chunk of her best crusty bread on to a wooden tray, which she then wedged on to Beth's ever diminishing lap. 'Get that down yer, my girl,' she said, standing before Beth with her chubby legs wide apart and her podgy fists on her hips. 'Every drop, mind,' she warned.

'You're an old tyrant,' Beth teased. But the rich warm aroma from the broth had made her realise just how hungry she was, and so, under Maisie's relentless scrutiny, she finished it off right down to the last spoonful, intermittently breaking up the crusty bread and soaking it in the thick relish of barley, onions, potatoes and meat. Afterwards she gave Maisie a cheeky smile, telling her, 'There! You don't have to stand over me now. Unless you want me to eat the bowl as well!'

'No,' Maisie replied with a smile. 'But I'll make us a fresh brew of tea, and the pair of us can sit an' talk awhile.' She bent to collect the tray from Beth's lap. 'What do you say to that, eh?'

'I say that's a lovely idea, Maisie,' Beth replied. She had her own reasons for wanting a quiet chat before the youngsters came home. And this time, she didn't intend to let her friend dodge the issue. Wedging herself deeper into the comfortable old rocking chair, she followed Maisie's movements as that busy little body went back and forth . . . filling the huge black kettle from the tap above the old pot-sink, then going with it to the firegrate, where she wedged it firmly into the glowing coals. Now she was reaching into the pine dresser and taking out two small pot mugs which she brought to the big square table, where the sugar bowl, milk jug and brown teapot were already prepared. And standing beside them was a plate of home-made apple macs.

The dresser and table were much too big for the scullery, but it was the cosiest and most lived-in room in the house. The only other pieces of furniture were the two big rockers placed one either side of the range, this being Maisie's pride and joy, and which she kept polished to a smooth black brilliance. At the far end of the scullery the window above the sink looked out over a small paved area which led down to the lavatory. In that same wall were two doors; one opening out to the yard, and the other enclosing the stairway that led up to the two bedrooms. Directly behind Beth was the door to the parlour. She glanced at it now, seeing herself in Mr Miller's arms when he had carried her through it some two days ago. Flushed with embarrassment, she looked quickly away. 'Maisie, you still haven't told me. How much do we owe the doctor?' It was a source of worry to Beth, for she was well aware that no doctor would make a house-call and attend to a sick patient, without remuneration of some sort. She knew also that Maisie was not fortunate enough to have made provisions for such an emergency.

'Now, don't you go worrying yerself about that, lass,' Maisie told her, fetching the two cups of tea and setting them in the hearth. 'You'll eat one o' me apple macs, won't yer, darlin'?' she asked disarmingly, promptly scurrying to the table to collect them. When Beth gratefully declined, she pushed the plate to the far end of the table, 'Oh, well . . . I'll not have one neither,' she said, momentarily keeping her back to Beth, and secretly hoping she would not pursue the matter of what the doctor was owed; because the plain truth was, the doctor was owed nothing.

'I want to know, Maisie,' Beth insisted.

'Oh, lass, stop your moithering. There weren't no choice, I tell yer,' Maisie assured her, turning round to face Beth's quizzical gaze. 'If that doctor hadn't come to attend yer . . .' She shook her head in an agitated manner and rolled her eyes upwards, spreading out her hands in a gesture of helplessness. 'Oh, lass! Yer looked like death . . . an' we were that worried.'

Beth's suspicions were already forming and she did not like the conclusions she was coming to. 'Who, Maisie?' she persisted. 'You said "we" were worried.'

'Well, me an' Cissie, o' course,' Maisie retorted, her face colouring up.

'And who else, Maisie?'

'What d'yer mean, lass?'

'You know what I mean,' Beth said in a firm voice.

Maisie laughed with feigned surprise, as though she

161

had only just perceived what was troubling Beth. 'Oh! You mean Mr Miller the rentman?' she said with exaggerated innocence. When Beth patiently nodded, she went on anxiously, 'Well, o' course, the poor feller were worried! Didn't he see the state o' yer? And wasn't it that poor bugger as carried yer up to the bedroom an' all, eh? Why, lass! It were only natural that he were worried. He might be the one as holds his hand out for the rent every week, but he ain't such a bad sort deep down.' She was rambling on, eager to divert attention from the question which she knew was already shaping itself on Beth's lips. 'It's the old man that's the real sod. What! That bugger would have us out on the street afore yer could say: "Where's me hat?" Oh, aye, it's well known hereabouts how the old man has his stepson under his thumb . . . rules him with a rod of iron, he does. Never did let the young feller have a life of his own, yer know, lass. 'Course, David Miller's not so young any more . . . going on forty, I reckon. An' thanks to that tyrant Luther Reynolds he's never had a woman. Ever since his mother died o' the TB he was roped in as his stepfather's right-hand man; then when the ol' feller's illness kept him from seeing to the many properties he's acquired over the years, he used his stepson to fetch an' carry for him. Played on his sympathies, he did . . . used him worse than a slave. With that old bugger pulling his strings, David Miller ain't got much to look forward to, an' that's a fact. What's more, I don't reckon Luther Reynolds is as much of a cripple as he'd have folks believe.' She screwed up her face into an expression of disgust. 'I expect it suits the canny ol' sod to have folks running round waiting on him!'

'Maisie!' Beth's cry brought her nervous rhetoric to an end. 'Was it David Miller who summoned the doctor?' she insisted, having already guessed from Maisie's frantic attempt to change the subject, that Mr Miller had done more than just carry her up the stairs.

'Well . . . yes, lass. He could see yer had urgent need of a doctor. We both could. Oh, Beth! I was so afeared for you and the babby.'

'And did he . . . did David Miller . . . pay for the doctor?' When Maisie said nothing, but lowered her gaze to the floor, Beth's worst suspicions were confirmed. She too remained silent for a moment, mentally assessing the situation and wondering why David Miller should put his hand in his own pocket in order to help her. A man she hardly knew, and with whom she had conversed on no more than three or four occasions. A man who only a short while ago had given Maisie notice that they would all be evicted unless the rent was paid sharply. To Beth's mind, it was a bad thing to be indebted to such a man. 'I must pay him back, Maisie,' she said in a serious voice.

'O' course, lass,' Maisie readily agreed. 'Soon as ever we can . . . we'll pay the feller back.' She came to the fireplace and sat in the rocking chair opposite, regarding Beth with a sorry look and saying, 'I knew yer wouldn't like it, lass. But I had no choice, don't yer see? An' Mr Miller himself went for the doctor . . . the very same as attends him an' his stepfather. To tell yer the truth, lass, I saw another side o' David Miller altogether. But, like yer say, it ain't right that we should be beholden to him. An' we *will* pay him back, soon as ever we can.' She leaned forward and took Beth's hand in her own. 'Aw, lass, I'm that sorry to have let it happen, but . . . well, I just didn't know what else to do.'

'I know,' Beth told her with a reassuring smile, 'and I'm grateful, Maisie, bless your heart. It's just that I don't trust him. After all, he did threaten to evict you, didn't he?' She paused, her face creased in a frown. 'I can't for the life of me understand why he should have summoned his doctor to me, and paid for him too, Maisie,' she said quietly. 'I wouldn't have considered him a compassionate man. Unless I've sadly misjudged him.' Her own words set her thinking.

'Aye well, happen . . .' said Maisie, nodding her head. She made no mention of her own suspicions – that David Miller had an eye for Beth, who with her abundance of rich hair and strong dark eyes was strikingly beautiful, even though she was big with child. But then again, some men liked to see a woman big with child. An' there was no denying that such women had a special bloom about them – although, in Beth's case, she was unusually pale and thin of face. Maisie couldn't help but worry about her. She knew Beth had things on her mind. Things concerning her family, and the baby's father. Things she had not volunteered to talk about. And, though she would have liked Beth to confide in her, Maisie never asked questions. It was not her way. It was enough for her to know that Beth had left a bad situation behind, and that she was trying to forge a new life for herself. As for the man who had put her in the family way, well . . . he couldn't have been much good, or he wouldn't be letting her face it all on her own. Maisie had strong views on that particular issue, and, without the facts, could only draw her own conclusions. She quietly regarded Beth now, seeing how troubled she was, and how deep in thought she had become, and her own heart was sore. Going against her natural instincts, she asked gently, 'Is there some'at else on yer mind, lass?'

For one weak moment Beth was tempted to confide in Maisie, to talk with her about all that had happened, about the way she had broken her father's heart and brought him close to death because of her love for Tyler Blacklock; and the way she had been deceived by this man whom she had loved and – God help her – *still* loved in spite of everything; and how she was

desperately unhappy at the thought of her child coming
into the world without a father. All of these things she
longed to tell Maisie. But she could not. There was
still too much shame, too much uncertainty ahead of
her. Besides, how could she burden Maisie with such
things, when that dear soul had her own troubles? All
the same, as she looked up into Maisie's warm kindly
eyes, Beth thought how comforting it would be to share
her thoughts, to lay bare all the things that plagued her
every waking moment.

'What is it, lass?' Maisie had seen the look in Beth's
eyes, the deep-down need to open her heart. 'Won't yer
let me help yer, eh?' she asked softly. 'Yer know what
they say . . . a trouble shared is a trouble halved.'

The conversation between Beth and Maisie might
have taken a much deeper turn, but in that moment
the door burst open and Cissie came tumbling in, her
blue eyes wide and wild. 'I didn't do it, Mam!' she cried
fearfully. 'It weren't me, honest to God, it weren't!'
When she saw Beth in the chair she screeched with
excitement. 'Beth! Oh, Beth, you're better . . . you're
better!' She launched herself at Beth who grabbed
her with wide-open arms and hugged her close, the
two of them rocking back and forth, laughing out
loud, the special love they had for each other lighting
their faces.

'Hey! Give over, our Cissie,' cried Maisie, clutching
the girl's arm and drawing her away. 'An' *you* should
have more sense, Beth Ward!' she chastised. 'Poor
little mite . . . squashed atween the two of yer.' She
pointed to Beth's swollen belly. 'An' you just out o' yer
sick-bed an' all.' Turning her attention full on Cissie, she
demanded to know, 'What were that yer screamed when
yer burst through yon door? What's all this about, my
girl? What is it you "aint done", eh? What mischief you
been up to now, for Gawd's sake?'

165

'Nothing. I ain't been up to no mischief at all, Mam,' Cissie retorted, but there was something in her voice that told Maisie otherwise.

'I'll be the judge o' that,' Maisie chipped in. 'I asked yer once an' I'll ask yer agin . . . what's all this about?'

'It's that miserable man who sells chocolates on the Railway Station. He said I pinched some'at off his counter. He says he's sending the bobbies after me. He's a liar, Mam. He's allus looking for trouble. Nobody likes him . . .' She was gabbling now, growing agitated. When the sharp insistent knock on the front door echoed through the house, she clamped her hand over her mouth, her whole body stiff and her blue eyes stretched wide as she stared up at Maisie.

'The bobbies!' Maisie's loud fearful whisper sent a shiver through the girl. 'Cissie Armstrong . . . may Gawd help yer if you've fetched the police to this door.' Maisie's warning was lost when the knock came again, this time with more insistence. When she saw that Beth was struggling from the chair, Maisie rushed forward and pressed her back. 'Stay right there, lass,' she told her. 'By rights, yer should still be abed.' She saw how the incident with Cissie had affected Beth, whose face was completely drained of colour. 'Don't worry. It won't be the first time I've dealt with the authorities.' She turned to Cissie. 'We've come through a lot since yer dad was took from us,' she said proudly. 'There ain't never been enough food, nor money. But we've none of us ever tekken anything that didn't belong to us. You think on that, my girl, while I go an' see what this 'ere bobby has in mind.' She kept her gaze on the girl a moment longer, before swinging away and departing the room, her deliberate footsteps echoing along the passage to the front door, the sound of them reaching whoever was on the other side of that door . . . and at once the knocking ceased.

'Come here, Cissie.' Beth beckoned the girl to her. 'Come and sit here beside me.' She patted the arm of her chair. When Cissie did as she was bid, Beth circled her arm round the girl, asking gently, 'Did you take anything from that man's counter?' When Cissie remained silent, but stared at Beth with sorrowful eyes, she asked again: '*Did you, Cissie?*'

Suddenly, the tears were rolling down the girl's face, her expression ridden with guilt. 'Whatever it was that you took . . . have you still got it?' Beth insisted. The girl nodded, wiping the tears from her face with the back of her hand. Beth hugged her, saying softly, 'Thank you for telling me the truth, Cissie. You know what you have to do now, don't you?' The girl nodded again, clinging to Beth when she embraced her closer. 'Go now, Cissie. Quickly! Before your mother comes in with the policeman.'

Pausing long enough to return her loving hug, the girl then fled across the scullery and out of the door, with Beth craning her neck so as to see her cross the yard and go out into the back alley that ran behind the row of terraced houses. In that same moment, the sound of footsteps coming down the passage told Beth that Maisie was indeed bringing the policeman into the house, although no doubt she had been given little choice.

Beth was astonished however when Maisie appeared at the door, because she was wearing a smile instead of a frown. 'There's a visitor to see yer, lass,' she told Beth. As Maisie ventured further into the room, Beth turned her attention to the tall slim figure following her. It was not a policeman after all. Relief flooded Beth's heart. But it was tempered with embarrassment, for the visitor was none other than David Miller! The moment his eyes locked on to hers – quiet brown eyes that greeted her with a warm smile – Beth felt curiously self-conscious. Instinctively, she spread her long slim hands across the bulge beneath her dressing-robe. She wondered what a dishevelled sight she must look, with her hair only fleetingly brushed and the mark of her illness still on her.

When he came forward, the smile deepening in his surprisingly pleasant face, Beth felt rigid with embarrassment and the colour rushed to her face. But then she instantly chastised herself. After all, what did it matter *how* she appeared to the rentman? But, strangely enough, she found that it *did* matter, though she could not understand why. Unless it was the thought of her mother, and the belief she had instilled in her daughter that: 'A respectable lady must always look her very best at all times. Nothing else matters.' But Beth knew differently now. It had taken Maisie Armstrong to show her that other things *did* matter. Being a 'lady' did not mean wearing expensive clothes and looking down on other, less fortunate people. Nor did it mean wielding power and riding in fine carriages. Maisie had neither expensive clothes nor the airs and graces so valued by Esther Ward. Yet she was more of a 'lady' than Esther could ever hope to be.

As though reading part of her thoughts, Maisie quickly gathered her own long, fringed shawl from the rocking chair, and wrapped it discreetly around Beth, who thanked her quietly and proceeded to tuck the shawl-ends in until hardly an inch of her dressing-robe was visible.

'Good afternoon.' David Miller made a strange little bow as he stretched out his hand in greeting, his brown eyes fixed on her face. 'I see you're well enough to leave your sick-bed? That is good news . . . good news indeed.'

When Beth seemed lost for words, he pushed his hand forward, obliging her to return his greeting. And, as she did so, Beth found herself thinking how soft his hands were in comparison to Tyler's. But then, this man spent his working day collecting money and living a soft life, while Tyler knew only hard demanding work that taxed him to the limit of his physical capabilities. But then again, who was she to judge the better man? Tyler had been her world, her life and her whole future. He had seemed deeply sincere, as much in love with her as she was with him. And yet he had both cheated and deserted her. Now, she was amused to find herself idly wondering what kind of man was David Miller. What manner of creature lurked behind those soft brown eyes and seemingly shy smile? Was he a man of passion like Tyler? Or was he the cold aloof individual she had imagined? Suddenly, she was playing a game, smiling back at him, watching his reaction, waiting for the moment when the purpose of his visit was revealed. As she said to Maisie, here was a man she could not entirely trust. Indeed, Beth doubted whether she would ever again trust another man for as long as she lived. 'I understand I owe you a debt of gratitude, Mr Miller?' she said, her smile growing sweeter. At the same time she was appalled at this uncharacteristic hardness in her; until she reminded herself of how this same man had threatened Maisie with eviction, and caused them all so much worry.

'I'm only glad I was able to help,' he replied, his smile encompassing Maisie, who had come to stand beside Beth.

When there was an embarrassing lull in the conversation, Maisie intervened with, 'By way of us gratitude, Mr Miller, would yer like to set with us a while? I've just made a fresh brew, an' there's a batch o' newly baked apple mac on the plate there, d'yer see? Still warm they

169

are.' Maisie was warm-hearted, and not one for bearing grudges.

'Well now, yes indeed, Mrs Armstrong,' he replied, looking from Beth to Maisie. 'I would like that very much.' He had taken his bowler hat off at the front door, and now he gave it into Maisie's outstretched hand. He watched while she carefully placed it on the unoccupied rocking chair, before urging him to, 'Set yourself at the table, Mr Miller, an' I'll pour yer a nice cup o' tea.' When he did so, taking every precaution to make sure that he was facing Beth, Maisie told him, 'Help yerself to as many o' them apple macs as yer fancy.'

'Don't be too greedy, though,' Beth warned good-humouredly, though not entirely disguising the serious intent behind her words. 'I'm sure you understand that money does not come easily into this house, and what with the rent taking priority, there is precious little left for luxuries such as apple macs.'

'Beth Ward!' Maisie was appalled, although she was in no doubt as to Beth's well-meaning motives. 'Shame on yer. Whenever are we so poor that we can't afford to ask a visitor to share us refreshments?' She stared at David Miller, who appeared to have been rendered both startled and shamefaced by Beth's words. 'What! I should be most upset if yer didn't taste o' my apple macs, Mr Miller,' Maisie assured him. 'What's more, I urge yer to take as many as yer like,' she affirmed. Whereupon the poor fellow was obliged to shovel two of the attractive-looking pastries on to his plate, and to make all manner of appreciative noises, while Maisie insisted, 'Now then, ain't them the best apple macs you've ever tasted, sir . . . ain't they?'

In between indelicate mouthfuls he was quick to assure her that they were indeed the most delicious cakes he had ever tasted; which they were, because his mother had never been renowned for her baking, and since her sad demise some few years after the death of her first husband, the Miller household comprised only himself and his stepfather, and an old woman who professed herself their housekeeper when in fact she was a woman from the town who called in each day to flick a duster about and serve their stodgy meals. Mr Reynolds had chosen the woman on the basis of her most valuable quality – that of grudgingly accepting the most meagre of remuneration for her time and trouble. She was slow and sometimes slovenly. But the old man made no complaint, especially when he thought of the money he was saving. He often sang the housekeeper's praises, even while he was choking on her 'apple pies'. David, however, had no fondness for the woman. He decided that if and when he took himself a wife, he would be rid of the housekeeper once and for all.

In between enjoying Maisie's cakes and replying to her polite but meaningless conversation, David Miller could not help but enjoy the cosy atmosphere in this tiny room. The smell of fresh baking mingled with carbolic soap and blacklead hung in the air, and for some reason he did not understand, it created a great longing in him. He missed his mother. He missed feminine company, and above all missed having another person who might intervene when his stepfather took it into his mind to be downright awkward and argumentative. His mother had often found cause to intervene. As far back as he could remember, she had been the one to keep Luther Reynolds in his place. She praised him when he was good and she scolded him when he was bad. She mothered her cantankerous second husband in the same way she had mothered that thin, uninteresting and timid boy who was her only child. And, even though he was not Luther Reynolds' blood son, they had been a family. And he did miss that, so very much.

David Miller was not a passionate man; he was

content to live a quiet unassuming life. Oh, there were times when his stepfather's cruel and demanding nature caused him moments of rebellion, making him wonder whether he should move out and make some sort of life for himself. But these moments were few and far between. It was not in his nature to be wholeheartedly rebellious, so he soon shrugged off these uncomfortable feelings. Besides, his stepfather was old now, and leaning more on his stepson with every day that passed; and even if that young man grew tired of his miserable life in that mausoleum of a house with the fiercely cunning, ageing scoundrel, how could he even begin to change things? Where would he go? What would he do? Apart from collecting rents, noting down whether a roof was becoming dangerously neglected or floorboards were rotting, and serving notices on tenants who were in arrears, he had no particular skills to speak of. But lately something was happening to him, disturbing the measure of contentment he had found within his own soul. That something was Beth.

Whenever his frugal and wasted life became darkly unhappy, and he would lie awake at night thinking of his childhood, certain memories would come to him – dim and happy memories that brought images of his mother into his mind. She, like himself, was not handsome, but was a tall reed-thin creature with a large face and small eyes, and a way of showing her disapproval without saying a single word. Yet, where his stepfather had never in the whole of his life shown the slightest kindness, his mother had had a warm, quiet heart. On certain occasions, mostly when he had read a Bible passage particularly well, or had sat silently throughout one of his mother's female gatherings, she had shown her approval by allowing him to put his two skinny arms round her neck and kiss her ever so politely on the cheek. Now, whenever his loneliness threatened to engulf him, he would remember these occasions. Even now, after all these years, he could recall that certain satisfied look on her face, the smell of camphor that lingered about her, and the feel of her skin under his mouth. That was the clearest memory of all: the feel of her skin under his mouth. Warm it was, and rough, like the leather binding that encased the Bible.

He cherished the memories, for they were the only ones in his life when he had actually touched another human being; except, of course, when as a small boy he was made to shake hands with the pot-bellied whiskered gentlemen who came to see his father. His mother's touch was somehow different, though. She would always be smiling, while often the gentlemen would be scowling. Besides, he had been allowed to embrace his mother, and to actually *kiss* her! Now, though, these few pleasant memories had been replaced by another.

On that day when he had taken Beth into his arms, it was as though she had awakened a new man in him, a stranger to himself, a man who was no longer content with memories. A man whose hands had felt a different kind of skin against him . . . smooth like silk, and warm as the blood that ran through his own veins. When he had lain Beth on the bed, her long rich hair had trailed across his arm, sending shivers through every part of his being. Oh, how he had longed to stay in that room with her, to see her being undressed, to savour all the delights that he imagined hidden beneath those cumbersome garments. That night he had not slept. Instead, he had paced his own bedroom, up and down, up and down, remembering . . . imagining . . . wondering. Only when his stepfather had rapped the adjoining wall with the handle of his walking cane had he made himself be still. But he could not be still inside. Nor had he been still ever since.

He had come to a decision. A remarkable decision,

which greatly excited him but also terrified him beyond belief. He had vowed to take Beth for his wife. Without revealing the name of his intended, he had said as much to his stepfather the very next morning. At first, and in the cruel manner which David might have expected, the old man exploded into laughter. 'You! Wed!' he screamed, his bloodshot eyes wide with astonishment. 'Never! You're not man enough, you bloody fool.' But then he had grown thoughtful, regarding his stepson with narrowed scathing eyes, as though seeing another facet to his character, and the stepson had stood his ground, meeting that old villain's scrutiny with unswerving courage.

'Say what you will,' David had replied with admirable dignity, 'I mean to take a certain woman for my wife.'

'Who is she, you fool? What's her name?' the old scoundrel wanted to know. Adding with the light of fear and suspicion in his eyes, 'A fortune-hunter, eh? Some bright-coloured bitch who's seen an easy living for herself, that's what she's all about, I'll be bound.' He laughed again, saying in a grating voice: 'You always were a fool. So! You've found a woman, have you? Huh! I don't believe it. What woman would want a sop like you for a husband, eh? Unless, as I suspect, she's not after you at all. Happen it's *me* the bitch is after, eh? Me . . . an' what few guineas I've managed to put aside for my old age.'

Little more was said that morning, except for David's confirming his intention to take a wife, and assuring the cynical old soak that: 'She's no fortune-hunter. Nor is she afraid of hard work. She is a woman of strength and beauty, and I could find no better.' He had left the house to the sound of Luther's cruel laughter following him down the street.

Over the next few days, he had suffered many jibes and commands to, 'Fetch her here. Let a *man* take a look at her. After all, if she's everything you say, we don't want you frightening her off, do we, eh?' It was painfully obvious that the old man thought his stepson to be suffering delusions, and that there was no wife, nor ever would be. Not that the old man was bothered about that, because he liked things the way they were, him in his own house with his hoard of shiny guineas, and his stepson doing as he was told for a wage that kept him totally dependent on the old fellow – and without the backbone to change the situation.

'I am right, don't you think, Mr Miller?' Maisie's voice cut across his thoughts.

'Oh! I do beg your pardon,' he apologised with a reddening face, straightening his back and looking from the bemused Beth to Maisie and back again. 'Somehow my attention has strayed, but I do assure you it was not meant as an insult.' He was appalled that he should have allowed himself to be sucked into such a deep and distracting avenue of thought.

'Aw, think nothing of it,' Maisie said cheerfully. 'You got to thinking, an' was carried away. There ain't no shame in that. I do it meself, y'know, all the time,' she explained, trying to put him at his ease and, at the same time, hoping to keep him here a little longer. She was no fool. Maisie would have given a whole batch of her apple macs to wager that what this hapless fellow was thinking about so deeply was her Beth. She had seen it from the minute the poor man had collected her in his arms and carried her up the stairs. She had seen it when he put his burden down on the bed. And she saw it now, as he stared into Beth's face with such longing that it showed in his eyes as naked as a newborn babe. 'All I said was . . . Beth's got a glow on her. She's mending well, don't you think?'

'Yes, I do.' He smiled, embarrassment fading. All the while he was speaking, he never once took his eyes away from Beth; he continued to stare at her with a hunger that kept him to the edge of his seat. 'Your aunt is right,' he said quietly, believing what he had been told, that Beth was a recently widowed niece come from London to stay with her dear aunt until the child was born. 'You certainly do have a glow about you. And I really am delighted that you seem to be recovering so very well.'

For a long moment, Beth stared back at him, her dark eyes growing serious and her voice betraying her deeper appreciation for what this man had done. 'I have you to thank for that, Mr Miller,' she told him kindly. 'But for you, I might have lost my child.' The light in her eyes dimmed with a kind of fear that touched him so deeply that he actually leaned towards her and put out his hand. When Beth thought it best to ignore the gesture, he fell back in his chair. 'Nonsense!' He gave a small laugh to hide his self-consciousness at having betrayed his feelings like that. 'I'm only glad that you're recovering so very well. Now, shall we let the matter end there?' He glanced at Maisie, who was eyeing him curiously.

'No,' Beth replied. 'I'm afraid the matter cannot end there, Mr Miller. As I say . . . you have my deepest gratitude. But there is still the matter of the doctor and his fee.'

'Oh, but you mustn't worry yourself about that,' he said, his confidence returning. 'No, not at all. Put it out of your mind, please. I have no intention of asking for compensation.' He turned to address himself to Maisie. 'I hope I did not give that impression?' he asked with a frown.

Maisie was suitably relieved. 'Well, now, that's exactly what I told her, Mr Miller!' she cried jubilantly. 'That good man don't want no such thing, I told her . . . what he did, he did outta the goodness of his heart.' She turned to Beth. 'Didn't I tell yer, eh? He won't want you fretting over such a little thing as money. Ain't that what I said, eh?' she lied.

All the same, Maisie was secretly relieved to hear the gent say the very same, because she hadn't cared for being beholden to her rentman, any more than Beth had. The trouble was that while Maisie had certain principles as far as stealing was concerned, she had no such qualms about taking that which was offered; while Beth was another kettle of fish altogether. Beth was a woman whose strong principles would not let her accept something for nothing, although she herself was generous to a fault. Maisie had seen these qualities, admirable or otherwise, ever since Beth had been under this roof, when she had insisted on paying her way and doing more than her share of housework, in spite of being heavy with child. To tell the truth, Maisie wondered how she had ever managed before Beth came to live here.

'There you are!' David Miller said with some relief. He sensed an ally in Maisie. It surprised him too, especially in view of the fact that he had been obliged to convey his stepfather's threat to have them evicted. He regretted that very deeply. In fact, there were any number of things that he was coming to regret.

'Maisie?' Beth's face was serious as she addressed the little woman.

'Yes? What's bothering you, lass?'

'I wonder . . . could you do me a great favour?'

'Well, o' course I can, darlin', if yer tell me what this favour is.' Maisie's curiosity was plain on her face as she got up from her chair and went to Beth's side. 'What is it, lass? What's bothering yer?'

'My sewing-box.' She met Maisie's surprised look with a dignified half-smile. 'Would you be a sweetheart and fetch it for me?' Under normal circumstances, Beth would never have asked anyone, especially Maisie, to do something which she herself was quite capable of doing; but she had little strength in her just now, and was afraid that the long steep climb up those narrow stairs would drain her of the small amount of energy she had left. The thought of being confined to her bed again was not a happy prospect. Besides, her concern for the well-being of her unborn child was paramount.

Maisie straightened up. Her expression changed from concern to annoyance as she continued to look down on Beth's lovely troubled face. Instead of giving her answer straight away, she turned about to face the visitor. 'Excuse me, Mr Miller,' she said in a firm though polite voice, 'but I expect you'll be wanting to be on yer way?' She knew very well that Beth kept the remnants of her little nest-egg in that sewing-box. She was acutely aware of Beth's present intention as well. However, Maisie had an intention of her own, and it was this . . . she was not going to allow Beth to give her few remaining shillings to this fellow. The determination in Beth's face was reflected in her own as she waited for David Miller's response.

'I would rather stay a while longer,' he replied with surprising boldness. 'That is, of course, if *you* don't mind?' he remarked to Beth.

'Oh, but I would very much *like* you to stay, Mr Miller,' Beth replied at once. She was surprised when his responding smile softened the deliberate hardness in her heart. Not for the first time, she felt his loneliness. 'Indeed, I *insist* that you stay,' she told him, a sense of regret tempering her purpose when his smile broadened and his kind brown eyes lightened. In that moment it dawned on her that David Miller was attracted to her in a way she would not have imagined. But no matter! Soon he would be gone from this house, and her debt would be paid. Yet some deep instinct warned Beth that, however hard up she and Maisie were, their first priority from now on must always be to keep the rent paid as it fell due. It would not be easy, but once the baby was born the way ahead would be that much clearer.

Her dark eyes returned to Maisie, who was obviously most reluctant to do as she was asked. 'Please, Maisie . . . the sewing-box?'

Sighing noisily, Maisie looked directly into those dark determined eyes and shook her head. 'All right, lass, whatever you say,' she returned impatiently. 'But . . . well, I hope yer know what yer doing!' she said in a low voice, hoping the rentman would change his mind and go. But he was too entranced with Beth to think of leaving. In fact, he had not taken his eyes off her these past minutes. Maisie doubted whether he had even heard a single word of what had just transpired. 'Yer sure, now, lass?' she asked pointedly.

'Yes, Maisie, I am sure,' Beth replied, becoming uncomfortably aware of David Miller's quiet attention, and wanting him out of the house as soon as Maisie had brought the sewing-box and she was able to discharge her debt to him; with her grateful thanks, of course.

Without another word, Maisie hurried from the room. At the foot of the stairs she paused to gather the voluminous folds of her skirt into her chubby fists, then with a frustrated backward glance climbed the stairs, loudly huffing and puffing, and seeming deliberately to take her time by way of protest at Beth's decision to repay the doctor's fee. 'After all,' she could be heard to mumble disgruntledly, 'the rentman did it wi'out being asked . . . so he had no bloody right ter ask for it back!' Oh, but he hadn't asked for it back though, she reminded herself, because it were Beth's idea. 'Well, it ain't one of her best, that's for sure!' she told herself as she paused for a breath on the steep stairway.

'Mr Miller, I should be obliged if you would not stare at me so.' Beth had grown increasingly embarrassed beneath his gaze. If she looked away, she could still feel the intensity of his eyes on her, and if she looked at him with an uncomfortable smile, he merely continued to stare at her in that intimate manner. It was all so unnerving.

'Oh!' At once, he also was embarrassed. 'Please forgive me, Mrs Ward.' The story he had been given by Maisie Armstrong was that, following the sad loss of her husband, this lovely young lady was left alone in the world, except for the child yet unborn, and her dear Aunt Maisie. Beth, whose name he had heard being spoken by both Mrs Armstrong and the girl, was far too young and beautiful a woman to be left on her own for too long. In her present condition, and finding herself inadvertently confined to the house, there had been little occasion for any man to see how incredibly lovely she really was. That in itself was most fortunate for him. However, it seemed to him that, as soon as the child was born, she would be inundated by determined suitors bewitched by her beauty. And if he was to wed this woman – which was an intention which had only been strengthened by his close proximity to her – then he should make his move now, before it was too late, and he saw her snatched from under his very nose, by some charming, worldly fellow, with the gift of the gab and dark, sultry looks that would sweep her right off her feet.

But, oh, how to begin? What could he say to persuade her into marriage? How should he appeal to her? Should he explain how he himself had given the matter much thought, and had come to the conclusion that it was only common-sense for her to accept his proposal. After all, was she not short of money? Was she not a widow? And did she not have the child's future to think of? All of these things were on the tip of his tongue. But these were practical things, cold calculated issues that did not betray his real reasons for wanting her. But how could he say he wanted her because she was the most beautiful, delightful creature he had ever seen? How could he tell her he lay in bed at night, dreaming of her warm and naked beside him? Could he really tell her what was in his heart? That he was so lonely, so unwanted, so needful of another human being who might look on him with pleasure and love in her eyes. Could he tell her of his great longing to have and to hold her forever more? No! He dared not. The last thing he wanted was to frighten her away.

He looked at her now, seated in the chair, her small straight shoulders leaning slightly forward, the pronounced bulge beneath her shawl, the long wild hair that tumbled about her shoulders like fallen brown leaves after rain, and her face, such a strong yet lovely face, with those classic features, small straight nose and eyes that seemed to him like pools of water under a midnight moon. Suddenly, he began trembling inside. Suppose he failed to speak up now? Suppose he paid for such a mistake by losing her to someone else? The prospect terrified him . . . made his blood run cold. He had to speak out! He must!

'Marry me.' The words were blurted out before he was even conscious of his own intention. Just two words, but they might have been two rounds from a shotgun, such was their impact.

Beth had been looking away. Now she swung round, her eyes wide with disbelief as she stared at him. 'What did you say?' she demanded in a quiet shocked voice. It occurred to her that she must have misheard.

Amazed by his own courage, David Miller returned her stare, and with a degree of warm persuasion in his voice, said tenderly, 'Forgive me for being so bold.' A hot rush of embarrassment coloured his face as he went on, 'What I said was . . . *marry me.*' After his proposal, his nervous smile slipped away to be replaced by an expression of anticipation. He waited for her answer. He prayed it would be the right one. The one to set his heart soaring, and to give him a purpose in life.

It was a moment before Beth recovered. She had not misheard after all. *He had asked her to be his wife.* David Miller, this stranger, had asked her to be his wife! There had been no warning, only the affectionate look in his bright brown eyes and the way his quiet gaze had followed her every move. Only minutes before, she had felt a murmuring instinct that he had taken a fancy to her. But she had had no idea how deep his fancy had gone, or how serious were his intentions. 'But . . . I hardly know you, Mr Miller,' she told him now. 'There is no question at all of my marrying you.'

'I understand,' he mumbled sadly, 'and I hope you will forgive me for daring to ask, but ever since the day I carried you in my arms to your bedroom . . .' he could feel himself growing hot with the memory . . . 'I have thought about you . . . thought and thought.' His voice tailed away and the ensuing silence was hardly bearable.

'Please don't go on,' Beth entreated. She found herself affected both by his acute embarrassment and the obvious depth of his emotion. 'The fault is equally mine. The reason I asked you to stay a while was because I must return the doctor's fee which you so kindly provided when I was in need of help.'

'No!' He was horrified. 'No, I will not . . . cannot accept it. Please. If you insist, it will be like throwing the money back in my face.'

Beth made no response, other than to regard him with a dignified curiosity. He was looking at her, appealing with such a forlorn countenance that she wondered for the first time whether she was doing the right thing in being so determined to repay him. In spite of her previous conviction that here was a man without a heart, a man who would not suffer the slightest compunction about throwing a family on to the streets, she began to harbour doubts. Perhaps Maisie was right after all? Perhaps he too was a victim, a mouthpiece, a man denied the opportunity to strike out and carve a life for himself beyond his stepfather's influence? But then she was forced to wonder why he would let himself be suppressed in such a way. 'I'm sorry, Mr Miller,' she began, 'if I seemed to encourage you into believing that I would ever consider . . .'

'Marriage?' he finished. 'No, you have not misled me in any way, I promise you,' he assured her. Suddenly his courage was returning, and with it all manner of reasons as to why she should not dismiss his offer out of hand, but instead see the advantages of it. 'Think, though, Mrs Ward, of what I'm offering you. Sadly – and you have my deepest condolences – you have lost your husband and find yourself alone in the world, except for the admirable Mrs Armstrong and her family. But as you see, life is not easy for your aunt, who also is without a bread-winner, and though I'm certain she's a kindly, amiable person who gladly accommodates you, this is a very small house. You must agree then, that the situation is not at all suitable. Not at all.'

'Are you threatening us?' Beth wanted to know. 'Is this your way of saying that the house is now over-crowded and it would be better if I were to leave?'

'No, no!' He was deeply offended. 'Please don't mis-interpret my words. All I am saying is that this particular situation must be uncomfortable for all concerned.' He raised his hand to stop her when it appeared she was about to interrupt. 'Soon there will be another little body. Another mouth to feed.' He paused for a moment, wondering whether his account of the situation here was having the desired effect; although judging by her expression, he was digging his own grave. Frustrated, he bowed his head a moment before going on in a gentler way, 'What I'm saying is this, Mrs Ward . . . let me help. Allow me to take on board some of your responsibilities. As you can see, I do feel affection for you. Nothing would give me greater pleasure and satisfaction than to take you for my wife. I would be a good father to your child, if you would only allow it. And there is no shortage of accommodation in my stepfather's house. It's a large residence, with only myself and him to occupy it.' Saying the words out loud made him see the miserable way of life he presently endured. And because of it, his boldness knew no bounds. 'Marry me,' he urged with conviction, 'and I promise you will never want for anything again.' He leaned forward in anticipation, his small brown eyes reminiscent of a puppy waiting for a bone.

For a moment, Beth was reluctant to heap more misery on the poor fellow, because to her surprise, she did have an inkling of sympathy for him. Indeed, she was warming to him by the minute. Unfortunately, though, not in the way he would have liked. She had no affection for David Miller, only a degree of compassion for his apparent loneliness and longing for a companion. She opened her mouth to explain that she was so very sorry, but what he suggested was out of the question, when Maisie appeared. So instantly and silently did she emerge from the foot of the stairs, that Beth wondered with some amusement whether she had been hiding round the corner listening. Later, it was confirmed that this was exactly what she had been doing and had been momentarily transfixed to the spot by what was being said between these two.

'Maisie!' Beth's surprise at the little woman's sudden appearance showed in her voice. 'I didn't hear you coming,' she told her, at the same time holding out her hands to take the sewing-box which was securely tucked under Maisie's arm.

Beth's hands dropped back into her lap when Maisie made no immediate attempt to hand over the box. Instead she kept a firm hold on it and said in a friendly apologetic voice: 'I wonder, Mr Miller, would you be so kind as to excuse me and this young lady for a while?' When he seemed surprised by her request, she hastened to add, 'We'll only keep you a moment, I promise. You can step inside the front parlour and admire my late husband's set of smoking pipes.' Her grin was infectious. 'Lovely they are.' Ushering him from his seat and propelling him across the room towards the door, she told him cheekily, 'Off yer go, then. I'll fetch yer in a minute.' As he went with amazing obedience into the parlour, she reminded him, 'I'll be fetching yer afore yer know it.' She then pleased him with a knowing wink and a whisper of, 'Our Beth's an obstinate little sod when she makes her mind up ter some'at, as you've soon found out, eh? But I reckon she's apt to be a bit too hasty at times. You just leave the lass ter me, sir. I'm a bit older in the tooth and a great deal wiser on certain issues, wouldn't yer say?'

She quietly chuckled, thrust him into the room and closed the door behind him. When she came back into the scullery, her smile was gone, and in its place was a look of utter frustration as she declared, 'What in God's name are yer thinking of, Beth Ward? What possesses yer even to *think* of handing over yer money to that fella? What! Him and his stepfather's got more money atween them than the pair of us will see in a lifetime.' She clutched the sewing-box fiercely. 'I say no. NO! Whatever's left in this 'ere box is for you and the babby. It's not for giving away to them as don't bloody well need it!'

'Whether he needs it or not doesn't come into it,

185

Maisie,' Beth told her with equal determination. 'I owe him that money. I'm grateful for his kindness, of course I am . . .'

'Well, yer wouldn't damned well think so!' Maisie interrupted. 'Not the way you've flung it back in his face, yer wouldn't. What he did, he did outta the goodness of his heart, not for any chance that yer might tek it into yer head to repay him. He never expected that, I'm sure. In fact, he said to me on that very day: "Think nothing of it, Mrs Armstrong. I'm only glad I was able to help."' She pursed her lips and sighed heavily, her breathing erratic and her calm still not regained. 'Oh, Beth! Beth! Can't yer just allow the poor sod his bit o' pleasure at having helped a lady in distress?' she wailed.

Having seen that Beth was unmoved by her tirade, she abruptly changed tack and put on her best persuasive manner. 'Aw, lass . . . he aint such a bad fella after all, is he, eh?' she asked in a cajoling voice. 'Don't yer reckon he'll mek some lass a good husband?'

'I'm not saying anything against him,' Beth patiently pointed out. 'All I'm saying is I don't like being beholden to him, or to any other man.' What happened with Tyler had long ago destroyed her trust in members of the opposite sex.

'What? D'yer reckon he'll demand payment in another way?' Maisie insisted. 'D'yer think he did what he did so he could have a hold over yer?'

'No.' Beth had to admit she believed nothing of the sort. 'I don't think that.'

'Oh!' Maisie sensed a weakening in Beth's argument. 'So you've nothing against the fella? Yer don't think he's got some kind of evil intent to make yer pay for his good deed? And on top of all that, yer mean to break yerself so's there'll be no money for when the babby's born? Now then, Beth, yer must tell this foolish woman what kinda sense that makes, 'cause I can't see no sense in it at all!'

After listening to Maisie's very reasonable argument, Beth remained silent, her gaze lowered to the threadbare fireside mat and her dark eyes deeply thoughtful. She was acutely aware that Maisie was waiting for a sensible answer, but the truth was Beth could find none. Her wish to repay David Miller was not prompted by material considerations, nor was it instigated by a sense of her own dignity. Nor did it have to do with the man's own character or his 'devious' intentions. It went deeper than all of that. Much deeper. It had to do with emotions, with love and cheating, and trust and betrayal. It had to do with her mother and father, with her turncoat brother Ben. With hopes and disappointments. All of these things combined to make her more careful, more independent, and, yes, perhaps she *was* being just a bit proud.

But now, because of Maisie, Beth had occasion to recall an old saying: 'Pride comes before a fall'. Of all the things Maisie had said in defence of what she thought was right and wrong, the one statement that stood out bold in Beth's mind was when her friend had scathingly demanded what was the sense of giving away those few remaining shillings when there was a baby soon to be born? Babies were notorious for needing things . . . little bonnets and shawls . . . maybe a perambulator to be pushed about in, and, if it was fortunate, a cradle that rocked at its mammy's touch. Thinking about all of these things softened Beth's aching heart. But then it ached a little more when she thought of one other thing a baby might want. Something more precious than all the cradles and bonnets in the world . . . a daddy to hold it close and make it laugh. A daddy to want it, and to love it like no one else could. Not even its mammy. Now the pain welled up in Beth's soul, spilling over until she was overwhelmed by a great and terrible loneliness.

'Hey! Hey, darlin' . . . whatever's the matter?' Maisie had seen the tears spill from her eyes, and in a moment was stooping to gather Beth in her chubby arms. 'Aw, lass. Me darlin' lass. Take no notice of a silly old woman,' she whispered, rocking Beth back and forth as though she was her own small bairn. 'I ain't got no right ter say the things I did. It ain't *my* few shillings that's tucked away in this 'ere box, and Lord knows you've spent enough of yer little nest-egg on us that don't deserve it.' She had dropped the box to the floor, but now she picked it up and set it on Beth's lap. 'Here yer are, darlin',' she said. 'Do what yer want with the blessed coins. If yer feel it's right ter send that fella packin' with his money paid back, then do it, sweetheart. I'll fetch the scoundrel this very minute!'

She would have wasted no time in doing just that, but she was still having difficulty in setting the box on Beth's lap; the truth was, with the baby being so big inside her and the entire uncomfortable bulge protruding towards her bent knees, Beth hardly had any 'lap' left at all, and Maisie's frantic efforts to set the box so that it wouldn't keep slipping forward towards the floor, were proving a difficult and exasperating exercise. Tears soon turned to laughter at the little woman's comical dilemma and when she saw how Beth's warm sense of humour had diffused a very delicate situation, Maisie too collapsed in a fit of giggling. 'Yer little sod, Beth Ward!' she cackled, 'I've a mind ter tan yer bloody arse.' After a while, she cuddled Beth to her, and gently stroking the wild wayward hair, said in a more serious voice, 'Shall I put this 'ere box back where it belongs?'

When Beth silently nodded, her eyes soft and glowing, Maisie planted a kiss on her pale forehead and made her way across the room towards the door. 'Right then, lass,' she said with a knowing smile. 'But first, I'd best put the poor fella next door out of his misery.' She paused for a moment, carefully regarding Beth, who was looking at her with affection, her heart quieter now, and her emotions less turbulent. 'This may not be the best time ter say it, lass,' Maisie ventured cautiously, 'but while yer reflecting on things . . . yer might give a thought ter what you've been offered this very day. It ain't often a lass that's big with child is smiled on by good fortune. An' that's what David Miller is, lass . . . good fortune smiling on yer. He ain't yet forty, I shouldn't wonder, and though he ain't no oil-painting, he's pleasant enough all round. Yer heard what he said with yer own ears . . . he possesses a big house and pots o' money. An' what's more, it's plain ter see that the poor bugger's been starved o' love. Happen the good Lord's been helping him to save it all up to heap on you and the babby, eh?'

'Don't, Maisie,' Beth warned gently. 'You've persuaded me on one issue this afternoon. Don't demand anything more.'

'Right!' she reluctantly conceded. 'I'll learn ter mind me own business, just see if I won't.' All the same, as she went to call David Miller, whose hopes had not dwindled since he'd been shut away with the late Mr Armstrong's pipes, Maisie was convinced that here was the answer to all of Beth's problems; a husband to give her the respectability she warranted, and a father to give the baby both a name and a deal of security. It was a certain fact that the lovely Beth was in dire need of a man to keep the wolves at bay. Once that babby was here and she was exposed to the outside world more often, there would be all manner of men who would make a beeline for her. And they wouldn't all be of a kind that might improve her lot in life, that was for sure! Round these parts, that kind of fella was few and far between, an' no mistake.

Still, there was a very real danger that any charming, handsome young man with only one underhand thing on his mind might turn Beth's head, because in spite of being part of Maisie's own family now, she was terribly lonely. Lonely in a way that neither Cissie nor her mam could help. Lonely for a man to ease the ache in her young heart; lonely for someone to cuddle up against at the end of a long day and talk about the future and her own family, the children she would have, and the man who would always be there, long after Maisie was under the ground.

As she threw open the door to tell David Miller 'Come on then, sir,' Maisie took a moment to observe the manner of this certain gentleman; the way he made a polite little bow as he turned from the fireplace where he was studying the small oak cabinet on the mantelpiece which housed the handsome collection of smoking pipes; the manner in which he smiled . . . easy-like, but nervous enough not to be arrogant; the cut of his polished leather boots, no doubt costing enough to feed Maisie's family for a whole month; and the way his brown eyes lit up when she told him, 'Our Beth has had second thoughts about the little money matter yer discussed earlier.' But when his eyes positively shone with delight she took him aside and whispered furtively, 'She don't like to be bullied, don't Beth. But, if yer intentions really are honourable . . . an' if they're *not* then I swear I'll skin yer alive meself! . . . all I can say is, don't give up too easy on the *other* matter, if yer get me meaning.' Maisie prided herself on knowing a good deal about character, and she felt in her bones that here was a good man who had been led astray by a bad 'un. Threats of eviction and the like had only ever been just that . . . threats. In fact, if she were to cast her mind back to the time soon after her darlin' man got himself killed, this 'ere David Miller had been most sympathetic. She had suspected then, and she knew it now, that he himself had put his hand into his own pocket to pay a two-week arrears on the rent. No man who was rotten at the core would ever have done such a thing. No, this one had a good heart, and Beth had won it over. It would be a crying shame to let it all go to waste.

Beth felt embarrassed anew at the prospect of having to explain to David how she had changed her mind and was content to leave things as they were with regard to the doctor's fees. Now, when he strode into the room, a smile on his lips and a shy look in his timid brown eyes as they swept her face adoringly, she thought about Maisie's words: 'Been starved o' love . . . happen the good Lord's been helping him save it up to heap on you an' the babby.' These words were still echoing in her heart when he sat down with his eyes still fixed on her face, and a kind of sadness about him. And try as she might to hold herself aloof from him, Beth was surprised and disturbed to find herself responding to his enthusiasm and gentle manner with a certain relaxation of her own. Her instincts told her that this man was harmless enough, even amiable. Yet, her deeper instincts warned her to be careful, for men were hard and unpredictable creatures who could smile sweetly while sticking you under the ribs with a carving knife! After all, the three men who had meant all the world to her, and one in particular whom she had thought to spend the rest of her life with, had each deserted her when she needed them most. It would take a good man, a very special man, to convince her that all men were not the same. Until that unlikely day, she would be on her guard.

Beth was not to know that the unlikely day was only three weeks away. Even now while the two of them were exchanging pleasantries, he bearing in mind what Maisie had confided in him and she thinking how truly

wonderful it would be if Tyler were to walk through that
door to claim her and his child, Fate was creating the very
circumstances that would draw her to David Miller in a
way that she could never have envisaged.

On a rainy Friday morning in March, some few weeks
after David Miller's astonishing proposal, Beth went
into labour. The evening before she had been fretful
and unsettled, not wanting to sit, unable to walk with
any degree of comfort, and her whole body feeling as
though it was burning up. 'What ails yer, lass?' Maisie
had asked, putting down her sewing and eyeing Beth
with a knowing look. 'In pain, are yer? Is it time, d'yer
reckon?'

She saw how Beth was unduly flushed and agitated.
Her own two had never taken her in that way, because
they'd arrived in the middle of the night without so much
as a minute's warning. But then, no two women were
the same. Maisie was acutely aware that this was a first
birthing. She was also mindful of the fact that Beth had
been dragged down by her recent illness. Except for
the huge mound at her middle, the lass was not as far
through as a matchstick, with her pitiful, thin face and
big lost eyes.

'I just feel so warm,' Beth explained. 'Uncomfortable,
like.'

'Is there any pain, lass?'

'No.'

'Has yer waters broke?'

'No, I don't think so.' Maisie had described to Beth
how she would first know when she was going into
labour. 'There'll be one o' two ways o' knowing,' she
promised. 'Either you'll go straight into labour pains
. . . dull, rhythmic contractions that increase with the
babby's intent to come into the world; or your waters
will break . . . that's ter say, the protective skin below

will break with the pressure, and the fluid which has cushioned the babby from harm will come gently away.' As far as Beth could tell, neither of those things had actually begun to happen.

'Aye, well, it don't mean ter say it ain't started,' Maisie said after some consideration. 'It might be as well if I sleep with one eye open tonight, eh?' she asked with a little smile.

And that was just what she did. Beth knew that, because she also could not sleep . . . tossing and turning this way, then that, perspiration breaking out all over her and a strange sense of urgency building up inside her. At quarter to four the following morning, she was out of bed and watching from the window as the sky began to flood with light, silhouetting the irregular skyline with its array of chimneys, monumental cylindrical pipes rising from the cotton mills, together with the nearer squat chimneys jutting from the endless rows of back-to-back dwellings. Already the ascending curls of smoke were darkening the coming dawn and shrouding the many tall, proud church spires. Yet, in spite of the grime and the black clouds already forming to disperse the daylight, Beth was always fascinated by the way night-time fell away and the world was lit once again; as though an almighty invisible hand had put a match to a huge gas-lamp just beyond the horizon.

She sat by the window, quiet as a mouse so as not to disturb Maisie, who in spite of her determined vigil had fallen asleep some time ago and was snoring to her heart's content. In this small room, and with the birth of her child so obviously imminent, Beth's deeper memories were awakened. Memories of another room not so unlike this one, a room where she and Tyler had lain in each other's arms and vowed their undying love. A stark, unwelcoming room made warm and cosy by their happiness. She recalled how she and Tyler had made wonderful love, afterwards lying content in each other's arms. She had not regretted it then and she did not regret it now; if anything, she thanked the Lord for His blessings. What she did regret was her naivety, the way she had hung on Tyler's every word, believing with all her heart that he meant every single thing he told her.

Those same words echoed in her mind now. 'Oh, Beth! Beth . . . you're all I ever want in life. I love you so much. So very much.' Now as she thought of the softness of his voice, the warm fervent touch of his mouth pressed against hers, the bitter-sweet emotions that rippled through her were almost unbearable. With his words came another's; the girl, brassy-faced and tearful as she revealed how Tyler had whispered the very same endearments in her ear . . . made her with child, then deserted her when she threatened to tell Beth what was going on. Even now, she questioned her own wisdom in believing the girl, yet the truth was she had no real choice *but* to believe her. When Annie showed her the brooch . . . given to her by Tyler, the same brooch which once had been her own, Beth was shocked to the core. Even then she would have given Tyler the benefit of the doubt, or at least listened to his side of the story. Now though, all of that was irrelevant, because if she had needed proof that Tyler had used her in the same way he had used that girl, she only had to look around her. It shouldn't be dear Maisie comforting her, it should be Tyler. He who had not bothered to seek her out, and for all she knew was even now charming some other unsuspecting girl into his bed.

'How could you do it?' Beth whispered now. 'Couldn't you see I would have moved heaven and earth just to be with you?' She watched the unfolding day a while longer, then when weariness overwhelmed her, she bent her head to the windowsill, crossed her arms to form a pillow, and drifted into a deep quiet sleep.

When Maisie woke to find Beth was not slumbering beside her, she was instantly alarmed. Sitting bolt upright she cast her sleepy eyes from one corner of the room to the other. When she saw the figure by the window, she breathed a sigh of relief. Scrambling out of bed and gasping when the cold lino met her bare feet, she called out, 'Beth . . . are you all right, lass?' When there was no answer she tiptoed to the window. 'Beth?' Still no answer and her old heart turned over. A little closer, and she saw at once why Beth had given no response. 'Why, the poor little sod's hard and fast asleep!' she told herself. Reluctant to wake her, for she knew that Beth, like herself, had suffered too many restless nights, Maisie went on soft footsteps back to the bed. She slid away the eiderdown, and then carried it back to Beth, with gentle movements draping it ever so carefully over Beth's huddled form.

A few moments later, Maisie was dressed and on her way out of the room. At the door she paused a while to look at Beth with great affection. 'Bless yer heart, lass,' she whispered. 'It's plain the babby ain't yet urgent, but it won't be long now. We shall have us a new addition to the family within the next twenty-four hours, I should say.' Delight spread over her face at the prospect of a new babby lying in her arms. 'Oh, it will be grand, lass. It's a long time since old Maisie felt a young'un nuzzling up to her. No, it won't be too long, lass,' she told the sleeping Beth. ''Til then yer must get what sleep yer can.' Here she shook her head, saying in a more sombre voice, 'Though I don't like ter see yer all bent up like that, yet I daren't wake yer. No, I wouldn't be so heartless.'

Making up her mind to return as soon as ever she could and risk making Beth more comfortable, Maisie scurried away to get Matthew off to his work, and to shake the sleep from that rascal Cissie whom she intended sending to school, especially after that suspicious business yesterday. No doubt the lass would give her a good argument as to why she should not be sent, and truth be told Maisie couldn't help but secretly sympathise with her; after all, she herself had not suffered the misfortune of being marched off to school to learn the rudiments of reading and writing and she hadn't come to any great harm for the lack of it, now had she?

'I hate it!' Cissie toyed with her food. Somehow her appetite had altogether gone and her mood was defiant as she stared up at Maisie. 'You wouldn't like it, would you, Mam?' she cried. 'Nobody in their right mind would like it. You don't know how awful it is, or you wouldn't make me go there. Honest to God, Mam, it's just like a prison! Worse! That's what it is, Mam . . . it's worse.'

'Give over, our Cissie,' Maisie told her impatiently. 'How in God's name can it be worse than a prison?' She was rapidly losing her temper. 'Yer ain't shackled to the wall, are yer?'

'No, but we might as well be,' retorted Cissie.

'Yer ain't! And that's enough,' warned Maisie. 'And yer ain't fed on bread and water, are yer?'

'We ain't fed on nothing, that's what.'

'And yer ain't made to wear them overalls with arrows on, are yer?' Maisie persisted.

'Well . . . no,' Cissie reluctantly conceded, realising with disgust and a sinking heart that she was losing the argument. 'But sometimes Mr Siniter flogs the boys with the cat-o'-nine-tails!' she added hopefully.

'And no doubt the buggers deserve it,' retorted Maisie, being wise to Cissie's ploy; although she didn't doubt for one minute that the boys were flogged, some of the lasses too she wouldn't be surprised.

'Oh, Mam!' Cissie rounded the table and tugged

at Maisie's apron. 'I hate being squashed in amongst ninety brats, and having my knuckles rapped when I don't understand what Mr Siniter's telling me. I don't understand sums, and all them strange words. Don't make me go. Please, Mam.'

'Yer have to go, lass,' Maisie argued. 'That there Gladstone fella made it legal that all childer have to attend school 'til they're ten year old. If that education bloke finds I've failed in me duty, like as not the bugger'll have me clapped in irons!'

'That's never worried you before.' Cissie was desperate enough to be unusually cheeky.

'Well, it's worrying me now!' Maisie retorted impatiently. Maisie might well have pursued the matter to its conclusion but she was in too much of a hurry to see the children away and get back upstairs. She turned away to attend to young Matthew, who had been sensible enough to remain silent throughout the bantering.

Cissie gave no reply and returned her attention to her breakfast, scooping the milky-pobs from her bowl and sucking at the soft wet bread that dripped on her spoon. Now and then she glanced at Matthew, wanting to say something, but afraid in case it got her mam all worked up again. 'It's not fair,' she muttered under her breath, quickly wolfing down her food when Maisie flashed her a warning look.

For the next few moments, all was quiet round the table, save for the occasional slurping sound when it seemed a pob of bread might slide from the spoon and plop back into the bowl. Maisie finished her breakfast as quickly as she could, without choking herself. But she felt sorry that she must force the lass to school, and now and then stole a glance at the miserable little face, a face that was beloved by her, a small peaked face with a pretty mouth and large expressive blue eyes that were presently turned down to stare dolefully at the newspaper that served as a tablecloth.

The newspaper had been given to Maisie by the man in the corner shop, otherwise it might have been thrown into the midden and that would have been a terrible shame – although it was too full of words and pictures of Gladstone to be of much interest to Maisie. There were several large holes in the newspaper where she had cut out the precious pictures of Queen Victoria, who strangely enough reminded Maisie of her dear old mam long gone.

Although she was glad that Cissie had managed to sieve at least some learning from her all too rare attendances at school, Maisie did not altogether regret the fact that she herself could make neither head nor tail of what was written on that newspaper but she knew the content well enough, because Beth had taken the trouble to read the articles to her.

'You should be kept informed of what's going on, Maisie,' Beth had told her seriously when she loudly protested how she didn't see no point in knowing all about umpteen things that made not the slightest jot of difference to the likes of her; such as how a fella called Daimler had got the first petrol-driven car; or talk of the Royal Jubilee; although she had been interested to hear how unions for ordinary workers were springing up all over the country.

'It won't last though,' she'd told Beth cynically. 'You'll see . . . the high and mighty buggers in government won't let ordinary folks have no say in nothing.' Maisie harboured no illusions where men in tall hats and carrying canes were concerned. 'They're all mouth and bloody trousers . . . don't know what it's like to go without a crust, or to have their bellies rumbling with hunger, or to lie in a damp bed and watch a cockroach crawl up the wall and on to the ceiling where it might fall on yer face in the middle of the night. What the bleedin' hell do they know, eh? What do they know of ordinary folk such as you and me?'

'Can I say cheerio to Beth, then?' Cissie asked, a smile returning to her face at the thought of a few extra precious moments.

'No, lass, yer can't do that, 'cause Beth's fast and hard asleep, and she ain't slept too well these past nights.'

'Aw, Mam,' Cissie moaned. 'Can't I wake her up, just for a minute, eh?'

'No!' Maisie was adamant. 'Yer can't do no such thing.'

'Well, can I peep in at her? I promise I won't make a noise.' Just the *sight* of Beth would gladden her sorry heart.

Maisie thought for a moment. 'Aw, all right. But mind yer don't open the door none too wide, and mind yer don't wake her up, our Cissie . . . else you'll be going to school with a sore arse as well as a sour face!' she warned. She watched as the girl went eagerly across the room and quietly up the stairs. Cissie would not wake Beth, Maisie was sure of it. If she was a jealous woman, she might well take umbrage at the way the girl adored Beth. But then, Maisie herself felt the same way about the lovely young woman who had come into their lives, so how could she resent Cissie's affection for her? If anything it was a joy to see, and the Lord alone knew Beth had been desperately in need of a friend when she first set foot in Blackburn.

'I can't eat no more, Mam.' Matthew pushed his plate away.

'But you've hardly touched it, lad,' Maisie said without reprimand. These past weeks she had been concerned about the boy. He seemed to be unusually quiet; although of course he had never been the lively little chatterbox that Cissie was. All the same, Maisie had noticed how withdrawn he'd become of late, and how he was always wanting to go to his bed afore time. Lately, too, he had not been eating enough to keep a sparrow alive. She looked at him now, with his floppy mass of brown hair and eyes as violet as her own, and she thought how tender he was at eleven years old to be working alongside grown men down in the mines. Not for the first time, she asked herself whether there could have been any other way she might have organised things. But the answer was always the same. When her darling man was lost in those same bloody mines, she had done the best she could; although there was never a day went by when she didn't regret the way young Matthew seemed to be paying the biggest price of all. 'Your dad would have been so proud of you, lad,' she said now in a choking voice.

When the boy smiled back at her, Maisie's heart went out to him. He did seem a sad little thing. 'What is it, luv?' she asked, bending her head to look into his face. 'Are yer poorly?'

'No.'

'What then? Are yer tired, eh?'

'Not really.'

'Is it to do with yer work then?'

'No.'

'But there is some'at on yer mind, ain't there?'

Matthew did not instantly respond to this particular question, but then he said something which surprised Maisie. 'How long will Beth be staying with us?'

'Beth?' Maisie thought she detected a note of resentment in the boy's voice, although she could not be certain. 'Why . . . as long as she needs to, I expect. And, like I've already told her, she's as welcome in this house as a ray of sunshine.'

'The babby too?' The boy kept his violet eyes on Maisie's disbelieving face.

'Of course the babby too.' When her answer sent the boy into a thoughtful silence, Maisie told him caringly, 'You know how Beth was dreadfully unhappy when she came here?' When he nodded, she went on, 'And it's allus been yer mammy's policy never to turn a wretched soul away?' He nodded again. 'So . . . d'yer think I were wrong? D'yer think I should have left Beth where she was . . . lying unconscious on the street with not a friend in sight? Is that what *you* would have done, son?' Maisie's pointed words caused him to think. He took a while to answer but when he did, it was merely to shake his head somewhat reluctantly. Maisie was glad in her heart that her son could see it was right to have taken Beth in. 'And d'yer agree that she has been a good friend to us all?' she insisted.

He nodded again, but this time his gaze fell away beneath Maisie's quizzical expression and, in a soft voice that betrayed his shame, he said, 'I know how she's dipped into her nest-egg to help us but . . .'

'Yes, luv?' Maisie secretly chided herself for not realising why her son had been troubled of late. 'While we're talking, and before our Cissie comes back, let's have it all out in the open, eh?' she persuaded him. ''Cause I can't let yer go to work without the air's cleared atween us.'

When the boy sat upright in the chair and levelled his handsome eyes at his mother, she was astonished at how grown up he seemed. His shoulders were broader than she remembered, and he had sprung up in height when she wasn't looking. There was a square strength about his chin that put her in mind of her late husband, and when he spoke it was with a quiet resignation that was both impressive and dignified. Yet there was something else too, something that worried her deeply but which she could not put a finger on; a kind of rebellious attitude, a hardness that occasionally flashed in his eyes and made them appear cruel. Taking a deep breath and seeming mentally to prepare himself, the boy told her determinedly, 'When our dad got killed, you said *I* was the man of the house. You said it was *me* that had to be the bread-winner now.' His courage grew. 'I liked it better before she came.'

Maisie saw it all now, and chided herself for being such a blind fool. In an instant she had rounded the table and was seated beside him. She had the greatest urge to take him into her arms and cuddle him, but her instincts warned her against it. Suddenly he was not a child but a man, with all the inherent responsibilities towards his family. There was a terrible sadness in Maisie as she looked at him, and a degree of helplessness. Her son had not really enjoyed the chance to be a boy, and now he never would. It was all too late. 'You'll *always* be the man in this house,' she told him in a voice that trembled with emotion. 'Nobody will ever take that from you, though I wish to God it could have been different, and yer father was here to take the weight from yer shoulders.'

'I *like* being the man of the house,' he said, staring at her in a forthright manner that warned her to tread carefully. 'But *she* won't let me be. She's spoilt everything. I expect, when the babby comes, you'll forget about me, won't you?' There were tears in his eyes, but he swiftly blinked them away.

'Aw, no . . . no, no.' Maisie was shocked. He was jealous! That was it. The boy was good old-fashioned jealous! 'What a thing to say,' she declared, returning his stare with a hurt look. She would have gone on to reassure him of so many things, but Cissie's quick footsteps could be heard on the stairs. Clasping Matthew's small but work-worn hand in hers, she whispered lovingly, 'We're all of us immensely proud o' yer, son, yer do know that, don't yer?' When he gave her a half-smile, she impulsively hugged him, thrilled when he didn't resist. 'We'll talk when yer come home from work,' she promised. 'Just you and me . . . on us own, eh? And between us, we'll thrash this thing out. Would yer like that, eh?'

'I'm sorry, Mam,' he said quietly. 'I've been thinking all sorts of things, and they all seemed right, but now that I've put them into words, well . . . they sound different . . . selfish.' Now, as Cissie came rushing into the room, he grew embarrassed and pulled his hand from his mother's. Scrambling from his chair he said in a brighter voice, 'I'd best get going, or I'll not get a lift on Ted Leyton's coal-waggon.'

'Huh! *I'd* rather be going to the mines on Ted Leyton's coal-waggon than to that rotten school!' Cissie told him.

'That's enough of that, my girl,' Maisie interrupted. 'Yer didn't wake Beth, did yer?'

'No. I bet I couldn't if I wanted to,' Cissie replied. 'She's fast and hard asleep. I bet if I shook her and shook her she still wouldn't wake up.'

'Yer little sod! Yer didn't, did yer?' her mam asked suspiciously.

'What?'

'Shake her.'

''Course I didn't, Mam.' Cissie was indignant. 'I just told her I was being sent to rotten school and that I'd see her when I got home, but she never even heard me.' In spite of the fact that Beth had slept all through her incessant chatter just now, Cissie could not hide her excitement. 'When will the babby come, Mam?' she asked with delight.

'Soon enough, child. Soon enough.' In view of her son's confidences just now, Maisie felt it was not the right time to discuss the new babby. She shifted her attention from Cissie to the boy. 'Ready are yer, lad?' she asked affectionately, rising from her chair and crossing the room towards him. 'Got yer snap-can, have yer? And yer clean hankie?' She always used to insist on her man having a clean hankie, even though it always came home black as the coal underground; but it was important for Maisie to send her man to work with a snap-can filled with sandwiches, and a sparkling white rag for blowing the coal dust from his nose and wiping the sweat from his brow. Her man had gone now, but here was another in the making. 'God go with yer, son,' she told him softly. Her eyes let him know she had not forgotten what they had talked about. 'We'll have us little chat tonight.'

'I'd best be going, Mam,' he replied, and Maisie noticed there was a light in his eyes that had not been there before. In a minute he had turned away, and for the briefest time Maisie's heart went with him.

Soon Cissie had followed her brother out of the door, and Maisie lost no time in clearing the table. She left the dishes in the old pot sink, and went to the long-case wall clock from which she took a small tin box. Out of this she drew a number of carefully saved coins, and counted almost all of them on to the table. Today was Friday. David Miller would shortly be making his rounds, and she must not give his stepfather any excuse to put them out. 'We shall have to pull us belts in this next week,' she muttered aloud, 'but, like Beth rightly said, we must first make sure of a roof over us heads.' Placing the coins with the buff-coloured rent book, she then made her way to the foot of the stairs. 'I shall have to wake yer, gal,' she chattered to herself as she climbed the stairs. 'Much as I'd rather let yer sleep, I can't see yer all buckled up like that, bless yer heart.'

Beth was already awake. When some short time ago she heard the front door close, she had lifted her head to see Cissie going reluctantly down the road, banished to school. She was tempted to knock on the window and give Cissie an encouraging wave, but she resisted the temptation, for it might have undermined Maisie's authority with the girl, and that was the very last thing Beth wanted. Besides, she had other things to occupy her mind right now. Not only was she stiff and uncomfortable from having slept in such a crooked position, but there were other things happening within her body that told her the babby might be on its way. And she was proved to be right. Maisie's face said it all when she came into the room to see Beth gripping the edge of the windowsill, her face deathly white and creased in pain. In no time at all, Maisie had everything under control. 'Breathe like I told yer,' she warned Beth. 'Remember everything I've said and you'll be fine, lass . . . just fine.' When she saw how Beth was struggling to breathe in that low easy rhythm that might ease the pain and allay the birth until the time was right, Maisie encouraged, 'That's the way, darlin' . . . nice and steady like. Do as old Maisie tells yer, and the little 'un will be here afore yer know it . . . slipping into the world with no trouble at all.'

Unfortunately, Maisie was wrong. By midday she was beginning to realise that the babby was not about to 'slip into the world with no trouble at all'. Four hours later, she was anxiously hoping that Cissie would come straight home from school and not go gallivanting all over Blackburn, as was her way. There was trouble here, desperate trouble that had Maisie sick inside; although she constantly reassured Beth that: 'Everything's all right, lass. Don't worry now', she herself was more worried than she would ever admit. Beth's first birthing was proving to be a long and difficult labour, and one right outside Maisie's experience.

Beth was exhausted. Sometimes the pain was like the blade of a knife slicing through her, and sometimes it was a dull insistent sensation that squeezed the very breath from her lungs. Sweat oozed from every pore in her body, trickling over her skin and sticking the long cotton shift to her back until she desperately wanted to tear it away. 'How much longer, Maisie?' she asked in a whisper. 'Dear God . . . how much longer?' Her breath was snatched away as she was riveted by a long shuddering spasm.

'Not long, lass,' lied Maisie, realising that she alone could not help Beth. She needed another pair of hands, and someone who was no stranger to birthing. The neighbour on the right was an old fella who was neither use nor ornament, and most of the women would be away to the shops on a Friday afternoon. That left only the neighbour on the left. Maisie was reluctant to recruit Meg Piper's help because, although she had given birth to fourteen childer herself, she had grown feeble of mind. Normally old Meg would not have been Maisie's choice for helping her bring Beth's young 'un into the world, but she had no option, not now, not with Beth so wearied by the event, and like as not the unborn itself was every bit exhausted as its mammy. If Maisie knew anything, it was this . . . nature had a way of giving a body breathing space. Up to now, Beth's pain and discomfort had not eased at all; but it would, Maisie told herself, it would! And so she whispered words of encouragement, and bathed Beth's steaming body, and all the while she spoke to her of holding the babby in her arms. 'Aw, it'll be a real little angel,' she said, smiling with delight, 'with rich brown hair like its mammy, and the same big dark eyes. Oh, an' the little sod'll be kicking and screaming for its titty, not knowing or caring what trouble it's caused.'

'Do you think so, Maisie?' Beth asked in wonder, her eyes veiled with anguish and her long slim fingers wrapped round Maisie's as though she dared not let go.

'O' course I do!' Maisie told her. 'Would I say such a thing if it weren't so?' She silently prayed the Lord would forgive her for assuming that He meant Beth and the little 'un to live.

Maisie was right about one thing though, because after a while Beth's pain eased and she was able to relax a little. Sighing deep within herself, she slid into a fretful and unnatural sleep; a sleep that brought its own kind of nightmare, a dark swirling dream filled with images of everyone she had ever known, all going before her as though in a mourning procession. Her father; her shrewish mother; Ben, the brother whom she had loved and who had turned against her; all those she had worked with; Wilson Ryan, the young man her parents had wanted her to wed; Tom Reynolds with his small devious eyes and silver hair; Florence Ball and her harlot daughter. They were all there, talking and laughing, smiling and waving as they went by. Only one paused a while, only one, and he was a tall strikingly handsome man with black shoulder-length hair and dark green eyes that were filled with sadness. Only he stopped to hold out his arms as though he might embrace her, his loving smile wonderful to see. But even as she moved towards him he was lost to her, disappearing into the distance, the smile gone from his face and a look of desolation written there. 'No!' Beth called him back. 'Don't go, Tyler. Don't leave me!' But he was gone, and with him went her will to live.

'Hold her down, Meg, or she'll tear herself wide open.' Maisie was frantic. She could see the small dark head emerging. 'Beth!' she yelled, at the same time stilling the girl's flailing arms and attempting to quiet her. 'It's all right, lass. Gently does it. Let the babby come gently.' When Beth seemed beyond her hearing, she yelled again, this time with a harsher voice to shake her out of her malaise. 'For gawd's sake, yer bugger, do as yer told!' At last her words found their way into Beth's dark troubled nightmare. 'That's it, lass . . . nice and easy, like old Maisie told yer,' she said, giving Beth a quick hug when she opened her eyes to realisation.

'It's coming, lass. The babby's coming, thank God.' There were tears in her eyes as she looked at Beth's weary grey face and those suffering dark eyes that bared her soul. 'It's all right, lass . . . it won't be long now,' she promised, her voice heavy with relief. Maisie had feared she would never see this moment. Death had visited this house today, she told herself. She had felt his ominous presence, almost smelled him beside her. He had been there, in Beth's eyes, in her own soul, and she had trembled before an almighty being who held them all in the palm of his hand. But now she prayed the shadow of Death was lifted. There was much to be thankful for.

At five-thirty in the afternoon Beth gave birth to a fine, lusty-lunged son, and all the doubts and suffering were forgotten as Maisie laid the crinkled bloodstained bairn in her outstretched arms. 'Oh, Maisie, he's so beautiful!' Beth whispered brokenly, the tears spilling over her dark lashes and a look of ecstasy on her face. 'Oh, Maisie! . . . Oh, Maisie!' she kept saying over and over. 'Oh, Maisie!' In all of her life she had never seen anything so wonderful. She was crying now, loud joyful sobs that shook her frail body. In a moment the joy had mingled with all manner of regrets, and sadness, and a feeling of bitter anger at the man who should have been here to share the most glorious day in her life. Tyler should have been here. *He should have been here!* But he wasn't, and so Beth hugged their son close to her breast, and looked into his face, and marvelled at the infant's strong features, his long fine limbs, the dark hair and the beautiful eyes that were not yet their true colour, but which had an intense marbling of green in them. Lost for words at such tiny perfection, Beth pressed him ever closer, looking up at the watching Maisie with eyes that spoke volumes, of love and gratitude, of pain and regret, and oh, such joy! The tears coursed down her face, emptying the pain inside.

'Aw, lass, isn't he the grandest little fella I've ever clapped eyes on?' laughed Maisie. But then she was sobered by Beth's tears, and by the heartfelt cry made when the girl was almost lost to them. In a quiet, meaningful voice, she asked slyly, 'Will yer call the little fella Tyler? After his daddy.'

Not realising how she had called out in that dreadful nightmare, Beth was momentarily shocked by Maisie's suggestion. Giving no answer, she merely looked at her friend with a puzzled and surprised expression, but was visibly relieved when Maisie told her how she had heard the name from her own lips. 'And being the canny old sod that I am, I reckoned the fella must be the one as left yer with child.'

Maisie's words opened old wounds. 'No,' Beth told her firmly, 'I won't be calling my son after his daddy because his daddy has not earned that honour.'

Maisie saw how deeply Beth was hurt. 'I'm sorry, lass,' she said solemnly. 'Will I never learn to mind me own bloody business?'

Beth laughed. 'No, Maisie,' she replied light-heartedly, 'I don't think you ever will. But then, I probably wouldn't love you as much if you did, would I, eh?'

At this point, Beth was made aware of the tall bony figure standing by the fireplace. As soon as Maisie saw Beth stretch her neck to see who it was, she called the woman forward. 'This 'ere's Meg Piper from next door,' she told her. 'And to be honest, lass, I never woulda managed without her.' From now on, when anyone said a bad word to her with regard to poor dimwitted Meg, she would put them in their place and no mistake!

'How can I ever thank you?' Beth asked her. 'How can I ever thank either of you?' Because of this woman and

Maisie, Beth had been delivered of a fine healthy son. She would be forever grateful for such friends.

'Enough of that,' Maisie warned. 'We're all of us bloody knackered, and there are still things to be done.' She wagged her head impatiently. 'Gawd knows where that bugger Cissie's gone,' she declared. 'No doubt she's getting back at me for sending her to school, but she'll get her arse tanned when she does come home and that's a fact!' Turning her attention to the other woman beside her, she said, 'Thank you for yer precious help, Meg, but it's done now, and yer must be out on yer feet. Take yerself off home, lass, and know that you've done real well today . . . aye, you've done real well.' She chuckled when a broad smile lit the other woman's gaunt face and she hung her head in embarrassment. 'No, yer have!' Maisie reassured her. 'You've done real well. And what's more, Meg Piper, I shall make it me business to let all and bloody sundry know what a godsend yer are.'

'I do me best, Maisie,' replied the shy soul, 'but sometimes, well, I can't do right for doing wrong.'

'Well, yer ain't done no wrong today, lass,' Maisie assured her, 'and you tell the buggers that.' Meg nodded her grey head and, after wishing Beth well with her new babby, ambled across the room. 'I've done real well,' she could be heard mumbling. 'Maisie said I've done real well.'

'Aye, yer have that,' Maisie called after her, 'and if you've a mind, there's some'at else I'd be glad for yer to do.' Meg turned, a ready smile on her face which told Maisie that she would be only too delighted. 'I've used all the hot water up here, lass,' Maisie went on, pointing to the fireplace and the big black kettle standing in the hearth. 'There's a fire lit downstairs . . . one fire alone ain't enough to provide all the water a body needs at such a time. So I wonder if you'd fill the pan with water and wedge it into the coals? I'll be down to fetch it soon as ever I think it's ready.'

Meg turned away, mumbling again and making gestures as though she was already filling the pan. 'Fill the pan with water and wedge it into the coals . . . Maisie'll be down to get it, soon as ever it's ready.'

'Mind, though, don't overfill the pan, Meg, or it'll spit on the fire and put it out. I don't want the fire out, now do I, eh?' she finished.

Once downstairs, Meg followed Maisie's instructions to the letter. First she collected the big coal-blackened pan from the hearth and filled it with water, just as Maisie had told her; but making sure it was not filled right to the brim, because didn't Maisie say she didn't want the fire put out? 'That's right,' Meg said aloud as she brought the pan back to the hearth. 'Maisie don't want the fire put out.' A frown creased her narrow face as she tried to remember what else Maisie had said. She shook her head, repeating her thoughts parrot fashion. 'Water in the pan. Wedge it on the coals, and Maisie will fetch it soon as ever it's ready. But she don't want the fire put out.' At this she smiled and nodded. 'Maisie don't want the fire put out.' Glancing at the fire, she saw how low it had died. 'Maisie don't want the fire put out,' she murmured again. She then looked at the coal scuttle and the black mound of coke inside, and noticed the slivers of kindling wood that were laid on a newspaper beside the fender.

With great deliberation, she placed the half-filled pan on the shag rug before going to the coal scuttle where she took the small shovel that Maisie used to dig out the coke. Plunging it into the scuttle, she scooped up a heap of small coke pieces and threw them on to the dying embers; then another and another, and still the fire was lazy. Next, she gathered up a generous armful of kindling wood, which she carefully set over the pieces of coke. Almost instantly, tiny yellow flames and miniature plumes of smoke began to lick round the wood. 'That's it!' she said with satisfaction, taking great pains to press the pan down flat on the heaped-up coals. That done, she went from the room and from the house, to take herself home as Maisie had suggested. And all the while she could be heard murmuring, 'Maisie says I've done a good job . . . I've done a good job.'

As she opened the front door, a gust of air travelled through the house, igniting and fanning the kindling wood with such ferocity that the ensuing sparks erupted into a silver crescent which then spilled on to the rug. Soon, it was smouldering, and the putrid stench of sulphur began to envelop the room.

Lying flat on her back, all of her energy drained, Beth followed Maisie's movements with fascination. Having made Beth as comfortable as was possible following such a traumatic and hard birth, Maisie set about cleaning the infant. With practised skill and tenderness, she turned the small pink body in her capable hands, her fat gentle fingers plucking at the caked blood and skin that still clung to its tiny features. 'By! He's a real bonny lad,' she told the smiling Beth. 'I know it took a deal of torture to fetch the little sod into the world, but, oh, Beth lass . . . the good Lord's blessed yer this day, an' that's a fact.' Maisie took a moment to look into her tired smiling eyes, and thought how hard these long endless hours had been, and all through it Beth had shown only strength and courage. Remembering, she slowly shook her head from side to side as though in disbelief. 'Aw, lass, me lovely lass,' she said in a croaky voice, 'if you've been blessed, then it's 'cause yer *deserve* to be!' Tucking the infant deeper into her lap, she reached out to take Beth's pale hand into her own. 'I love yer,' she said simply, the tears brightening her eyes.

'And I love you, Maisie,' Beth told her softly. She
might have said more. She might have told Maisie how
she had been more of a mother to her than her own. She
might have revealed how terrified she had been in the
worst of her confusion and agony, and she could have
confessed to Maisie how, in the darkest depths, she had
longed with all her heart for Tyler to be with her; how
even then, she would have forgiven him. She could have
bared her soul to Maisie, told her things that she had a
right to know. But she did not. It was still too entrenched
inside her, too private and painful to share with anyone,
even with Maisie. Instead she told the little woman,
'The good Lord already blessed me when He brought
me to your door.' For a while there was no need
for words, only a brief span of quiet contemplation while
these two reflected on their relationship; two women,
each without a man, each lonely in a way few could
understand. Now there had developed between them a
deep undying bond. The birth of Beth's son had drawn
them closer still, firming a friendship that each would
cherish for as long as she lived. In this world there was
no stronger love than that which transcended sadness,
and hardship, and loneliness; all the things that might
otherwise break a body's spirit.

At length Maisie drew her hand from Beth's in order
to attend to the struggling infant. 'The little bugger's
after its titty,' she told Beth with a chuckle. 'Here, you'd
best take him.' She gave the small bundle into Beth's
outstretched arms. 'I don't expect you'll have much milk
yet, lass,' she remarked, 'but let him try anyroad, eh?'
She chucked the infant under the chin, then brushed her
fingers over his generous head of hair which was already
rich and dark. 'I was wrong, me beauty,' she confessed
to Beth. 'He ain't got hair like yourn, has he?'

Beth suspected Maisie was fishing for information
about his father. All she gave away was, 'No, Maisie,

he hasn't got hair like mine. His hair is just like his father's.' She gazed down on that small face and a well of love flooded her sorry heart when he looked up at her with eyes that might have been Tyler's. 'I think he'll have green eyes too like . . .' She didn't know whether it was emotional and physical relief that the ordeal was over or the deep knowledge that now she would never know a day when Tyler was not with her; he was here now, in this tiny boy, who had brought meaning to her life. But suddenly she wanted to cry, to release all that painful emotion that she had bottled up inside her for too long now.

'Go on, lass,' Maisie urged. 'Say it. Say his name, and be done with it . . . He's like his daddy. Like Tyler.' She paused a moment before going on in a quiet loving voice, 'I don't know the ins and outs of why your fella ain't here today, and I'm not prying. No doubt you'll tell me if and when yer want to. But I do know this much, lass . . . whatever it was that took place atween the two of yer, well, I can see that it's a painful thing. If yer ask me, there's only one way to deal with some'at painful, an' that's to get rid of it. Spit it out. Yer son's like his daddy . . . like Tyler. Ain't that right, lass?'

Beth had not wanted to cry. Not now. Not when she was holding the most precious thing in the world here in her arms. Her son! She was holding her son! Now, though, when Maisie spoke those wise kind words, her heart opened. The tears that came were tears of joy, and with them came a strange sense of healing. 'You're right, Maisie,' she confessed, 'I know you're right. And, yes, my son is like Tyler.' For the first time in many months, she had spoken his name out loud. It was a tingling shock on her lips, but, just as Maisie had predicted, once it was spilled out, the hurt inside her was somehow eased.

The regret was still there, and the anger. But it wasn't so sharp, nor so unbearable. She wasn't alone any more either. She had her own dear son, and Maisie, and Cissie, and Matthew; though Beth had long felt the boy's deep-seated resentment of her. Matthew would not be so easily won over, because of the way his father's untimely death had effectively forced him to be the head of the family. He saw Beth as a cuckoo in his nest. She sensed that, and though she had never mentioned it to Maisie, Beth had lately wondered whether she shouldn't be making plans to move out once the baby was born. Maybe that was what she should do.

Suddenly, her mind was made up. As soon as she was up and about, she would ask David Miller whether he had a small dwelling place, not so far away that she couldn't keep in close touch with her new family, but far enough away for Matthew not to feel threatened. Beth pulled her thoughts up sharply. How would she pay the rent? How would she ever furnish a house, however small? On top of that, how on earth would she feed herself and the child? But then she reminded herself that, even if she were to stay here in this house, which would not really be fair in view of Matthew's feelings, she would still need to find a weekly income. She realised the whole thing would need a great deal of careful consideration. But right now, she was bone-weary and her brain was fudged with recent events. There was a tiredness on her that dragged her down. Later, though, she would think it through.

'Right then!' Maisie saw how Beth was unconsciously sinking deeper into the bed, desperate for much-needed sleep. At once she was easing the bundle from her arms and arranging both mother and child into a more comfortable position. 'Like I said, yer ain't got no milk yet, and the little bugger's wore himself out sucking at nothing,' she declared. 'The pair on yer can rest a minute while I go downstairs.' She tapped the child on its dimpled hand. 'So, yer little rascal, yer can't go nodding off for long, 'cause though we had enough hot water to wash yer mammy, we need to fetch the pan o' water from downstairs afore we can clean the day's journey off you.' Here, she chuckled and pulled a wry face. 'That's if Meg Piper had the good sense to put the bloody pan on the coals in the first place.' As she struggled to rise from the old bed whose mattress springs had long ago collapsed, she looked towards the window.

'Our Matthew won't be long afore he's home.' She hadn't forgotten the talk she and the boy had promised each other. And she hadn't forgotten how he'd kept such unhappy thoughts to himself these past months. But she would put his mind at rest, that she would, or perish in the attempt! 'Gawd knows where our Cissie is!' she said frustratedly. 'Singing outside the railway station, I shouldn't wonder . . . trying ter scratch a few pennies together. But she'll cop it from me when she does get home, I'm telling yer.' She glanced at Beth and the child, both sleeping, both utterly worn out. 'God love and bless the pair on yer,' she murmured.

As Maisie opened the bedroom door, the smile lingered on her face. In a minute though her whole expression was changed to one of horror when the acrid smell of smoke filled her nostrils. 'Jesus, Mary and Joseph! There's some'at afire!' she exclaimed, going more hurriedly down the narrow staircase. At the foot of the stairs she paused, her instincts warning against opening the stair door. Normally, because there were no windows to lighten the enclosed stairway, the stair door was always left open. Obviously, Meg had closed it behind her.

Lowering her gaze in the half-light, Maisie was alarmed to see dark puffs of smoke drifting through the gap at the bottom of the door. The air was stifling, and even as she stood there frantically working out her next move, which was to get Beth and the infant safely out, the smoke intensified. 'Christ Almighty, Meg, what have yer done? *What in God's name have yer done?*' she gasped. 'Dear Lord above, what am I to do? There ain't no other way out but through this door,' she told herself. When she put her fist to the doorknob, the searing heat made her swiftly recoil.

On trembling legs, she began her way back up the stairs, all the while forcing down the rising panic inside her, and muttering her way through a plan of escape. 'Happen we can somehow get outta the window . . . attract the neighbours . . . lower Beth and the babby down?' The smoke was stinging her eyes and causing her to cough and splutter. 'Don't let yerself panic, Maisie Armstrong,' she told herself firmly. 'There's not only yerself to think of here.'

Rushing into the bedroom she slammed the door shut behind her, momentarily leaning on it to gather her breath and to say a small prayer. 'Thank God the childer ain't here. But, oh, if Maisie ever wanted yer help, Lord . . . she wants it now!' Still spluttering from the smoke that had found its way into her lungs, she scurried across the room, calling, 'Beth! Rouse yerself, lass.' In spite of her determination not to panic, she could not altogether disguise the terror in her voice. 'We've got to get out. We've got to get out quick!'

Beth had not slept. In the few minutes that Maisie was gone from the room, she had drifted in and out of a strange lethargy, disturbed by the unusual heat in the room and what she imagined to be sulphur emitted from the coal in the fireplace. She could hear Maisie calling her. 'Got to get out, lass . . . there's a fire . . . ain't got much time.' And though she struggled to respond to Maisie's hands pulling her from the bed, something else pulled her back. But when an attempt was made to take her son, she resisted, clinging to him and pressing him into her body. 'That's right, lass,' she heard Maisie say, 'keep his face covered . . . the smoke . . . the smoke!'

She was vaguely aware of Maisie tearing a segment of sheet and dipping it into the soiled water in the bowl; she understood when the wet cloth was thrust into her hands, and straight away held it close to the child's face. Now another piece for her and one for Maisie, then Beth felt herself being ushered across the room; her legs were like jelly beneath her, and the child was a dead weight in her arms, but when Maisie tried again to prise him from her, she cried out: 'No! He's safe, Maisie. He's safe!' And Maisie must have realised that Beth would never let go the precious bundle for she made no other attempt to take it from her.

Peering through the gathering smoke, Beth realised what Maisie had in mind. *The window!* Maisie was desperately trying to thrust the window up in its frame, but it wouldn't budge. Beth could have told her the window was prone to jamming. All of Maisie's stout efforts came to nothing. Down below in the street, the neighbours were congregating.

'Smash it!' came the shout as they saw the women struggling to release it. 'For Christ's sake, smash the bloody thing!' came a frantic scream. 'Stand back! Protect yerself!' Almost instantly the missile broke through one of the panes, but it was impossible for any man, woman or child to squeeze themselves out of such a small opening; let alone a body of Maisie Armstrong's size, and a woman who had only just been through a terrible childbirth, and whose lifeblood was even now slowly trickling away.

'We can't get out this way, lass,' Maisie said breathlessly. 'Can yer make it downstairs? There's no other way . . . we shall have to brave it, God help us.' When Beth quickly nodded and took hold of Maisie with her free hand, she smiled bravely, saying, 'All right, lass.

Keep right behind me, and hold that wet rag across yer mouth. Mind yer do the same for the young 'un, and God willing, we'll come out all right.'

Beth gave no reply other than to look at Maisie with a world of love and gratitude showing in her dark eyes. There was little strength left in her now, but she would not let Maisie down. Nor would she let this tiny boy lose his life when he had only just tasted it. 'Good gal,' Maisie whispered. She had seen how Beth was bleeding from below, and she knew why the girl had said nothing, and loved her all the more for it.

In a minute, they were at the door. Maisie slowly opened it; smoke poured in, but not flames, thank God, not flames. Down the stairs they went, feeling their way, silently praying. At the bottom of the stairs, Maisie hesitated, reluctant to open the door but knowing it was their only chance to escape a dreadful inferno; these houses were rich in timber and would go up like so much matchwood. On the other side of the door could be heard the ominous sound of crackling wood, and beyond that the sound of men's voices, shouting, desperate; although it was unclear what they were shouting, both Maisie and Beth realised they were willing them on, and help was not too far away. In her heart Beth wondered if it would be too late for her, and so she prayed for her son, and for Maisie.

'Press yerself against the wall, lass,' Maisie ordered as she wrapped a piece of wet rag round her chubby fists and prepared to open the door. Without question, Beth did as she was told, folding the child close to her body. She could feel the hairs on her arms being singed. The air was almost black now. It was hard to breathe and the heat was intense. Suddenly, the door was flung back and black clouds exploded over them.

The last thing Beth heard was a terrible scream, followed by a multitude of shouting voices, and another horrendous sound that could have been an outer door being wrenched from its hinges or the whole house coming down on top of them. All of Beth's instincts told her to crush the child to her . . . keep him safe . . . keep him safe. Keep him safe. When the darkness and heat washed over her it was like a haven, so quiet and peaceful, lulling her away, carrying her sore aching body as though it was a feather, drifting, drifting.

The afternoon sky was like a black inferno, with every street for half a mile swallowed up in putrid smoke. It rained down in grimy droplets that stuck to the rooftops and darkened the pavements below. Cries went up on every street corner and the sound of running footsteps echoed across the cobbles as people rushed to the scene of mayhem on Larkhill. 'Where did it start?' they cried. 'How many dead?' Nobody knew. They only knew what they saw with their own eyes: the awful black smoke, and the tonguelike flames that leaped above the chimneys from Larkhill, and threatened to engulf their own tiny hovels.

'What did you say?' David Miller had been on his usual weekly round, collecting rent from his stepfather's houses, when it became evident that a terrible tragedy was underway only two streets from where he was standing. Grasping the arm of a man who would have fled straight by him, he yelled above the din, 'The fire? Did you say it was on Larkhill?' Uppermost in his mind was the Armstrong family, and Beth. He could not keep the fear from his voice.

'That's right, matey,' the fellow replied, struggling to release himself from the iron grip that held him. 'They reckon the whole o' Larkhill's on fire . . . people trapped . . . dying!' When his words visibly stunned the other man, he took the opportunity to wrench himself free. Without a backward look he went away at a run and was soon lost in the rush of bodies all heading for Larkhill. David Miller followed, running until he thought his heart would burst; he could see all his hopes dying before his eyes.

Thrusting his way through the mob, he emerged to a scene of carnage. The fire was still raging, though the hoses were now playing on it, spewing water into the heart of the flames and causing the smoke to billow like huge clouds to blot out the daylight. At least three houses were completely gutted by the fierce fire, and another half dozen badly damaged. Higher up on the pavement, far enough away from the devastation, a number of people were gathered; some obviously in authority, some possessed by morbid curiosity, and others openly weeping. 'Three dead,' someone whispered, and to David Miller the news was like a hammer to his heart. He began walking towards those pitiful misshapen bundles that lay beneath the blankets. 'Three dead,' someone had said. 'Three dead.' But who? Who?

'Get back, sir.' A firm hand was spread against his chest, pressing him away. 'Make way for the Infirmary waggon.' The burly officer stretched wide his arms and flattened himself against the straining bodies, forcing them to retreat as the waggon threaded its way towards the figures on the ground, the horses up front wildly snorting, the whites of their eyes like glittering diamonds in the fierce light. Like everyone else, David Miller craned his neck to see what was happening. Suddenly a child was crying.

'No, lass, come away. There's nothing more to be done.' Beth heard the tender voice as though from a long, long distance away. She felt the gently restraining hands, and other firmer hands that meant to save her life but which would also prise her from her beloved Maisie. She pushed them away. Maisie needed her! Maisie, that darling little woman who even now was smiling. 'Do as they say, lass,' she told Beth. 'There ain't nothing to be done for old Maisie.' The pain showed on her blackened face, and her poor burned hands reached out to touch the child which Beth had wedged between them. 'You've a child o' yer own now,' she said brokenly, 'but I wonder if you'll do some'at fer yer old pal as loves yer like her own daughter?'

Choking back the painful lump that filled her throat, yet letting her tears flow unashamedly, Beth made no resistance when two other arms reached down to take her child lovingly from her. Instead, she cradled that dear little woman in her arms, holding her as close as she could bear, and all the while silently praying that they were wrong, and Maisie would recover. 'Don't you talk like that,' she said in a firm voice. 'Please, don't say such things.'

'But will yer do as I ask, darlin'? Will yer?'

'Oh, Maisie. You only have to ask. You know that.' When Maisie just stared up at her with fading eyes, Beth's heart turned over. 'Maisie! Listen to me. Remember what you told me . . . so many times when I've almost given up . . . be strong, you said . . . trust in the Lord.' She was sobbing loudly now, her vision of her friend's face hopelessly blurred. 'Maisie!' There was anger in her voice as she spoke now in Maisie's own rough way. 'Don't die on me, you old bugger. Don't you dare leave me and the young 'uns.'

In spite of all Beth's persuasion there was a greater power calling, and she could feel Maisie fading in her arms. 'Please, Maisie.' She could hardly talk for the sobs that racked her frail body. 'Don't leave us. We love you so much.' She began feverishly stroking the familiar face, pushing the singed wisps of hair from that deep crinkled forehead. There was no hope in Beth's heart now. Only a bitter sad resignation, and a fervent prayer that Maisie was going to a better place. 'What is it you want me to do?' she asked now. There was no reply. No response. And yet Maisie was still warm and alive in her arms.

Desperate that she would never know what Maisie had wanted from her, Beth persisted. 'A favour, you said, Maisie. What is it you want me to do? The children. Is that it? You want me to look after the children? Oh, but I would do that as naturally as breathing, you know that, don't you, Maisie?'

The violet eyes flickered and opened. 'The childer,' she murmured, her whole body wincing with such pain that it made Beth cry out; her own pain as nothing beside that of her friend. 'Mind the childer, lass.' She waited for Beth to speak, but there was too much sorrow, too much grief. All she could do was nod. It was enough. 'Bless yer heart . . . I know . . . you'll look after 'em well, lass.' Astonishingly, Maisie softly chuckled. 'He's waiting fer me, lass,' she murmured. 'My fella that's been gone these past years . . . the old bugger's . . . waiting fer me. He won't be too pleased though . . . not when he sees what a terrible sight his Maisie is. Oh, but I have missed him though. God knows I've missed him.'

She smiled then, a glorious brilliant smile that shone from deep within. Beth thought it was the most beautiful smile she had ever seen, and wondered whether that darling woman's husband was waiting in an unknown place only Maisie's eyes could see; waiting with a smile to match his Maisie's, and with his arms wide open. Somehow, the thought brought a degree of peace to Beth's frantic heart.

When Maisie closed her eyes, Beth knew she would never again see them, laughing, mischievous, chastising. Never again. And now, as she kissed that quiet face, Beth gave herself up to those who waited to help her. In that moment when she felt herself sinking, three people came to her. Three people whose lives were inextricably bound with hers. Through her fading senses, she was aware of

Cissie, bursting through the barrier of curious solemn faces; her screams terrible to hear. 'Mam! Mam!' With a cry from the soul, she threw herself down, locking her small arms round Maisie's still figure and rocking her back and forth, back and forth. 'Mam! . . . Oh, Mam!' She would have willed Maisie back from that place where she had gone, but Maisie was beyond hearing. The girl was inconsolable.

The boy remained a short distance away; not so far that he could not see his mother and sister, yet close enough for Beth to see the silent suffering in his eyes; violet eyes that were painfully like his mother's, and yet not like hers, more serious and secret. Now, as they turned on Beth, they were filled with intense loathing. She could not hear what he said, but when he mouthed the words she knew; in her heart she knew what he was saying 'It's *your* fault! You killed my mam.'

'You'll be fine, Beth.' Another voice filtered through the haze. A voice that was familiar to her, a kind quiet voice, a friend's. 'You're not to worry about a thing, because when you and the child come home from the Infirmary, I mean to take good care of you.' Realising that David Miller still had hopes of making her his wife, she slowly shook her head. His answer was to stroke her hair and assure her, 'I'll make you a good husband, Beth. You'll never again want for anything. I heard the promise you made to Maisie, and I'll help you keep that promise. I'll help you take care of the children . . . just as Maisie asked.'

When they carried Beth away, he went too. And when she asked for her son, it was David Miller who placed the tiny infant into her arms. 'You saved him, Beth,' he told her. 'With your own body, you kept your son safe.'

In the years to come, whenever she recalled the horror and sadness of that night, she invariably remembered the three people whom Fate had woven for ever into the strands of her life; Cissie, the darling girl who was to grow more like her mammy with every passing year; Matthew, made old before his time and constantly seeking retribution because of it; and David, kind, generous, but fatally weak and flawed in character. In their turn, each of these three people would bring heartache and joy to Beth. Like a tall tree whose roots went deep, she would be blown this way and that, destined to be ravaged by time and the elements. And through it all, she would keep a strong heart, and a powerful determination to rise above whatever obstacles Fate might put across her path.

Part Three

1887

ENEMIES

Chapter Six

'We're in trouble, I won't deny it.' Esther Ward was clearly agitated, her bony fingers plucking at the frayed leather of the desk-top, and a nervous look in her unusually penetrating blue eyes that sent a shiver through the man standing before her. 'Richard blames me, I know it. They *all* blame me. It's the chance they've been waiting for. I know what they're saying. . ."Only men understand the complexities of business", that's what they're saying. "When a woman tries to think like a man, no good will come of it".'

Thumping her small fist on the desk, she spat the words out. 'Fools! Pompous fools! They know as well as I do that it has nothing whatsoever to do with who heads a company. All around us development opportunities are drying up. There's an acute shortage of good land. Money is harder to come by, and all in all it's a depressing time. Even Richard, with all his fancy ideas and determination, can't stop the company from going under.' She chuckled. It was a most unpleasant sound. 'He deserves what's coming to him. He has a few more shocks coming his way yet. Fool that he is! It won't be only the company he loses.'

Seeming not to have heard her last remark, Tom Reynolds spoke bitterly. 'I knew there were problems,' he said, 'but I thought things were beginning to look up?' She had not yet spoken the words he dreaded, but he sensed they were imminent.

Esther shook her head, oblivious of the stray wisp of hair that fanned to and fro across her forehead; hair that had once been a soft shade of brown, but which now was streaked iron grey. Her features had not softened with the passing of almost three years; if anything her face was more chiselled and her blue eyes harder. She regarded the man for a while; the wiry frame and sharp shrewish expression, the startling white hair and eyes which, in a certain light, seemed more pink than brown. Tom Reynolds had been a loyal and useful ally but now his usefulness was almost at an end. And yet she was reluctant to let him go. She saw him as a reflection of herself, devious and cunning, her partner in many a conspiracy; the most successful of which had been the manipulation of that slut of a girl in Tyler Blacklock's lodging house. She gloated inwardly at the memory. So easy! So satisfying. Not only had her clever plan discredited the young man whom Beth had set her heart on, but in the process had driven Richard's daughter to her knees.

She knew how Beth had gone to the lodging house on the night when her own father disowned her; how she had run to her lover only to be turned away from there broken-hearted when the girl claimed that Tyler was the father of her own mythical child. There was also the unexpected but most gratifying development of the girl's jealous lover and his mate beating Tyler within an inch of his life. Esther could not have planned that particular episode better if she had intended it.

When she learned from her son that Beth and Tyler were never reunited, Esther was beside herself with pleasure. There was a hatred for Beth within her; a hatred that spanned more than Beth's own lifetime. It delighted her to think that the girl had gone into the night, alone and unloved and growing with child. Indeed, it occurred to Esther that Beth could well be dead by now. No matter. It was no more than she deserved. If she had come to a pitiful and desperate end, this woman for one would not be sorry.

Now another image raised itself, making her inwardly fume. If Beth had got her just rewards, Tyler Blacklock had carved himself a very different destiny. Against all odds, he had emerged from the gutter to haunt her! Over the years he had not only made himself a small fortune, but in the process gained something of a respectable reputation. While he rose in stature, the Ward Development Company suffered crippling misfortunes, until now its back was to the wall, and Esther Ward was a desperate woman. If Tom Reynolds was devastated by her next words, it was no more than she was herself. 'I'm afraid if things don't soon improve, you may have to find another employer.'

'What other employer?' The words exploded from him. 'You've just said yourself that times are hard in the development industry. There's not one single company taking on. They're laying off more like. Every street corner tells its own story. You know that!' He had awful visions of himself walking the streets, demeaning himself to look for work. In his wildest nightmares he had never thought it would come to this. And it wouldn't, by God! Not while he had a canny bone in his body.

'What would you have me do, then?' She thrust back the chair and strode round the desk, her two hands locked together and her whole figure trembling with rage. 'There's no money, damn you. Do you hear what I'm telling you . . . *there is no money!*'

He smiled now, and facing her boldly, said quietly, 'You conveniently forget, I think. It is *I* who am handling the sale of the lease on the office premises. And, if my memory serves me right, you stand to rake in a tidy sum on that. Also, have you forgotten the lucrative deal which I again masterminded on that commercial

231

property north of the Thames?' He could have gone on, reminding her of his own incredible bargaining skill, and revealing his knowledge of certain holdings still owned by the company, though truth to tell they were neither large nor especially lucrative.

To Tom Reynolds' mind, there were two causes for the rapid downfall of the company. One was Esther herself, who had never been accepted into what was essentially a man's world, and who, in her desperate efforts to prove them all wrong, had made one too many a mistake. Unfortunately the damage was already done by the time Richard was fully recovered, and in spite of his commendable efforts to rescue what was left of the business he had built from his own sweat, it was far too late. The other cause of the present crisis was Ben, a man of few principles, whose only view of life was through the bottom of a tankard, riddled as he was with guilt and arrogance.

'You see, I know there *is* money in the coffers,' Reynolds reminded his employer. 'I do hope you're not working up to telling me that you won't be able to pay me what I'm due? That would be very foolish of you.' The threat was unmistakable. 'I have no intention of seeing my dues gambled away by your wastrel of a son.' Increasingly, he realised with a certain satisfaction that this was a family of shame and scandal. So far, Esther Ward had manage to keep the scandal contained to a certain degree, but he wondered how much longer it could all be brushed under the carpet.

Enraged that he should take it on himself to tell her the state of her own business, and bristling at the manner in which he spoke of her precious son, Esther said sharply, 'Whatever is or is not in the coffers is nothing whatsoever to do with you! You're an employee, nothing more, and maybe not even that for very much longer. You would do well to remember your place.' Dismissing him with a gesture, she began walking towards the door which she meant to bang closed behind him. When she realised he had no intention of following her, she paused and jerked round her head, staring at him with those glittering blue eyes. 'Get out,' she hissed.

'Oh, you want me to leave, do you?' he asked with a devious smile, at the same time drawing a large scroll from inside his waistcoat. 'Surely not. At least, not until you run your eye over what came my way this very morning.' Ignoring her repeated instruction for him to get out, he unrolled the scroll and began spreading it over the desk, using the paperweight and penholder to secure its curling corners. Still, she did not move. Undeterred, he kept his gaze averted, saying quietly, 'I have something here which may yet put the company back on an upward spiral.' When still she made no move, he chuckled and made as if to put the document away again, pausing when he saw out of the corner of his eye that she was returning to the desk, albeit hesitantly.

'What is it?' she asked suspiciously, curiosity getting the better of her. In a moment she was beside him and leaning forward, her narrowed eyes poring over the detailed plans, and excitement growing within her. The plans showed a warehouse of enormous proportions. However, it was not the warehouse itself that was of interest, but the extensive parcel of land on which the building was situated. Furthermore, the details showed that the building was derelict, and permission was already secured for it to be demolished. Added to which, the entire parcel of land, totalling some fifty acres in all, was earmarked for residential development, or commercial enterprise.

'What do you think?' Tom Reynolds was utterly captivated with himself. 'Clever of me to acquire such information, don't you agree?' Then without disclosing how – if he had the money to proceed on his own, he would not now be displaying that same information on Esther's desk – he pressed her for a response. 'Of course, if you're not interested, there are those who would snap my arm off to get at this piece of land.'

'Have you shown this to anyone else?'

'I'm astonished that you should even think such a thing!' He sounded suitably offended.

'Hmm.' Esther turned her head and glanced up at him, her blue eyes alight with suspicion. At length she said with a devious manner to match his own, 'And *I'm* astonished that the thought had not occurred to you. No matter. Either you have not shown these plans elsewhere, in which case I owe you an apology . . . or you have touted them round, and the fools can't see what's in front of them.'

A fever grew inside him as he gazed on her. Esther was no beauty, but she had a certain handsomeness about her, a particular wickedness he had not seen in other women. Wickedness excited him. Esther excited him. She was the reason he had remained with the Ward company, even after he was made to suffer the humiliation of having his wages paid by a woman. Time and again, that woman had shown herself to be as scheming and ruthless as any criminal-minded rogue he had ever come across; with the exception of his good self, of course. 'I can see I don't need to explain how this parcel of land is only a few hundred yards from the newly designated railway lines. This is a rare opportunity to acquire a most valuable asset.'

'I can see that for myself,' she reminded him, but suddenly her manner was more subdued, her words more cautious. 'But it's a long-term investment and, as I've only just explained, I haven't got that kind of capital. Besides, it won't come cheap, I'm thinking. There'll be others who see exactly what you and I see. And no doubt they will have the capital to take advantage of it.'

'You have the capital.'

'Not enough. Besides, I have a house to run, and my husband's medical expenses. We have outstanding wages and other debts that must be met. Even with the few remaining assets, there is very little margin to work on. I dare not spend another farthing, and it would be suicide for me to go to the bank, even if Richard agreed, which he won't.' She stopped to peruse the plans once more, a greedy glint in her eyes. 'It would rankle, though, if it went to one of our rivals. And I do believe I still have some influence with my husband.' She stared at Reynolds. 'All the same, it is long-term. As I say . . . going for this land could cost me everything.' She looked at the man, waiting for his reassurance. She was not disappointed.

In a hoarse whisper that betrayed his obsession with the idea, he told her, 'If it was me, I'd beggar myself to acquire it.'

Not for the first time, his manner alarmed her a little. She needed more time – time to think, time to weigh up the consequences. 'I don't know,' she mused aloud, stroking the palm of her hand up and down her throat. 'It would not be easy to raise the capital needed,' she said at length. 'I would be forced to deposit certain deeds with the bank. You realise that if I'm unsuccessful, they will foreclose and we'll be paupered.' Suddenly, she saw the folly of it all. 'No.' Shaking her head, she said, 'Richard would never take the risk, and I'd be a fool to even consider it.'

'You would be a fool *not to*!' She had unwittingly touched a nerve, sending his memory back over the years, to when he was a young man. For the briefest and most uncomfortable moment, he was made to think of the father he'd left behind in the North of England, a man just widowed and with a stepson whom he disliked intensely. Tom Reynolds remembered how he had quarrelled with his father, a quarrel much like the one he was leading up to with Esther Ward.

He could hear his father's words now: 'Thomas Arnold Reynolds . . . if you walk out on me, there will never again come a day when you'll be welcome in my house.' Fearful that this might well be his last chance to secure his own future, he persisted, 'Don't be afraid to strike out, Esther. In this world, you have to grab what you want, before somebody else does. Besides, how do we know the sale will be well attended? Not everyone is as perceptive as you and me. Not everyone will have seen the *real* value of that land.'

Having worked himself into a highly nervous state, he clenched his fists against his sides, saying in a grating voice, 'My own father lacked the courage when it came right down to it . . . I begged him to strike out when land was there for the taking, but he was a small thinker . . . a loser. *I have no time for losers!*' There was bitterness in his voice, and a degree of loathing.

Encouraged by the curiosity in her expression, he drove the argument on. 'What's the alternative? Will you sit tight in your little kingdom, and watch it crumbling all around you? The office will be gone soon. You've already given notice to the work-force, though you haven't paid them their dues. Most of your capital is spoken for, and the creditors are closing in. Think about it. The way things are, you might struggle on for a few months. A year maybe. But you're bound to go down eventually. You *must* take this opportunity, Esther,' he urged. 'Afterwards, you can sit back and watch the investment grow handsomely, before you offer it out to the highest bidder and make a killing. What have you got to lose?'

There was a long painful silence while she deliberated

on his words. There was never any question in her mind. Some time back, when the warning signs were becoming clearer and Richard was incapacitated, she had been cunning enough to transfer certain holdings into her own name. These represented a tidy sum, not a great fortune but enough for her to be comfortably off. If it came to it, she would sell up and move away, taking Ben with her. As for Richard, he had been a thorn in her flesh for too long now. 'We'll see,' she said cautiously. 'We'll see.' And with that vague promise, she bent her head to study the plans.

If anything was growing at an alarming rate, it was the network of railway lines running out of the centre of London to outlying suburbs. Any land remotely near such construction held unlimited potential. Not only would any subsequent residential development be wonderfully placed to take advantage of the new route into the heart of the city – thereby making the houses attractive to those whose business was in the city centre – but past experience had shown more often than not that the railway barons could well pay a fortune for any land they needed. 'We might be on to something here,' murmured Esther, her scheming mind leaping ahead. 'I would certainly hate to see this land knocked down to another developer.'

'I knew you'd see it my way.' The man's voice came in an intimate whisper. 'We think alike, you and I.' Putting the flat of his hand over the plans, he pushed them aside. The woman remained in a half-bent position facing the desk, her arms bearing the weight of her body, and her gaze fixed on the table. She could feel his fingers tracing the curve of her neck.

He could not know how his words had affected her. She was a woman with many needs. For too long now, she had been starved of one particular need, the kind a respectable woman should not dwell on for too long, a deepdown need that only a man could satisfy. Disillusioned with the ruthlessly ambitious woman he had married, Richard had long ago turned his back on her. Consequently, her needs had intensified. The feel of a man's hands on her caused her to shiver; her shivering excited him, made him bolder. Leaning forward, he pressed himself against her back, his mouth kissing the nape of her neck, and his hands raising her skirt, creeping fingers against her thighs, touching her in that most private part. Trembling and a little afraid, she gently struggled, vaguely aware that her husband was in the next room. But she would not be denied, not now. It was too late.

Frantically he began tearing at the small buttons that ran from her waist to the collar of her dark blouse. 'No.' She bowed her head, moaning with pleasure, ceasing her efforts to pull away. Encouraged by her lack of resistance, he tore all the harder at the blouse. She could feel his hard member pushing into her spine, the sweat on his face as it rubbed against her neck, and her own need was all consuming. Laying her hands on his, she stilled them. Turning towards him, her face flushed, her fingers reached down, searching for and caressing the hard nakedness there. He was groaning now, his face turned upward, eyes closed, his whole body trembling. Suddenly, he was bent forward, his hands thrusting apart her blouse, his mouth wetting the dark erect nipples. Lifting her with incredible ease, he laid her across the desk and prising her legs open, spread his half-naked body over hers. Now, as he pushed himself into her, she cried out with joy, locking her arms round his neck and thrusting herself forward, making a noise like an animal devouring him, wanting him heart and soul.

Driven by a fever long suppressed, neither of them heard the door open. Neither saw the man who stood there, a sad bulky figure in the doorway. He remained only a moment then, head bowed in shame, Richard Ward turned away. He did not look at the woman who passed him in the hallway. His thoughts were too personal, too painful.

Tilly Mulliver had seen the look on his face, heard the sounds emanating from the study, knew what he had witnessed, and her heart went out to him. Unlike that gentle man she was neither shocked nor surprised because she had seen the way Tom Reynolds silently lusted after his employer's wife; she knew also that Esther was no better. Pausing to watch the big man stride away, his broad shoulders bent as though beneath a great weight, Tilly despaired that she could do nothing to help him. She had always considered Richard to be a fine and good man, a man not possessed of ambition, or of the ruthlessness required to succeed in business, a man with principles and a certain dignity. Unfortunately, it was his high principles that had obliged him to reject the daughter he loved; a sad deed that had left its mark on him. Watching him stride away, hurt and humiliated by the shocking scene he had just witnessed, she wondered whether she should tell him her secret.

But then she reminded herself of the promise she had made to another whom she loved. She could not reveal the truth, because it was not hers to tell. For now, she must keep her own counsel. When the time came, he would be told. When the time came, she would no doubt lose him for ever. But then, that was as it should be. Someone else had first claim on Richard. Someone else who loved him every bit as much as she did. *But not* more, *never* more. On silent feet, she returned to her duties, mindful of her place in the order of things.

* * *

It was three o'clock the following morning when Tilly Mulliver was woken from a shallow sleep. Voices resounded through the house, voices raised in anger. At first she did not recognise the man's.

'You're a slut! God almighty . . . all these years, and I've been blind to what's been going on right under my nose.' There was a pause, then a loud bang as though someone had thumped their fist on a table or sent an object flying against the wall. 'I want you out of this house! You and that useless son of yours.'

'He's your son too, Richard Ward, and don't you forget it. What's more, if anybody leaves this house, it won't be me and it won't be Ben. If anybody leaves, it will have to be you, I'm afraid. You see, this house is mine now. Together with certain other assets . . . all legally signed over. You yourself signed the papers. You gave me power of attorney. While you were wasting in your sick-bed, it was me who had to make all the decisions. It didn't bother you then, and now there is nothing you can do, unless you want to broadcast to the world how your own judgement was sadly impaired. Of course, everyone knows you gave up your place at the helm a long time ago. Be careful, Richard! If I thought you were a real threat, you know I would stop at nothing to discredit you.'

Tilly Mulliver had been shocked by the revelations, but she was also delighted that Richard was incensed enough to raise his voice in such anger. At last, at long last, he had seen his scheming wife for what she really was. Now, though, his voice was strangely quiet. 'I hope you appreciate the seriousness of what you're saying?'

'No! It's you who needs to know the seriousness of what I'm saying, Richard. This house and certain parcels of land acquired by me while you were indisposed . . . they're all in my name.' She paused, allowing him to digest the information. 'No doubt if you had made a speedier recovery, I might not have enjoyed such a free hand; but then, your illness was prolonged by your feverish attack of conscience with regard to your precious daughter! In spite of the fact that you turned her away, I was afraid that your love and devotion to her might make you forget how she had shamed you. I don't forget how often you have threatened to throw Ben on to the streets; knowing full well that if he went, I would go with him. When I saw the opportunity to strengthen my own position and lay claim to that which rightfully belonged to me, I brought you the papers, and, being the trusting fellow you are, you made no bones about signing them. Of course, you never did read the small print. Believe me, Richard, there is no court in the land that would believe you did not know what you were signing. After all, it wasn't your *mind* that was ill, was it? Now, you would not want such a thing bandied about, would you?'

'So you're adding forgery to your many other dubious talents.' The calmness of his voice belied the cold fury inside him. He had been all kinds of fool. And yet he did not blame her. There was no one to blame but himself. Now he knew the real extent of her cunning, he was on his guard, his mind searching for a way out of what was a very dangerous situation. Knowing Esther, she would have executed the whole devious scheme with the utmost care. He realised with a sense of desperation that he would have to be twice as cunning as his wife if he was to recover that which she had taken from him. Paramount in his mind was the thought of his daughter. Even so, Beth had shamed herself and brought the family name into disrepute. He could not forget that.

'Forgery! Oh, dear me, no. Certainly not forgery. As I say . . . you yourself signed the papers.'

'Then, of course, I did not know what I was signing.'

'That I can't deny. But don't reprimand yourself too

241

much, my dear. After all, you really were quite ill for a long time. I must admit, it was rather cruel of me to take advantage of your amiable nature. But then, if I had waited until you had your full wits about you, you might have realised my intention and signed the house over to your daughter and her bastard.'

'Beth was wrong in what she did, I won't deny that, and I don't know if I can ever forgive her. But whatever she is guilty of . . . she can never sink to your level. Remember that. Remember this also: you had better enjoy your little triumphs while you can . . . because they won't last long. You have my word on it.'

'Do your worst. It can only amount to nothing.'

As the cruel words died away, there came the sound of a door slamming, followed by Esther's tinkling laughter and the spiteful jibe: 'I can't abide you near me. You've forgotten how to be a man, Richard. Do you hear me? I was a woman today! For the first time in years . . . I was made to feel like a woman. You're nothing to me. NOTHING!'

Unable to sleep, Tilly got from her bed. She put on her robe, lit the candle and went on tip-toe down the back stairs and into the kitchen. Realising that she would probably be dismissed on the spot if Esther should discover her, she closeted herself in the pantry and proceeded to pour herself a glass of sarsaparilla from the big earthenware jug there. Still incensed by what she had heard earlier, she began mentally planning a short journey for the morrow. Bad things had taken place here this night. Things that she must not keep to herself. Above her, in Richard's bedroom, she could hear the slow deliberate footsteps striding heavily back and forth across the floor. 'Oh, Richard, why ever did you stay with such a woman?' she murmured. But then she knew why, didn't she? It always came back to his daughter. Beth, who was conceived in love, born in shame, and raised in jealousy and resentment. 'Wherever you are now, Beth, I hope you never know your father's unhappiness. I pray you've found a deal of contentment with your young man,' she murmured kindly.

Suddenly there was movement in the hallway; whispering voices and soft footsteps. Blowing out the candle, Tilly crept to the kitchen door and gingerly opened it. The lamps were still burning either side of the front vestibule. Esther's slight figure could be seen coming furtively through the door and into the recess. There was a man leaning heavily on her arm; the man was Ben and, as usual, he was the worse for drink. As they neared her hiding place, Tilly shrank back into the shadows.

Esther's voice was scathing. 'You fool! He might have heard you. When will you realise that everything we have is at stake? Time and again you've promised not to drink, not to gamble, and still you waste yourself. Look at you!' From her hiding place, Tilly saw the dark spreading patch that ran down his collar. It was not the first time he had come home covered in blood. 'Oh, you fool, Ben! You fool! One of these days you'll get yourself killed,' his mother cried. As she passed beneath the wall-lamp, Esther glanced up the staircase, her face drained white and haggard. 'It's all for you,' she whispered to her son. 'All of it. All the lying and scheming, all for you. You're the only worthwhile thing in my life. Beth never belonged here with us. All of this is yours by right, and I won't let you throw it all away. I'll make a man of you yet.' Here her voice fell lower, taking on an edge that frightened the listening woman. 'I swear I'll make a man of you yet. Or kill you with my bare hands!'

'I saw him again tonight.' He pushed her away, but quickly clung to her again when he almost lost his balance.

'Who? Who did you see tonight?' She was obviously

humouring him, anxious to get him safely into the sitting room.

'Blacklock . . . Tyler Blacklock.' He laughed, a quiet cruel sound. 'The fool asked me about Beth.'

'What did you tell him?'

'Oh, don't worry. I told him how deliriously happy she was.'

'So, Blacklock still believes her to be married and living the good life? He still doesn't know that her father turned her out? Presumably he doesn't even know that Beth was carrying his child?' The idea amused her. 'You're quite certain you said nothing that might make him suspect?'

'What do you take me for?' He lurched against her, flinging both his arms round her scrawny neck. 'You old bitch,' he mumbled. 'You enjoy these rotten little games, don't you, eh? I'm glad I told you now . . . it's worth it just to see the look on your face.' He drew her to a stop and swung her round so he could see her face in the half-light. 'You hate Beth, don't you? You've *always* hated her. I remember when me and her were kids. Even when it was me that was in the wrong, you'd always blame her . . . punish her . . . shut her away in the cellar or the attic. Why? It's always puzzled me. Why do you hate her so much?'

'Shut up, you drunken idiot!' Unknowingly, he had touched a raw nerve. Thrusting his hands from her shoulders and threading her arm round his waist, she urged him on. 'If he hears us, we'll both follow Beth on to the streets and that's a fact.' She had not told Ben that the house was now in her name. Knowing his weakness for cards and drink, she thought it wiser to keep such information to herself.

He allowed her gently to propel him towards the sitting room, all the while murmuring, 'Always puzzled me . . . always puzzled me.'

'Don't let it bother you, son. She's not worth a second thought. She's no good, and never has been.' Her instincts told her that Ben was suffering a pang of conscience with regard to his part in this little deception. It wouldn't do for him to reveal the truth to Tyler Blacklock, because then that young man would no doubt turn heaven and earth upside down to find his sweetheart. He was eligible too, and well on his way to being rich. The thought of Beth having both the man she loved and an easy life was too disturbing.

'Well, it's too late now anyway.'

'What do you mean?'

'Tyler's got himself a woman. He was at the club with her. Talking about wedding bells, she was. Nice enough creature, I suppose – leggy, dark hair. But she doesn't hold a candle to Beth.' He stopped again, leaning heavily on her arm, his voice low and tearful. 'I'm drunk, Mother,' he said, 'but I know what I've done. And I can't help but wonder whether Beth's all right.'

'Well, you'd better stop wondering about her, and start wondering about yourself. Things can't go on the way they are. I won't put up with it, I tell you. The business is going downhill fast, and things are even worse between me and your father. You're no use to me the way you are. I've warned you before, Ben, either you stop keeping bad company, or . . .'

He laughed in her face. 'Or what, Mother dear? Throw me out, will you? Disown me? No . . . I don't think you'd do that to your little boy. You couldn't bring yourself to punish me when I was a child and guilty of all manner of things . . . you'd rather punish poor little Beth, wouldn't you, eh? It's me that's in the wrong now. But you're still punishing her, aren't you? You still haven't satisfied my curiosity. What is it with you and Beth? Why do you loathe her so?'

'Be very careful what you say, Ben. It's a dangerous

thing to let your tongue run away with you,' she told him. The warning was enough to silence him. He had never heard her talk like that before, at least not to him. It had a sobering effect. Without another word, he let himself be led into the sitting room.

The watching woman waited until the sitting-room door was closed on the two secretive figures. After a moment she retraced her steps to her own modest quarters. She did not go straight to her bed. Instead she stood with her back against the door. Such things she had heard this day! Such wicked things. Tomorrow was her day off; she would have much to report. First thing in the morning, she would make her way to the big house where she intended to relay everything she had learned. It was not an errand she would enjoy, because she knew the sorrow it would cause, but her specific task in this household was to be the eyes and ears of her dear companion. Unpleasant though it was, that was the reason for her being here, that and no other. Her explicit instructions were not to get involved, nor ever to reveal her real purpose there. And like a faithful friend, she had carried out these instructions to the letter; with one unforeseen eventuality. She had come to like Richard Ward, and like had deepened to love. But he saw her only as part of the furniture, and so her guilt was lessened. In that one respect only she had failed her dear friend. But though she had wished things might have been different, she consoled herself with the knowledge that it could come to nothing. And no one would ever know.

'She's mending now, Miss Mulliver, but she was real poorly . . . cried out for you, she did, but I had no way of knowing how to contact you.' The maid was growing more and more flustered. She was desperate to ensure that Miss Mulliver should not think her irresponsible.

'Poorly, you say?' Tilly Mulliver's only concern was for the state of her friend. 'I hope the doctor was called. What did he say? When did this happen? It's only been a week since I was here, and she was in perfectly good health then.' Without stopping to take off her hat and coat, she hurried down the hallway with the little maid scurrying behind her. In a moment the two of them were running up the wide curved stairs. 'I knew this would happen! I should be here . . . my place is with her.' She had never liked the arrangement that had installed her in the Ward household, but having heard the tragic story, and knowing how much it meant to the woman who had rescued her from a life of loneliness, how could she refuse?

'I did call the doctor, madam . . . straight away.' Not used to rushing about in such a manner, the maid was breathless. 'He said I was just to keep her warm in bed, and feed her on soft broth. She were only poorly for three days.' Anxious to be seen as having made all the right decisions, she added with a little pride, 'There weren't no need for a nurse, 'cause I looked after the mistress myself . . . stayed up all night when the fever took her . . . mopped her brow and talked nice and low 'til she come through it. This morning I boiled her a nice fresh egg, and she ate the lot. Like I said, the mistress is mending well now.' If she thought to gain praise for her endeavours, she was disappointed. 'Madam' was only interested in hurrying to her friend.

'It's all right, Margaret.' Tilly was relieved at the sight which greeted her as she entered the bedroom; a large bright room where the sunlight found every corner, and the furniture was regal. 'You can leave us now,' she said, taking off her outdoor clothes and handing them to the maid. 'But I would welcome a pot of tea and a slice of your fruit loaf.' She glanced at the woman sitting in the bed; a long-limbed creature with gentle brown eyes and chestnut-coloured hair that was now streaked with silver. 'I understand you've had only a boiled egg this morning,' she said meaningfully, then returning her attention to the maid, ordered, 'Make that tea for two, Margaret. And a double helping of your delicious cake.'

'Very well, madam.' The maid gave a knowing little nod and backed out of the door with a smile on her face. She was glad Miss Mulliver was here. There wasn't another soul in the whole world who could handle the mistress like her, and, if the truth be told, she had been really concerned about the mistress's bird-like appetite.

'I'm not at all hungry,' the woman protested, but then her whole face lit up in a brilliant smile as she held out her arms. 'But, oh, Tilly . . . you don't know how glad I am to see you.' When the other woman folded herself into the delicate embrace, she was shocked at how thin her friend had become.

'Oh, Elizabeth, why didn't you send for me?' she demanded, gently drawing herself away yet keeping the long pale fingers entwined in her own small hand. 'If I had known you were ill, nothing on this earth would have kept me away.' She was saddened and alarmed by the white face and big dark eyes that stared back at her from a thinner face than she remembered.

'Now, you're not to fuss,' Elizabeth reprimanded. 'You know how I can't stand to be fussed over.' She slid her fingers from her friend's grasp and pulled herself up in the bed, a smile lighting up the ageing beauty of her face. 'What news have you?'

'No news at all,' she warned, 'until I know how you've been . . . and whether you are on the mend.' She had been sitting on the edge of the bed, and now she leaned forward to take the other woman's hand again. 'What ails you, Elizabeth?' she asked in a tender voice. 'You were in good health when I saw you only a week ago today.'

'Something and nothing, that's all it was.' She laughed, but to the listening woman it held a hollow sound. 'It might even have been Margaret's fruit cake, for all I know.' When she saw Tilly would not be so easily put off, she sighed loudly. 'Oh, Tilly . . . it really was "something and nothing". The fever came on me out of nowhere. I have no idea what caused it. The doctor seems to think I took a chill while out walking on Tuesday last. If you remember it was a blustery day, and you know how easily I take cold.'

'Then what in God's name were you doing out on such a day?'

'I just felt the need. There was no particular reason. I was not on an errand, if that's what you mean.' For the briefest moment her eyes clouded over. 'I would never do that again. I should never have done it on that day.' A look of alarm spread through her features. 'Oh, Tilly, it was a foolish thing . . . supposing he had seen me standing outside his house?' She gasped now, putting her fingers to her mouth as though to stifle the horror of her thoughts. 'What if *she* had seen me?'

'No one saw you, Elizabeth,' Tilly assured her, 'and no one knows how close you are.'

'They must never know!'

'They never will . . . unless you want them to. Certainly, they will never know from me.' Here she paused, looking deep into Elizabeth's eyes. 'Would it be so terrible if they knew?'

'Don't even say that! You don't know.' Her voice broke in a cry. 'You can't know what dreadful memories would be unleashed. Such jealousy, such pain.' She shook her head vigorously. 'No! I could never do that to him. Not to him. Not to . . . Richard.' As always when she mentioned his name, her eyes filled with tears and she bowed her head, as though steeping herself in memories that were both painful and exquisite.

'You still love him, don't you? After all these years, you still love him.' Realising her own love for the same man, there was a sadness in Tilly Mulliver's voice.

'I will *always* love him. You know that.' Surreptitiously wiping her eyes, Elizabeth asked eagerly, 'What news have you? How is he? And Beth . . . what of Beth?'

'Goodness me! So many questions, and I'm hardly in the door.' Tilly regarded the woman with concerned eyes. 'First, tell me, Elizabeth, are you really mending?' She suspected that her friend had been more ill than she admitted.

'Yes.' The answer was given with conviction. 'When you come next week, I'll be up and about, as good as ever.'

'I don't mean to leave my next visit for another week, Elizabeth,' she insisted. 'In fact, I had intended to persuade you to give up this present arrangement.' She fell silent for a moment before going on quietly, 'I want to come home, Elizabeth. I miss being with you.'

'No! Oh, dear me, no.' There was desperation in her voice. 'I miss you too, but you must stay near him, at least for a while longer.' She had not told her friend the truth. Her illness would develop. Soon, she would be at peace. Until then she must know his every move. She needed to live his life with him, if only through the eyes and ears of her dearest friend. Through shame and fear she had lost him once, a long time ago. She must not lose him again. 'Please, Tilly. You know I wouldn't ask you to do this unless it was important to me. Please, a while longer. You've been such a good and loyal friend to me all these years, and I know it was wrong of me to ask something so demanding of you, but . . .' The tears threatened and she could not say the words.

'All right, Elizabeth. I know what you're trying to say.' Miss Mulliver knew this woman like she knew herself, and loved her dearly. 'Of course, I'll do as you ask . . . for a while longer.' She had long understood that it was not a healthy situation for any of them, and the sooner Elizabeth realised that, the better. She could have refused to go back to the Ward house, but she owed this woman everything. After her own parents died and she was left destitute, Elizabeth had found her wandering the streets. Out of the goodness of her heart, and perhaps because she also was lonely, she had taken Tilly home to be her companion. That was ten years ago. Since then the two of them had become almost inseparable. Until the day, some time back, when Elizabeth had discovered where Richard and Esther Ward lived.

She had told Tilly the whole story, about the man she adored, and whose child she had brought into the world. She told about the shame, and the heartbreaking decision she was forced to make under duress. She revealed how, since that fateful day, her life had not been worth living . . . the loneliness, the bitter regrets and the lingering shame that rose above all else. When she saw the post of maid in general to Esther Ward advertised, she used all her powers of persuasion to convince Tilly that it would only be for a very short time: 'Just so I know how he is . . . how my daughter Beth is faring.' Against her better judgement, Tilly had agreed. Now she was afraid that Elizabeth's initial interest had become a dangerous obsession.

Today, though, was not a suitable time to raise the subject of it all coming to an end. Also, Tilly had decided that she could not now reveal the news she had brought with her this morning; shocking news, news that told how Richard had been cheated and deceived by his own wife . . . and devastating news of Beth . . . how she was not safe and happy with Tyler Blacklock, as they had first thought, and how she also had been betrayed, both by

251

her own brother Ben, and by the woman who had raised her from a child.

How could Tilly tell of these things? How could she explain the loathing in Esther Ward's voice, and the awful contempt in which she held both Richard and Beth . . . the very people whom Elizabeth idolised? Tilly realised now that she could never tell her these things, and yet, she knew that the gentle Elizabeth had a right to know. But not now. She could not tell her yet; not until Elizabeth was completely strong again. With a sinking heart, she also realised that she must go on living with the Ward family, at least for now. And after all Elizabeth had done for her, heaven only knew it was little enough to ask in return. Besides, her own secret affection for Richard Ward was calling her back. And so she would return, to watch and listen, and to hope against hope that all would come well for both Richard and Beth. She smiled now, a smile that put her friend at ease. 'I won't let you down, Elizabeth,' she said fondly. 'You know that.' And yet she felt bound to warn, 'But, there has to come a time soon when you must let go of the past . . . or go to Richard and Beth with all that is in your heart.'

Elizabeth shook her head, a great sadness on her. 'I can't go to them. I can never go to them.'

'But why? I have never understood why.'

'Because I sinned against them both all those years ago. I sinned and brought shame down on all of us. It was shame that crippled four lives.' Now, when the memories poured over her, she faltered. 'Shame is a terrible thing, Tilly. It never goes away. I have no right to intrude on their lives. Not now. Not ever.' She would not be on this earth much longer. It was too late for confrontations. 'But, oh, I do cherish the little things you tell me . . . the things he laughs at, the way he strides out with pride. Wrong though it is, I still love him. You keep him alive in my heart. Through him . . . through you, my dearest friend, I have a purpose in living.' As she spoke, joy brightened her face, and the love she still felt for this man was alive in her every word. 'And Beth . . . so lovely, you say? So delightful. Sometimes, I would give everything just to let her know the truth.' The tears coursed down her face. 'She would never forgive me, and neither would Richard. I made my decision a long time ago, and now I have no rightful place in their lives. I've caused enough heartache. I won't be the cause of any more.'

'Oh, Elizabeth, Elizabeth!' Embracing her friend, Tilly asked herself whether, given the same circumstances, she herself would have acted any differently? The answer was the same as on every previous occasion she had asked herself that question. When she was young and maybe a little wilful, Elizabeth had made what she deemed to be the right decision, and she had suffered because of it. Now, almost a quarter of a century later, she was suffering more than ever, because she could not forget, and because she needed to feel close to the ones she still loved. Who could blame her? Who could say she was wrong? Certainly not Tilly. She had her own shame, and could not rid herself of the guilt that came from loving a man who was not hers to love. She felt no wrong in inventing things to tell Elizabeth. If she could ease her pain, then she would gladly make any sacrifice that was asked of her. If it had not been for Elizabeth taking her in off the streets and giving her a home, then Tilly's own life would have been empty. She adored Elizabeth, this good kind soul who had asked for little in return.

'In a moment you can tell me all about Richard. But first, is Beth happy with her young man? What was his name . . . Tyler? Yes, that's right. I remember now.' Suddenly she was young again, living through her daughter, like every mother does. 'And tell me again how she has a look of me.' The questions spilled out excitedly and her dark eyes shone. 'You will tell me everything, won't you, Tilly? You won't leave anything out?'

'No, I won't leave anything out.' Her conscience pricked her as she went on to lie, telling Elizabeth everything she wanted to hear. Good and happy things that would not cause her heartache. Things that took her back to when she was young. Things that filled her with joy and drew her into the everyday lives of the two people she had loved for so many lonely years. Through her friend, Elizabeth captured so many dreams, building memories that were, by their very nature, second-hand. But she cherished them, and hung on every word that Tilly uttered.

'Richard looks so proud and handsome,' she related, and when it was said, it came from the heart, because it was what Tilly herself saw, the man whom Elizabeth had never stopped loving, and the man who had captured her own heart. When it came to telling Elizabeth about Beth, how she 'seemed happy enough', Tilly prayed it was so.

Elizabeth listened with rapture to everyday incidents of family life. Richard and Beth were hers at last, the family she had been cruelly denied; because of love, and guilt and shame, they were closer now than they had ever been. Elizabeth had lost a lifetime of belonging. It was snatched from her by a woman without heart or conscience, a woman driven by greed. Esther Ward had more reason to be ashamed than her vulnerable sister Elizabeth, for she had taken advantage of the forbidden love which had grown between Elizabeth and Richard, and she had never once opened her heart to the innocent girl-child who was born out of that love. Yet she saw only admirable virtues in herself, and badness in others.

* * *

'Liverpool!' she cried with surprise. After they made love, he had left the warm bed and her possessive arms. Like so many times before, he had gone to the window where he stared out across the night sky, his thoughts a million miles away. When, sensing that he had left her alone in more ways than one, the woman asked him to come back to bed, he had not turned to look at her but instead remained silent a moment longer. After an agonising lull, he told her quietly, 'So often I've left London, only to return, yet I can't settle. For a long time now I've intended going North. There are growing opportunities there, especially in the major cities where, like London, the population is spilling into the suburbs. As yet the land is still relatively cheap. Its potential isn't even tapped. So far I've been very fortunate in that I've been in the right place at the right time; buying land and property in a subdued market then selling it on when demand is high. There have been ups and downs, yes, but on the whole my fortunes have grown. There's an auction in Liverpool soon. I'm tempted to attend.' He nodded as though reassuring himself. 'Yes, I have a good feeling about it.'

Clambering out of bed, the tall dark-haired woman flung a silk robe around her slim figure. Going to him, she wound her arms into his smoking-jacket and snaked them about his naked body. 'I love you,' she murmured.

He smiled into her eyes, his heart filled with kindness and gratitude; but not love. He could never love any other woman. Not when Beth was so alive in his mind. 'I know,' he whispered.

'And you would still leave me?'

He smiled again, a sad, lonely smile that told her he was still not hers. She believed he never would be. 'Come with me, if you want to,' he whispered. He owed her that much.

'Not as your wife though?'

He shook his head, 'Is that so important?'

Now it was her turn to lapse into thought. Being the wife of Tyler Blacklock was important. But she would never admit it. During the year they had been together, she had seen him time and again in the dark quiet hours when he believed himself to be unobserved. She had watched him, standing by the window, tortured, lonely, a man in pain, a man in love. But it was not her he was in love with. 'No,' she lied. 'It's not important.'

Relieved, he drew her into the haven of his arms. 'You're a good woman,' he told her.

She laughed dryly. 'But not the marrying kind, is that it?'

'Something like that.'

'It's her, isn't it?'

'What do you mean?'

'I don't know who she is, Tyler. I only know that she has your love, and that she is a very lucky woman.' She asked a question then that tore him apart. 'Why aren't you with her instead of being with me?'

He shrugged his shoulders, but gave no answer.

'She's married. Is that it?' She saw the agony in him. 'Oh, Tyler, I'm sorry. You've been good to me. I should learn to mind my own business.'

Drawing her tighter to him, he assured her, 'If you want to come North with me, you can. You know that, don't you?'

'Of course I want to come with you,' she told him. 'Don't decide to settle there though, will you?' She shivered. 'North seems a long way away, and they tell me it's cold there.' When he laughed, she tugged at his arm. 'The bed's still warm though.'

'Not yet,' he said, gently freeing himself. 'In a while.'

Disappointed, she turned away and slid back between the sheets. From there, she peeped at his tall muscular figure, so solitary, always alone. Except for the woman he kept hidden in his heart.

Chapter Seven

'To hell with you!' Luther Reynolds clenched the sides of the chair, his large fists curling and uncurling, and his fiery dark eyes glaring at the determined face of David Miller, the stepson he had come to resent with such bitterness that he could taste it. Yet he must contain the depths of his feelings, his hatred, his fervent wish to see his stepson come to a sorry end. It wasn't easy, having David under the same roof. But there were times when he had to hold his tongue, if only to ensure that he could keep on using this fool for his own ends.

It amused him to see how the gullible idiot deferred to him, even when they were in the midst of a vicious argument. David Miller was never vicious though; he was too lily-livered for that. 'Useless! That's what you are,' the old man screeched now. 'You never were any bloody good to me.' He moaned aloud and rolled his eyes to the ceiling. 'God give me strength,' he yelled, instantly turning his attention back to the younger man who stood before him, and whose woebegone expression would have been comical were it not so pitiful. 'What the hell are you staring at me like that for, you ungrateful bugger?' shouted the old man, thrusting his powerful frame forward in a threatening gesture. 'If it weren't for me giving you a roof over your head after your mother had the gall to die on me, you would have ended up in the bloody workhouse! And what thanks do I get, eh? None at all, that's what. None at all.

Nothing but whining and whinging, trying to run my life . . . My life! Bloody cheek. How would *you* know what I'm capable of? You're useless. Do you hear me, Miller? I said you're useless.'

Here his voice took on a devious note and his eyes slanted so that all light and expression were shut out. 'Where is she? Where's that wife o' yours, eh?' When David appeared to ignore the pointed question, he asked again in a lewd voice, 'Worn her out, have you? Oh, I heard you again last night . . . pushing your attentions on her . . . mating like dogs. But there aren't any brats to show for it, are there? You still haven't proved yourself a man, have you, eh? With three years to make your mark, your wife's belly should have been permanently swollen.'

He cocked his head sideways and looked at his stepson with a wicked expression on his face. 'She doesn't like it, does she, eh? That fancy wife of yours doesn't like you touching her, does she? Well, I can't say as I blame her because if I were a woman, *I* wouldn't like your paws on me either . . . and that wife of yours is no ordinary woman either. Special, isn't she? Too bloody good for the likes of you, wouldn't you say? Haughty and beautiful, isn't she? *Proud*, that's what she is . . . too sodding proud. No woman on this earth has any right to be proud, least of all one who comes to her husband with three brats in tow. But she's proud all right. And you're going the same way, I can see that! But you're making a mistake if you think you'll ever be a better man than me. You're too weak. You've always been too weak . . . got no spunk, and never have had. So don't think you're man enough to tell *me* what to do. What! Even bent and old like I am, I'm a better man than you'll *ever* be.

'I'm going to that sale, because I want that land. I want it badly, and I can't trust you to get it for me. Oh,

yes, I mean to be there. I'll show the buggers that old
man Reynolds isn't done yet. I can still give them a run
for their money. Every time they put in a bid, I'll be
there to force the scoundrels beyond their limits . . .
and I'll keep on forcing until that land deed has the
name of Luther Reynolds written on it. It's *land* I'm
after, not houses. I'm done with buying houses built on
somebody else's land. You never really own any part of
it, don't you see? Look at Larkhill. I'm buggered every
which way I turn because the ruins are mine, but the
land beneath is somebody else's. I can't rebuild without
paying through the nose for the privilege, and even if I
did build, getting rent is like getting blood from a stone!'
He jerked his head angrily. 'I'm caught between a pig
and a poke, blast it. It's land that makes the profit. Land,
that's what I want. And don't you tell me I'm not fit to go
to this bloody auction!' His eyes were bulging out of his
head, and if he could have easily sprung from the chair,
he might have locked his hands round the younger man's
throat.

As it was, he sat bolt upright, his cane propped against
the chair and his legs jutting rigidly before him. 'I'll be
there, I tell you. What's more, *you'll* be taking me,
because if you refuse I'll have the lot of you out of this
house before you can turn round . . . you, that haughty
bitch you married, and the three bastards she brought
with her. Now then, what have you to say to that?' His
lips clamped together and he raised one corner of his
thin mouth in a spiteful leer, his large bald head nodding
deliberately to and fro while he waited for the younger
man's response.

'If David doesn't take you, then I will.' Beth's quiet
voice defused a situation that David was incapable
of handling; she knew that. Worse, Luther Reynolds
knew it also. Now, when the old man jerked his head
round in astonishment, she looked past him to smile

encouragingly at her husband, saying, 'Forgive me for interrupting, David, but I was within earshot and, as you know, I take great exception to Mr Reynolds' particular brand of cruelty.'

Beth's forthright remarks brought a roar of laughter from the old man. 'Oh! "Cruel" am I?' he said mockingly. 'How's that then . . . pray do tell me, Mrs Miller?' He laid emphasis on the 'Mrs', at the same time bowing his head in a servile manner. 'And why would you want to take me to this auction? Do you see yourself as being given some sort of payment, eh? Or perhaps you've an idea that you might worm your way into my affections, is that it? Well now, if that's your little game, you can bloody well think again! You'll not get a penny of my money. Not now, and not ever. I'm warning the pair of you . . . my solicitors have got their instructions. When I'm put beneath the ground, every penny I own . . . every piece of property, every square inch of land, every stick of furniture and even the clothes on my back . . . it's all to go my son. My real flesh and blood.'

'Your real "flesh and blood"?' Beth made a puzzled face. 'Oh! You mean the son who deserted you when he realised you might be a burden on him? The son who helped himself to your money before running off? That brave young man who hasn't contacted you these many years? Why, of course you must leave all your worldly goods to him. It would be unthinkable for you to consider David here, who has been more of a son than you ever deserved . . . the stepson who stayed by your side when your own son deserted you; and who even forgave you when his beloved mother died because of your neglect.' There was a cold fury in her voice now.

'Shut your mouth, woman!' His eyes grew bulbous and a small trickle of spittle crept from the corner of his mouth. 'Shut your wicked mouth, or get out of my house, do you hear?' He lurched forward with intent to swipe at her but lost his balance and was thankful to fall heavily back into the chair. After enjoying so many years of unquestioning servility from David, it infuriated him to know that Beth did not feel threatened by him.

'If that is what you want, Mr Reynolds, then I'm sure David can be persuaded to leave with his family,' Beth told him icily; though in fact she despaired of ever persuading him to leave this house. She had long realised that while Luther Reynolds lived, David would always be there to pander to his every whim. But she was not intimidated by the old man's manner which could sometimes be childishly cajoling, sometimes violent as it was today. Nor was she concerned by his threat to put them out of the house. Almost from the day she and the children had been brought to this large dilapidated dwelling on Buncer Lane, Luther Reynolds had made it painfully clear that they were not welcome. Not a single day or night had passed without him making life as difficult and miserable as was possible. But he had stopped short of throwing them out, because then he would only be punishing himself. Whether he liked it or not, this despicable old man was dependent on his stepson.

'No, Beth.' The gentle-hearted David was shocked by the cold vehemence between these two people whom he loved more than anything else in the whole world. 'There'll be no talk of us leaving. This is our home, and this is my father. He needs me.'

'Need you!' The old man sneered, but he was more subdued. 'Have I ever said I bloody well need you?' he demanded. Secretly, though, he was thankful that David had intervened. Although he would be glad to see the back of the lot of them, it wasn't yet time. Lately, he had been of a mind to trace his son Arnold Thomas, but until such a day as he might be fortunate in that respect, he had no one except the lily-livered David. And, though he would never admit it, his stepson was the only person he could trust to handle his business interests.

'Now, don't be foolish, Father,' David gently reprimanded. 'If I wasn't here to take care of things, how on earth would you manage? And what would happen to the business, eh?' He knew only too well what would happen; no doubt his stepfather would have the daily help to come in and take care of him, but as far as the business was concerned, it would likely be whipped from under him by the many land sharks who would prey on the defenceless old man without the slightest compunction. The thought was horrifying to David.

During these past ten years, he had learned a great deal about his stepfather's business; not only did he trudge the streets collecting money, which he then took to the bank after it had been religiously recounted by Luther, but he was the one who made all the entries into the ledgers; he was the one who always met with accountants and reported back to his stepfather, who constantly grumbled that he was 'too ill and racked with pain' to weigh himself down with the burden of meetings and ridiculous men in ridiculous suits, with their ridiculous ideas that a man should always invest the money he earns with the sweat of his brow . . . 'Twaddle!' the old man would say. 'There's only one place for money, and that's a safe place . . . a place where it can make a healthy profit without being subjected to the fluctuation of bonds and shares and suchlike. Never take risks. That's always been my way.' And he never did. He was too wily, or too much of a coward.

'So you'll do as I ask, and take me to the auction in Liverpool next week?' Luther Reynolds sensed his stepson's weakness, and he knew the argument was going his way. He was wily enough to recognise that he did need his stepson; more than David himself would ever know; or at least needed him until his own son could be found and persuaded home. All the things that bloody woman, Beth, had said were true, but his old mind was not so sharp as it once was. His body was fading and he had need of his own son beside him. Yes, Arnold Thomas had done a bad thing in deserting him just when he needed him most, and he had been a rogue of the worst kind to have stolen money into the bargain; but if he could only find his son, he would tell him that all was forgiven, and that he wanted him here, in his rightful place, at the helm of his father's business.

Unbeknown to his stepson, the old man had already been scanning the local papers with a view to hiring some kind of enquiry agent to search far and wide for the son who had absconded all those years ago, but as yet he had not been given the opportunity to do anything positive. However, it was only a matter of timing. Meanwhile he had to tread very carefully, because if David suspected that his talk of cutting him out of the business was more than just *talk*, there was no telling how he would react. Even a worm occasionally turns. He knew the man whom he had grudgingly raised from a boy. David was loyal to a fault, and in his naive understanding quietly expected the same kind of loyalty in return. The old man silently cursed himself for blurting out his intentions just now . . . about how he would leave nothing to David, yet everything he had to his own undeserving son. The woman knew he meant every word he said, but he was counting on the fact that she would never convince her husband of it. In future he must guard his tongue or risk everything. And it went without saying that, if he was not prepared to take a risk with his money, he most certainly was not prepared to take a risk which might lose him the one person he could trust. David might not be his real kith and kin, but he was honest, and he was hard-working . . . willing to be at his beck and call and to labour long hours, with only a pittance for his troubles. Luther knew that he might search long and hard, from one end of the earth to the other, but he would never find such an incredibly forthright and loyal employee. Instead, he might be cursed with one who would rob him blind and charge him three times the wages for the privilege.

So, with the exception of the boy Matthew, who was marked with the same ruthless stamp as himself, he grudgingly tolerated the 'intruders' brought under his roof, and whom he had come to resent beyond reason; perhaps because he saw in them his own failure as a family man. Or, and this was more likely, he found Beth too lovely, too desirable, too much like the women he had longed for as a young man, and never had the fortune to find. Twice he had wed, and neither woman had truly satisfied him. Beth stood before him now, a dignified creature, her slim shapely figure taut with anger, her wild brown hair loose to her shoulders, and her dark flashing eyes daring him. He wanted her! Had wanted her since that first day. But wanting only frustrated him more. Want was all he could do, for his body had long ago ceased to function in that way. But his mind was quick, and his memories were all intact; and the longing never really went away, that awful persistent longing that could find outlet only in frustration and anger, and a wish to do bad things; to hurt and to insult like he did now while he waited for David to concede defeat and agree to take him to the auction after all. 'I don't want you here,' he snapped at Beth. 'This is between me and him. What the hell has any of this to do with you, anyway?'

'Oh, but it has everything to do with me,' she replied. Realising the vindictive nature of this man, and knowing how he had conditioned her husband since he was a child, Beth felt obliged to look out for the interests of those she loved. Less than one month after she and David were married, and knowing that he himself would never have the courage to ask, Beth had gone to Luther Reynolds with a certain proposition. 'Either you increase my husband's wages to reflect the work he does on your behalf, or I might find it my duty to persuade him to look for other employment, perhaps with one of the many property owners hereabouts.' She hoped such a threat would put the fear of God in him, not least because he had a particular loathing for competition, and the idea that his own stepson might join forces with the opposition and take with him all manner of secrets was too much to stomach. The princely sum of one guinea a month was agreed on, and though it was not as much as Beth would have liked, it was a welcome increase, and one that positively staggered her disbelieving husband.

As a result, she had been able to put away a few shillings every week, and over these past three years the shillings had mounted until now the bag of coins which she kept hidden under the bedroom floorboards had swollen to a tidy sum. Her biggest regret was that she found it necessary to keep its existence from David. Somehow she could not help but suspect that he would think it immoral to squeeze extra wages out of his stepfather, only to hoard them beneath the floorboards.

Beth had soon discovered that David Miller had many weaknesses, but the one that concerned her most, and gave her reason to fear for the future, was his blind love for and loyalty to the monster who had raised him. It was an unnatural devotion which, to her mind, could end only in disaster. A strange relationship, it was built on love and hate, uniquely tender on one side, and unspeakably cruel on the other. More and more, Beth found herself acting as the buffer between them, and

curiously enough, at times when she sought to protect
him, it seemed as though she was actually having to fight
her own husband.

She looked at him now, a pathetic and solitary figure almost like a small boy as he stood before the
man who had always dominated and manipulated him;
certainly, there was an air of obedient subservience
as he fidgeted uncomfortably, his dark brown hair
falling lankly over his forehead and vivid brown eyes
large with sadness. He seemed so thin and haggard.
Beth remembered how Maisie had said David Miller was 'going on forty I shouldn't wonder'. The fact
was, he was ten years younger. David had been eighteen when his mother died, after a surprisingly short
illness, which Luther Reynolds had insisted was, 'Nothing more than a cold.' The weight his stepfather had
put on the young man's shoulders had made David
seem much older than his twenty-eight years. Never
once had he shown him any kind of affection. And
still David would not hear a word against his beloved
stepfather.

Aware that she was causing David a deal of agony just
being in the same room as Luther, Beth turned to him
now, saying with some tenderness, 'And you, David?
Would you rather I left the room?'

For a brief moment, she actually thought he would
defy the old man, but then her heart sank when he
sheepishly replied, 'Perhaps it *would* be for the best,
dear.' Having said that, he self-consciously dropped
his gaze from her disappointed eyes and turned it to
the multi-patterned carpet. Pausing just long enough
to sweep the old man's triumphant face with an antago-
nistic look, Beth turned from them both and went, head
high, out of the room and into the hallway, where the
late March sunshine found its way through the tall
arched windows, and where the air seemed relatively

fresh compared to the musty damp smell of the old man's den.

As Beth went through the house, from the wide spacious hallway and into the dark-panelled sitting room, it struck her again how lovely the old place could be. Buncer Lane itself was a delightful road, flanked on both sides mostly by detached houses, with fancy lead-light windows and wide impressive doors. The houses were surrounded by gardens, some with a little front wall, and some with high laurel hedges, or holly trees that scratched you as you walked by. Luther Reynolds' house was the largest of them all, a red-bricked dwelling with pretty decorative fan-lights above the windows and door. Some time ago he had ordered that the front garden be flagged over, and now the weeds were pushing up between the paving slabs and the stones themselves had sunk in the ground at one end. There was little that could be done to improve the overall unkempt appearance, except to dig the whole lot up and start again, but, as Luther Reynolds told David on one occasion, 'I don't use the bloody garden, so why should I waste precious money on it?' And so it remained, an eyesore and a danger, although Beth herself regularly cleared the weeds from the path.

The house consisted of two reception rooms, each furnished with black oak monstrosities that created a dark and depressing atmosphere. Then there was a smaller room at the front of the house where the old man counted his money, and which he called his 'den', and, to the rear of the house the kitchen, a large, well-designed place with windows on two sides; one looking out to the side of the house where the undergrowth reached waist height, and the other two situated at each end of the wall that overlooked the rear garden. When Beth first came to the house, the rear garden was derelict. After a little more than a year, she alone had transformed it into a place where the children could play in safety, a stretch of patchy grass with a few well-cared-for roses round its border, and an immensely high wall skirting the garden from one end to the other. Beth had persuaded David to mend the rustic oak bench, and it was here that she would spend her happiest times, sitting beneath the old apple tree, watching the children at play.

Looking out of the window on this pleasant Sunday afternoon, she smiled as she saw the three children engaged in various activities at the far end of the garden. Her son Richard, whom she had named after her own father, was now a sturdy three year old, with a serious nature for one so young, although he had a mischievous and exasperating streak. With his thick black hair and sea-green eyes, he was the living image of Tyler. Every time Beth looked at him, the pain almost cut her in two. The love that had been denied her was always there, together with fond recollections of the father who had never seen him. The torment never really went away, but she had learned to live with it.

Even now, as she smiled at her son's antics – he was laughing and clapping his little hands together and making mischievous faces at Cissie, who adored him – memories of Tyler besieged her heart. 'I can't forget you,' she murmured softly. 'After all this time, I still love you.' She wondered at her own weakness in craving for a man who had professed his love for her and made her with child, only to walk away without even a backward glance. In all fairness, Tyler had not known about the child. But then, would he have cared? Hadn't he also got his landlady's daughter with child? And didn't he desert her in the same heartless way? All of these things Beth constantly reminded herself of; together with the fact that she was now a married woman and should reserve all her thoughts for the man who had put a ring on her finger, even though she had a son, and both of Maisie's children. In spite of all the weak traits in his character, David Miller had kept his promise to Beth. 'I'll take care of you,' he had said, 'I'll help you to raise Maisie's children.' He had done all of that, and she would always stand by him because of it. Yet, somehow, in her secret heart, he never seemed to reach the same stature as Tyler Blacklock. Beneath all the doubts, all the hurt, there still lingered something . . . something she could not put a finger on. Now she had stopped denying her love for Tyler. Hidden away, pushed to the darker recesses of her mind, it was a tangible presence that gave her a degree of comfort in the terrible loneliness of her marriage. Yes, she still loved him. She probably always would.

Not for the first time, Beth asked herself how she could so readily condemn David for being so weak as to love someone who had treated him in such a callous and despicable manner, when she herself was guilty of the very same weakness! She had affection for David, and a deep gratitude towards him. She endured his lovemaking, sometimes she even enjoyed it, but for the greater part she could not love him in the way he truly deserved. Inside, she was like his stepfather's room . . . dark and secret, allowing David into only a small part of it. She felt guilty, always guilty, thinking how she should be opening her whole heart to him. But then, how could she, when her heart was already given?

From her vantage point, Beth watched the children a while longer. She gave thanks to God for her precious son, and for the opportunity to raise Maisie's two children. If she had any misgivings, they were for Matthew. He had never forgiven her for intruding in what he had seen as his family, his responsibility, the only inheritance his father had left him. These past three years he had grown sullen and morose, keeping himself at a distance, always watching her, silently blaming her for Maisie's tragic death. With his dark brown hair and expressive violet eyes, he was an incredibly handsome boy, not yet fifteen, but tall and with a broad back which was a legacy from his boyhood in the mines.

Only last year, on the instructions of Luther Reynolds, David had brought the boy out of the mines and begun to teach him the way of business; Matthew often accompanied him on his rounds, and though he made little attempt to befriend David, the boy worked, and learned, and spent so many hours closeted in the 'den' with the old man, that Beth was obliged to voice her concern. All the same, her protests went unheeded, and each day that passed she could see Matthew becoming more and more influenced by old Luther. Sometimes she would lie awake in the dark hours when David was sound asleep, and talk to her old friend Maisie. 'I'm so sorry, sweetheart,' she would whisper, 'I feel I've failed you where Matthew is concerned. But he's so bitter, so filled with resentment, and I can't promise that I will ever be able to change that. But I won't give up, I promise you that, Maisie . . . I won't give up.' With a lighter heart, she would tell Maisie of her other child, Cissie, who was now going on thirteen, a lovely girl who was the same forthright and delightful character as her mam before her.

Beth's attention focused on the girl now, slim, her hair more fair than dark, but fine like Maisie's. She was playing with Richard, teasing him with a fallen branch from the apple tree, and snatching it away when the child made to grab it. Their laughter was a tonic to Beth, and she was glad that Cissie had finally begun to forget that terrible night when Maisie was killed, along with poor Meg, and another neighbour who perished while asleep in his bed. For many months afterwards, Cissie had suffered awful nightmares, when she would scream for her mam. It seemed to Beth as though nothing would

ever console her. But she showered the girl with love
and affection, sitting with her night after night, to talk
and reminisce, recalling Maisie's antics, and laughing
and crying together until after a while Cissie began to
emerge from her grief and the bond between her and
Beth grew ever stronger.

Matthew, though, allowed himself no respite from
his black crippling grief; he kept it close, deep inside
him. He never talked of Maisie, nor of that night, and
whenever Cissie broached the subject of their mam,
his reaction was violent. He would lash out at her and
afterwards hide himself away in some shady corner
where he would sit, his head lowered to his knees,
engulfed in a dangerous brooding mood that lingered
until the day's end. After a while, Cissie learned not
to speak of Maisie, but she confided her sadness in
Beth. 'Matthew doesn't love me any more,' she would
whisper. 'But I love him . . . even though he makes me
afraid sometimes.' He made Beth afraid too. Yet she
suffered his grief with him, wanting to share his sorrow,
hoping that she could alleviate some of his pain. She
knew he was suffering, because even though he tried
to hide it, Beth saw it in his eyes. She tried so hard
to help him, to talk with him and show him how much
she cared . . . how much they all cared. But he would
not let her near, and her heart was saddened because of
it. Only the old man got through to Matthew, and even
though David argued his stepfather was showing only
kindness, and 'had the boy's interests at heart', Beth
was not convinced.

Time had only confirmed her fears. And yet it was not
all bad news, she reminded herself, because Matthew
was no longer condemned to go underground in order
to earn a living, and David had told her how amazed he
was at 'the boy's remarkably quick mind and business
acumen'. All the same, in spite of David's assurances,

Beth was uneasy. Her instincts warned her that no good could come of this unhealthy alliance between Matthew and the old man. She looked at the boy now. Isolated from the other two, he was leaning against the apple tree, his hands deep in his pockets and a surly look on his face. His eyes were watchful, unfriendly. Now and then he would smile, as though enjoying some dark secret thought. Shaking her head forlornly, Beth turned away.

Suddenly, the still afternoon air was rent by a piercing scream, then the sound of the child crying and Cissie's angry voice: 'Go away, Matthew! You're horrible . . . horrible!' Swinging back to the window, Beth was horrified to see the girl pressed against the apple tree with her arms wrapped protectively round the little boy, the two of them bent double, cringing together while Matthew flayed them viciously with the branch. Even from where Beth stood, she could see the blood trickling down Cissie's arm. In a minute she had rushed from the house and was running down the garden. 'STOP THAT!' she yelled, but Matthew took no notice. Instead, he laughed aloud and beat them all the fiercer.

'Mummy! Mummy!' The boy clung to Cissie, his eyes wide with terror as he cried out. His cries became screams of pain when the branch whipped against his face, causing blood to spurt from his nose, staining his shirt with crimson raindrops.

'Keep down, Richard . . . Cissie! Keep your faces down.' Beth feared for the children's sight as she lurched forward to grab the branch. If she thought Matthew would stop once she had hold of the other end, Beth was badly mistaken. Far from letting go, he wrestled like a mad thing, kicking out with his boots and laughing like a maniac when the branch flicked across her throat and drew blood. But if he was determined, Beth was equally so. Gripping the sharp branch with both hands, she

272

worked her way along it until she was close enough to see the whites of his eyes. His laughter was terrible to hear. In that moment, she thought he had gone completely mad. But then, without warning, he turned his head and spat across the garden, simultaneously snatching his hands from the branch and sending Beth crashing backwards into the tree trunk! The force of the impact knocked the breath out of her.

'You rotten coward, Matthew!' Cissie was the first to recover, and there was no doubt she would have chased him to the ends of Kingdom Come if Beth hadn't thrust out an arm to stop her. 'He deserves a proper thrashing,' Cissie protested, fiercely indignant that she had been unable to defend herself while her cowardly brother took delight in whipping her. 'He's bad, Beth. Matthew's turned out real bad.' And though she would dearly have loved to deny it, Beth remained silent. Cissie was right. Maisie's son had turned out bad.

'Nothing but a prank, I tell you.' Luther looked deep into the boy's eyes and smiled wickedly when he saw the truth lurking there. Shifting his attention to David, who was still holding the boy by the scruff of his shirt collar, he told him solemnly, 'He's different from you, isn't he? You were never spirited, even as a boy. So I don't expect you to understand how harmless the incident was.'

'It was a wicked and spiteful thing to do.' David was urged on by Beth's insistence that he 'talk some sense into the boy, or watch him go from bad to worse'. David's answer had been to bring the boy before the old man. He wondered now how he might explain to Beth that his stepfather saw no real harm in what Matthew had done. In fact, David himself believed it would have been far better to have let the whole matter drop. The old man was right as always. In all probability it really had been nothing more than a prank.

Luther Reynolds now addressed the boy. 'Did you mean to be wicked and spiteful?'

'No, sir.'

'Did you set out to hurt the children in any way?'

'No, sir.'

'And . . .' Here, he hesitated, his narrowed eyes sending messages to the boy '. . . do you intend to say sorry?'

The boy did not answer immediately. He returned the old man's stare, his expression at first defiant, but then his hard features relaxed into a knowing smile. 'Yes, sir,' he replied quietly.

'Good!' The old man sank back into the chair, a look of satisfaction on his face. 'Say it then . . . "I AM SORRY".' He felt himself in danger of laughing out loud, so cleared his throat and addressed the boy in a firmer voice. 'Go on. Say it, damn you!' He stared as Matthew mutinously bit his lip, lowering his gaze to the floor and fidgeting from one foot to the other. After what seemed a long time, but was in fact only seconds, an almost inaudible whisper issued into the room. 'What was that you said? I didn't hear you!', the old man bellowed, enraged.

'I said . . . I'm sorry.' The boy was visibly shaken.

'There! He's sorry,' Luther told his stepson, smiling freely now and licking his lips like a dog might lick the juice of a bone from his chops. 'Will that satisfy your good lady?' When it appeared that David was unsure, he roared, 'Damn and bugger it, man! The boy has said he's sorry.' Each word was accompanied by a clenched fist thumping on the chair arm. 'What more do you want? Would you rather I thrashed him within an inch of his life? Should I cut off his fingers for daring to draw blood from your precious wife?'

'Well, no, of course not. You know I couldn't stand the boy being submitted to physical punishment,' David was quick to assure him. 'Two wrongs never made a right.' He himself was satisfied with Matthew's apology, and wanted the unpleasant business over and done with; but the thought of Beth waiting outside the door made him unusually bold. Turning to the boy, he said firmly, 'If you ever again raise your hand to either of the children or your mother, I shall . . .' His courage wavered as the two of them continued to stare at him, each daring him to go on. 'I shall . . .'

The old man intervened, 'Yes? You'll what?' There was disgust in his voice and, much more humiliating, a suggestion of amusement.

It was this that made David Miller bristle. 'I shall flatly refuse to take him with me on my rounds,' he declared. There! It was out. And he felt all the better for it.

The old man sniggered. 'Do you hear that, boy?'

'Yes, sir.' The boy kept his glance on the floor.

'So you had better behave yourself, hadn't you?'

'Yes, sir.'

Craning his neck, the old man looked up at his stepson. Without speaking a word, he continued to scrutinise the young man and to feel greatly satisfied when he saw how he was unnerving his victim. What he saw in David was not a man, but a boy. A frightened boy, a boy who, in spite of trying with all his might to please the man who had married his mother, had only succeeded in doing the exact opposite. When he was small, David Miller had been every bit as spirited and mischievous as any boy, but he had been bullied into believing otherwise. The result was a timid, indecisive creature, a thing to be ridiculed. Just for a second, for one brief surprising second, the old man admitted to himself that it was he who had created this pitiful excuse for a man, and his conscience, that bothersome thing which he had buried long ago, rose to haunt him. The experience was a frightening and unwelcome one. 'Get out!' he yelled. As David prepared to usher Matthew before him, there came another instruction. 'Leave the boy with me.' He chuckled, 'Perhaps I can make him see the error of his ways.'

Coming down the stairs, Beth saw her husband emerge from Luther's den. She saw the disappointment on his face, and realised with a sinking heart that the boy would not be punished.

Soon, the sound of low wicked laughter echoed through the house and, hearing it, Beth's blood ran cold. 'Oh, Maisie,' she murmured, raising her dark eyes heavenward. 'What have I got us into?' Turning her footsteps, she hurried towards the kitchen where she had already begun preparing the tea. As she went along the hall, she wondered how she might persuade Maisie's son to be a better person. She had tried. God alone knew how she had tried. The sad truth was, Matthew enjoyed being cruel. Luther Reynolds had fostered a sadistic streak in him that frightened her. Time and again, she had cast her mind back to before Maisie was lost in that tragic fire. The questions she asked herself were always the same. Had he changed so much since Maisie's death, or was he always vindictive? If so, why hadn't she seen it in him? Why hadn't Maisie seen it in her son?

Beth had convinced herself that it was all her fault. If she hadn't come into the family . . . *his family*, would Matthew have turned out the way he was now, or would he have grown into a fine young man with a greater sense of responsibility towards his sister? And, the greatest guilt of all, if she had not been in Maisie's house . . . if Maisie had not been tending to the birthing . . . then the fire would not have happened and that darling woman would be alive today. That was the truth! Beth could never dwell on it too long. It was too painful, too heart-breaking. That was why she could not, *must not*, give up on the boy. She had made a promise to Maisie, and somehow, whatever it cost, she would try with all her might to keep that promise. Nothing on God's earth would turn her from it.

In spite of his loathing for her, in spite of the wickedness that had taken hold of him, Beth would persevere. She had to! The boy had lost the father he adored, and soon after had lost his darling mother also. His hatred since was channelled towards Beth, and, in all truth, she could not blame him for it. He was so very young, so hurt and confused by all that had happened in his life, it seemed only natural that he should want to lash out. And if it was her he was lashing out at, so be it. She was strong enough to take a certain amount of punishment if it meant that, in the end, Matthew would rid himself of that core of hatred which was slowly eating him away.

One thing Beth would not tolerate, though, and that was his deliberate cruelty towards the children. Richard was only an innocent babe, and as for Cissie, there was no more delightful child on this earth. As Beth had reminded the boy on more than one occasion, his sister also had lost her parents, and the home she had been raised in. Secretly, Beth admired Cissie's strong character, and the way she had come to terms with the tragedies in her life. It was a pity that Matthew was not made of the same admirable stuff. And yet, she believed with all her heart that there was a great deal of goodness in the boy, buried beneath the sorrow and the hurt.

In the kitchen she found Cissie occupied in laying the table, while Richard was already seated there, his small chubby arms folded before him and his watchful green eyes following Cissie's every move. When he realised his mammy was at the door, he swung his legs out of the chair and came rushing to greet her. With a cry, she swung him up, a squealing, squirming bundle, throwing his arms round her neck and covering her face in smacky wet kisses. 'Hey! Let me breathe then,' she laughed, giving him a big hug before putting him to the floor. As he ran back to climb into his seat, she thanked God for blessing her with such a healthy and adorable son. Richard would soon be four years old. The boy had grown sturdy and handsome, his green eyes and dark hair so reminiscent of his father. Sometimes the fact was a source of comfort to Beth. At other times, mostly when he smiled in that particular way of Tyler's, leaning his head sideways and looking at her with incredible love in his sparkling green eyes, she found it unbelievably painful.

The warm, delicious smell of home baking emanating from the kitchen made Beth realise just how hungry she was. Saturday was the day when she and Cissie rolled up their sleeves and turned out enough pies and bread to last the whole week, more often than not with the dubious help of Richard. Somehow, the wonderful aroma lingered on for days after. If Maisie had taught Beth anything at all, she had taught her how to look after a growing family.

Beth had thought her son and Cissie were still in the garden, so was pleasantly surprised to see the two of them already in the kitchen; Richard eagerly awaiting his tea, and Cissie fussing with a place setting. 'Well, now, you have been busy, haven't you?' Beth remarked. 'Thank you, Cissie. You've done a wonderful job.'

Glancing at the table, she saw that the girl had done everything just as she had shown her . . . the big brown teapot had pride of place in the centre of the table, with the pretty rose-patterned milk jug and sugar bowl beside it. There was the bone china three-tiered cake stand, each layer nicely laid out with slices of home-made cake. On the larger bottom tier were several rather chunky pieces of Beth's fruit loaf, baked in the manner which Maisie had taught her; then came the apple cake wedges; and finally, making a pretty pattern on the smallest top tier, the tiny sponge cakes, each one displayed in a pretty white doily and finished with a half cherry on top. There were several other plates dotted about the table, one containing best gammon sandwiches, another holding generous helpings of pork pie, and the others mostly displaying white and brown triangles of bread and butter, to be heaped with a liberal spoonful of the plum preserve from the small barrel-shaped pot nearby. Cups and saucers were arranged at just the right angle beside the small plates, and the bone-handled knives were correctly positioned to the right of each plate.

While Beth regarded the beautifully laid table, Cissie stood opposite, her big blue eyes proud and smiling. Suddenly, a look of horror spread over her face. 'Oh!' she cried, flinging herself towards the drawer in the table and snatching out a handful of spoons. 'I forgot to put the teaspoons out.' She quickly dropped one into each saucer before standing back and looking at Beth with a forlorn expression. 'I've done it again,' she said, twisting her lips in that way she had of showing disappointment with herself. 'I coulda swore I'd remembered every-thing.' Clenching her small fists, she folded her arms across her chest. 'The surprise is ruined! I've spoilt it, ain't I?'

Suppressing the chuckle that might well have relayed the wrong message, Beth went to her. Putting her arm round the girl's painfully thin figure, she said warmly, 'It's a wonderfully set table, Cissie. I couldn't have done better myself. I'm very proud of you, sweetheart.'

'Honestly?' The smile returned to Cissie's face.

'Honestly.' Beth chuckled now. 'What's a teaspoon between friends?'

Laughing and relieved, Cissie clung to her a moment longer. 'Oh, Beth, I do love you,' she said: the two of them laughing all the more when a little voice piped up from its place at the table, 'I do love you too!'

They waited tea for another twenty minutes, before Beth addressed the two impatient children with the solemn words, 'If the others don't have the good manners to come to the table at the proper time, then we'll start without them.' And that was just what they did, although Beth only picked at her food, her heart too full to eat.

She was not altogether surprised by her father-in-law's absence, because right from the start he had taken particular pleasure in taunting her in this way. 'Of course I'll be joining you for Sunday tea,' he would say charmingly, then would purposely keep them waiting until, fretful and concerned, David would leave his place at the table to remind his stepfather, only to be told that they should: 'Start without me. I'll be along.' But to this day he had not once sat down at a table prepared by Beth, and both she and David knew only too well that it was a deliberate snub. Worse, Luther would lock himself in his room until the table was cleared and the kitchen was empty. Then he would go in there, turn everything out of the cupboards, eat his fill, and leave the place looking like a herd of swine had trampled through it.

Beth had long ago given up the idea of winning the old man over. In fact, she was quietly grateful for the fact that he chose not to sit down to table with them. The ordeal of suffering his ogling eyes on her at mealtimes would have been too much, even for someone with Beth's strong constitution. It had not taken her long to realise that here was a vindictive old villain, bent on making her life as miserable as he possibly could. Over the years she had learned to stay two steps ahead of him. Her first step was to leave the kitchen exactly as he left it; if he thought she had any intention of clearing his mess up behind him, then Luther was very much mistaken.

The kitchen was a great echoing place, with high beamed ceilings and quarry stone floor. There were two grand old pieces of furniture in there, a huge square pine table with thick bulbous legs and four small drawers beneath the overhanging table top and a pine dresser of enormous proportions, with a cupboard beneath, two stout deep drawers and four shelves that reached to ceiling height, each stacked with blue willow pattern plates and festooned beneath with pretty china cups hanging from hooks. From the brown hide couch in the sitting room, and the two matching armchairs set either side of the old range, the pretty cottage paintings and floral drapes throughout the house, the many ornaments that decorated every room, Beth was able to glimpse the nature of the woman who had lived and died here – David's mother. There was a certain warmth and cosiness in this great dilapidated old house that only a gentle soul could create. On the one occasion she had broached the subject of his mother, David had looked at her with cold eyes, saying in a hard voice, 'My mother was her own worst enemy. She must have known she was dying and yet she did nothing to help herself.' That was the only time she ever heard him sound like Luther. It was also the last time she ever mentioned his mother.

When David first brought her to this house as his wife, Beth had hoped she could fit in, make this place a proper home for all of them. Sadly, she was frustrated at every turn, and all her efforts went to waste. Luther Reynolds ridiculed David in front of her, belittling him in such a way as to destroy any respect she might have had for her husband; although she could not help but like him a little. He was a strange man, still lonely in spite of taking her for his wife, and kept his own counsel, never discussing his thoughts with her, keeping his troubles deep, and always ensuring that she had whatever she

281

needed. In that respect, David Miller kept the promise he made her.

Yet she was lonely too. Oh, she had the children, and she treasured every moment with them, but she was unfulfilled, possessed of a deep longing which she could not understand. There was something missing in her life. Warmth maybe? A companion who would sit and chat with her, like she and Maisie used to chat? A lover who would hold her close and whisper in her ear? Someone she could share all her intimate thoughts and dreams with? All of these things amounted to one person . . . Tyler Blacklock. In spite of her determination to forget the man who had wronged her, never a day went by without her thinking of him, remembering, longing for such a love again. And all the while, her son Richard was there to remind her . . . sleeping, waking, looking at her in that special way that was Tyler's. He touched her heart, awakening the love, stirring the pain.

And then there was Matthew, always resentful, always looking to hurt; and her father-in-law, leading the boy into bad ways, moulding him in the same pattern as himself. Luther was the devil in disguise. From the start, Beth had seen him for what he really was. Right away they were sparring, wary of each other. The first time she discovered the awful mess he had deliberately left in the kitchen, Beth was determined she would not be used as a skivvy. When David had asked her to clear the mess away, for fear of inciting his stepfather's rage, Beth had astonished him by refusing. 'If he wants to behave no better than an animal, then let him wallow in it,' she told him, and no amount of cajoling would persuade her otherwise.

Confused by her rebellious attitude, David himself had cleaned up the kitchen behind his stepfather, and so the pattern was set. Luther would wait until dark, when the rest of the family had vacated the kitchen, then would take everything from the larder, spreading it on the table, spilling it on the floor, and generally inflicting mayhem on a hitherto spotless environment. After he had taken his fill and sampled everything, he would then collect a jug of ale from the pantry and depart along the hallway with the tap-tap of his walking cane making an ominous rhythm on the tiled floor; the sound becoming muffled as he made the difficult journey up the wide ornate staircase to his bedroom. Once there he would guzzle his ale, and cough and belch, and laugh and curse, until his bloated body was overwhelmed by slumber, and the house grew peaceful once more.

On every Sunday previously the pattern had been the same. When the kitchen was clean and the children put to bed, Beth and David would go to the sitting room, where he would sit at the circular table, head bent over documents and rent books.

But now the meal was over, and David had only just made an appearance. She was clearing the table when she heard the slow deliberate footsteps of her husband approaching the kitchen. When the door creaked open, she did not turn around but carried on with her task. 'We waited for you,' Beth told him. 'We were disappointed that you decided not to join us,' she said, keeping her eyes intent on the table. She hoped with all her heart that he was not going the same way as his stepfather; and yet, the signs were already there. The same secretive manner, the way he considered his own wishes to be paramount, the odd furtive way he stared at her when he thought she was not aware of it. David Miller had unwittingly, or maybe deliberately, mimicked so many of Luther's attitudes. Thankfully, though, there still remained one stark difference between the two men; because where Luther had a cruel and vicious streak in his character, David was a gentle soul, generous and accommodating to a fault.

'I'm sorry, Beth,' he replied softly, crossing the room and coming to stand beside her. When she paused in her work and turned to look at him, he saw the disappointment in her dark eyes. 'It was not intentional, I promise,' he told her. 'I got to glancing through the ledgers, and before I knew it, the time had flown.' He slid his arm round her narrow waist and bent to kiss her on the forehead. 'Forgive me?' he asked.

Beth nodded. 'Consider yourself forgiven,' she said, knowing from experience that there would be no point in saying otherwise. 'I can't speak for the children though.'

'Where are they?' He turned to look out of the window.

'You'll find Cissie and Richard in the garden.'

'And Matthew?' He quickly returned his attention to her, his quiet brown eyes growing anxious. 'Did he come to the tea table?'

Returning his gaze with a directness that answered his question, Beth shook her head.

'And Father?'

Again, she shook her head. 'That doesn't concern me. We did not miss your father,' she said in a hard voice that betrayed her contempt for the man. 'But something has to be done about his influence over Matthew. It's a great source of worry to me, David, and the boy won't hear me out. You know he blames me for his mother's death?'

'That's nonsense.' He knew of Matthew's bitterness towards Beth, and deplored it. But if Maisie's son would not listen to her, he would not listen to David either. 'As for my father's influence over the boy, I do believe you're exaggerating, Beth. He has shown Matthew a great deal of kindness, and you have to admit that, were it not for my father's offer of friendship, Matthew would be a very lonely soul. After all, he refuses to mix with boys of his own age, and rarely leaves this house except when I take him on my rounds.'

'Doesn't that give you cause for concern?' Beth asked pointedly. 'That an old man is all the "friend" Matthew has? Has it not occurred to you that it's your father who dissuades Matthew from making friends of his own age . . . talks him out of seeking other work? Don't you realise he doesn't want the boy growing away from him? Think of the many hours when the two of them are closeted in the den. Ask yourself what they do, David. What do they find to talk about for so long?'

'What are you implying?'

'I am implying that it's unnatural, and I want you to talk to your father. Heaven knows *I've* tried talking to him, but it gets me nowhere. I don't like what's happening, David, and I want it stopped.'

She felt him recoil from her. 'The trouble is you see only bad in my father,' he retorted.

'And you see only good!' she snapped. It was no use. David would not intervene, she knew that now. Neither the old man nor the boy heeded a word she said. She had tried everything . . . appealing to common sense, persuasion, threats . . . but it all fell on deaf ears. Now, as on other occasions, David had scoffed at her fears. All she could do was to keep vigilant, and to hope against hope that Matthew would soon tire of the old man, or that the old man would soon tire of deliberately using the boy in order to antagonise her. Maybe, if she appeared to be unruffled by his underhand behaviour, Luther would seek other means by which to destroy her peace of mind.

'There's no point in continuing this conversation, Beth. I can see it will only raise ill feeling between us.' David remained close for a brief moment, perhaps hoping that she would retract her words, but Beth only looked at him in that certain proud manner which told him she would not change her mind. Disgruntled, he turned sharply away, leaving her staring after him and shaking her head, disappointment and frustration written on her face.

A few moments later, squeals of laughter and delight heralded the arrival of Cissie and Richard; the kitchen door burst open and they tumbled in one behind the other, the boy first, and the girl pretending to chase him, her hands making pointed ear shapes behind her head, and her small pretty features twisted into a fearsome expression. 'Oooh . . . Ooooh!' she wailed, her voice growing louder the more he screamed. When the boy fell into Beth's arms, Cissie collapsed in a fit of laughter, grabbing the boy to her, and the two of them rolled about the floor, giggling and fighting.

'Well, thank you very much, Cissie Armstrong,' Beth chided good-naturedly.' 'Now that you've got him all excited, it'll be hours before he can get off to sleep.'

'I'll read to him, then.'

'About monsters and hobgoblins, no doubt!' Beth laughed. 'Not a good idea, I think.'

'No, Beth!' Cissie seemed astonished that she should think such a thing. 'I wouldn't read frightening things like that to him. At least, not just before he goes to sleep.' Cissie had a love of reading, especially since Beth had helped her to master the longer words that she had never really understood. 'And Richard likes me to read to him.' She addressed herself to the boy now. 'Don't you?' she asked. He nodded his dark head and turned to Beth. 'Please, Mammy,' he said, his handsome green eyes appealing.

A deal was made between the three of them. Richard could play outside a while longer, while Cissie and Beth washed the dishes. Afterwards, Beth would choose a story, and Cissie would read it to the boy until he fell asleep. Normally this was Beth's favourite time

. . . when her son was lying sleepy in his bed and she would read him a story about creatures and little people; gentle stories that soon sent him into a peaceful slumber. Cissie also loved to read to him, and considered it a real treat when Beth gave the privilege over to her. There had grown between Cissie and the boy a strong abiding love that was wonderful to see. It was a source of great pleasure and comfort to Beth, especially since Cissie's own brother appeared to have turned his back on her. It was a sad thing to Beth, and one which only made her all the more determined to draw Matthew back into the family fold. To that end, she tried to keep alive Cissie's love for her brother, although it was proving more and more difficult as the girl frequently pointed out, 'He ain't the same, Beth. He ain't like my Matthew no more.'

It was eight o'clock when Cissie collected the tin bath from the outside shed. Already, the darkness was closing in, and there was a real winter nip in the air. When she returned to the kitchen, she found Beth sprinkling a shovelful of coals on to the fire. 'Draw the curtains, Cissie, and keep the cold out.'

In no time at all, the fire was blazing cheerfully, the curtains were drawn against the night, and Beth was pouring the water from the kettle into the bath; a spill of cold water from the ewer, then another drop from the kettle, and the water was just the right temperature, the warm steam rising nicely and filling the room with a comfortable warm smell. 'Come on, Richard,' she told the boy. Going to the chair where he was already dropping off to sleep, she gently pulled him to his feet and began peeling the clothes from his back.

'I'm tired . . . don't want a wash,' he mumbled, leaning his small sturdy figure against her, and twisting both hands into his dark hair until it made a tangled mass.

Ignoring his protests, Beth stripped away his under-garments and lifted him into her arms. 'We'll make it a quick wash then, shall we?' she asked, kissing his warm round face and pressing him to her. When he murmured and clung to her all the more, she was tempted to put him in his night-shift and take him straight to bed, but Sunday night was bath night, and he would sleep all the better for it, she thought. Setting him to his feet, she tested the bath water once more. Satisfied, she helped him into the bath and began soaping him all over; as usual, he bawled loudly when it came to washing his hair. Next came the rinsing, then the part he liked best of all . . . standing naked before the warm fire, while his mammy dried him with the soft towel that wrapped round him like a cloak. In no time at all, he was scrubbed shiny, dressed in his night-shift, and seated in the big armchair, with the heat from the fire drying his hair and making him feel all sleepy.

'I'll take him up to his bed, Cissie,' Beth told her, at the same time taking the boy by the hand and leading him towards the door. 'Mind you wash all over. I'll be down in a minute. Meanwhile, stay away from the fireplace, like I've always told you. I'll help you dry your hair when I come down.' Beth was always very careful to put a safety screen across the fire, but ever since the tragedy that had taken Maisie, she suffered from a real dread of accidents. Once, when she caught Cissie with her head down, drying herself in the heat from the fire with her hair hanging over her eyes and dangerously close to the flames, her heart had turned somersaults.

'Don't worry, Beth,' Cissie called after her. 'I won't even be washed by the time you come down.'

'Oh, yes, you will, my girl! And don't use any more hot water, or there'll be none left for me,' Beth told her sharply. She knew Cissie well enough to recognise a ruse when she saw one. Cissie hated going to bed, and she hated getting up in the morning, but she thoroughly enjoyed lazing in the bath, and finding every excuse not to say goodnight. 'I want to see you washed and almost dried by the time I come down. I don't want you turning up late for the shop tomorrow morning. It's your first day, and you need to make a good impression.' Cissie had been most reluctant to surrender her independence and take up employment in Moll Sutton's flower shop. Beth, however, was determined that she should enjoy a more stable position, with a regular wage; though even she had to agree that it was merely a pittance.

Beth had long been concerned about Cissie's 'wanderings'. There were too many unsavoury characters lurking about, and Cissie was not only young and pretty but had a friendly loving nature that could easily lead her into trouble. As she went from the room, Beth could hear Cissie moaning behind her, and knew they would be going through the same old argument when she returned to the kitchen.

Smiling to herself, she led the boy across the hall and on up the staircase, then along the galleried landing towards the far end of the corridor and Richard's room which was situated between the larger room that was Cissie's and the bright pretty room that was Beth's and David's. He would have preferred that the children be positioned a greater distance away from them, but she had insisted, particularly in view of Cissie's broken nights and fits of terror following the fire in Larkhill. Her nightmares had deeply affected Richard, and so Beth had told her husband, 'Either they stay close by where I can hear them should they need me . . . or I'll arrange for the children, *and myself*, to move to the east end of the house.' She was not surprised when he withdrew his objection.

For some time now, and urged on by the old man's taunts, he had been intent on fathering a child of his own. David's need for a son had become an obsession. It was an ordeal for Beth to be used for this night after night, but she comforted herself with the knowledge that he truly loved her and was always both gentle and considerate. She felt guilty that the love between them was all one way, and yet there was nothing in this world that she could do to change her feelings. What she felt for David was not love but gratitude, with maybe a scattering of affection. The kind of love he wanted she could never give, and had never made any pretence of. In her heart, Beth sensed that he knew the way of things, and this only made him all the more determined to have a son of his own. He had never insisted that Beth's son call him 'Daddy', and she was immensely thankful for that. Richard was Tyler's son.

One day in the future, when he could understand, she would tell him about his father; she hoped she might be able to explain the facts without revealing how Tyler had deserted them. Often she had seen David looking at her son, a look that was filled with longing and, sadly, a measure of envy. Beth had a love for children, but how she wished she could have borne them for the man she loved, instead of the man she was indebted to. All the same, if it happened that David made her with child, she would bear the child proudly, and be glad that she had brought him a degree of happiness. So far, though, there was no sign of it.

'Can I have a story, Mammy?' In the light from the lamp the child blinked his weary eyes, his question muffled by a long noisy yawn.

Tucking him deeper into the bed, Beth leaned forward to kiss his face. 'I promised, didn't I?' she reminded him, going to the dresser and opening the drawer there. Taking out the small leatherbound book, she held it beneath the flickering light. 'A tale from Lamb,' she muttered, opening it on the first page. 'Cissie won't be

coming up for a while,' she said, making her way back
to the bed, 'do you want to wait? Or shall Mammy read
it?' The last word was shaped by her smile. The child
was already fast and hard asleep. Going on tiptoe to the
dresser, Beth replaced the book, then taking the oil-lamp
with her, drew the curtains; but not right across, for she
knew how the boy liked a chink of moonlight to shine
through. After another fond peep at his sleeping face,
she crept out of the room, softly closed the door, and
gathering up her skirt in order not to trip over the hem
on the way down the stairs, swiftly retraced her steps
back to the kitchen and Cissie.

When Beth pushed open the kitchen door, she was
taken aback to see that Cissie was not alone. Matthew
was there. Cissie was kneeling on the rug, her back to
the fire and her slim body bent forward over the bath.
Her hair was dipping into the water and, stooping above
her, Matthew was carefully pouring water from the jug,
making a cascade over her hair as it washed the soapy
water back into the bath. For some reason she could
not instantly understand, Beth was riveted with shock.
Neither Matthew nor the girl was aware that she had
come into the room, and as Beth's eyes went from the
unique expression of wonder on the boy's handsome
face, to the girl's slender form . . . the small budding
breasts, and the young limbs that were already shaping
into those of a young woman . . . a strange sense of
revulsion shivered through her.

'Matthew,' her voice startled him. As she came forward, he almost dropped the jug, his face pink and
confused as she continued to stare at him. Taking the
jug from his hand, she said in a cool voice, 'I'll take care
of Cissie.' So many unpleasant thoughts were spilling
through her mind that Beth was made to recall her
husband's words with regard to Luther . . . 'You see
only bad in him'. Was that really true? And was it also

true that she saw only bad in Maisie's boy? A rush of guilt caused her to temper her attitude. 'Perhaps you would be so kind as to empty the bath for me later?' she asked, forcing a half smile and putting herself between Matthew and his sister.

'I don't think so,' he replied sullenly, unrolling his sleeves and going to the chair, where he collected the burgundy waistcoat given to him by the old man. 'I have other things to do.' Pushing his arms into the waistcoat, which he then buttoned up the wrong way in his confusion, he pointed to the girl who had lifted the veil of wet hair from her face and was peeking out of one eye. 'I thought the children were already in bed,' he said guardedly. 'Luther sent me to see if it was all right for him to come and get himself something to eat.'

At the mention of the old man's name, Beth's hackles rose. 'Well, you can tell him it's *not* all right!' she snapped. 'What's more, he, like you, was asked to join us for tea. If the pair of you would rather stay away, then so be it; but you must not be surprised if the rest of us refuse to be inconvenienced by such behaviour.' No sooner were the words out of her mouth than she regretted them. Every time she vowed to get closer to Matthew, she only succeeded in driving him further away. However, she had been somehow unnerved by finding him here in this way. One other thing had to be said, and she said it now. 'What do you mean, Matthew . . . you thought the "children" were in bed? You would do well to remember that you yourself are little more than a child. Certainly, you are not yet a man, although I've no doubt that one day soon, you will make a fine young man.' She was visibly astonished when a strange little giggle broke from him, after which he stared at her defiantly. It struck her then just how quickly he really was becoming a man. In all these months when Matthew had kept out of her way, he had changed from the boy she had known when she first came to Maisie's house. Now, Maisie's beloved son had grown much taller, possessed of the broad shoulders of a man, his face having acquired a gaunt handsome profile that held a certain arrogance. The eyes that were violet like his mother's were strangely secretive, seeming to frown and smile at the same time. The way he looked at her now disturbed Beth deeply. Suddenly, he shrugged his strong shoulders, before deliberately turning his back on her and strolling from the room.

Beth had a mind to go after him, but then Cissie called out, 'I'm cold, and my hair's dripping all over the place.' Beth went immediately to her assistance. Intent on getting the girl dried before she caught a chill, she did not see Matthew push open the door to stare at his sister, then at Beth. When the door quietly swung to, she paid it no mind. There were too many thoughts pressing on her, too many instincts that bristled inside her. Before she finished here and made her way to the sitting room, there were certain things she must say to Cissie, and she must say them without alarming the girl, yet, at the same time, make her aware that she was no longer a child, that she already had the mark of a woman on her. Beth called herself all kinds of a fool, for she herself had not realised how quickly the girl was growing up. From now on, when Cissie was taking her bath, that door would be locked, just as it was when Beth herself was bathing. The men, Matthew included, always had a strip-wash in the outer scullery.

'Right then, my girl.' Dipping her two hands in the neck of Cissie's night-shift, Beth drew out the long brown locks, spreading them over the collar and fanning the hair out as it was not altogether dry. 'Get yourself off to bed. Like I said, I don't want you being late your first day at the shop.' She had spoken to Cissie about ensuring that the door was locked in future when she was taking a bath. Beth had been surprised to know that Cissie herself had been thinking along those very same lines, and it only told her that she was right about Maisie's children – they were growing up fast. She had not realised it until now.

Cissie had also been entertaining secret hopes that Beth just might change her mind about sending her to work at the flower shop. When she saw that her hopes might come to nothing, she was horrified. 'Oh, Beth! *Must* I go and work in that shop? I'd rather be out and about, finding my customers in the market-square or the boulevard.'

'You want to learn all there is to know about selling flowers, don't you?'

'Yes . . . but . . .'

'And you want to be the best flower-seller in the whole of Lancashire, don't you?'

'You know I do.'

'Then you can learn a great deal by working in Moll Sutton's shop, *and* get paid in the process.'

'I can't learn no more than I already know!' Cissie protested.

'What exactly *do* you know, Cissie?'

'Well . . .' Beth's forthright question had taken her by surprise. 'I know which are tulips and which daffodils, and I know what to charge . . . a tanner for a big bunch, threepence if they're past their best bloom, and a penny for a sprig of heather.' Her grin ran from ear to ear. She felt very pleased with herself.

'Do you know anything about how the flowers appear in the warehouse? Or where they all come from? Or what they cost to buy in?' When Cissie looked like breaking in, Beth went on, 'What about cartage . . . and how long will they keep in certain conditions? What margin of profit is there?' She paused to let the girl reflect on her questions. 'Well?' she asked at length. 'Do you think you know as much about selling flowers as Moll Sutton?'

'I know if I happen to find a bunch that's been thrown out 'cause it's past its best, I can likely get a threepenny piece for it at the railway station. That's good profit, ain't it?' she remarked cheekily.

'Ah! But it won't buy you a shop, now, will it?' Beth was quick to point out. 'Wouldn't you like to know how Moll Sutton made so much money that she could get herself a shop?'

'Naw. I don't want a shop, Beth.' Cissie was adamant. 'I only want to sell me flowers wherever I find meself a customer.'

'You can argue until you're blue in the face, my girl,' Beth told her firmly, 'but it won't do you any good. In my book, if you set your heart on a particular way to earn a living, then you should find out everything you can about it.' They were her father's words and she had never forgotten them.

Sensing Beth's quieter mood, Cissie was intrigued. 'What do *you* know best?' she asked, slipping her arm round Beth's slim waist as the two of them sauntered to the door.

'Oh, I know a bit about land development,' she confessed, 'and I suppose I know about children, and the things your mammy taught me.'

'What did your own mammy teach you, Beth?' It suddenly occurred to Cissie that Beth had never spoken about her own parents. 'You have got a mammy, haven't you, and a daddy? Why don't you ever talk about them?' Her big blue eyes swivelled upwards, watching Beth's changing expression. She felt guilty when she sensed Beth's deep sadness. 'Aw, I'm sorry. Me and my big mouth, eh?' she said, lowering her gaze and wishing she knew when to hold her tongue.

Hugging the girl close to her, Beth replied quietly,

'It's all right, Cissie. It's only natural that you should want to know about my parents.' She laughed softly in a bid to put the girl at ease. 'After all, I know all about *you*, don't I?' She fell silent for a moment, grateful when Cissie decided not to press her. At the door, Beth held the girl at arm's length, then, looking into those mischievous blue eyes that betrayed Cissie's delightful nature, told her softly, 'One day, Cissie, I will tell you all about my family, I promise.' In her mind's eye she saw the face of her father, and her heart was heavy. 'Now off to your bed, young lady.'

Cissie had seen Beth's sadness. 'You know I love you,' she said with childlike simplicity.

Beth's dark eyes grew moist as she pulled the girl to her. 'I know,' she said. 'And I love you too.'

'Goodnight, Beth.' Reaching up, Cissie kissed her lightly.

'Goodnight, God bless.' After Cissie had gone, Beth closed the door and stood with her back against it, her eyes downcast. In her innocent curiosity, Cissie had opened old wounds. After all this time, Beth had hoped that the memories would be less painful. They were not. And yet, if she could turn the clock back, would she change anything? Would she not want to know the joy she had experienced in Tyler's arms? That wonderful love they had shared and which had given her the precious gift of a son. How could she not want that? If her relationship with Tyler had brought her a deal of heartache, it had also brought her so much more. No, she would not want to change that . . . only to have it go on, with Tyler wanting her as much as she wanted him. But that was not to be. Tyler's love was only a passing thing, or he would be here now, loving her, helping to raise their son, and making her lonely life complete. 'Put it behind you, Beth, once and for all!' she told herself firmly.

'You must let the past go or you'll drive yourself out of your mind.'

So many times she had told herself that, and each time she knew it was an impossible thing to do. It wasn't just Tyler. It was her father, and her brother. It was Esther Ward, the mother who had never really been a mother. There was something in her that made Beth afraid. She had always felt that, although she never knew why. She suspected that something had happened many years ago between her parents, something strange and secretive that had left its mark on them both. There was no way of knowing what. From an early age, Beth had sensed the quiet sadness in her father, and the resentment in her mother. No! More than resentment. What she sensed in her mother was a dreadful loathing. If only Esther had shown her daughter the love she craved, Beth would have returned that love, and things would have been so very different. Whatever it was that had happened between Richard Ward and his wife, it must have been a bad thing because, to Beth's mind, it had brought nothing good. Even the marriage itself was devoid of love. Even as these thoughts careered through Beth's troubled mind, she was forced to compare her own marriage with that of her parents. Wasn't it strange how history seemed to repeat itself?

The clock on the mantelpiece struck the tenth hour. The house was quiet. Beth felt refreshed after her bath, and content in the knowledge that all three children were safe in bed. This was the time she enjoyed most; when she could relax in the cosy drawing room, with its pale green walls and deep floral armchairs, and with the cheery fire-glow sending out waves of warmth that made her deliciously sleepy. It had been a long, tiring day . . . first this big house to be cleaned, then the uphill trek to church and Sunday service; next came the lunch, which took hours to prepare and only minutes to devour; this was followed by the inevitable mountain of washing up. There followed a short time for recreation, which Beth enjoyed with Cissie and Richard; then there was the mending to do, and the tea to prepare; afterwards, there were the children to wash and bed. In spite of it being claimed that Sunday was the Lord's day and therefore a day of rest, all in all it was one of the most tiring days of the week.

Without realising it, Beth's thoughts turned to her husband. She had hardly seen him all day. It crossed her mind that he might well be keeping out of her way after his failure to secure some kind of punishment for Matthew's cruel and unacceptable behaviour earlier in the day. Suddenly, her thoughts materialised as David came into the room, bringing a cold blast of air from the outer hallway.

'Ah! There you are, my dear.' He appeared delighted to see her. Closing the door behind him, he strode into the drawing room, a broad smile on his face as he went straight to where Beth sat. Kissing her tenderly on the forehead, he remarked sharply, 'What with one thing and another, I've seen very little of you today.' Separating the tails of his jacket, he seated himself in the opposite chair, a frown creasing his forehead as he glanced about the room. 'The lamp isn't lit,' he said with surprise. 'Why isn't the lamp lit?' He rose with the intention of going to light the lamp, which was in its usual place in the centre of the table.

'No . . . please. I would rather you didn't,' Beth told him.

'As you wish,' he said, returning to his seat.

Anticipating his question, she added, 'I prefer the firelight.'

For a moment he remained silent, his curious brown eyes quietly appraising her; he thought Beth looked especially lovely tonight. She was wearing a taffeta skirt of burgundy, with a pretty close-fitting cream blouse that complimented her rich chestnut hair and dark eyes. As always, on a Sunday evening after she had bathed, she had left her hair loose. It tumbled over her slim straight shoulders in deep shining waves that reached almost to her waist, and her beautiful, heart-shaped face shone like a child's. 'You look very lovely,' he murmured, his voice husky, his eyes betraying the need inside him.

The compliment might have delighted any other woman, but the whispered words made Beth's heart sink. Tonight she had wanted to be alone with her memories. She raised her head, hoping he might realise how tired she was; her dark eyes were looking into his, exciting him all the more. In the firelight's glow, her eyes appeared uniquely beautiful, shining and alive, possessed of magic. Aware of his thoughts, she quickly looked away.

In a moment, he was beside her, his hands caressing her hair, his body pressing against her, the roughness of his jacket brushing against her face, abrading her skin, the warm smell of cloth invading her nostrils. Now, his hands stroked her neck, fell to her breast and followed the small tight curve there. He was breathing harder, then he was on his knees before her, his open mouth finding her lips, pressing . . . probing. His fingers wrapped themselves round her ankles, sliding upwards, making her skin tingle. Shame swept through her, shame, and disgust . . . and desire. Pulling away, she struggled from the chair, from his searching hands. But he would not be rejected. 'Go to your bed,' he told her. There was anger in his voice, and a love so desperate that it smothered her.

Without a backward look, Beth went from the room, along the softly lit hallway and on to the bedroom which she shared with her husband. She knew he would not be

far behind her. She wished she could take her son and
Maisie's children, and go from this place. A woman
with three children . . . where would they go? How
would they live without money? Oh, she had the bag
of coins beneath the bedroom floorboards, but it was
no fortune, and with four mouths to feed it wouldn't
last very long. She was trapped! Who would offer a
woman and three children a roof over their heads?
She thought of Matthew, of her promise to Maisie.
'Take care of the childer.' Beth was convinced that
Matthew would run away if she took him from this
house, then what would become of him? She thought
of Tyler, and there was bitterness. She remembered
David's kindness, and there was gratitude. He was
her husband . . . for better or worse, he was her husband. And she was a woman. Where was the shame?
There should have been none, but there was. There
was!

She never watched him undress. Somehow, it made
her feel wanton and increased her shame. Every sound,
every movement, told her what he was doing . . . the
shoes placed neatly side by side, the braces flicked down
over his shoulders, the trousers carefully folded and laid
across the back of the wicker chair, his footsteps coming
to her over the creaking floorboards; every sound, every
movement . . . he was touching her now, warm, tickling,
smooth, his naked body moving up and down against
her, his voice in her ear, soft and loving, fingers probing,
his mouth on hers; the gasp of excitement when he
entered her, jabbing, hard, growing excited. 'I love
you,' he murmured. 'Love me Beth . . . love me . . .
love me.' But there was no love in her heart. No love.
Only a loneliness too painful to bear. Tears coursed down
her face, but he did not know. There was much he did
not know.

* * *

'Shh!' The old man slid his gnarled hand over Matthew's face. 'Don't make a sound.' His voice was like grated glass, near and frightening. The warm acrid stench of his breath was unpleasant to the boy. In the flickering candlelight, the withered features took on a grotesque appearance. Trapped beneath the twisted fingers, Matthew wriggled uncomfortably, his brown eyes round and bulbous with fear. 'It's only me . . . Luther,' the voice whispered hoarsely. At once Matthew relaxed, his eyes creasing in a smile as he wondered what the old man was up to. When the fingers drew away, the boy's spittle clung to them, making a delicate spidery line that soon snapped and fell apart. 'Shh! Not a sound,' the old man warned as the boy climbed out of bed and quickly dressed.

Holding the candle before him, Luther led the boy to the far end of the landing, his awkward movements impeding his progress. Intrigued, and a little afraid of the gyrating shadows that loomed like feathery figures on the walls beside them, the boy kept close to the bent figure, curiosity alive in him, and a strange excitement driving him on as it always did when he was with the old man. 'Where are we going?' he asked in a whisper. He had never been this way before.

Occasionally pausing to gather his breath, the old man half-turned and put his finger to his lips, his thick unkempt eyebrows throwing weird shapes over the sockets of his eyes. The gesture was enough. Matthew remained silent, going stealthily after the crooked figure as it squeezed through the tiny opening, then upwards with difficulty, climbing the narrow winding staircase that seemed never-ending. After what seemed an age, they came into a small room where the roof beams straddled above them like great barren trees, and the wind whistled through the tiny cracks where the moonlight shone through.

'Where are we?' The boy dared hardly speak. His every limb was shaking. Suddenly the old man grabbed him and whispered in his ear, 'Shh! Shh! . . . look, there.' He found himself looking towards the floor but could see nothing, and so shook his head. The old man's face wrinkled into a grin. He pointed again, pushing Matthew to the floor. 'Oh!' He could see it now . . . the softest light in the room beneath. Carefully, oh so softly, the old man and the boy folded to their knees.

'It's them . . . mating like dogs.' Luther chuckled, an ugly sound. 'She doesn't like it, though,' he rasped, his rubbery lips touching the boy's ear. Instinctively, the boy pulled away. 'See there.' The words were mouthed; they must not be detected.

Intrigued, Matthew bent nearer to the light, pressing his face to the chink in the floorboards. For a moment he could not see clearly . . . and then he did! Far below, the tiniest candle-flame sending out the smallest light, flickering, subdued. In the bed, there were two figures; the man was paramount, rising and falling, moaning and whispering. Beneath him the woman's face was pale and passive, her arms bent above her head, her rich hair spilling over the pillow. In a moment the man was still. The next moment he was climbing from the bed, the ferocity of his passion still evident on him. The woman turned away. Tears glistened in the flickering light.

'There!' The old man was beside himself with excitement, his hand trembling so that the candlelight danced and spurted like shooting stars. 'Did you see?' he asked in a whisper. 'DID YOU SEE?' He licked his lips, mouth hanging open, trembling. When the boy gave no answer, the old man took him by the arm and propelled him to the far end of the room, down the narrow stairway, through the tiny door and back to the safety of his own bedroom. 'Say nothing!' he warned the boy before leaving. 'Or I'll not take you again.' He smiled, a wicked ugly smile, and then he was gone.

It was a long time before the boy could settle. There was a crippling sense of guilt on him. He had seen things this night that touched him deeply. He had seen two people making love. The experience had shattered him. He had heard the joy of one, and seen the tears of another. It was the tears that haunted him. 'Why did you cry, Beth?' he murmured into the silence. There was no answer. Only a deeper silence that sucked him in. Suddenly he was crying too, deep racking sobs that took him back to a night long ago, soon after his father was killed. He recalled he had suffered a terrible nightmare; so vivid that even when his eyes were open and he was screaming for his mammy, the nightmare would not leave him. Only when Maisie came to hold him and soothe his fears did he feel safe. She said something to him that night . . . something he would remember to his dying day. 'Yer mammy's here, darlin',' she had whispered, 'and yer mammy won't ever let yer cry alone.'

In his despair, Maisie came to him now, that familiar loving face with its bright violet eyes and a profusion of greying hair that was never in place. 'Bless yer heart.' He could hear her voice as though she was here in this room, her own unique aroma all around him. 'There ain't nothing wrong wi' crying, sweetheart, but yer must always share yer troubles wi' them as love yer. Don't cry alone. Don't ever cry alone.' Oh, how he missed her, how he loved her. 'Oh, Mam! Mam!' His own cry opened a door in his heart and the crippling pain spilled out. Long into the night he sobbed, weeping for what he had lost, and for what he had become.

When morning dawned he knew he would never again follow the old man up to that room. He would get himself a job, and he would be the man his mammy had always hoped he would be. But he did not belong here, in this house. Right now he had no idea what would become of him, yet this much he did know – there was a sense of peace in his heart at last, and the bitter core of hatred had melted with his tears.

All the same, there was still a hardness in him towards Beth. Much as he wanted to, and much as he had been moved by her tears, he could not find it in him to forgive her. Deep down, he still blamed her for taking his mammy from him. The bitterness was still there. He believed it always would be. But not the badness, not any more. Not now his mammy had spoken to him.

Chapter Eight

On 14 July 1892, Maisie's son boarded a merchant ship and sailed away from his homeland. The sun was shining, and the docks at Liverpool were thronged with people. People laughing, people crying, some boarding vessels, others disembarking, and others waving good-bye to their loved ones. In the distance, a band was playing, though the music was drowned by the lusty yells of porters and traders all plying for business.

Beth stood alone, a quiet solitary figure, heavy with child, biding her time until she might be called to say goodbye. Just as she had predicted, Matthew had become a fine young man, tall and strong, and markedly handsome, with his wayward mop of brown hair and those dark violet eyes that still held a world of bitterness whenever they looked on her. As she gazed intently towards the small group that was her family, a great sadness filled Beth's heart. In these past two years and more, since Matthew had been employed with David, distancing himself from the old man and returning to the family fold, Beth had never stopped hoping that one day he might turn to her with affection. But she had hoped for too much, and Matthew remained unforgiving, not actively unfriendly towards her but always out of her reach. It was a sorry thing, and one which caused her a few silent tears.

But for all that, Beth was delighted at the way he had come to share the love of his sister, Cissie, and her own son, Richard. His relationship with David also was a good one, in which he benefited from the older man's advice and experience. When he expressed his desire to go to sea, David had attempted to dissuade him, saying, 'It's a hard life, Matthew. Much more demanding than overseeing a terrace of houses and collecting rents.' He spelled out the dangers without being too alarmist, but it only served to make Matthew more determined to become a sailor. Eventually, it was David who found him a good ship and carefully guided him through the process. Now the day had arrived, and it was time for Matthew to say goodbye.

Beth never took her eyes off the little group; Cissie, who was now a young lady of exceptional prettiness and who was hugging her brother for the umpteenth time; and Beth's own son Richard . . . now six years old and growing more like Tyler every day; and David, a quiet man, a man who was too gentle, a man still dominated by the monster who had raised him. In different ways she loved them all; even her weak-natured husband, who showered all of them with affection, and who was filled with excitement that, at long last, he was about to become a father in his own right.

Beth looked forward to the birth of their child; with Richard growing so fast, she missed that special feeling of holding a small warm being in her arms. She would not claim to be content, because contentment came with having the man you loved lying beside you on a cold night; it came with that certain wonderful intimacy which Beth had experienced once long ago, and which was lost for ever. Contentment came when your life was fulfilled, which hers was not. But she had found a deal of happiness in her family. If she had had it in her power to change anything in that one moment, it would be for Matthew to come to her as a friend. She was both proud and fearful for him and, as she continued to look on him, thought of the vast and mighty oceans he would cross, the loneliness of such journeys, and prayed he would not regret his decision to leave them.

'Mammy! Mammy!' Richard was running towards her, dodging between the legs of many passing travellers, a broad grin lighting his face and an air of excitement about him. In a moment he had gripped her hand in his and was pulling her away from the bale on which she had been resting. 'Come and say goodbye,' he urged, tugging at her with all his might. 'David says you're to come and say goodbye to Matthew.' In his enthusiasm he lost his cap and when Beth stooped with difficulty to retrieve it, she almost lost her balance as he insisted on pulling her forward. 'Quick, Mammy . . . quick!' he cried. And so Beth allowed herself to be taken at an awkward pace along the wharf and on to where David and Cissie were saying their final farewells.

Unfortunately, when Beth was only a few feet away, Matthew raised his head and his eyes met hers. He appeared sad for a moment, but then his neck stiffened and his eyes grew harder. Beth sensed the hostility, and instinctively paused. At once, Matthew swung away and was quickly gone from sight, leaving Cissie chasing down the wharf to catch one final glimpse of her brother. 'Oh! He's gone, Mammy. Matthew's gone.' Richard was crying now, pressing his face into the deep folds of her skirt. Beth was crying too, crying inside, and she wondered whether she would ever again see the young man who had been left in her care. 'God go with you, son,' she murmured. 'We'll always love you.' The tears threatened, but she fought them back. This was not a time for tears. It was a time for thanking God that Matthew had turned his back on the badness that might have dragged him down. Besides that small miracle, her own regret at having lost him seemed very small.

'Well, the lad's away,' David emerged through the

crowd to tell her. 'All we can do is hope he'll be safe. I would rather he'd stayed at home with us, but it was his choice, and he's not a child any longer.' Cupping his hand beneath Beth's elbow, he looked deep into her eyes and said in a quieter voice, 'Don't feel bad. I'm sure he'll turn to you, in his own good time.'

'I hope so,' she murmured. 'Oh, I do hope so.' One last lingering look at the place where she had last seen him, but he was gone from sight, gone from her now. Turning away, she smiled when Cissie began softly singing, and her heart was filled with joy that at least she still had her and Richard. Strange, though, how it was Tyler and not David who was uppermost in her thoughts in that moment. But then, he was always with her. He was with her now . . . skipping along beside her, holding her hand, laughing and chattering, smiling at her with those winsome green eyes. In Richard, she had the very essence of his father. That was a blessing she gave thanks for every moment of every day. There were many regrets in her life, but her beloved son was not one of them. 'Let's go home,' she said, returning the boy's loving smile. 'I think you've had enough excitement for one day.'

'Oh! Can't we stay and watch the ships, Mammy?'

'Now, Richard, you heard what your mammy said,' David reminded the boy quietly. 'It's time we all went home.'

It was Cissie's turn to persuade him. 'I'll read you a story if you like,' she said, mischievously flicking at his cap. 'That is . . . if you can catch me!' Laughing aloud, she took to her heels, and made for the outer doors. Screaming for her to stop, the boy went after her, his short sturdy legs quickly gaining ground; but that was exactly what Cissie had planned. When she allowed him to 'catch' her, the two of them rolled about on a pile of hessian rope, screeching and laughing, until

David reminded Cissie that she was 'a young lady of certain years' and that Richard should remember how he had only been allowed to come to the docks on the understanding that he be on his 'best behaviour'. And, such was their remorse, the two of them were instantly subdued. When David led the little group out onto the street, where he quickly hailed a Hansom cab, Cissie had linked arms with Beth, and was walking tall and proud like a 'young lady' should. Richard was holding Beth's other hand, but he was not so composed because everything around him was too exciting for a boy of such tender years, and so he skipped, and laughed, and sang, and teased Cissie about her 'po-face'. And Beth walked between them, a smile in her heart, and a twinkle in her eyes.

From a distance, the tall dark-haired man watched with disbelief, his handsome green eyes following Beth's every step. In that first heart-stopping moment when he realised that it really was her, his impulse had been to run to her, to grab her in his arms and smother her with kisses, to chide her for not waiting until he came back to make her his wife. He wanted to tell her he had never stopped loving her, that never a single day had passed without him thinking of her, wanting her in his arms or by his side, sharing the success which life had bestowed on him. 'Beth . . . oh, Beth.' He shook his head slowly from side to side. Reproach mingled with anger – anger that she did not wait, anger that another man should so easily have taken the woman he loved, anger that she should be heavy with another man's child. According to Ben, she had waited for him and he had failed her; never mind that the real fault was not his, or that he had lain at death's door, or that he had been loath to go to her as a cripple, with nothing to offer but a life of struggle. The fact remained that he had waited too long. Like a fool, he had wanted to return for Beth, carrying the world to place at her feet. Now, he had the world, but it was a lonely, loveless place without her. In the pursuit of his fortune, he had deliberately travelled many long and distant journeys, always seeking to escape from memories of Beth and their time together. He had quickly learned that it was a futile exercise, for she was with him wherever he went.

He looked at her now, thinking that time had made her more beautiful. Even though her hitherto slim figure was heavy with child, there was a beauty about her, a certain dignity, that made him proud. Dressed in a gown of deepest blue that complemented her dark eyes and rich hair, she was the loveliest creature he had ever seen. Tearing away his gaze, he studied the children at her side. He wondered about the pretty fair-haired girl – a relative of Beth's husband, perhaps? Certainly she was too old to be Beth's daughter, although it was obvious that the girl had a great affection for her. The boy, though . . . five, six years old? A handsome little fellow and filled with mischief as boys should be; no doubt this was Beth's son, and, taking into account the years between, no doubt begot in the early weeks of Beth's marriage. He could see the man now, striding ahead of his family, a tall fellow in a black tail-coat, sombre trousers and high grey hat. It was impossible to see his face, but Tyler assumed the man to be Beth's husband, Wilson Ryan, who according to Ben was a man of considerable reputation in the millinery world, not without fortune, and most certainly the ideal partner for Beth.

Tyler Blacklock had little interest in the millinery world, for he hardly ever wore a hat and so did not move in such circles; neither had he made enquiries with regard to Beth or her husband. As he had told

Ben: 'I'm glad she's happy.' And he was. He never sought to discuss her. It would have been too painful. He wondered in passing what Mr Ryan might be doing so far north; perhaps seeking to expand his chain of hat shops? After all, wasn't that the very reason why Tyler himself was here . . . to expand his own business by bidding for a valuable piece of land which was shortly being offered here in Liverpool?

His curiosity was short-lived, for he could think only of Beth. If only . . . if only. No! Beth was content with her family. Nowadays, she probably never even gave him a second thought. Yet he could not forget her. God only knew how he had tried to replace her in his thoughts and in his heart – striking relationships with one woman after another, lurching from one crisis to the next, building his business with her in mind . . . driving himself like a man demented and amassing a fortune, yet knowing all the time that he was striving for the impossible. However many women he took to himself, they were not Beth. Not his true love. And yet, he could not accept that he would never again hold her in his arms. But he must accept it! He must! But then if he did, what was there worth living for? Without Beth, there was no purpose.

And so he went from day to day, from one business deal to the next, pouring his heart and soul into his land agency business, trying to forget, always trying to forget, but being made to remember all the more. And now here she was, and he was all at odds, wanting to go to her, knowing he could not. Like a phantom she moved in his sight, lovely and compelling, her dark beauty drawing him against his will, his thoughts calling out to her.

In that moment Beth turned and looked into his face. It was like a hammer to his heart, seeing her dark eyes widen with surprise, her hand spread across her mouth as though to stifle a cry. He stepped forward, but then his companion returned, smiling up at him, taking his arm possessively and wanting to leave. Afraid and thrown in turmoil he allowed himself to be drawn away, but he could not push that lovely face from his thoughts. In his shocked heart, Beth went with him, her dark eyes burning into his, astonished at first, then intensely accusing. Over and over he told himself: 'You failed her, and she hates you for it. Now, there is no place in her life for you.'

'What's the matter, Beth?' Cissie had been stripping the excess leaves from the stems of a bunch of slender white tulips, which she then lovingly arranged one by one in an earthenware vase. For some minutes now she had been disturbed by the way Beth was pacing to and fro in front of the great fireplace, a deeply thoughtful expression on her face, and her whole manner one of extreme agitation. 'Is it the babby?' Cissie asked now. 'Is the little tyke up to its tricks again?' She knew Beth had suffered many sleepless nights of late, because she herself had been kept awake into the small hours, thinking of Matthew and wondering how he was faring.

'No. The child is quiet,' Beth told her.

'Then is it Matthew?' Cissie wanted to know. 'You've been restless since that day at the docks, when we saw him off.'

Beth shook her head. 'No, it isn't Matthew, although I pray he made the right decision.' All the same, Cissie was right in one assumption: Beth's peace of mind had been shattered on that particular day. All these years, she had carried Tyler's image in her heart, and suddenly there he was, looking at her, startling her, his gaze finding its way into that secret part of her that she had always kept hidden. If she had entertained any doubts before, they had gone for ever. *She still loved him*. In spite of the fact that he had let her down badly and – most devastating of all, even though he now had a new love – Beth still pined for him. Since that day she had not been able to sleep, or to think straight. Of all the people in the world she least wanted to see, yet most wanted to see, Tyler had walked back into her life to turn it upside down. Their eyes had met for only the briefest moment, but it had seemed like a lifetime. She wanted to hate him, but she couldn't. She wanted to go to him, but she couldn't.

For all her life, Beth would cherish the time they had had together, and she would always regret their parting, and yet, and yet, he was a scoundrel of the worst kind. Time and again she told herself she was fortunate to see the back of him, so often she reminded herself of the despicable way he had behaved. It didn't matter. Oh, she knew well enough that if he were to walk through that door now, she would not entertain him; her pride would not let her. But secretly she would go on loving him. She could never change her deeper feelings because he was still a part of her growing up, part of her life, her first awakening of passion. Nothing could take that from her, and so she clung to the memories. Fate had parted them for ever, but she would never know any other man in the way she had known Tyler. He was her first love. And he would be her last.

'If it ain't the babby, and it ain't Matthew, what else is troubling you?' Cissie laid the flowers on the rug and came to stand before Beth, her pretty face frowning. 'Something's bothering you, I know,' she said quietly. 'Won't you tell me, Beth? Won't you let me help?' When she saw the pain in the dark eyes, she went on, 'Please, I ain't a child no more.'

'Oh, Cissie . . . Cissie, what a comfort you are to me.' Reaching out her arms, Beth enfolded the girl to her, resting her face against Cissie's fair hair and saying in a softer voice, 'Do you remember years ago when you asked about my family?'

'Yes, I remember . . . when I said you never talked about your parents, and you told me that one day you would tell me all about them. Only you never did.' She was astonished to see the tears flowing down Beth's face. 'Oh, it's your family, ain't it?' she cried. 'Some'at's happened to make you feel bad.'

Choking back the tears, Beth forced a small laugh. 'No, it isn't my family, bless you,' she said, adding thoughtfully, 'although . . . in a way, I suppose, it is.' She took a deep breath, her mind assailed with doubts. She wanted so much to confide in Cissie, to share her secret, and after all Cissie was right in saying she was no longer a child. She was turned fifteen now, and had a wise old head on her shoulders; in many ways, the girl reminded Beth of Maisie; like two peas from the same pod they were. Beth did not fool herself that it would be an easy thing to talk about what she had kept hidden all these years, but somehow she felt it would be a natural thing for her to confide in Cissie.

'Come and sit here with me.' Beth moved towards the settee, the girl followed. When the two of them were seated, Beth told her, 'You're so special to me, Cissie. You're very perceptive, because there *are* things playing on my mind, and yes . . . it would help me so much if I could talk them over with someone. I've never been one for making friends, you know that. I was always a solitary child, and my making friends was frowned upon.' She smiled. 'It's hard to escape from the teachings of your childhood.'

'Were you not happy as a child, Beth?' Cissie thought of her own happy childhood. She had come to forget the horror of a certain night, and all her memories were pleasant now.

'No, Cissie, I was never happy as a child.'

'Will you tell me about it?'

Again Beth hesitated, thinking it wrong that she should use this lovely girl in order to lessen her own burden. Suddenly the decision was taken out of her hands when the door was flung open and there was David, grey-faced and tired, his sleeves rolled up and his hair dishevelled. Whenever he buried himself in the ledgers and account books, he lost all sense of time. Often he would go hours without food, keeping the study door locked against all intruders, and invariably emerging dog-weary and irritable. Today was Monday and, as always on a Monday evening, he was kept busy balancing the books from the rent collection on Friday; already, he had spent most of the day closeted in the study with his stepfather. Looking at him now, Beth could tell that something was wrong. 'What is it?' she asked. 'Is everything all right?'

'Of course it is,' he replied tersely. 'Is there any reason why it shouldn't be?'

'Well, no.' The private moment between herself and Cissie was lost. 'I made a fish pie. Enough for you and your stepfather,' she told him. Beth still saw it as her duty to provide for the old man, though he rarely ate anything she prepared. 'I'll arrange a tray,' she said, rising from the settee. When David had gone into consultation with the old man earlier, she had been instructed not to disturb them. She had learned from experience that it was unwise to argue.

'No food,' he told her, 'just a pot of tea. And a jug of cider for my stepfather.' He glanced at Cissie. 'No doubt you'll bring it in,' he said. 'Beth should stay off her feet wherever possible.' His gaze roved round the room. 'The boy?'

'I put him to bed half an hour ago,' Beth explained.

He nodded, his expression still serious. 'The tea,

Cissie,' he reminded the girl. 'And a jug of cider . . . *now*, if you please.' Without another word, he departed the room and returned to the study where Luther was waiting for him.

'Hmh! What's the matter with *him*?' Cissie asked, staring at Beth with a puzzled look. 'He's got a face like a fish on a slab.'

'That'll do, Cissie,' Beth gently chastised. 'Do as you're asked, there's a good girl.'

'Then we can talk?'

'I don't think so.' Beth was oddly relieved that she had not confided in Cissie; not that she didn't trust the girl, but because she had never spoken to anyone about her family, or her reason for leaving them all those years ago. Before she and David were married, Beth had secured his promise that he would never probe into her past, and would not pester her with regard to young Richard's father. He had kept his word – although she knew there had been times when he was sorely tempted to ask her the questions that must have played on his mind. To discuss these things now, with Cissie, seemed in Beth's view to be wrong. She was not proud to have been the cause of splitting her family up; nor could she forget how her father's love had turned to disgust; and how could she easily reveal the shame which she had brought down on the Wards? How could she possibly expect a girl of Cissie's years to understand how a woman could love so deeply that there seemed no shame in it at all? Maisie had asked her to 'look after the childer', and that must be her main concern. Her own sordid story could only be a bad influence on such a young and impressionable mind. Beth knew how Maisie had believed her to be a widow. That impression was passed on to the children, and then to David. Beth never denied it. She thought it best to let well alone. David was a man of high principles, and if he suspected the truth, that she had conceived her son out of wedlock, well . . . it didn't bear thinking about. 'When you've taken the tray, Cissie, I think you had better finish your flower-arranging, then get yourself ready for bed.'

'But it's only eight o'clock!' Cissie was pouring the cider from the larger jug into the smaller one. As she turned, surprised and disappointed at Beth's instructions, the cider spilled over. With a moan, she replaced the jug and mopped up the mess.

'You know how long it takes you to wash and get yourself into bed,' Beth reminded her. 'And don't forget you have a busy time ahead of you tomorrow. Isn't it Preston market-day?'

Beth held the door open while Cissie manoeuvred her way through it with the wooden tray. She was not surprised when the girl turned to her with the dark remark, 'I wish he hadn't come in just then.' Beth remained silent. Contrary to Cissie's opinion, she herself was glad that David had stopped her from opening her heart to this impressionable young girl.

'You're a good friend,' Beth murmured.

'And do you promise that if you need a shoulder to cry on, you'll come to me first?'

Laughing softly, Beth gave her a gentle push. 'Promise,' she said, adding with more urgency, 'Get that tray along to the study, or there'll be murder to pay.'

'I'm no thief, damn you!'

The voice echoed through the house, waking everyone from their slumbers, and shocking Beth to her roots. In the six years and more that she had been David's wife, not once had she heard his voice raised in such dark anger.

'Mammy! Mammy!' The boy's frantic call spurred her on. Clambering out of bed, she grabbed her robe, wrapping it round her swollen form as she went in haste along the landing towards her son's room, calling to him, 'It's all right, sweetheart. Mammy's here.'

In a matter of minutes, she had gathered the frightened child in her arms, soothing him, lulling him back to sleep. But then the uproar began again, this time the voice of the old man. *'You're a liar! A bloody liar. What kind of man are you, to steal from the hand that fed you all these years?'*

The boy was past sleep now, his trembling form clinging to Beth and his green eyes wide with fear. When Cissie appeared at the door, Beth held out her arms and the girl fell into them, and there the three of them remained huddled while the unholy row raged below.

David's face was drained white. He had never before been accused of stealing and it did not sit well with him. His brown eyes dark with anger, he stared the old man out.

'In all the years you've known me, I've never taken what wasn't mine,' he said in a hard voice. 'Since I was old enough to carry a money-bag, I've trudged round the streets, knocking on every door of every property you own . . . aye, and sometimes I've had a fist in my face for the trouble, but never once have I let you down. Never once have I dipped a finger into that money-bag, however fat it bulged and however heavy it weighed; it was always brought straight home to you . . . every farthing that crossed my palm.' He gasped as though someone had stabbed him through the heart. 'And now you say I've thieved from you? Never! Not while there's a breath left in my body would I steal from anyone . . . let alone my own father. . .'

He stopped when he saw the twisted grin on Luther's face, and it made him remember with a falling heart that this man was not his real father. Suddenly all the anger emptied from him, and in its place there was anguish. He shook his head and continued to stare at the old man, but there was pleading in his voice now. 'You know I would not steal from you,' he said quietly.

The old man was breathing hard, his pig-like eyes fixed on the other man's face. He hated him. Oh, how he hated him! At the same time, he needed him. 'All I know is, there's money missing!' he growled. 'And if you ain't got it, then who the bloody hell has? Answer me that, go on! There's four guineas missing here.' He gestured towards the numerous piles of shiny coins spread out before him. 'Four guineas, I tell you, and you don't leave this room until they're accounted for.'

He leaned forward and crooked his bony arms round the neat piles of money, protecting it, coveting it, his eyes fixed on his stepson's face. He made a strange sound, like that of a wounded animal, dropping his face into the money and swivelling his eyes upwards. 'You're robbing me,' he accused in a pitiful voice, 'robbing a helpless old man of his livelihood.'

'No!' David took a step forward, stretching out his hand as though he might touch the old man, but a hard forbidding glare stopped him in his tracks. Taking the ledger from under his arm, he opened it at the relevant page and slid it on to the desk. 'I swear to God . . . I checked every coin. There's no mistake, see for yourself.' Grabbing the pile of cloth money-bags from the corner of the desk, he turned them upside down one by one. 'Examine the ledger again,' he begged. 'It's all there, I tell you.'

Luther waved his arm impatiently. 'Get out,' he said. 'Not satisfied with stealing my money, you're trying to tell me I'm senile into the bargain, is that it?' He cocked his head to one side as if he had just realised something awful. 'You want me put away, so you can take everything!' His back stiffened and he swept the money towards his chest. 'You and that wife o' yourn

. . . you want me put away. You want to finish me off. That's why you took the boy away from me . . . sent him away to sea.'

'Now you're imagining things.' David's anger was returning. 'Matthew went to sea of his own accord. As for putting you away, nothing could be further from my mind, Father. Even if I didn't love you as I do, I know my duty. As long as I live, I'll take care of you, you can be sure of that.'

'Fine words, easy said. I've no doubt you'll "take care of me" . . . and I know why, you canny bastard!' Luther laughed without opening his mouth, making a deep rattling sound that was frightening to hear. 'You'll "take care of me" because you see yourself as getting it all when I breathe me last, don't you, eh? Well, you're a bigger fool than I took you for.' He paused, enjoying the confusion on the younger man's face. Suddenly his withered features crumpled into a surprising smile. What he said was even more surprising. 'In all truth, I can't see that you'd steal from me,' he muttered cautiously, smiling deeper when the other man visibly relaxed. 'Mebbe you lost the money,' he said, 'but no matter. It's only four guineas. I'll stop it from your wages at the end of the month.' It pleased him to see the shock his words delivered, and before David could protest, he lied, 'You've been a help to me since my old bones went crook, and I'll see you get your dues when the time comes. But there's something else playing on my mind at the minute.' He sat back in the chair. 'You know the land that's coming up for auction?'

'You mean Tobias Drew's properties?' The old man had pointed the article out to him some time ago, but David had thought it unwise to consider such a large project.

'I intend to bid.'

'You know my thoughts on that, Father. You've

already built your holdings up to over a hundred houses, plus some useful parcels of land. I'm worried that you're taking on too much.'

'Oh, aye? Concerned for my health, are you? Or is it that you're worried about having to work a bit harder for the grand wages I give you . . . wages that's been strangled out of me by that bloody woman o' yours?'

'That's uncalled for. I won't deny I find it harder to keep pace, what with collecting the rents, keeping the books ready for the accountant, and overseeing the more recent purchases, like the six acres of land in Accrington which we're negotiating to sell on. Then there's the matter of Larkhill, and the houses that were made derelict by that tragic fire.'

'Bugger Larkhill! If it weren't for that bloody fire, you'd never 'a' brought that damned woman and her brats to this house.' Sensing he was going too far, the old man was more cautious. 'Water under the bridge,' · he mumbled. 'As for Larkhill, I don't want to know. I've told you . . . that's *your* responsibility. I'm sick to death of the worry it's brought, what with the leaseowners demanding money from me, when I've no bloody rents to collect there . . . I don't know which way to turn. They want to finish me, that's what it is! The buggers want to see me go under. I've asked 'em to sell me the land so I can develop it but they won't see sense. They're keeping me to the contract . . . wanting their pound o' flesh. I tell you it's an impossible situation! The agent knows you've got full authority as far as Larkhill's concerned. Do what the hell you like with it, only I don't want it being a bloody millstone round *my* neck. The authorities are already threatening me with letters claiming the derelict houses are a public danger.'

Unlike his stepson, who favoured building houses for sale or rent, Luther Reynolds was a cold and calculating thinker, a man who thought with his emotions; a legacy, no doubt, of being starved of love for so many years.

Much later, when the children were asleep and the house was quiet once more, Beth lay in bed beside her husband. His head was lying in the crook of her arm and the flat of his hand was spread over the bulge of her stomach. On coming upstairs, he had turned to her for comfort, desperate to make love, needing to feel the growing swell of her body that was his own flesh and blood and, as always, he was moved to tears by it. He was quiet now, his physical needs satisfied, and the hurt cried out of him.

Beth lay very still. Her arm was aching from his weight, and her body was sore from his eager love-making. Inside her, there was a small life forming, something precious and wonderful; but there was also a deadness in her, weighing her down like a physical burden, a burden that grew harder to bear with every passing day.

The house was so quiet. So deathly quiet, the eerie stillness broken only by the gentle snoring of the man beside her. She turned towards the window. The curtains were partly open, allowing the merest glimmer of moonlight to creep in. Her thoughts began to wander. Somewhere out there, in a room perhaps much like this one, Tyler was with his woman. His image rose in her mind now. The years had not changed him too much; he was still as she remembered, the same virile, darkly handsome man who had won her heart, held her as close as any man could hold a woman. As close as he was now holding the other woman . . . *the other woman*. Her lips formed the words, a small cry. 'Oh, Tyler.' Torturing herself, she pictured him now, him and the other woman, lying in a bed much the same as the one she herself was lying in . . . making love.

He whispering endearments in his lover's ear, the joy of lying in each other's arms . . . the ecstasy afterwards, the contentment of just being together.

Beth remembered it all as though it was only yesterday; it was etched on her mind and in her heart for all time. She wondered if he ever thought of her. She was curious as to how he felt when he saw her at the docks the other day. He must have noticed that she was with child. Was he just the slightest bit jealous? Maybe he was riven with guilt? Did he think her attractive still? Was there even the slightest echo of the love they had known? But, no, of course not! How could there be?

Turning from the window, she gazed on the face of her husband, a kind face and not unattractive, with its straight features and good skin, and the unruly mop of hair that tumbled over his forehead; he stirred in her arms, whimpering like a child, and pressing himself against her. Suddenly, the very touch of him was obnoxious to her.

Sliding her arm from beneath him, Beth got out of bed and, wrapping her robe about her shivering form, went first to the window, where she looked out at the moonlit night. Then, not wanting to return to bed, she made herself comfortable in the wicker armchair, her eyes gazing on her husband's sleeping face. 'How like a child you are,' she murmured, unable to quell the feeling of disgust that he sometimes wrought in her. His needs were insatiable. Yet she had needs too. Needs he could never understand. She did not want a *child* to walk through life beside her. She needed someone strong of heart, someone to talk with, to make plans with, someone who made her laugh, who understood her in the way a man understands a woman. David could never do those things. He would not know how to.

From somewhere in the lower regions of the house, laughter told Beth that Luther Reynolds was still awake.

The thought made her shiver deep within herself. Glancing once more at the figure in the bed, she could not bear the thought of climbing in beside it. Instead, she curled deeper into the chair, closed her eyes and was soon asleep.

Downstairs, the old man gathered together the piles of coins and laid them in the tin chest. He then placed the ledger on top, and locked the articles into the sturdy cupboard beside the chimney breast. Afterwards, he returned to the desk, where he opened one of the smaller drawers, and from it counted out a number of shiny coins . . . totalling four guineas in all. Chuckling wickedly, he thrust them into his waistcoat pocket, collected the lamp from the desk top, and quietly departed the room. 'I'll go to Liverpool,' he whispered as he hobbled up the stairs, 'and I shall outbid all of them.' His face was a study in cunning as he told the paintings of his ancestors, 'It's all for him . . . all for my son Arnold Thomas.' He chuckled again. 'The bugger said I'd never make a businessman. Well now, Arnold Thomas will eat his harsh words when he's living in the lap o' luxury.'

A small sound caused him to turn his head 'What's that?' he said into the darkness. It was only the night, the sound of an old house creaking, and the dark deceit in his own cold heart. Unnerved, he pushed forward. His voice was the merest whisper as he stared down the landing towards a particular door, his mind imagining the two people behind it; two people he resented beyond words.

'Sleep in a warm bed while you can, because you'll be in the gutter soon enough, the lot of you.' He chuckled as he went on his way. 'Wherever you are, son, your old father means to find you, to put things right between us before his old bones is laid into the ground,' he muttered. 'I still ain't forgiven you for what you said, but when all's said and done, blood's thicker than water.'

Discounting all the years during which his stepson had sacrificed a life of his own to follow an old man's dictates, he pressed on to his bed. 'There's much to be done,' he mumbled to himself. 'Much to be done.'

Two weeks later, on the morning of the auction, a determined knock on the door sent Cissie flying headlong down the hallway from the kitchen, with Beth in close pursuit; young Richard was already upstairs with his newly appointed day-tutor, and David was closeted in the den with Luther, going over the final details for the auction.

'It's two men,' Cissie whispered, peering through the keyhole, her blue eyes squinting into the daylight and a look of mischief on her pretty face. Much to Beth's disapproval, Cissie had lately taken to observing visitors through the narrow chink, seeming to derive great pleasure from the knowledge that they could not see her. She began giggling. 'Rough-looking blighters, they are,' she told Beth who was now alongside her.

'Come away from there!' Beth chided, tugging at the girl's smock and edging her away. But then she opened the door and was ready to agree with Cissie; the visitors really were 'rough-looking blighters'.

'Top o' the morning to yer,' said the older one, grabbing his tatty beret off his black unruly mop of hair. 'Would there be a Miss Elizabeth at this 'ere address?'

'Yes,' Beth replied in a curious voice. 'There would.'

'And is that yourself?'

'It is.'

The fellow smiled a broad toothless smile, looking from Beth to his companion, then back again. 'Ah, well.' He dug deep into his jacket pocket, the grin fixed on his face and his bloodshot eyes regarding Beth with interest; at length he drew a mangled envelope from his pocket and, flourishing it grandly, explained, 'This 'ere's from a lad we come across in a foreign port.' He made a loud noise through his cavernous nostrils. 'The lad asked a favour of an old shipmate, and being as he was most polite, how could that shipmate refuse, I ask you? How could he refuse, eh?' He glanced at his young companion; a thin scrag of a man, with a long thin nose and small sunken eyes.

'Well, you *couldn't* refuse, matey,' this companion acknowledged. 'Not seeing as how politely the young feller asked an' all.' He smiled at the other man, then smiled at Beth, then at Cissie who, struck with horror at the thin man's strikingly unpleasant face, pressed herself closer to Beth.

'Accept the letter then, Miss,' the older man insisted, holding it out for Beth to take. 'The lad said you might be glad of word as to his daring adventures. A nice enough lad . . . Matthew. Aye, that were it . . . the lad's name were Matthew.'

'Matthew!' Cissie had only now realised that these two merchantmen had brought news of her brother. 'Oh, Beth. It's a letter from Matthew!' In her great excitement she thrust herself forward and grabbed the older man by the hand, which she shook up and down, crying, 'God bless you, sir. God bless the pair on you.'

'Well, I'm buggered!' said the scraggy one. 'Whoever woulda thought a lad could leave such a pretty little gal to go off on some faraway adventure, eh?' He glanced at his mate, then feasted his eyes on Cissie once more.

'Thank you both,' Beth told them, at the same time stepping between the men and Cissie; she did not like the way the younger man was regarding the girl. Reaching into her skirt pocket, she brought out a silver shilling which she placed into the older man's hand. 'Please divide that between you,' she said. 'And I really am most grateful for your errand.'

Knowing when he was dismissed, the older sailor turned to leave, taking the other fellow with him. Ramming the cap back on his head, he nodded. 'Good day to yer, Miss.'

'One thing.' Beth hesitated to keep them lingering, but she had to ask, 'The boy . . . Is he well?'

The sailor chuckled. 'First of all, the "boy" ain't such a "boy" no longer . . . life on board a ship in the middle o' the ocean ain't for no boy.' He displayed his empty grin once more. 'I reckon you'll find this 'ere boy will come back a man. And, yes . . .' He fidgeted and gave a sideways look to his mate '. . . yer could say as 'e were well. Aye, yer could say 'e were well enough.' With that, he swung away and strode quickly out of sight, the thin fellow hurrying beside him. Once away from Beth's searching dark eyes, he turned to his mate and said, 'That boy does have the makings of a man, it's true. But, like a man, he'll need to learn that yer don't break yer heart over them as you've left behind, 'cause yer tied to your ship fer as long as the cap'n says so. And yer learn ter keep the tears inside. That way, yer fellow shipmates don't take the tar outta yer, and make yer life one long misery.' He shook his head forlornly. 'Oh, aye . . . the lad has the makings of a man. But he's still a long way to go, poor little sod. But then, we all 'ave to learn the hard way, more's the pity.' He grinned, 'Still, we managed to keep all that to us selves, didn't we, matey?'

'We did right, I reckon, 'cause there ain't no sense in causing upset, that's what I say.'

'What does it say?' Cissie was impatient to know the contents of the letter. She was on Beth's heels all the way back to the drawing room, and now, when Beth was seated in the big armchair and eagerly slitting open the envelope with the tortoise-shell letter-knife, Cissie was kneeling on the floor beside her. 'Go on,' she was urging. 'Read it. Tell me what it says!'

Unfolding the letter, Beth swiftly ran her dark eyes over it. Satisfied that it contained nothing which might distress the girl, she read aloud:

Hello, Beth

I thote you and Cissie, and everywun there, wuld like to know how I wus geting on. Well, I'm on bord ship just now, and I'm keping watch with an old hand by the name of Mr Margetson. He's a gud frend to me and the uther yung fellers. I'm wurkin hard and lurning to be a sailor, so you can be prowd of me.

I don't know wen I'll see you agen, but I'm sorry for the things I did, and I'm ashamd. Tell Cissie I luv her, and Richard. David is a gud man.

God bles all of you,
Matthew

When Beth finished reading, she sat still and silent for a moment, her heart aching, and her mind alive with memories of her old friend. She prayed that Maisie could somehow see how well her boy had done for himself, and how he had come to regret the hatred that almost destroyed him. When she raised her head, there were tears in her dark eyes; Cissie's eyes, too, were bright and full. The letter had subdued them both. Without speaking, she crooked her hand round the back of Cissie's head, pulling her close until the girl's head nestled in the dip of Beth's shoulder. 'Oh, Cissie,' she murmured, 'aren't you just so proud of your brother?'

'I wish he'd come home,' Cissie replied with a small sigh. Then, raising her head slightly, she placed the flat of her hand against the round bulge beneath Beth's blue gown. 'Do you think our Matthew'll be home afore the babby comes?'

'It all depends how far away he is,' Beth explained. 'It may be impossible for him to get home in just a few months.'

'That sailor said Matthew would come home a man. We won't know him, will we, Beth?'

'Of course we'll know him.' She laughed softly. 'Don't forget, we all change. Every day we change a little, but you wouldn't expect Matthew not to know *us*, would you, eh?'

Cissie shook her head. 'All the same, I wish he'd come home,' she insisted. 'The sea makes me frightened.' She recalled the docks, and the way the sea screamed and wailed like a soul in torment, throwing itself against the piers with a wild vengeance that struck terror into her young heart. 'It's like a real person,' she said, 'it gets angry, and it drowns people.'

'That's a fine way to talk, Cissie Armstrong!' Beth told her in a reproachful voice. 'Matthew's gone to be a sailor. Sailors know all there is to know about the sea.' She held the girl at arm's length. 'Are you saying Matthew won't make a fine sailor?'

Beth's ploy worked. At once, Cissie was indignant. 'Our Matthew'll make the best sailor there ever was!' she declared. Now, when Beth smiled knowingly, the girl saw how she had been manipulated, and soon the two of them were laughing.

Luther did not laugh, though. When David proudly took the letter to him, he scanned it and threw it aside. 'The young bastard!' he hissed. 'Not one word for old Luther who took him in! Never a mention of the one who spent many an hour teaching him the way of things. Ungrateful bugger! Serves him right if the sea rises up and drowns him!'

No sooner were the words out of his mouth than he glanced anxiously about, his unattractive features relaxing when he saw that his words had fallen only on his stepson's ears. If 'that bloody woman' had heard him utter such a curse, she would have ripped into him with a piece of her mind, then he would have whipped her with his tongue, then this sop of a man before him would have got between them, and afore you knew it, there would be a full-scale war waging – and in the heat of the moment he might foolishly betray his devious plans to boot the lot of them out of his house and out of his life. And that would be soon as ever he had his own son safely established back under this roof, where he should have been all along! For the moment, he was canny enough to see the wisdom of keeping his stepson sweet, and that would not be achieved by stirring up a hornets' nest.

As for Matthew, the old man had to admit that, despite his anger at the boy for having deserted him, he still felt a murmuring of affection towards him. He chuckled inwardly, thinking that maybe the boy was not altogether lost to him. Boys had a way of doing things in a great hurry and then regretting them afterwards. Adventure might seem exciting, but all too soon it could seem like a prison sentence, especially when it meant living aboard a ship with all manner of rogues and scoundrels. Happen it wouldn't be long afore he was back here, and then they would see. Yes, indeed . . . they would see.

'The lad made his choice,' he told his stepson now. 'I've other things on my mind at the minute.' Draping a cloak round his crooked figure, he leaned on his cane and shuffled awkwardly to the door. 'Let's be having you!' he grumbled, impatiently donning his top hat. 'Or have you forgot we've a sale to attend?' A thought suddenly occurred to him. 'You remember what I told you? I've no intention of paying for a Hansom all the way to Liverpool. The railway's cheaper, and it'll get us there just the same.'

'No, I've not forgotten,' David sighed wearily. There were times when he almost believed that Luther feigned his disability. Certainly he seemed surprisingly agile in that moment. He still could not understand the old man's fever to acquire yet more land. 'The Hansom will take us to Blackburn Railway Station, then from there we'll travel to Liverpool and should arrive with time to spare.'

'Good! Then don't stand there dithering, you bloody fool. Let's be away!' He groaned. 'If it weren't for me old bones and the fact that I might be overlooked when the bidding starts, I wouldn't want you within a mile of that sale room. Sometimes you're worse than bloody useless.' He flung the door open and waved his cane impatiently. 'Come on! Come on!' he snapped, thumping the end of his stick on the floor and glowering from beneath his unkempt eyebrows.

As they passed the kitchen, Cissie came rushing out. 'Don't go without me!' she reminded them. Usually Beth accompanied her to town, but, seeing as the Hansom would be going right by the flower-shop, she had arranged for Cissie to be dropped off there. As the party filed through the front door, the girl called out, 'Cheerio, Beth. I'll see you later.'

Beth was standing in the kitchen doorway, the dish-cloth in her hands and a serious expression on her face. ''Bye, sweetheart,' she returned, at once shifting her gaze to David. Neither of them smiled, but each knew the other's thoughts. Beth had heard the manner in which the old man had addressed her husband, and it would have gladdened her heart to hear him snap back; just for once to tell the old villain to 'Go to Hell!' Yet, she knew he wouldn't. He looked at her

331

now, a sheepish half-smile on his face that said, 'I'd better not antagonise him further by passing a minute with you.' Instead, he allowed the old man to usher him along and occasionally jab at him with his stick. Beth could not bear to witness such humiliation, and so she averted her gaze and returned to her work.

She heard the front door close. Putting the dishcloth on the drainer, she spread out her hands on the rim of the sink and leaned her weight forward. Glancing at the big old wall-clock, she saw that it was still only eight-thirty. The day loomed unending before her. Young Richard would be kept busy with his learning for some considerable time yet, Cissie would not be ready to come home until tea-time, and David had warned her that it would be late when he and his 'father' returned, especially as Luther had expressed a desire to 'celebrate afterwards'. He obviously meant to have the land that was being auctioned, and when he set his sights on something Luther Reynolds usually got his way.

By ten-thirty, Beth had cleared away the breakfast things, washed the dishes and stacked them into the big dresser, wiped down the kitchen table, taken the coconut matting from the floor and hung it over the line outside where she beat every speck of dust from it before replacing it over her freshly scrubbed quarry tiles; all that done she was now enjoying a cup of tea, before setting about the drawing room. She felt strangely restless, wanting to throw herself into every small task that awaited her throughout the house. There was an energy about her, a drive that told her, 'Keep going, Beth. Don't give yourself time to think . . . to think about Tyler!'

When the daily help came through the back door and into the kitchen, she found Beth sitting at the table, breathless and dishevelled. 'Why, Mrs Miller! Whatever have you been doing?' A quick glance told the plump jolly creature that most of her work had already been done. She was horrified; not only because she could see how Beth had thoroughly exhausted herself, but because she had been taken on two weeks ago by Mr Miller, who had told her categorically, 'I don't want Mrs Miller tackling any of the heavier domestic tasks, you understand? Her condition is advanced now, and one can't be too careful.' He had explained that, 'Mrs Miller is a woman not used to being idle and will sweep clean through the house with fearsome enthusiasm if she isn't watched. Be here on time and do your work well and I might consider hiring you on a regular basis once the child is born.'

Eager to secure the position, the girl had fervently assured the master, 'Depend on me, sir. I'll watch Mrs Miller like an 'awk. I shan't let her do a thing, 'cause I'll be two steps afront of her all the time.' She had been taken on straightaway, and was now settled in the position. Having just wed, and her husband laid off from the cotton mill only four days since, her wages were now the only ones coming in, and she lived in fear of being put out of work.

'Don't fuss, Peggy,' Beth told her. 'I can't see the sense in leaving all the work to you, when I have so much time on my hands.'

'But, if you'll pardon me, ma'am . . . it's what the master pays me for. He partic'ly said I wasn't to let you lift a finger about the house.' She nervously dipped the top half of her body forward in a half-hearted curtsey. 'Mr Miller'd skin me alive if he could see you now,' she said in a pitiful voice. 'You look fair worn out.' She glanced from one end of the kitchen to the other, noting the sparkling sink without a cup or plate in sight, and the gleaming table top, then the freshly scrubbed floor that was still damp in the corners; the coconut matting

333

beneath her feet bristled from its merciless thrashing. 'The master was most partic'lar,' she said lamely. 'Most partic'lar.'

Smiling mischievously, Beth leaned forward. 'I won't tell if you won't,' she whispered as though imparting a secret. Pointing to the chair opposite, she told the girl, 'Come and sit with me a while, Peggy. Tell me all about your weekend. Has your husband managed to find a position yet?' When the girl made no move, she realised that instead of putting the poor creature at her ease, she had only succeeded in heightening her anxiety.

'Begging yer pardon, ma'am, but . . . well, I'd rather get on with me work, if yer don't mind. That is . . . begging yer pardon.' She repeated the half-curtsey, her big round eyes going over Beth's face and a sense of panic taking hold of her. She didn't like the unusually high colour of the mistress's face. 'Are yer all right, ma'am?' she asked, looking desperate.

'Of course I'm all right,' Beth reassured her. 'Hard work never killed anyone that I know of. And please, Peggy . . . I would rather you didn't curtsey. It makes me nervous when you keep dipping unexpectedly like that.' Suddenly, a wave of tiredness swept through her and she closed her eyes for a moment, during which the girl remained quiet, but visibly agitated and eager to be getting on with her work. Sighing wearily, Beth opened her eyes and told her, 'You're right, Peggy. I think I went into the work with a little too much exuberance this morning.' She smiled warmly, and not for the first time the girl thought how incredibly lovely her mistress was. She had a nice nature too, not like some of the gentry; although, of course, the Reynolds weren't really 'gentry' as such.

Everyone knew the story of how old man Reynolds had come up from nothing to be a landowner. There was a time when he owned only this great mausoleum, and that piece of derelict land at the bottom of Shorrock Hill. That son of his . . . what was his name? . . . Arnold Thomas, yes, that was it. Well, the story was that Arnold Thomas was the ambitious one, while the old man was content to live on the money he got from leasing the land to them as paid the price, usually folk who wanted a storage area or distribution centre. At one time, Mr Jarvis the coalman paid a pretty penny just to park his waggons there. But Arnold Thomas smelled a bigger profit from the up-and-coming developers who were looking to build back-to-backs for the mill-workers. The old feller would have none of it! Time and again they argued, with the son wanting the land sold on the open market, and old Luther arguing that he would 'do what the bloody hell I think fit with me own land!' He were always a bit of a tyrant.

In fact, Peggy remembered her own mam saying as how there were certain folk, including herself, who believed it were Luther Reynolds' fault when his second wife died of the fever. Weeks she'd been badly, and he wouldn't hear of spending a penny on a doctor. After the poor woman died and his own son deserted him, the old man took his bitterness out on the little stepson left behind. Yet, in spite of everything, David Miller grew up to idolise the old rascal.

Looking at Beth now, the girl was made to wonder whether she had ever regretted coming to this house. Certainly, there were times when the mistress had a strange faraway look in her eye, a look that belied her busy nature and preoccupation with the children she adored: a haunted lonely look. She seemed to find it difficult to make friends, and the fact that she hardly ever wandered far from the house only added to her loneliness.

'You rest there a while, Mrs Miller,' the girl said with

unusual boldness, 'and I'll make you a fresh brew of tea before I start on the drawing room.' She frowned at Beth when an awful thought suddenly occurred to her. 'You ain't already been in there as well, 'ave you, ma'am?' Her whole body relaxed when Beth told her with a measure of amusement, 'No, Peggy, but I might well have done if you hadn't come in when you did.'

'Then, is it all right if I get on, begging yer pardon, ma'am?' She flushed with guilt when Beth took a few moments to reply. Against her better judgement she added hastily, 'I'll stay if you really want me to. If you're lonely, ma'am, that is?'

Deliberately ignoring the girl's last comment, Beth replied in a more serious voice, 'I'm sorry if I've made you anxious, Peggy. You go about your work.' She pushed her chair back and stood up, one hand across the bulge of her stomach and the other holding the small of her back. 'If you should need me, I'll be in my room,' she said. She had risen this morning with the intention of going into town and meandering among the shops, perhaps treating herself to a new bonnet, or buying Cissie those pretty boots she had so admired some days ago when the two of them had walked up and down Ainsworth Street, browsing in all the shop-windows; afterwards, Beth might have called in to the delightful tea rooms at the corner of the boulevard. Now, though, she only wanted to sit in her room a while. Later, when her son was finished with his learning, she and he might make their way to Corporation Park, where they could stroll through the gardens and enjoy the sunshine of a beautiful July afternoon.

With this thought in mind, Beth went from the kitchen and along the landing, then up the stairs towards her room. Outside the nursery, she paused and quietly inched open the door. Seated at his tiny desk beneath the window, Richard was intent on the word-pictures being held up by the kindly faced tutor. Unobserved, Beth closed the door and went softly into her own room.

Here she went to the dressing table where she sat down and regarded herself in the mirror. Looking back at her was a young woman in her thirtieth year, with trim shoulders and strong handsome features. Her hair was loosely coiled into the nape of her neck, and at her throat was a pretty cameo brooch given to her by her husband last birthday. As though suddenly observing a stranger, Beth looked down at her hands, small dainty hands that were now red from scrubbing the floor. She looked at the bump beneath her gown, and touched it with tenderness. Sighing, she raised her head and stared once more into the mirror, into those dark eyes that rarely revealed what was in her soul. In the secrecy of that room, where she had lain so often in David's loving arms, her eyes now betrayed all. Soft tears blurred the image in the mirror. When they spilled over, she did not wipe them from her face. Instead, she remembered what Peggy had said just now: 'I'll stay if you're lonely.' The ghost of a smile flitted across her sad features. Another ghost walked her heart, reawakening old wounds, reviving old memories. 'Lonely?' She nodded her head and smiled, murmuring the words which no other living soul would ever hear. 'Yes, I am lonely . . . lonely for him. Lonely for what might have been.'

Shaking off the nostalgia that threatened to overwhelm her, she went to the window and threw it open, startling a tiny robin that had been resting on the sill. As it flew away, the songs of many starlings filled the air. The sun was already hot on her face, and down below in the garden two doves stalked the lawn, looking for titbits. Soon, July would be gone, she thought, and with it, the turning of the year. Suddenly, she felt lighter of heart, ready to face the truth she had long denied herself. Yes, there were things she would never experience in life, special things which a man and woman in love might enjoy; she would never carry Tyler's child again, nor would the two of them grow old together, content in each other's love. But she was blessed in so many other ways. She had her health and strength and the tiny life forming inside her; she had security and a comfortable home; then there was Cissie whom she adored, and her own darling son who was so like his father that her joy in him must always be mingled with pain. Besides all of that, Beth reminded herself that she had the love of a good man; although, sadly, she could never return his love, she was bound to remain by his side until the end of her days.

Looking up to the blue sky, she watched the many birds flying overhead, chattering and screaming as they passed out of sight. The world was beautiful. Life was beautiful. Now, as she prepared to close the window, the robin returned, standing only inches from her hand and eyeing her with great deliberation, his tiny head cocked to one side and his bright eyes glinting in the sunshine. Suddenly her mind was made up. In no time at all, she was hurrying down the hallway towards the nursery, where she swept in to announce, 'It's such a glorious day, Mr Turnbull, I think we'll cut short Richard's lessons and I'll take him out in the sunshine.'

The tutor appeared unsure, but the boy jumped up from his place, rushing to Beth and grabbing her by the hand. 'Where are we going, Mammy?' he cried excitedly. 'Can we go to the park? Can we?'

'First, we'll go down to the kitchen and pack a small picnic,' she told him, 'then, yes . . . we'll make our way to Corporation Park.'

He gave a squeal of delight, turning round on the spot and throwing his little arms around her. 'Can we stay all day?' he said breathlessly. 'I want to feed the ducks, and I want to play in the sandpit. Can I climb the cannons?

Oh, can I, Mammy?' The questions tumbled from him as he went hand in hand with Beth, down the stairs and into the kitchen, where Peggy was soon caught up in the excitement. 'I'd best fetch the smaller basket,' she said, 'on account of your condition, begging yer pardon, ma'am.' Soon, the wicker basket was packed with fruit, slices of pork pie, daintily cut sandwiches and a small earthenware jug of sarsaparilla. 'Gotta have enough, ma'am,' Peggy remarked. 'Small boys have such enormous appetites, don't they?'

It took Beth only a few minutes to put on her bonnet and best shawl while Peggy dressed the boy for outdoors. Soon, the two of them were ready and going through the front door. 'Begging yer pardon, ma'am,' Peggy whispered hesitantly, 'you won't go climbing no steep hills in Corporation Park, will yer? Not seeing as yer . . . I wouldn't want anything to go amiss,' she finished, blushing bright pink.

'Bless you, Peggy. Of course I won't go climbing hills,' Beth assured her with a light peck on the cheek to show that she was not annoyed at the girl's being so forward. With that, Beth and her son went hand in hand out of the house and down the street, the boy's constant chatter filtering back to the watching maid and causing her to smile. 'Have a good time!' she called out, over the hustle and bustle of passing carriages. Beth's smile in return gladdened the girl. She had been so worried about the mistress, and it wasn't just because of the way she had torn into the work this morning, nor because of the bairn growing heavy inside her and making life uncomfortable. No, the girl's instincts told her there was something else that deeply disturbed the mistress, something secret that maybe even her own husband didn't know about.

Craning her neck, she caught a last glimpse of Beth and the child. She looked so slim and young in that cream shawl above her blue taffeta gown, with the pretty frilled bonnet over her gleaming hair; she had a way of walking, thought the watching girl, with just a little envy . . . so easy and graceful, even though she was with child. Now and again the small boy at her side would look up, and Beth would lean towards him, no doubt answering his lively questions. All the way down the street he jumped and fidgeted and laughed and chatted, and Beth held his hand, keeping him close, keeping him safe. After all, Tyler's son was the most precious gift of all.

The woman loved the feel of his nakedness, the muscles in his chest hard against her back and his arms wound round her thighs. Softly, so as not to wake him, she turned her long slim form until she was face to face with his sleeping figure. For what seemed an age, she studied his features, strong lean features which she had come to know so well. She had never loved any man, never really wanted to. She had not wanted to love this man, especially when she knew he could never love her back. And yet, she wanted him like she had wanted no other. Not for the first time she wondered cynically whether she craved Tyler Blacklock because he was tall, darkly handsome and unattainable, or because he was fast becoming a very rich and influential man. Certainly, it was these qualities that drew her to him in the first place, but now . . . these were not the true reasons why she stayed with him. She had tried hard not to fall in love with him, preferring to play the field and maybe trap a man whose heart was fancy free.

She laughed softly. Things never turned out the way you wanted them to. This man was different from any other she had known. He was thoughtful and caring, but strong-willed and quick-minded. From a lonely boyhood to being left for dead in some alley, he had never looked to others for strength. Instead, like the powerful and determined man he was, Tyler Blacklock had risen above it all to become a formidable but respected businessman. Tenderly, she stroked his face, running her slender fingers over the newly grown stubble on his chin, tracing the classical lines of his nose with the tip of her finger, and all the while gently thrusting herself against him, arousing him, wanting him. Placing her mouth over his, she murmured teasingly, running her fingers along the nape of his neck, watching his face so she could smile into those magnificent green eyes when they opened to gaze on her. Soon he was responding to her love-play, softly moaning, his arms tightening about her and his nakedness fusing harder with hers. Suddenly his moan became a soft, broken cry. 'Beth . . . oh, Beth.' He felt her stiffen in his arms. His eyes flickered open to see the horror on her face. At once he pulled away, confused and angry with himself.

Sitting on the edge of the bed, he bowed his head, clasping his hands over his face. 'I'm sorry,' he told her simply. She made no reply but climbed out of bed. He watched as she poured water from the jug into the bowl and quickly washed and then dressed; not once did she look at him or speak one word. He knew how she must be feeling, and he hated her. But he hated himself more. She had been a good companion; she did not deserve this from him. 'Are you leaving?' he asked quietly, his loneliness intensifying.

'What the hell do you think?' she demanded, swinging round to face him, her eyes blazing. When he looked away, she realised she would lose him for ever. She didn't know if she could bear that. In the wake of his softly spoken words her anger subsided and she went to him. 'Don't let me leave,' she said. 'You can stop me if you've a mind to.'

He looked at her now, dark eyes green as the ocean

depths, unfathomable, like the man himself. 'You must do what you think fit,' he said, rising from the bed and brushing past her; her gaze followed him, sweeping his nakedness. There was no anger in her now, only fear. 'You won't go away penniless,' he promised her. 'You know that, don't you?' The emotion in his voice was not unkind. But it was not love, she realised that. Cupping his hands in the large jug, he splashed cold water over his face and chest, rubbing it up and down his arms before towelling himself down. Taking his trousers from the chair-back, he slid his legs into them and buckled the belt round his waist. 'Do you really want to leave?' he asked.

'You know I don't.' Her relief was evident in the small cry she made. 'Oh, Tyler . . . must it always be like this? Must she always come between us?' He gave no reply, but went to the window and drew back the curtains, letting the morning light spill into the room; a room which, without being pretentious, bespoke his new standing in life, a large, well-furnished room, with a grand bed and expensive decor, and velvet curtains with fancy frills. When he turned to look at her with some compassion, she walked the few steps that kept them apart and, staring at him with desperate eyes, insisted, 'That woman in the docks . . . it was *her*, wasn't it? She's the one you can't forget.' He shaved his face clean and combed his thick unruly hair, then continued to dress, hurriedly now, for she was touching on memories that were precious to him. 'For God's sake, Tyler, why can't you put the past behind you?' In her desperation she was relentless.

He fastened his boots and shrugged his broad shoulders into the dark jacket. He was ready. 'I'll see you to the station,' he said, 'if that's what you really want.' He went from her now, with that familiar slight limping stride that only made him more attractive. 'When I've seen you safely on the train, I should still have time enough to get to the auction.'

'Is it all you can think about . . . buying land . . . building your fortune?' She almost spat the words out. 'Is it for her? Is that why you drive yourself, Tyler? For her? Do you live in hope that your fortune might tempt her away from her rightful husband?' Even before she'd finished speaking, she knew she had gone too far. In one stride he had her in his grip. For one awful moment she feared he would strike her; instead he looked down at her, his contempt far more painful than a blow. 'I'm sorry. I didn't mean that,' she whispered. Her voice was sincere, but in her heart she meant every word she said. Everything he had ever done was for the woman he could not forget. 'I should not have said that,' she reluctantly admitted. When he released her it was with such force that she almost fell to the floor. She had never seen him so agitated.

'We'd best get started,' he said. The rage had gone from him and she was afraid that it was all too final. She could see her easy life becoming harder. The years passed quickly and too soon beauty was a fading thing. She hesitated and he understood. 'You don't have to leave now,' he reminded her, his voice softer, a smile playing about his handsome mouth. 'But our relationship can never be a permanent one. I've never led you to believe otherwise.'

Suddenly she wanted permanence more than anything. She had tasted the fear of being cast out, and it left a bitter taste in her mouth. Why couldn't he love her? Why was it so impossible for him to make their relationship more secure? The anger was rising in her again. 'This woman . . . wasn't it long ago? She's probably forgotten you. Can't you put her firmly in the past?' she wanted to know.

He had been standing by the door which was now

partly open. He was preparing to leave. He quietly closed the door and, leaning his back to it, he dropped his gaze to her upturned face, before tilting his head upwards and staring at the ceiling, his anguished thoughts in turmoil. She had asked why he could not put Beth firmly in the past. How could he give her an answer when he did not know the answer himself? Looking into her face he repeated her words on a long drawn-out breath. 'Put her in the past.' He shook his head. 'If only I could. But, don't you realise, the past is the present, and the present is the future?' He laughed cynically. 'We can never dismiss yesterday as though it never happened, because we carry it with us from moment to moment until the end of our days.'

'Surely you must know you can't have her? She's content with her family around her. You must accept that she wants no part of you. Not now, not after all this time.' Reaching out, she touched him, a compassionate look in her eyes. 'She has no love for you, Tyler . . . no need of you, can't you see that? Don't you know that whatever was between you is over for good?'

'I know it.'

'Then forget her!' She edged closer to him, her voice soft and pleading. 'Make a life with me, Tyler. You said yourself that I'm good for you.'

'I know that too.'

'Then . . . ?'

He reached out to touch her, but his arms fell loosely by his sides. His eyes appraised her face, a lovely face, a sad face – because of him. He regretted that, but the awful truth was only a murmur away. '*I love her.*' His voice was a mere whisper, but such was the effect of his words on the woman that he might have shouted them from the rooftops.

She knew she had lost him. The slender hold she'd had on him was broken because of her impatience. Silently she cursed herself for being such a damned fool. Yet she had known from the start that he would not be easy to keep; he was a man deeply in love, relentlessly loyal to that one love, with no room for any other woman. Her frantic mind recalled the young woman at the docks, and she was not surprised that he adored her. Even with child the woman was incredibly lovely, a graceful creature with an aura of that unique beauty few women possessed. But more compelling were her dark expressive eyes, eyes that had widened with shock on seeing Tyler there, eyes that might have spoken to him of anger but instead had betrayed something much deeper, and far more dangerous.

Until now, the woman had been careful not to reveal how she had witnessed what passed between him and that lovely creature at the docks. She had seen something in those dark tragic eyes, something akin to the anguish betrayed now in Tyler's. She did not pretend to understand such depth of feeling. It made her both uncomfortable and afraid, and now she could see the delicate security she had achieved slipping through her fingers. She would try anything . . . anything to hold on to it.

When she spoke now, there was a cruel plan forming in the back of her mind. 'I can't bear to see what's happening to you,' she told him. 'How you drive yourself . . . punish yourself. Don't you realise how ruthless you're becoming? Can't you see how your bitterness is changing you? Oh, Tyler . . . Tyler! You're so very different from the man you once were . . . warm and giving, enjoying the rewards which your hard work brought you. Now it's only the work! You don't laugh any more, Tyler. You've closed your heart and locked her inside it. All this time you've been living a dream, and now you've seen that dream in the flesh you torment yourself even more.' She looked at him and felt his pain, but he had shut her out again. There was nothing more to be said. Unless . . . unless . . . Careful, though, she must bide her time, think it through. He did care for her, she knew that, but was it enough? Was it enough? She had to take the chance before it was too late. 'I'm with child,' she lied, her voice trembling slightly, the words echoing through the silence that had descended between them. When he remained silent but stared at her, visibly shaken, his dark green eyes seeming to see right through her, she began crying. 'I'm afraid,' she murmured. 'What will I do? Where will I go? Are you angry?'

His answer was to take her in his arms and press her close to him. 'Maybe it really is time I settled down,' he said, holding her at arm's length and smudging her tears away with his thumb. She raised her head, astonished and relieved that he had not seen through her. But, then, men were always blind to a woman's wiles. There was a moment's silence before he smiled. 'If you want to be wed in London . . . you'd best get packed.'

'You mean it!' Her little plan had worked. He would never know the truth, because there were many ways a woman could fool a man. 'You really mean it?' she asked breathlessly. 'We're going to be wed?' Her eyes were big and shining. In that moment she had no conscience. She only knew her good fortune lay in that Tyler Blacklock was an honourable man.

He laughed, a sad bitter sound. 'We wouldn't want my son to come into the world without his father's name now, would we, eh?'

Exultant, she went to the bed and withdrew the portmanteau from beneath. It took only a few minutes to pack their belongings. Another few minutes and she was ready to leave with him. During this time he had remained by the door, his expressionless gaze following her every move. She stood a while, intently regarding him, her hand steadying the portmanteau on the bed, and only the merest glimmer of guilt colouring her face. Afraid that he might guess at her deceit, she began talking, laughing, making plans, distracting his attention from what she had wickedly led him to believe. Buttoning the long fitted jacket over her expensive cream gown, she went to him on determined footsteps. Her heart leaped. He was so handsome. And now, he was hers. 'I'll make you a good wife, Tyler.' She was gabbling now. 'You won't regret it. Oh! It'll be wonderful, you'll see.' She threw herself into his arms, sighing deeply when he half-heartedly returned her embrace.

Her triumph would have been short-lived if she had seen the smile slip from his face and a look of regret shape his expression; his quiet eyes were drawn to the window, to the skyline beyond. And his heart soared to wherever his Beth was in that moment.

Chapter Nine

'Damn and blast!' Luther Reynolds clambered from the carriage with considerable difficulty, his crooked frame making it awkward for him to pass easily through the narrow doorway and on to the small step which the driver had lowered. 'Get your paws off me!' he yelled when David went to assist. 'You're no sodding help at all.' He thrashed out with his cane. 'Piss off out of it. Useless! That's what you are. Bloody useless!'

The edge of his stick caught David a glancing blow to the side of the head as he stooped to guide the old man's unsteady legs on to the step. Undeterred, he gripped the open door with one hand, stretching his other arm to the side of the carriage and forming a barrier to stop the old man missing his footing. With abuse being hurled at him all the while, he remained so until Luther Reynolds was safely to the ground. His reward was a surly look and the instruction to, 'Get out of my way, bugger you . . . fussing and bothering as though I were a sodding infant.' Now, it was the driver's turn. 'What the hell are you staring at?' the old man snarled, thrashing out with his cane and causing the fellow hastily to retreat into his driving seat up top, out of harm's way. Once there, he could be heard to mutter, 'Fornicating old sod, you want that bloody stick wrapped round yer bleedin' ear'ole!'

Having paid the driver and quietly apologised for 'my father's temper', David pointed out the entrance to the auction rooms just a few feet away, and together the two of them made their way there, the old man shuffling and leaning heavily on his stick, and the younger man walking protectively alongside, positioning himself between his father and the many horse-drawn vehicles which sped up and down the road, a great number of them stopping to discharge their passengers right outside the sale room; one in particular drew to a halt behind the two men, who kept their backs to the traffic and concentrated on reaching the large arched entrance without being trampled underfoot.

Climbing from the carriage, Tyler instructed the woman, 'Wait here. I shan't be long.'

'Take as long as you like,' she said, smiling sweetly. 'I won't be going anywhere without you.'

'A moment only,' he explained. 'I don't intend to wait for the sale to begin, but it would be a pity to come all this way and not to leave a bid.' He had been greatly excited by the prospect of bidding in person, but now somehow his enthusiasm had been dampened by another less satisfying prospect, that of exchanging wedding vows with a woman he did not love in the way a man should love the mother of his child. Without waiting for her reply, he closed the carriage door and called to the driver, 'Wait here.'

The driver nodded, touched his flat cap and replied, 'As you say, Guv . . . as you say.' His bleary pink eyes followed Tyler's tall hurrying figure which, in spite of the noticeable limp, was athletic and commanding. 'As you say, Guv,' he mumbled. 'I ain't in no hurry neither.' There had been a 'going away' in the family, and what could be more of an excuse to have a merry binge than a son emigrating to far-off America in search of his fortune? The entire family had seen the young man off on Saturday, but the celebrations were still going on. It had been a hard night, and he felt like death warmed up.

Coming into the foyer, Tyler pressed on through the crush of bodies all surging in the same direction. From the information he had received on the sale, he was aware that Tobias Drew had left a considerable quantity of land, located at the two extremes of the country. Judging by the crush here, Tyler realised he had underestimated the interest it would attract. He said as much to the clerk who now took details of his bid, a sum which he had increased from the original figure in view of the crowd that was already gathering, even though the sale was not scheduled to take place for at least another two hours.

'You must know yourself that land is at a premium,' the clerk said. 'There's many a man here would murder to get his hands on some of the prime development pockets that's being put up today.' He scoured the milling crowd with narrowed eyes before shrugging his shoulders and bending to write out in meticulous copperplate the handsome figure that Tyler had quoted. 'There's no doubt you'll be in the running, sir,' he said, without raising his head. 'This 'ere's a very sensible sum, if you don't mind me saying . . . a very sensible sum indeed.'

'You think there'll be none better, do you?'

The narrow-faced man straightened from his task. 'Well now . . . let me see.' He ran his astute eyes over the many faces that were gathered in that small timbered room. Then he made a sound that might have been a cough. 'Well now,' he repeated, looking directly at Tyler with a meaningful expression.

'You'll not find me ungrateful for useful information,' he assured the fellow with a smile.

'Ah.' He sniffed, signifying satisfaction with Tyler's answer. 'Look there, sir.' He gestured with his head to a balding gentleman in a long-tailed coat who carefully carried his top hat under his arm as though it was a precious parcel. 'D'you see how he strolls about with a casual air?' he asked. When Tyler nodded, he went on, 'You musn't be fooled by his disinterested expression, sir.' That's one of our local landowners. Part of his estate includes a grand house and considerable acreage out Langho way, and he runs four very lucrative cotton mills hereabouts. He goes by the name of Jules Barker. If you were to ask me, and of course, you have,' he continued slyly, 'I would say that Mr Barker was your main rival.' He winked. 'Some of it, or all of it. It don't matter which to him, I reckon.'

'You mean, the fellow wants to buy land in the South?'

'Land is land, wherever it is, sir. Besides, there's a greater shortage of it in the South than here, or so I'm told.' Tyler nodded in agreement and so he continued, 'See that gentleman there?' He looked across the sea of top hats towards the far end of the room; Tyler followed his gaze. 'That crooked old fellow by the rostrum is Luther Reynolds . . . a tyrant by anybody's standards.' He visibly shivered. 'But I'll tell you what, when it comes to business he's a canny old scoundrel . . . never used to be, though. Oh, no. It were his son that changed him, so the story goes. His only son walked out some years back, and ever since it's been like Luther Reynolds has been driven by the Devil!'

'You think he's a serious contender then?'

'Without a doubt, sir. He goes after every property that comes available. Oh, he don't always get it, mind, but he's landed some very lucrative deals. One thing's for sure . . . old Luther Reynolds wouldn't be here today if he hadn't set his sights on some . . . or maybe even all . . . of what's going under the hammer here. Right old Scrooge he is an' all. Thinks nothing of screwing the last farthing outta ordinary hard-working folk whose misfortune it is to reside in one of his run-down properties. But, you see, ordinary folk don't get much choice in where they live. My own mother still inhabits a disgusting damp hovel down Larkhill.'

He eyed Tyler with curiosity, recalling the distinct London accent. 'Being as you're not from these parts, you wouldn't be acquainted with the facts regarding Larkhill, now would you, sir? Larkhill being a street of back-to-backs, and one of that old fellow's most infamous holdings.' He paused only to draw breath before going on, 'Burned down it did . . . almost the entire stretch of Larkhill on one side. Burned to the ground by a fire started in Maisie Armstrong's place . . . had a lodger she did. The word was given out was that the young widder were a relative. Anyway, the fire took Maisie and two other good souls beside.'

His eyes misted over as it all came back. 'Dreadful it were. Dreadful! The young lady who was staying with Maisie, well, folks laid the blame at her door 'cause Maisie herself were a very careful woman, an' no mistake. Of course, it didn't help matters when the young widder upped and married the landlord's stepson; although by all accounts old Luther Reynolds gives her a hard time . . . hates her he does, so they say, and that stepson of his . . . well, between you and me, sir, David Miller might have a good heart and a measure of sympathy for the tenants old Luther treats badly, but when it comes to backbone – well.' He spread his hands. 'He certainly weren't blessed with much of that particular quality.

'Still, there isn't a soul on God's earth who can tell Luther Reynolds what to do. He's a cussed old bugger, if you don't mind me saying. And I don't mind telling you, it makes my blood boil, sir. Since the fire that devastated Larkhill, that canny old villain has wriggled out of every opportunity to put the street to rights. My own mother lives in fear of her very life, what with fire-ravaged timbers hanging loose in mid-air, and rats running free round the rubble. It's nothing short of a nightmare for them that's left in Larkhill, and that old scoundrel still demands four shilling a week rent. Can you imagine that, eh? Four shilling a week, and most poor working folk have only twenty shilling a week between themselves and the workhouse! But do you think anybody gives a cuss. No, they don't!'

'I'm sorry to hear that,' Tyler said with genuine concern. Certainly, the fellow's story had aroused his curiosity in the surly faced old man by the rostrum. But now he was impatient to be away, for it was a long and tiring journey back to London, and he had various other things on his mind that had taken precedence over the proceedings here. All the same, he did not want to throw away the opportunity of acquiring at least some of the late Tobias Drew's legacy. Taking the pen from the fellow's hand, he spun the bid-docket round and quickly crossing out the figure written there, scribbled another, larger figure above it. 'D'you think that will do it?' he asked the startled fellow.

Glancing again at the docket, the fellow gasped. 'If that don't put you in good stead, sir, I don't know what will.' Realising that he might have been just a shade too friendly with this gent of consequence, he quickly reverted to his best business manner. 'Now then, sir, you'll need to state which lots you want the bids put forward on, and what way you want this sum to be proportioned.' He pushed the docket forward for Tyler to enter his separate bids; no sum was mentioned out loud, for fear of eavesdroppers, and the docket was kept very close between them, with a queue now beginning to form behind. 'Thank you very much, sir,' he declared when Tyler returned the docket into his keeping. 'Your bids will be properly put forward at the appropriate time.' His smile broadened when Tyler slid a silver coin into his hand, this being speedily despatched to his waistcoat pocket before other eyes might catch the glint of it.

On his way out, Tyler was obliged to pass within a few inches of Luther Reynolds, who glowered at him when he had the effrontery to say politely, and with the secret hope that his own bid would at least put Reynolds out of the picture: 'You'll have to be sharp today, sir. It seems the whole of Lancashire has turned out for the event.'

The old man's answer was a black look and the curt remark, 'I don't know you, nor do I want to, so kindly keep your observations to yourself.'

Reynolds was further irritated when Tyler smiled down on him and, making a sweeping gesture with his arm and with the parting remark, 'Good day to you then,' strode away without looking back. If he had lingered a moment longer, he might have made the acquaintance of the old man's stepson, the same man who had also figured in the clerk's account of Reynolds; the same man who had wed 'the young woman from Larkhill'. And how great would Tyler's astonishment have been if only he had known that the man he had missed by just one minute, was the same man who had wed his own lovely, tragic Beth.

Outside, the streets of Liverpool were bustling. Barrow-boys and costermongers were shouting the qualities of their wares; carts and beer-waggons were lazily trundling along; and some way down the street an old woman in a long black dress and shawl was setting out her many flowers for sale. Women in fancy hats strolled by with their handsome escorts, and above it all, the sound of barrel-organ music floated on the warm July breeze.

Out in the fresh air once more, and feeling reluctant to return to the carriage where his companion was patiently waiting, Tyler paused on the steps, his gaze encompassing the busy scene. Some short way from where he stood, two elderly men with handlebar moustaches were deep in argument, one declaring: 'If the motor vehicles are already running on French roads, why the devil do you say they'll never find a place here in this country?' The other gentleman, who was by far the more vehement of the two, replied stiffly: 'Because there are people . . . such as myself . . . who would turn Heaven and earth to prevent it, that's why. Motor vehicles indeed! There's nothing wrong with the horse and carriage, and I for one will never put my trust in a contraption that spouts black smoke in its wake and goes at some God-awful speed, enough to frighten the life out of every decent citizen.' The argument quickly moved on to other things, including the enviable life style of Oscar Wilde.

Smiling to himself, and wanting now to escape back to London where, given time, he might even enjoy the state of marriage and learn to live without regret, Tyler stepped down to the pavement. Almost at once, his attention was caught by a certain gentleman approaching at a rather hurried pace, his weasel-like face lifted high as he searched ahead, and his thick white hair shockingly conspicuous amid the dark top hats and extravagant bonnets around him. 'Good God, it's Reynolds!' Tyler muttered, recognising the fellow at once as Esther Ward's trusted clerk.

In that instant their eyes met, causing the smaller man to halt in his tracks as he stared at Tyler, his mind racing back to a certain conspiracy which he and the mistress had connived between them, designed not only to cost Tyler Blacklock the opportunity of acquiring work, but in addition to discredit him in Beth's eyes. Tom Reynolds had eagerly entertained the idea that Beth might then turn to him, instead of which she disappeared. The mischievous scheme therefore had backfired to a certain extent. However, it had caused the perpetrators a considerable degree of satisfaction when Ben disclosed how Tyler believed his sweetheart to have married another. Both guilty parties were aware that Tyler would have searched the four corners of the earth if he had only known the truth.

The fact that Beth had been devastated by their malicious doings did not touch their consciences, even for a moment. Indeed, for different reasons, both derived their own particular satisfaction from her unhappy situation. In Tom Reynolds' case, he was still smarting from her rejection of him, and was delighted that Tyler Blacklock had not succeeded where he himself had failed. Besides which, he had not entirely given up hope that Beth would eventually be forced by adverse circumstances to return to her father's house. Much to Tom Reynolds' surprise and frustration, up until now that had not happened.

But, in the time between, he was not too preoccupied with that, being much too concerned with more pressing matters, although Beth was never far from his mind. He had wondered at Esther's motives for wanting Beth isolated from the family, although he long ago sensed the animosity between them.

He had long suspected there was much more to it all than what appeared on the surface, although he was never interested in what had sparked such dislike between the two women. It was a known fact that mothers and daughters were frequently at each other's throats. Tom Reynolds had no way of knowing the truth.

There were others also who might never know the truth, including Beth's brother Ben, and even Beth herself. Had Tom Reynolds been given just the slightest intimation of the dark secret in Esther's heart, he would have had that impossibly proud woman at his mercy and lined his own pockets at her expense. As it was, she had always paid him handsomely for his troubles; but how much more satisfying it would have been if he could have added Beth to his 'rewards'.

In the quietness of a lonely night, Tom Reynolds had often thought about Beth, dreamt vividly about her, and never a day went by when he didn't toy with the idea of searching her out; but that would cost both money and time, and he was not a man to waste such precious commodities, certainly not in the pursuit of a mere woman, and definitely not in the pursuit of a woman who might turn up at any day, desperate for his help. He had hoped that Beth would show herself before now, and yes, he was bitterly disappointed that she had not. But he was a patient fellow, who doggedly believed his time would come. Looking on Tyler now, and with all the guilt of his own wickedness writhing through his mind, he thought for one awful moment that his 'time' had come in a way he had not envisaged.

In spite of his dislike for the fellow, Tyler was tempted to pass the time of day with Richard Ward's clerk. He watched the slight figure come closer, a struggle going on inside him. He had never taken to Tom Reynolds, whom he considered to be a devious character, but Reynolds remained close to the Ward family, and all news of Beth must reach his ears. But then, Tyler reminded himself that he had already seen how content Beth was in the bosom of her family. What else could Tom Reynolds tell him that he did not already know? More importantly, did he really want to discuss his lovely Beth with the likes of Reynolds? Thinking it wiser to make a discreet exit, Tyler hurried to the waiting carriage, ordered the driver to make haste to the railway station, and prepared to climb inside. He was dismayed therefore to see the figure of the obnoxious Reynolds purposefully bearing down on him.

'Mr Blacklock . . . *Tyler Blacklock*!' Reynolds' shrill voice called out above the hubbub and in a moment he was standing alongside the carriage and looking up at Tyler with a cunning smile, safe in the knowledge that the other man must know nothing of his own part in driving Beth out of his life, for if he had Tyler would have pulled him apart with his bare hands. 'Surely you don't intend going without passing the time of day with an old colleague?' he asked boldly.

Nodding his head in recognition, Tyler simply said, 'Forgive me, but we really are in a hurry.'

'You don't seem surprised that we meet some two hundred miles from home?' Reynolds pointed out.

Looking towards the building he himself had just left, Tyler replied, 'No. I'm not at all surprised. After all, we're in the same line of business . . . obviously we read the same publications. No doubt, like myself and countless others, you will have seen the schedule referring to the late Tobias Drew's land holdings.'

'Ah!' Reynolds nodded his head. Realisation dawned, causing the smile to slide from his pointed features. 'Of course,' he murmured. 'How unperceptive of me. Of course, you're here with the same purpose as myself . . . to beat off rival bids and go home with a deed or two tucked safely in your pocket.' His mood was abruptly changed by the fact that he and Blacklock were here as rivals – although, all things considered, it was the most natural thing in the world. Indeed, he should have been more surprised if Blacklock were *not* at the sale.

'Like I said, Reynolds, we are in the same line of business.' Tyler was impatient to be gone. 'But I wish you well,' he added. 'I assume you're here on behalf of the Ward Company?' It was no secret that the company had struggled to fend off trouble these past years and was now in very real danger of going under. But then, there were many companies in the same boat – some managed to stay afloat, and others went down without a fight. But Esther Ward was not a woman to go down without a battle, although there were those who rightly despised her and would willingly speed her on her way. And, if the company did fold, Tyler had no doubt that both Richard and Esther were wise enough not to lose everything they owned; that was, if they hadn't been foolish enough to let their wayward son Ben get his hands on any reserve funds. As for Beth – well, she at least was financially secure in her marriage.

'I do believe you mean that!' remarked the other man with astonishment. 'And, yes . . . I am here acting on behalf of Esther Ward.'

'Please give the family my regards,' Tyler told him. What he wanted to say was: 'Is Beth really happy? Does she pine for me? Is Wilson Ryan the husband she had hoped he might be?' But the questions remained in his heart. Grabbing the jamb of the open door, he placed one foot on the step and prepared to swing himself into the carriage.

'I'm surprised you mean to go without asking after Beth.'

The words stopped Tyler short. Turning round, he stood squarely facing the other man, his eyes dark with pain and so many questions on the tip of his tongue. When he spoke, the calmness of his voice belied the turmoil inside. 'I saw Beth only the other day,' he said. Unaware that his remark had come as a great shock to the little man, he went on, 'I could see how content she was. But when next you meet, please give her my fondest regards.' He wondered how he could be so calm when every nerve-ending in his body was screeching. He wanted to say, 'Tell her I need her. She only has to say the word and I'll follow her to the ends of the earth.' Oh, but hadn't he forgotten something . . . someone? Here in the carriage – the woman who was carrying his child, the woman he was pledged to marry. And hadn't he forgotten how happily wed Beth was? Fool! When would he realise that it was over?

'You . . . saw Beth?' Tom Reynolds' smile hid the fact that Tyler's words had been like a blow to the stomach. Elizabeth Ward was here in Liverpool? 'Was she alone? Did you speak to her?'

'Sadly, no. Beth and her family were too soon lost in the crowd, but it pleased me to see how well she looked.' He might have said 'considering she was with child', but the words stuck in his throat. Instead, he made a comment that was further from the truth than could ever have been imagined. 'Seeing you just now, I thought perhaps you had all travelled North together, you and Esther with her family?' He wondered whether Beth had grown closer to her mother over the years. Had he been one to gossip and socialise, he might perhaps have learned more, but he was by nature a loner. Besides, the Ward family also kept themselves to themselves and did not broadcast their business to all and sundry.

It took but a moment for the little man to recover, and when he did it was to say with careful cunning, 'But of course, Blacklock, that's exactly what happened.' He needed to be alone in order to digest what Tyler had just told him. Elizabeth Ward was here? He was gripped by a feeling of great excitement. If she was here then he would be in no hurry to return South. If Beth was here, he would look for her. When he raised his head, Tyler was already seated in the carriage and closing the door. 'Er . . . just a minute, Blacklock.'

'Yes?'

Reynolds smiled nervously. He was on the verge of questioning Tyler further with regard to Beth, but then he stopped himself in time. What the devil was he thinking about? The last thing he wanted to do was to arouse the other man's suspicions. With lightning cunning, he asked, 'Aren't you attending the sale?'

Tyler would have replied without giving his reason for leaving just now, but having heard the conversation and now the question that indirectly concerned her, the woman leaned forward. Smiling down on Tom Reynolds, she told him, 'We're in a hurry to get back to London. You see, Tyler and me are to be married straightaway.'

'Married?' Reynolds could hardly hide his pleasure, his small piggy eyes roving over the attractive figure now edging itself closer to Tyler. 'Well, let me be the first to congratulate you, Miss . . . Miss . . .' He never liked to be told half a tale – especially when he knew the tale would be of interest to Esther.

Tyler surreptitiously pressed his companion back against the seat before leaning out of the window and yelling to the cloaked figure up top, 'Away, driver!' Then, 'Stand back!' he told the little man as the carriage pulled quickly away, leaving Tom Reynolds reeling from the news he had just learned – two snippets of information that made his trip North just that bit more gratifying. The fact that Beth's lover had not married in all this time had always been a thorn in Reynolds' side. In spite of Tyler believing that Beth was living in splendour in the Surrey countryside, in wedded bliss with Wilson Ryan, Reynolds was always nervous about his own part in such a deception. It had not escaped his attention, either, that should Beth ever return and find Tyler to be the affluent and eligible bachelor he now was, she might be tempted to forgive and forget, and that would be disastrous for Tom Reynolds in more ways than one. With Tyler Blacklock married though, and he being an honourable man, the likelihood of such a situation was very slim.

His face broadened by a smug smile, Tom Reynolds

swung round, almost careering into a gang of young ruffians who were engaged in a pavement game of Put and Take. The ensuing cries of: 'Watch where yer going, yer clumsy bugger' and 'Are yer blind, matey . . . is that it?' would normally have brought a string of threats and abuse in retaliation, but not on this particular occasion. 'Oh, I beg your pardon' he told the scowling youths, bestowing on them a smile that rendered them silent as he went on his way.

It was a more composed and confident Tom Reynolds who now entered the sale room. Yet, as he stood by the entrance, his pale eyes scouring the hall, he was not to know that in a matter of minutes he would be dealt yet another shock. A shock which would have a profound impact on his fortunes, and consequently affect the lives of those unfortunate enough to be acquainted with him.

David Miller saw him first. Having returned with a glass of refreshment for his father, he was standing protectively beside the old man, his keen eyes observing the faces of passersby, and in between dutifully answering the old man's insistent questions. 'Who's here, eh? Fat cats from London, no doubt . . . come to take what belongs to us Northerners. Bloody cheek! Who else? Do you recognise anybody? What about Jules Barker? Can you see that fellow, eh? Though he's got a sodding nerve to show up here after he stole that block o'dwellings on Rosamund Street . . . right from under me nose, the scoundrel. What! Let the bugger try and keep up with me on this one, eh?' He chuckled low and hugged himself gleefully. 'Leave him licking his wounds, I will!' he promised. 'Same as I'll do to any manjack as intends to do me out of this one.' He sank back in his chair and began tapping the wood-block floor with the end of his stick, muttering to himself and glowering at all and sundry from beneath frowning eyebrows.

'If I had my way, we wouldn't be here at all,' David told him. He glanced down at the old man, but then looked away again when he saw that his words were going unheeded. As he raised his head, it was then that his gaze fell on the man at the far end of the hall. For a moment he was unsure, but there was something about the slightly built figure and the startling mop of white hair that held his attention like a magnet. The more he stared, the more certain he became, *and the more afraid*. He had cause to remember his half-brother, and he had cause to fear him. Arnold Thomas Reynolds had left his mark on the young boy who had come into his father's house all those years ago. Like Luther, Thomas had a particularly vicious streak which he had all too often exercised on the shy young innocent who had been introduced as 'your new brother'.

'What you gawping at, eh?' The old man prodded his stepson with the tip of his cane. 'Who is it? Who've you seen? . . . Jules Barker, is it?' When David gave no answer, but continued to look towards the far end of the room, a strange disbelieving expression on his face, Luther jabbed him harder and groaned, 'Useless! Yer bloody useless!'

Using his cane as a lever, he pulled himself up in the chair and, screwing his eyes into tiny glittering holes, looked first at David and then followed his curious gaze – *straight to the face of Tom Reynolds*. Making a sound as though he was choking, the old man visibly folded in the chair, his eyes now round as silver shillings and his mouth falling open. For a moment he lapsed into a profound silence, his whole attention fixed on the man who was his son, and who had appeared like a ghost from the past. 'It's him!' he whispered. 'It's my son.'

He tugged at the younger man's coat. David looked

down to see the old man's aged features crumpled like old leather, the tears running down his face. 'Arnold Thomas,' he said brokenly. 'My son.' He kept his gaze riveted on the slight figure. 'It is him. God Almighty . . . it is, ain't it?' he asked pitifully.

David stared again at the man, then he returned his gaze to the old one who had been the only father he had ever known, a father who in spite of everything he had idolised beyond all others, and there was a great sadness in his heart. Somehow he knew instinctively that with the return of Luther's own blood son things could never be the same. Yet he shared the old man's joy, for he had never seen such intense happiness on the face of another human being. 'Yes, Father, I do believe it's him,' he replied in sober mood.

'Fetch him then!' The old man scrambled to get out of the chair, all his doubts and astonishment giving way to the excitement which had been mounting since he first set eyes on his beloved son. It did not matter that this son had heartlessly deserted him. All was forgiven now. He was home, and that was enough. 'Hurry! Hurry, before we lose him again,' he told David, at the same time gripping the other man's coat and yanking it back and forth. 'Go on, damn you!' He thrust his arm out and almost tumbled over in his great enthusiasm.

'Sit down and then I'll fetch him,' David told the old fellow in a surprisingly authoritative voice, and so taken aback was Luther that he promptly sat down, trembling all over. In a moment, David was hurrying towards Tom Reynolds, and the old man was jumping up and down on his seat. He saw the two men meet. He watched as the older one stepped back with an astonished look on his face; then a conversation that seemed to go on for hours when in fact it was only a matter of minutes, and oh, Tom was looking across the room now, staring at the old man. It was too much!

365

Luther could contain himself no longer. Struggling out of the chair he began an unsteady path towards them, calling out, 'Arnold Thomas! Oh . . . son . . . son!' Tears blinded him and he was sobbing loudly. People stopped to regard him with curiosity, and someone was heard to say, 'It's Luther Reynolds . . . whatever ails him?' The sight of such a hard-bitten old rogue actually shedding tears was something to behold. But he paid them no mind. Instead he stumbled into the arms of his son, laughing and crying at the same time, content just to hold his own flesh and blood close, and to look into that face which already was showing remarkable similarities to his own – the small sharp eyes, the long narrow nose and loose jowls that came with maturity.

And while these two embraced and turned back the years between them, David stood aside, a lonely forgotten figure, heavy of heart yet deeply thankful that he had a woman waiting at home, a woman soon to give him a son of his very own. All the same, there was a terrible sadness in him as he looked at these two men, one he would willingly die for, and the other who had robbed his father of a son – yet that same son was held in greater esteem than he had a right to be.

The two men walked away deep in conversation, the younger one's head bent in concentration while the older one gabbled on about: 'The house, the money I've kept for you . . . it's a small fortune built up over the years, for you, son, only for you.' Now and then he would stop and gaze into Tom Reynolds' face, as though to convince himself that it really was his son come home again. 'I always knew you'd be back,' he told him. 'Ever since that day when you said I'd never amount to anything . . . that I lacked the guts to make something of myself . . . I swore I'd show you. If it was the last thing I did on this earth, I'd leave you a fortune to show you how wrong you were about your old dad.'

'A fortune, you say?' Tom Reynolds had been astonished when David told him that he and the old man were here to bid for some, or even all, of what was being offered here today. He was even more astonished to learn that his father meant it all for him. Something niggled at him. He leaned towards the old man. 'All these years, you've built up a fortune, you say?'

'That's what I said, son, and that's what I mean.' Luther chuckled. 'You don't believe me, is that it?'

'Oh, no! No. I believe you all right, Father,' he replied with a placatory smile. 'It's just that, well, how far did . . .' he glanced over his shoulder at the younger man who was following them as a dog might follow its master '. . . I mean, did he help you to acquire this fortune?'

'Never!' the old man snapped. 'The man's useless, always has been.' His answer satisfied Tom Reynolds, who turned to smile deliberately at his stepbrother. Through his teeth he murmured, 'If he's useless, then we won't be needing him much longer, will we, Father?'

'Oh, don't worry about him,' the old man said. 'Now that you're back, they'll be out of the door bag and baggage, him, the brats, and that damned wife of his!'

'Brats? Wife? He wed, then?'

'Oh, aye, he's wed all right,' the old man disclosed with a scowl. 'One of the women as lived down Larkhill . . . stroppy bugger she is.' He chuckled. 'Though if I'd been younger, happen I would have bedded her just for the fun of it, eh?'

'Attractive, then?'

He chuckled again. 'Oh, aye, she's that all right. Too good-looking for the likes of that useless sod, although she's got too much of what the cat licks its arse with for my liking. He's welcome to her. The brats ain't his though . . . they came with her. But he's finally filled her belly after three years!' He chuckled. 'Never thought he'd do it, mind. Like I said though, now that

you're back, son, they'll be given their marching orders.'
And so he went on, making plans, crawling all over Tom
Reynolds, eagerly filling in the details of events since
he'd been gone, and asking the same in return. Tom
Reynolds gave only enough information to satisfy the
old man's curiosity – his chosen profession, and that he
was here on behalf of his employers. He did not reveal
that he had never married, just in case the old man was
expecting a whole string of heirs to this 'fortune' he had
accumulated. Nor did he give his address.

Tom was a man who played his cards close to his
chest. At the same time his devious mind was ticking
over frantically, dark sinister thoughts beginning to take
shape. The old man, for his part, revealed everything,
although in truth there was little enough. However, he
also was careful not to disclose a particular snippet of
information, in case he had made the wrong decision.
No matter, though. Now that Arnold Thomas was
home, the two of them could discuss that little issue
later. There was plenty of time, he told himself. All
the time in the world. 'You'll not be bidding against
your old father, now, will you, son?' he asked, keeping
his voice at a discreet whisper.

'Only if I was all kinds of a fool, which I'm not.'

'Take me to the front, son. I want to see the whites of
their eyes while I'm bidding. It'll be like taking sweets
from a bairn.' The old man glanced back to see David
walking quietly behind, pushing his way forward in
order not to lose sight of them. 'You don't have to
stay,' Luther told him sharply. 'Arnold Thomas is here
now. I've little need for you.' Still David pursued them.
Irritated, Luther told his son, 'Like a barnacle he is.
All these years he's stuck to my arse like a bloody
barnacle!'

'Never mind that now.' Tom Reynolds could see
everyone surging forward to find their seats before the

rostrum. Suddenly he had a new and exciting reason for being here. 'We can talk about all that later, Father,' he said reassuringly, deliberately fussing round the old man and searching for the most comfortable seat in which to place him. 'Right now, there are more important matters to attend to.' And what could be more important than adding another property to a 'fortune' which had been sitting there waiting for him, while he had never known?

'Sod and bugger it!' Luther's voice sailed above a lull in conversation in the Queen's Head public house. 'I'm disappointed,' he told the two men. 'I'm more than bloody disappointed.' He turned to Tom with an apologetic look on his face. 'I especially wanted to succeed for you, son. You know that, don't you, eh?' He took another long noisy swig from his jug of ale. 'Damn the fellow, that's what I say,' he grumbled. 'The whole bloody shooting match!' he said with incredulity. 'He took the whole bloody shooting match, and with a *written bid*! I've never heard the like. What's more, he paid well above the odds, whoever he is.' He swivelled his bloodshot eyes from his son to David, then back again. 'What are you staring at?' he demanded. 'Think I'm drunk, d'yer? Well, what if I am? What if I sodding well am, eh? I'm celebrating, aren't I? My only son's come home. There's a *real* man to watch out for me now.' He leaned forward to say with a cruel tongue, 'So you see, David Miller, I won't be needing you no more, will I, eh? You and that bitch you wed, and them brats – well, you can all piss off out of it.' David's continuing silence infuriated him. 'D'you hear what I'm saying? I want you out! All of you. Out of my house by the morrow!'

Realising that things were moving a little too fast for his liking, Tom Reynolds intervened. 'Now wait a minute, Father, don't be so hasty,' he suggested. 'After all, there's much to be discussed, and I can't move in with you just like that. I have a life and a home of my own.' He was careful not to alienate the old man. 'Although, of course, I'll be moving back home with you just as soon as I've sorted things out,' he added reassuringly. 'Besides, David and his family will need time to find a place.' He smiled at his stepbrother. 'Isn't that so?' His mind was racing ahead; he wanted everything the old man had kept for him, but he had no intention of moving in with the old fool. In fact, his intentions were far more sinister.

David looked at the other man for a long moment. He saw two things . . . the same cunning, grasping creature who had deserted his own father when he needed him most, and a man who represented a very real threat to his own contentment. There was something else, too, something about those smiling eyes that sent a chill through him. His instincts were warning him. Of what? He wasn't altogether certain. One thing was sure, though. He would not leave his stepfather alone in that big old house, nor would he rest easy knowing that Arnold Thomas was there with him. That man might appear to be everything his father had ever wanted in a son, but as far as David was concerned, a leopard never changed its spots. Luther Reynolds' son had been a bad one. He was a bad one now. And he was playing a game which David did not fully understand. It was obvious that he had no intention of coming back to live in Blackburn. It was even more obvious that he held little affection for his father, in spite of fawning all over the old man as though he had been filled with joy to see him again after all these years. David knew differently. If Arnold Thomas had missed his father so much, why had he not come back before now? The truth was he hadn't come back at all, at least not to see his father. If it hadn't been for his employer sending him to that sale in Liverpool, the obnoxious little man would not now be sitting here, buttering up the surprisingly gullible old man, and leading him to believe that he was planning a homecoming. Addressing himself to Luther, David said patiently, 'Don't you think it's time we made our way home?'

His response was violent. 'Do what the hell you like!' he yelled, thumping his fist on the table and causing the drinks to spill over. 'You ain't listening, are you?' he demanded. 'I said I want the lot of you out of my house by the morrow. What's more, you'll take nothing with you, because what's in my house is mine, d'you hear? It's mine!' He scowled a moment longer, his boozy bloodshot eyes taking in his stepson's wounded expression, then, flinging one arm round Tom's shoulders, he chortled wickedly: 'That's told him, ain't it, eh?' Raising the half-empty jug of ale to his mouth, he slurped at the remainder, ignoring the trickle of brown liquid that meandered down his chin and on to his shirt collar. 'There you are, son,' he said, digging into his waistcoat pocket and slapping two silver coins on the table. 'You and me, we'll drink us health 'til they chuck us out, what d'you say?' He leaned heavily on the other man, laughing in his face and hugging him close. 'You and me, we'll show the buggers, won't we, eh?' He flung one arm wide as though to brush David from his sight. 'We don't need nobody . . . just you and me,' he said, his mouth almost touching that of his son.

Sickened by the old man's foul-smelling breath, Tom Reynolds half-turned his face away, though he was careful not to betray his disgust and loathing for this person who might as well be a stranger for all he knew or cared for him. Summoning David to help him, he said, 'For once, I think you may be right. We've done enough celebrating for one night. Now I think we'd best get Father to his bed.' The sooner he was rid of the pair of them, the better he would be able to think.

In the carriage, the old man gleefully outlined his plans for Arnold Thomas. 'Of course, you'll take over now, son. The business will flourish under you, I know it, and you'll not regret coming home, I promise you that.' He went on and on, tripping over his words with such excitement that he let slip something he would rather not have revealed just yet. He had been talking loudly, but suddenly he leaned closer to the other man's ear, saying in a low whisper, 'It's all yours, son. I want none of it. So long as I have you, I'm a happy man. There is one thing, though.' He glanced sidelong at David. 'It's all yours. *All but one little parcel.*' He chuckled as though at some private joke, then, sitting back in his seat, stared at David, saying loudly, 'It wouldn't be right if I didn't pay me dues, now would it, eh? When old Luther Reynolds is buried and under the ground, they'll not be able to say he didn't know how to pay his dues.' He chuckled again, and settled himself back in the red leather seat, leaving the other two men to ruminate on what he had said.

For David's part, he wouldn't have cared whether the old man had left him anything or nothing, he loved him too much. But he had a family to care for now, and there had been no opportunity to save a nest-egg, not from the wages paid to him over the years. All the same, it filled him with grief to think there would come a time when his stepfather was no more. He pushed it from his mind. It was too painful, too awful to contemplate.

Tom's thoughts could not have been more different from those of his stepbrother. Inwardly, he was seething. First the old man had led him to believe that he had left everything to him in his will. Now, he had intimated how he had reserved a certain title-deed for David, in return for his loyalty all these years. But what amount of land had he given to him? Was it a large holding? Was it the big house and the considerable plot on which it stood? Was it a block of terraced dwellings, which yielded a handsome sum every week? What had he left to his stepson? Tom had no way of knowing. One thing he did know, however, was that he wanted *everything* – every house, every square inch of land, every corner of what the old man had built up over the years. It was his, and he was not prepared to stand by while part of his rightful inheritance slid through his fingers!

By the time the carriage reached the mainline Liverpool station, Luther was more in command of his faculties. David had decided not to tell Beth that they were likely to be evicted. For his part, the scheming Tom had formulated the plan which had been taking shape all evening.

It was David who helped the old man down the carriage steps, but it was the favourite son who was summoned to see his father on to the platform. Biding his time, and hoping he might be able to make the old man see sense once they had time to discuss things, David stayed close behind as they all made their way past the ticket-desk and through the huge iron gates that opened out directly on to the platform, where the last train to Blackburn was due to arrive in ten minutes.

'You are coming home with me, aren't you, son?' Luther insisted in a worried voice as they pushed their way through the milling crowd. When the affirmative answer was quickly given, he chuckled and, nodding his head, mumbled, 'Of course you are, son. Of course you are.'

There was hardly room on the platform. It seemed as though everyone had left their departure from Liverpool until the very last minute. There were small groups of people gathering, eager to be the first to board. Men outnumbered women by two to one. There were couples of all ages, young and old alike, all chattering, all full of their day out, and pressing against each other as the minutes ticked away to when the train would steam in to carry them home. Men began to jostle their way forward, some dressed in long-tail coats and looking very formal, others wearing well-used and baggy brown trousers, with flat caps and grubby white scarves tucked into the necks of their jackets. These men were mostly younger, louder in voice, and enlivened by a jug or two of ale at the local inn. The noise grew until it was deafening, and the press of bodies mingling with the ale fumes sent up a warm acrid stench. Being hemmed in on all sides, and irritated by the sound of raucous laughter nearby, the three men pushed forward through the fidgeting bodies. Soon they had reached a vantage point from which they could easily board the train. 'We'd have done better if we'd carried straight on to Blackburn in the carriage,' David pointed out. He was painfully aware that the old man had consumed far too much ale.

'Be buggered!' retorted Luther Reynolds. 'And who'd have to foot the bloody bill, eh? Me! That's who.' He turned on David vehemently. 'I've already told you . . . you're free to do as you like. If you want to ride all the way to Blackburn in a fancy carriage, then sod off! Go on . . . sod off. But mind you've enough brass in your pocket to pay for it, afore you climb on board, 'cause you've seen your last penny from Luther Reynolds.' He doubled forward and laughed aloud, swinging out with his arms and causing a man nearby to grab him. 'Steady on, old fellow,' the man told him with some concern. His reward was a mouthful of abuse and the curt instruction to, 'Bugger off and keep your paws to yourself!' Realising the cantankerous old soul was the worse for drink, the man discreetly edged away.

From a distance, the train whistle could be heard,

once, twice . . . nearer and nearer. The noise rose to a painful crescendo as the crowd surged forward in anticipation. Tom Reynolds had waited for his chance. When it came, he was ready. 'Hey! Stop your pushing!' he yelled to some imaginary figure behind him. As he turned, he put out his knee and slyly thrust it into the old man's side. Suddenly there was mayhem as Luther fought to keep his balance, his eyes wide and terrified as the train hurtled into sight. Somewhere far off a woman screamed and every soul there was sent into a fearful panic. 'NO!' David's terrified cry split the air as he lurched forward to grab his stepfather's coat. But it was already too late – in that split second the old man stared into the bold eyes of his son and saw the wickedness there. It was a wickedness he himself had bred in Tom, and he saw the irony of it all. He was still smiling when he toppled over the edge to fall beneath the thundering wheels, taking David with him.

Beth glanced again at the grandfather clock. Its mournful persistent ticking echoed through the room, seeming to heighten her fears. Laying her sewing on the arm of the chair, she went to the window from where she looked out into the dark night for the umpteenth time. 'Where are you?' she murmured into the silence, her dark eyes troubled. It was not like David to stay out so late. True, he had warned her that he and Luther Reynolds would not be back early, but it was now past midnight, and still there was no sign of them.

Closing the curtains once more, she returned to the fireplace and wedged the big black kettle on to the still-glowing coals in the firegrate. She would make herself a cup of tea and think of pleasant things to while away the time. Suddenly a saying of old Maisie's came into her mind and she was forced to smile. 'It don't matter what troubles you got, darlin' . . . a cup o' tea will allus lift yer spirits.' So while the water in the kettle quietly began bubbling, Beth resumed her sewing and softly hummed a tune. David would be home soon, she assured herself.

It suddenly occurred to her that if it wasn't for him, she would be a woman alone in a harsh world. Worse, she would be a woman at Luther Reynolds' mercy. It didn't bear thinking about, and so she forced herself to muse on other things . . . everyday things that happened all around her, things like Cissie growing increasingly restless in her work at the flower shop and wanting to 'branch out on me own, Beth. Be me own boss!' Beth had seen how the girl was becoming more and more determined to go her own way. It was a source of anxiety to her, because times were hard and making a decent wage was not easy. Then there was Matthew. Though his letter had made it sound as if he was coping well with sea-life, Beth's instincts told her that all was not as it seemed. Yet, until such time when he might be allowed home on leave, there was no way of telling.

At that moment the door opened and Cissie came in, her hair tousled and her eyes swollen with sleep. 'Why haven't you come to bed, Beth?' she asked, going to the fire and warming her back.

'Come away from there!' Beth warned her. 'It only needs your night-shift to catch light and there'll be no saving you.' She had not forgotten the fire that had taken Cissie's mammy. There were times when she woke up in the night, haunted by the memory. It was one of the things that would go to the grave with her.

Knowing full well what was on Beth's mind, and seeing the fear in her eyes, Cissie hurriedly did as she was told, coming to kneel on the floor beside Beth, from where she could still feel the cheery warmth of the fire. 'Why are you up so late, though?' she persisted, glancing at the clock and seeing that it was already morning.

376

'I'm waiting for David,' Beth replied. 'There's no need for you to be down here. Go back to bed.' The kettle sent out a spurt of water, its shrill whistle startling both Beth and the girl. Almost in the same instant there was a loud knock on the door, a pause, then another series of urgent knocks. Something about them turned Beth's heart over. Pulling herself up from the depths of the armchair, she crossed towards the door, at the same time telling the girl, 'You stay here.'

'But who is it?' Cissie too was afraid. It was odd that someone should be thumping the door at the turn of midnight.

'I expect David's forgotten to take his key,' Beth called over her shoulder, forcing a matter-of-fact tone into her voice. But her heart was pounding. David *never* forgot to take his key! And even if by some remote chance he had left it behind on this occasion, Luther always kept a bunch of keys pinned to the inside of his waistcoat pocket.

As she made her way to the front door, the sound of Richard screaming for her caused her to ask: 'Comfort him, Cissie.' Even before she got to the door, Cissie was bounding up the stairs. At the top of the landing the girl looked back to see Beth staring up at her. In that moment when their eyes met each knew the other's fear. There was a link between them, a great abiding love that bound them together, and Beth was deeply grateful for that; although she could never have envisaged in her wildest dreams how much she would come to need Maisie's girl in the harrowing weeks ahead. 'All right, all right,' she cried out when the knocking resumed again. Placing her hand on the door knob, she asked: 'Who is it? What do you want?' From the corner of her eye she saw Cissie and the boy going quietly into the sitting room.

'Don't worry, Mrs Miller,' the voice came back;

a stranger's voice, but kind and soothing. 'It's the constable and a colleague . . . come to talk with you, my dear. Be so good as to open the door.'

Stooping to peer through the letter-box, Beth could just make out the dark uniforms with their shiny buttons. With trembling fingers she slipped the sneck and, turning the knob, inched open the heavy wooden door. Much later, when she came to reflect on this fateful night, she recalled the way the door creaked and groaned. David had meant to grease the hinges, but he never found the time. 'Yes?' The word seemed so inadequate, but she dared not voice her fears. She dared not ask what was on the tip of her tongue.

The taller of the two officers was the first to speak. Leaning forward, he said gently, 'I think it might be best if we come inside, ma'am.' When she nodded and stepped back, he ushered the other constable in and followed behind. Without looking at them, and yet acutely aware that they were standing only an arm's reach from her with their faces set in serious expressions, Beth swallowed hard to still the fluttering fear that had risen to choke her. With deliberate calm, she swung the door to and clicked the sneck across. Then, turning, she merely nodded her head and gestured for them to follow her. Bypassing the room where the two children were waiting, she went straight to the drawing room, wide dark eyes filled with fear, and with a heart that silently prayed to God that the news was not too awful.

In the adjoining room, the two children huddled close in the chair which Beth had vacated only moments before. They had heard the passing footsteps, and they wondered. From the next room they could hear the low drone of voices. Almost immediately there followed an eerie silence, during which Cissie instinctively drew the boy close to her. When Beth's cry cut the air, it shook them. They had never heard her make such a sound, such an agonised sound it put the fear of God into them. They clung closer and waited. The silence seemed never ending. Soon footsteps could be heard returning along the hallway. 'It's all right, darlin',' Cissie told the boy, when he began violently shivering in her arms. 'It's all right.' But she was afraid, her instincts telling her that something dreadful had happened this night.

The footsteps stopped outside the door, the handle slowly turned, the door was pushed open, and there was Beth. Her face was chalk-white, and she was trembling. The two men stood directly behind her. The one with the dark curling moustache was staring away, seemingly unable or unwilling to look at them; the taller man gazed compassionately at the two children huddled together. It was a pitiful sight and touched his heart, for he had a young family of his own. 'Look after Richard, please, Cissie. I have . . . to go . . .'

Beth's voice faltered and she made a choking sound. Quickly composing herself, she came into the room, holding out her arms to take the boy into her embrace. 'Be good,' she said, kissing him tenderly. 'Mammy has to go out for a while. Constable Maitland here will stay with you both.' She looked at the girl, an imploring look that spoke volumes. Stooping to put Richard down on the floor, she leaned forward to tell Cissie in a whisper, 'There's been an accident . . . David is in the Infirmary.' She thought it best not to say any more. But then, how could she tell this impressionable young girl that Luther had stumbled to his death beneath the wheels of a train, and David . . . foolish, kind David . . . had been badly injured in his effort to stop the old man falling? 'I have to go to him, Cissie,' was all she could say, then she averted her eyes from the girl's entreating stare and quickly hurried out of the room to collect her shawl from the hallstand. One last glance at the constable, and she was ready.

'Beth!' Cissie had followed her to the door; the boy was clinging to her night-shift, his frightened green eyes following Beth's every move. 'Will you tell David . . . tell him I . . .' A sob caught in her throat. When Beth swung round at the girl's words, she realised there were tears in Cissie's eyes. 'Don't worry.' Her expression showed that she understood. 'I'll tell him you're think-ing of him, sweetheart.' Collecting her purse from the hallstand, before flinging the long brown shawl round her swollen figure, she waited for the constable to open the door. 'Look after Richard, please, Cissie,' she told the girl, adding with a reassuring smile that belied the turmoil inside her, 'You'll be all right.' At the sight of Constable Maitland, who had come up behind the children, she gave one more instruction before running down the steps into the waiting police-waggon. 'Keep them away from the fire.' He nodded, and in a moment she was gone. The house was deathly quiet. Placing one hand on each child, the kindly constable turned them back into the room. The kettle was whistling as he closed the door.

'I'm sorry, Beth,' he said. That was all. The words were spoken in a gasp, his broken body lying twisted beneath the sheets and his cold fingers limp in hers. Even in the grip of pain, and knowing that he was breathing his last, the eyes remained infuriatingly gentle.

Long after they led her away from his side, Beth could still feel the incredible strength in his fingers during that last moment before he closed his eyes for ever; a strength that had astonished her, for David had never shown that side of himself before.

Now, as she sat in the doctor's office, her head bowed in her hands and the image of her husband still vivid in her mind, Beth wondered whether, in that one final moment when he knew they would be parted always, he had regained the strength that his stepfather had sucked from him all his life. She thought it odd that he did not ask for Luther, nor question whether he himself would live or die. His smile was strange to her, yet curiously beautiful, as though he believed that in death he and the stepfather he idolised would be reunited where no one could come between them. He did not ask after Cissie or the boy, merely reached out to place his hand on the swell of her stomach, his smile bathing her tearful face, and those three words softly whispered: 'I'm sorry, Beth.' Not that he loved her. Only that he was sorry. Sorry for what? she asked herself. Sorry for dying? Sorry for not saving his stepfather? Sorry because he knew she would now be alone? Why was he so sorry? Anger took hold of her. He should not have been sorry! He should not have thrown his life away on a cruel old man who never loved him! He should not be dead now! Three times she had gone back into that small side room where he lay. Three times she had touched his kindly face and asked him: 'Why?' But he gave no answer, for he was gone from that place. Gone with the man who meant more to him than his own life. If God decreed that Luther Reynolds should burn in Hell, Beth was sure that David would elect to burn with him. She could never understand such blind adulation, especially as that wicked old man had only ever shown him the utmost contempt and loathing.

'There was nothing we could do, you know.' The doctor was seated behind his desk, studying her bowed figure and trying to call her back. 'It was already too late when they brought him in.' Still Beth did not look up. He came round the desk to stand before her. 'Are you all right, Mrs Miller?' His tone was anxious. 'You really should go home and rest quietly. There is the baby to consider.'

Beth looked up, her eyes brimming, and hysterical

laughter threatening to overwhelm her. Only a woman could understand how futile his words were. 'Go home and rest quietly,' he urged. When only minutes before she had watched a kind, unselfish soul take his last breath, her husband, a man who wanted her to love him when she could not, a good man, a man she had much to thank for. But, no. The doctor was right about her going home. She had two children waiting there. Wearily, she pulled herself up out of the chair. 'Thank you, doctor,' she told him, her dark tragic eyes sweeping his face. 'I know you did everything possible.'

'The constable is waiting to take you back.'

She shook her head. 'No. Tell him thank you all the same,' she said, 'I have money enough for a Hansom cab to take me to the station, but I'll walk part of the distance.' She glanced out of the window. Already the sky was bright with the promise of a lovely July day. She had lost count of time, but was surprised when the clock on the wall showed that it was now ten minutes past four in the morning.

'Walk?' He seemed astonished. 'Is that wise in your condition, Mrs Miller . . . and in view of what has happened?' He studied her face with those dark expressive eyes and shining hair that fell loosely about her shoulders, as though she had just risen from her bed; but then, she could be forgiven that. It had been past midnight when the officers called on her, and she had been through a most traumatic experience. There were women who could never cope with such things. This one was strong. Even if her heart was breaking, she would not show it.

'I need to walk a while,' she said now, 'I need to breathe.' Stooping to collect the brown paper bag from her chair, she half-smiled. 'It isn't much to show for a man's life, is it?' she asked in a dry voice. In her mind's eye, she could see the nurse spreading out the contents on her desk. The small bone toothpick, his front-door key, the brown pig-skin purse containing two guineas, a handkerchief, and a small leatherbound notebook which he carried everywhere – mostly for reckoning Luther's fortune!

'Surely you would rather wait and let your brother-in-law see you home?' The doctor saw the shadowy rings beneath her eyes and knew that she was immensely tired. 'He won't be long, you know. He's made his statement and now he's collecting his father's belongings. Won't you allow him to take you home, Mrs Miller?'

Beth was visibly shocked. 'Brother-in-law?' she said, looking at him as though he had made some kind of mistake. And yet she did have a brother-in-law, she reminded herself. However, until this moment, no mention had been made of Luther's son being here. How was he summoned so quickly? Where did they find him? Even Luther did not know the whereabouts of his ungrateful son, Arnold Thomas. 'He's here?' she asked. 'In the Infirmary?'

'He was with his father and your husband when the accident happened. Apparently, they met up in the sale room and afterwards were making their way home together. There was another witness, a gentleman who seemingly had a small set-to with your father-in-law some minutes before he fell.' He wondered at the look of astonishment on her face. 'If you'll wait just one minute, I'll let your brother-in-law know you're here. He was informed earlier that you were on your way, but the authorities have kept him busy.' He smiled wryly. 'We can never escape from the legalities of life, I'm afraid,' he said, glancing at the official papers which Beth had signed a few moments before. His smile was now quickly replaced by the abrupt professional manner with which he had originally greeted her. 'Please sit down, Mrs Miller. I'm sure you'll only have a moment to wait before he's finished.'

'I don't want to see him.' Beth's mind was in chaos. Luther Reynolds' son had been with him and David when the accident happened! She knew instinctively that she would not like Luther's son any more than she had liked the old man himself. And what was going to happen now? Would he turn them out of the house? It seemed likely, because any son who could walk out on his own father would not think twice about claiming what was his, and she had not forgotten how Luther had taken great pleasure in telling David, 'It's all for my own flesh and blood.' Suddenly, she needed to get out of this place. She couldn't think straight here. 'I have to go now,' she said, wrapping the shawl about her shoulders and hurrying to the door. 'I'm sorry.' Before the doctor could protest further, she was gone and the door was clicking shut. He stared after her for a moment, then he shrugged and returned to his mountain of paperwork.

As Beth fled from the building, Tom Reynolds emerged from the side ward where he had been 'dutifully' paying his last respects to his unfortunate stepbrother. The officer had gone in with him, and now he turned to Tom with a look of sympathy. 'Dreadful business,' he said. 'Dreadful! But accidents happen, I'm sorry to say. It's times like these when I'd rather sweep the streets than be an officer of the law.' He waved a paper in the air, the long and detailed statement of what had taken place. 'Terrible accident,' he said again, 'I'm very sorry, but certain formalities have to be followed, even at a time like this.'

Tom Reynolds' expression was suitably sad. 'Of course,' he said. 'I understand. But now, if you don't mind, I would like to be alone with my grief.'

The constable's voice was kindness itelf. 'My condolences, sir,' he said, shaking his head, 'a terrible tragedy.

Terrible!' With a slow heavy tread, he made his way along the corridor, then out of the door through which Beth had passed only moments before. Outside he stood a moment, enjoying the fresh air, then wedging his helmet securely over his thick thatch of ginger-coloured hair, went away at a jauntier pace. He was glad the job was done. 'Rum thing,' he muttered to himself, 'losing your father and brother in one fell sweep.' He quickened his pace as though eager to get away for fear he might be contaminated with the ill-fortune that had struck that poor grief-laden man back there.

'Of course I am sorry to have missed my sister-in-law,' Tom Reynolds explained to the doctor, 'and from what you tell me, I need to hurry after her and make certain she arrives home safely.' He lied with conviction, hoping he was portraying himself as a grieving but concerned individual. He was not the slightest bit interested in his stepbrother's wife. If anything, he was delighted that their paths had not crossed just now. First, there were papers to sign, and certain arrangements to be made; after which Tom Reynolds hastened from the building, under the pretext of being anxious about his sister-in-law. But it was not his hapless stepbrother's wife who filled his mind as he travelled directly to Liverpool Railway Station, where he would begin his journey back to London. No indeed! It was his own success at having effectively got away with the heinous crime of murdering his own father, and dispatching David Miller at the same time. It was this realisation that played on his thoughts and lifted his spirits.

As for Mrs Miller, well now . . . let the poor bitch enjoy her short stay in Luther Reynolds' house, because soon it would belong to his only son, and there would be no place there for David Miller's 'mistakes'. Soon as ever the funeral was over and the will read out, there were plans to be made. Plans that did not include anyone but Tom Reynolds! If the old man was as good as his word, everything he owned would go to his only son.

Recalling the last conversation he had had with his father, Tom was reminded that a small legacy had been made to David. That was a real pity, because now it would no doubt pass on to his wife. Suddenly he saw his stepbrother's wife in a different light! His curiosity was aroused and he wondered whether he should have made her acquaintance after all. What exactly had the old man left to David? he wondered. Of course, Luther could have written a clause into his will stipulating that in the event of David's untimely demise, all should revert to his own blood-kin; that being Arnold Thomas himself. But for the moment there was no use racking his brains. He had no idea at all what had been left . . . either to himself or to his stepbrother; although, of course, the old man had intimated that he had built up a considerable fortune over the many years since he last saw his son.

Climbing into the train carriage, Tom leaned back into the seat and closed his eyes. Greed overwhelmed him but he must be patient and contain himself: the contents of Luther's will would not be known until after the funeral. Until then, there was much to arrange, much to think about. He laughed softly when the image of Esther came into his mind. Wouldn't she be envious though? Oh, wouldn't it be wonderful to rise above that family who, for too long, had looked down on him? He might even go so far as to seek out the lovely wilful Beth. When a man had a fortune, there was no limit to what he could do, or which woman he might entice into his bed. The thought was exhilarating. The taste of success was intoxicating. He couldn't settle. Getting out of his seat, he began pacing up and down the empty carriage. The day of the funeral could not come fast enough for him. And then . . . oh, what a great time he would have, counting the fortune which had so carefully been built for him. And with such devotion!

His laughter rang out from one end of the train to the other. Those who cringed from the awful sound might have been forgiven for thinking that the Devil himself had joined them on their journey.

Chapter Ten

In that beautiful quiet church, Beth stood behind the first pew, alone and resolute, her dark eyes focused on the two coffins that stood side by side before the altar. The voice of the priest drifted to the high rafters, his prayers echoed in Beth's heart; but her prayers were not for Luther, whom she still blamed for her husband's death. Her silent prayers were for that humble, quiet man who had taken care of her and the children.

It saddened her to know that David would never see his own child in the flesh. When she had first conceived, Beth had felt guilty because she had not wanted the child with all her heart. Yet, over the weeks, when she had felt it growing inside her, she had come to know and to love it. Now she thanked God that David had lived for a reason. The child was his legacy. A small person in his own likeness. Beth vowed to tell the child all the good and admirable qualities its father possessed, but she would be careful not to reveal the weakness which ran through his character and made him only half the man he might have been. That 'weakness' was Luther Reynolds. No, Beth did not pray for him. She would leave that to the priest.

Word had been sent ahead that Luther's son had been delayed. In fact, he never arrived; not for the service, nor for the lowering of the caskets into the ground. Now, when it was over, Beth found herself still alone. 'God go with you,' the priest said, and then he too departed. She smiled and watched him hurry away, a tall man in black ankle boots that were covered in mud. It made her smile. Even a man of God could not rise above the earth on which he walked. After it was all over, she went back into the church where she knelt on the hard boards and raised her face to the crucifix high on the wall. 'Help me, Lord,' she prayed; the desperate plea ran round that huge empty place and seemed to carry to Heaven itself. 'Tell me what I must do.' She waited a while, as though allowing the Almighty to think about what she had said. Then, bending her knee and making the sign of the cross on her forehead, she left the church and hurried home to the loved ones who waited for her. For one fleeting moment, she allowed herself to indulge in thoughts of Tyler. In that wonderful moment, her burden was lightened and her sorry heart was lifted with joy. But it was gone all too soon. Like memories of Tyler, it drifted into that secret part of her that was forever closed. Now and then she would peek inside, but the happiness it brought was short-lived. Just like the dream. A dream that never came true.

Today was Thursday. Blackburn centre was always quiet on a Thursday. Folks had long spent out and were biding their time until the next pay day. As Beth went down Ainsworth Street towards the flower shop where she had left Richard in Cissie's charge, she gave thanks for the girl's small wage. Times were really hard, with fewer tradesmen on the streets and almost all of the shops empty of customers. The flower shop was no exception. Now, letting her eyes rove over the many beautifully arranged flowers that spilled in a riot of colour into the window, Beth was disturbed to see that they were virtually the same as when she had called in with Richard this morning. Nothing appeared to have been sold. It was true that when folks had to cut back, it was always the little luxuries that went first; and what could be more of a luxury than a vase of fresh flowers?

As Beth went into the shop the tiny bell above the door rang out, bringing both Cissie and Moll Sutton rushing. The matronly woman emerged with a ready smile on her large, plain face, obviously expecting a customer. When she saw it was Beth, she made an effort to keep the smile, but it soon fell away. Cissie, however, came hurtling across the shop into Beth's arms, 'Oh, I'm glad you're back!' she said breathlessly, hugging her hard. Cissie had been wary about Beth attending the funeral, because the accident and the ensuing ordeal at the Infirmary had told badly on her. Her appetite had gone, and she spent most nights pacing the floor of her bedroom.

This past week had been especially hard, and it was showing. Moll Sutton remarked on it now. 'You really are looking peaked, my dear,' she said, bidding Beth to follow her into the back room where Richard was seated cross-legged on the floor, playing with a small wooden toy. On seeing Beth he scrambled up and came to wrap his arms round her. 'Can we stay a bit longer, eh, Mammy?' he asked, his green shining eyes looking up at her pleadingly.

'Well, I never!' she said in mock horror. 'Here's your mammy come to take you home, and you don't want to go with her.' She smiled secretly at the other woman, who for some reason seemed agitated.

'Just a bit longer?' He glanced at the wooden toy on the rug. It was a beautiful replica of a tram, pains-takingly carved out of beechwood and painted in bright dazzling colours. 'I want to finish my game,' he said forlornly, making her ashamed that he had no real toys to speak of. Being dependent on Luther's generosity, she had been careful not to waste money on trivial things, although Richard had not been made to go without toys altogether.

Beth was firm, though. It had been a long and distress-ing day, and she was impatient to be within her own four walls. She stilled her thoughts, being quick to remind herself that 'her own four walls' were not hers at all. No doubt the letter of eviction would soon be on its way. It was something she dare not think about, although at the back of her mind there was a last forlorn hope that the worst would not happen. 'No, Richard,' she told the boy, 'I imagine Mrs Sutton has had quite enough of you for one day.'

'As a matter of fact, Beth,' Moll Sutton appeared to be slightly embarrassed as she went on, 'there's something I want to talk with you about.' She picked up the toy and gave it to the boy. 'You keep it,' she said to everyone's surprise. 'My son outgrew it years ago, and I'm sure I don't want to play with it.' She laughed now as the boy clutched the toy to himself, his eyes imploring his mother not to make him hand it back.

'Oh, Mrs Sutton . . . are you sure?' Beth could see how well the toy had been cared for. It seemed such a precious thing to give away.

'Of course. I want the boy to have it,' came the reply. 'But if you have a moment, can we let him play while we talk in the parlour?' She turned to Cissie, who had been preparing to leave with Beth. 'Keep an eye on the shop,' she instructed. 'We'll only be a minute.'

Cissie reluctantly nodded. She would much rather be going home straightaway with Beth. She wanted to know about the service; after all, she had liked David a lot. It didn't seem fair to her that Beth would not let her go to the church, although on reflection she supposed it was right. Her thoughts changed course as she wondered what Moll Sutton had to discuss with Beth. She peeped into the shop. It was empty. It had been empty for most of the day. It was almost four now, and it was plain that there would be no more customers coming through that door before Moll Sutton put the bolt across. In fact, there had been only two all day long, and they only wanted buttonholes. Oh, and of course there was the beautiful spray which Beth had taken with her to the church.

Inside the back parlour, Moll Sutton ushered Beth into one of the two black horsehair chairs that were positioned either side of the fireplace. 'I dare say you're gasping for a cup of tea,' she said kindly. The table was already laid with a large daisy-patterned tray containing one dainty bone-china cup and saucer, milk jug and sugar bowl, and a small porcelain teapot. Moll Sutton had been a widow these many years and her only son lived miles away in the Midlands. When Beth replied that yes, she would welcome a cup of tea, it took but a moment for the other woman to get the kettle boiling on the rusty old gas ring, and soon she had collected another cup and saucer from the high, narrow cupboard. Soon she was seated and addressing Beth. 'Firstly, I want to say that my heart goes out to you in your tragic circumstances,' she began. Lowering her own cup to her knee and holding it there, she continued to stare at Beth for a moment before averting her eyes, seemingly lost for words. The ensuing silence was awkward. 'You'll be wondering why I asked you back here,' she ventured. Her hands were trembling, and she was obviously in great difficulty.

'I think I know why,' Beth told her in a quiet voice. She hated to see this kindly woman so distressed. 'I'm not blind,' she said with a half-smile. Inside, her stomach was churning because she realised what was on Moll's mind. 'You want to let Cissie go, don't you?'

'Oh, I don't want to!' the other woman protested, yet she was greatly relieved that Beth had spelled it out. 'But lately the business hardly brings in enough to keep me, let alone pay Cissie's wages.' She went on to assure Beth that: 'Should business pick up, I'll be knocking on your door, I can promise you that. Cissie's a good worker, and the customers like her merry chat.'

Beth nodded, and smiled, and wondered what would become of them all. She politely finished her tea while listening to Moll's tale of woe, and then she left the woman with a few kind words of reassurance before leaving the premises with Cissie and the boy laughing and chatting beside her. They did not yet know what had transpired, and so thankfully were unaware of the hardships that lay ahead.

On the following Monday morning, Beth walked the half mile into Blackburn town centre, where she reported to the offices of Marriott and Pikesley, the firm of solicitors who had taken care of Luther Reynolds' affairs when he was alive, and now were in charge of executing his will. Beth was extremely nervous as she was shown into the waiting room by a young woman with an authoritative air and an irritating habit of screwing up her nose in order to save her tiny spectacles from sliding over the tip of it. 'I'll keep that for the moment,' she told Beth, taking the long brown envelope in which was the letter informing her of the time and place of the will-reading. Beth had been tempted to stay away and wait for the bad news to come to her, but at the last moment had decided she would rather face it head on. 'There are some magazines on the table,' the young woman said in a squeaky voice. 'Mr Marriott won't be too long.'

The hard wooden chair struck cold as Beth sat down. The room was surprisingly austere, as the partners in this firm undoubtedly raked in a considerable income from their many business clients. The walls were an unwelcoming shade of green, the carpet threadbare in places, and apart from the half-dozen chairs positioned around the walls, there was only one other piece of furniture – a rather scratched and unattractive small oval table in the centre of the room.

Half an hour later Beth was still waiting, and growing

increasingly anxious. She wondered whether Cissie and
the boy were all right. Normally, young Richard would
be in the middle of his lessons by now, but Beth had
found it necessary to give the tutor notice, and she herself
had taken over responsibility for Richard's schooling.
Although she enjoyed the challenge, she was well aware
of her own limitations. The situation was not to her
liking, but it was the best solution in the circumstances.

Sitting in that cold, unfriendly room, chilled to the
marrow and convinced that soon she would be told to
leave the house in Buncer Lane, Beth was besieged by
all manner of doubts and anxieties. This past week she
had trudged from one end of Blackburn to the other,
searching for rooms where she and the children might
set up home. Every answer was in the negative. 'Sorry
dear, we don't take children' or 'With no man, how are
you going to pay the rent? Oh, no, I'm afraid I can't help
you.' No one with any room to let was prepared to take in
a woman with two children and another on the way, and,
in all truth, she could not really blame them. After all,
they had a living to make, and even Beth could not see
how she would be able to pay the rent after her meagre
savings were depleted.

Cissie was an angel . . . going out early in the morning
to lend a hand to anybody that needed it, and returning
each night with a few coins that she would give to Beth
– 'To keep us out of the workhouse' she would say with
a wry little smile. Beth had also earned her keep by
taking in two of her neighbours' children and charging
one shilling each child for five mornings' tuition. She
would have recruited more, but there was much suspicion of Luther Reynolds' daughter-in-law. It was too
well rumoured how she had been the cause of the tragic
fire in Larkhill when three people lost their lives. The
people of Buncer Lane had long kept their distance from
the feared and disliked Luther Reynolds, and saw no

reason to acquaint themselves with the woman who had been a mere lodger in one of his rundown properties.

The sound of the heavy oak door opening into the reception area startled Beth out of her reverie. But what happened next shocked her to the core. She heard footsteps coming closer, ever closer. In a minute a man was at the reception desk, his voice addressing the young woman. 'Arnold Thomas Reynolds, to see Mr Marriott.' His voice came to her out of the past, striking dread to her heart. In her confusion, Beth heard the woman's polite reply, 'Mr Marriott has a client with him, but he won't be long, sir. Mrs Miller is already here, in the waiting room. If you would care to join her I'll inform Mr Marriott that you're both here.'

'Ah!' Tom Reynolds was curious to meet his stepbrother's wife, especially as he suspected she might be due for an inheritance of sorts. 'Then I'll keep her company, but make sure you let Mr Marriott know I am a busy man and have come all the way from London for this meeting.'

Tom Reynolds! Shaken by the sound of that familiar voice, Beth had gone quietly to the door where she remained half-hidden from sight, her wide, shocked eyes watching as the man approached; the same slight figure, the shock of white hair, the inherent arrogance which had always infuriated her. It all came to her now . . . Arnold Thomas . . . Tom Reynolds . . . was Luther's son! Panic took hold of her. Frantically, she searched for a way out. The only means of escape was by the door where she was now standing; it was the only way in or out of that small room. There was no escape. What to do? What to do? With every second he came nearer. 'Take hold of yourself, Beth,' she murmured. 'What does it matter if he sees you? What does it matter?' Oh, but it did matter! Just the sight of him sent shivers through her. Tom Reynolds had always gone out of his way to antagonise her. He was her mother's closest ally, and would be only too thrilled to run back to Esther with the tale of her downfall. He was a bad sort, and Beth suspected he had created all kinds of mischief for Tyler and herself. He was a man without conscience, a man eaten up by greed, a man tarred with the same wicked brush as her mother. Thinking of it now, she was not surprised he had been created from Luther Reynolds' seed.

She had to get away! He must not see her! Desperate, she flattened herself against the wall, her heart pounding. Maybe she could slip away as he came into the room? Perhaps he would go straight past? Too late! The room darkened as he appeared in the doorway. She swung round, her horrified eyes meeting his. For a long fearful moment he stared at her, his pinkish eyes bulging out of his head and his mouth partly open as though he was suddenly struck dumb. Then, drawing his thin lips back over his teeth, he smiled; a smile that spoke of evil. 'Well! Well! Well! Elizabeth Ward,' he hissed in a soft caressing voice. His eyes devoured her, looking her up and down, pausing with surprise when he saw that she was with child. But then he smiled again. 'You are . . . David's wife!' He shook his head. He too had received a terrible shock, but he was a man of cunning and quick to adapt.

'Sit down, my dear,' he invited. 'We obviously have a great deal to talk about.' He stepped forward when she refused his invitation, his hand stroking her arm and his face close to hers. 'Not so high and mighty now, are you?' he murmured wickedly. 'Not so proud, eh? I'm given to understand that my father left me everything.' He laughed softly. 'Isn't it ironic that you could well be living in *my* house? Oh, but of course . . . I wouldn't mind that, my dear. Not if you made it worth my while.' He could not believe his good fortune.

It was the feel of his hand on her arm that snapped

something inside her. Without a word, she thrust her way past him, colliding with the receptionist as she fled the room. She could hear the young woman calling after her, but was too shocked to reply.

The walk back to Buncer Lane gave Beth time to think, clearing her mind enough for her to realise that she could not stay in the house a moment longer. The shock had left her feeling physically sick. Why had she not realised before? Some years back, Tom Reynolds had confided in her in a moment's weakness, explaining how he had walked out on his family years ago when, 'I could see there was nothing to be gained by staying.' His North-country accent was still evident, even after living in the South for so long. He had chosen a career in land development, the very profession which came so naturally to Luther. Like father like son! Made out of the same mould. Why had she not seen the resemblance between the two men? Arnold Thomas, Tom Reynolds. Why had she not realised?

She had gone to the solicitors that morning, hoping against hope that Luther's son might be persuaded to let her and the children stay in the house, at least until the baby was born. Now her every hope was dashed. Oh, he wouldn't mind her living in his house. *'Not if you made it worth my while.'* Beth was left in no doubt as to what that implied.

Fearing he might have followed her, she quickened her steps. She had to get home to the children. There were plans to be made, and quickly!

She had no time. No sooner had she arrived home to be greeted by two boisterous and inquisitive children, than a carriage drew up and out stepped Tom Reynolds. Cissie saw him from the sitting-room window. 'Look, Beth,' she cried, keeping out of sight. 'There's a man watching the house.'

On seeing who it was, Beth's heart fell. Tom Reynolds had dallied on the pavement, his small sharp eyes taking stock of the house and, more particularly, the sizeable piece of land on which it stood. She could almost read his mind. Buncer Lane was in a good area for redevelopment, and where this house stood there was room for any number of smaller dwellings. 'Come away, Cissie,' she told the girl.

'Who is he?' she wanted to know, reluctantly following Beth and the boy into the kitchen.

Realising that she should pick and choose her words until she knew which way to turn, Beth replied, 'He's Arnold Thomas . . . Luther's son.'

Sensing Beth's nervousness, Cissie went on, 'Did you meet him at the solicitors? Did the old man leave everything to him? Will he let us stay in the house, d'you think, Beth?'

She took a moment to answer. How could she explain?

'Well, I don't like him!' the boy suddenly blurted out. 'I don't want him to come here and live with us.'

Forcing a smile, Beth told him, 'Don't worry, sweetheart. It won't come to that, I promise you.'

Cissie had been quietly watching Beth. She knew instinctively that something was wrong. 'You don't like him, do you?'

Realising that both Cissie and the boy were becoming anxious, Beth was determined that they should not know what was in her mind. When the knock came on the door, she told Cissie, 'It's a lovely day. Take Richard into the garden for a while. Mr Reynolds and I have much to discuss.' Though her ready smile appeared to satisfy the boy, it did not altogether deceive Cissie.

Waiting until the boy had gone on ahead, Cissie asked Beth in a worried voice, 'If he puts us out on the street . . . where will we go?'

'He hasn't told us to leave yet.'

'But he will, won't he?'

Beth shook her head. 'I don't know what will happen,' she said truthfully. No sooner were the words out of her mouth than the knock came on the door again. 'Please, Cissie. Do as I ask and keep Richard happy in the garden until Mr Reynolds has gone. We'll talk then.'

'And will you tell me the truth?' Cissie had been horrified to see how ill and anxious Beth had seemed on returning from the solicitors earlier. In her heart, she knew that Beth was not telling her everything. There was something going on here that was bad, and as far as she could see the worst thing that could happen was for Mr Reynolds to turn them out. Yet, she had the feeling that there was more to it than whether they would be turned out. She had seen the look in Beth's eyes when the knock came on the door. She was keeping something back, Cissie was sure of it.

Beth looked at her now, her expression serious and her voice little more than a whisper. 'There are things you should know,' she said at length. 'And, yes, I will tell you,' she assured the girl. 'Now, will you please do as I ask?'

Cissie regarded her curiously, thinking how strained and pale she was, and how the light had gone from her lovely dark eyes. 'If that's what you want,' she said softly, leaving Beth to make her way along the passage, her heart in her mouth as she saw Tom's shadowy image through the stained glass in the top half of the door. Taking a deep breath, she mustered her courage and swung the door open.

His bold eyes appraised her, then he smiled slyly, saying in a hard voice, 'I'm afraid you can't object to my seeing my own property.' When she hesitated, he waved an official-looking envelope in the air. 'We need to talk,' he added. Beth gave no reply, simply stepping aside while he came into the hallway. As he brushed past her, he deliberately touched her breast with his arm. From that moment on she was on her guard, her suspicions heightened.

He smiled at her, a crafty smile which put her in mind of Luther; then, faced with her stony expression, the smile slipped away. In silence he followed her to the kitchen, his narrowed eyes undressing her as she hurried along the passageway ahead of him. This was his house now, and as far as he was concerned, Beth came with it.

Outside, the boy had soon forgotten their unwelcome visitor, enthralled by the toy which Moll Sutton had given to him and which he took everywhere. Lying flat on his stomach at the foot of the old apple tree, he chased the wooden tram up and down the tree roots which were pushing up from beneath the earth and making small hills. Cissie sat on a low branch, occasionally watching the boy and smiling at his antics, but her attention was drawn more towards the house. From her vantage point, she could see right into the kitchen without being observed. So far, she had not caught sight of Beth, and wondered about the conversation that might be taking place between those four walls.

'I'm hungry.' Richard paused in his play to look up at Cissie with appealing eyes.

'You'll have to wait,' she told him firmly. Realising that Cissie meant what she said, he gave a small moan and resumed his game – only this time he was a make-believe train, chugging round and round the garden, until he was running full pelt and making noises which Cissie told him were 'enough to frighten the dead'.

Remaining in her tree perch, she continued to watch the house. Soon her patience was rewarded when Beth appeared close to the kitchen window. But there was something wrong! The man was too close, too angry. He had come up behind her, and when Beth swung round, he spread out his arms to pin her there. She lashed out, and soon the two figures were furiously struggling. Realising that Beth was in difficulty, Cissie hurriedly scrambled to the ground, going at a run over the considerable distance that separated her from the house.

'You're a fool! Think what I'm offering you, Beth. You can stay in this house as long as you like. All I ask is that you keep me warm whenever I choose to stay.' Tom Reynolds had her in an iron grip, and no amount of fighting or pleading on Beth's part would induce him to let her go.

'Never!' She continued to struggle, twisting her face away from his, and trying desperately to push him from her.

'Leave her alone!' The loud cry made him swing round, his mouth open in astonishment as he found himself staring straight into a pair of ice-blue eyes. Holding herself tall and proud, Cissie told him, 'Get out of here, or I'll call a constable to you.' She stood framed in the doorway, a slight but determined figure. He stared at the girl a moment longer, then turned to look at Beth. Her quiet smile infuriated him, but also whetted his appetite to have her. 'I'll be back,' he shouted threateningly, 'you've got four weeks to think over what I said. It will take me that long to put my own house in order.' He laughed, straightened his cravat, then gathered his hat and cane from the table. 'Four weeks, Beth,' he reminded her grimly. 'Think on it.' He pointed his cane threateningly at Cissie. 'Out of my way, girl,' he hissed. When, glaring at him, she stepped aside, he went from the room, along the hallway, and out of the front door without a backward glance.

'Are you all right?' Cissie ran to where Beth was leaning over the sink, her hair dishevelled and her clothes in disarray. She had smiled at Tom Reynolds with defiance, but he had hurt her badly. 'Come and sit down,' Cissie pleaded. But Beth would not be persuaded. Instead, she went painfully into the drawing room from where she watched him climb into the waiting carriage. Leaning close to the window, her dark distraught eyes followed the carriage as it rumbled away down the road, its wheels spinning against the cobbles with increasing speed until in a moment it was out of sight. Cissie had come up behind her.

'Garn, piss off!' she called after it. Casting a sideways glance at Beth, she obviously expected to be chastised for using such strong language, but all Beth did was to shake her head in disapproval, thinking how Cissie's remark had echoed her own sentiments exactly. All the same, she would have a word with the girl when the time was appropriate. For now, she was in considerable discomfort, her body aching from top to bottom and her mind feverish with the threat which Tom Reynolds had issued. Having satisfied herself that he really was gone, Beth put her arm about the girl's shoulders. 'Don't be worried by what he said,' she murmured; it was enough that she herself was deeply concerned.

'He said we were to get out in four weeks,' Cissie reminded her. 'Where will we go? We ain't got no money, Beth.'

'That's for me to worry about,' she said with a reassuring smile, thinking all the while that Cissie had only spoken what was on her own mind. Things were bad. Suddenly she was seized by a painful spasm that took her breath away. The smile froze on her face and became a grimace of pain. She quickly turned away before Cissie could see. It took all her strength and a great deal of will power to walk the considerable distance back to the kitchen, where she told Cissie, 'Keep Richard happy while I wash and tidy myself.'

Cissie's answer was to come closer. Looking into

Beth's face, she said softly, 'If that man ever touches you again, I'll kill him.' Realising how deeply serious Cissie was, Beth was careful to reply light-heartedly, 'It wouldn't surprise me if you've frightened him away for good.' She fell quiet for a moment, reliving the incident in her mind and seeing Cissie standing at the door, her blue eyes blazing and her voice trembling with anger. 'Thank you, sweetheart,' she murmured, her dark eyes misting over. She wondered where it would all end, and silently prayed that she would find a home for them somewhere. She did not fool herself that the task would be an easy one. 'Leave me now,' she told Cissie. 'I don't want Richard to see me like this.' She glanced at her torn blouse and the raw scratches that ran from her shoulder to her elbow. When Cissie hesitated, she urged, 'I'll call you in a few minutes, and you can both help me get the meal.'

'Are you sure you'll be all right?'

'Of course. Go on now.' When Cissie turned to leave, Beth reached out to stop her, saying in a low voice, 'When Richard's in bed, Cissie, you and I can have a heart to heart talk.' She knew how curious the girl must be. 'I owe you the truth.'

Cissie made no reply, but nodded her understanding before going out into the garden where the little boy was still engaged in his solitary game, unaware of the drama that had taken place. On seeing Cissie emerge from the house, he came across the garden to run rings round her, launching into a high-pitched scream that was meant to be a train's whistle, and which nearly split Cissie's eardrums.

When, a moment later the boy had run to the far end of the garden, Cissie looked towards the kitchen. She could see Beth moving about in there, preparing for her wash. There were no words to tell how much she loved her because, though no one could ever take the place of her mother, Cissie had come to look on Beth as the dearest person in her life. She had never been so afraid as when she ran into that kitchen. She had looked at Beth, at how frantic she was, how distraught, and had felt such fury that it frightened her. She had wanted to fling herself at that man and tear his face apart with her nails; seeing Beth fighting him off like that, and her with child . . . it was a sight Cissie never wanted to see again. He had hurt Beth, and Cissie wanted to hurt him.

In the kitchen, bathing the angry scores on her flesh, Beth also was reflecting on what had happened. She deeply regretted that Cissie had to witness such a thing, yet at the same time had been immensely thankful for the girl's intervention. There was much Cissie didn't understand. Tom Reynolds was a dangerous man – more so now that he had come into a considerable fortune. But according to what he had told her on first coming into the house, he had not been the sole heir to his father's legacy. Luther had reserved a part of his fortune for another, although he had left nothing at all to David. It was Matthew who had been mentioned in the will. He was bequeathed that part of Larkhill which was irretrievably damaged – a millstone round his neck, a ruin that would cost a fortune to clear, a liability which would no doubt cause him a great deal of worry and heartache. Luther had a warped sense of humour. No doubt it was his way of punishing the boy for turning his back on him. Tom had asked about the boy, wanting to know, 'Who is this Matthew? What did he mean to the old man?' He had also shown an interest in Larkhill. Beth wondered whether he might challenge the will, but then smiled at the thought. Not even an avaricious creature like Tom Reynolds would want to take on such a burden as Larkhill, with all its inherent problems. But then, with Luther gone, she hoped that the legal responsibility of Larkhill might be rendered null and void. No doubt it would all take a while to disentangle.

It was five-thirty when Beth and the children sat down to a meal of crusty bread, mild cheddar cheese and muffins with fresh gooseberry preserve. Having played himself out and eaten his fill of muffins, the boy was soon complaining that he was tired. By eight o'clock, he was washed and tucked up in bed, and the kitchen was once more spick and span. Beth and Cissie had taken their hot drinks into the sitting room, and were seated either side of the fireplace. The fire was not lit, though the big old house became quite chilly even on a summer's evening. Beth was of a mind to get to her bed early, because she needed to be out and about tomorrow, searching out somewhere for them to live. 'Are you sure you're all right?' Cissie had noticed how unusually quiet Beth had been since she and Richard had returned from the garden.

'I'm fine,' Beth assured her. In truth, she was far from 'fine'. She was incredibly weary, and though she was not in any great pain, there was an irritating sensation of restlessness deep inside her. 'I'm tired, that's all,' she said. An awkward silence descended between them, and Beth knew what the girl was thinking. There would be no better time than now to tell Cissie of her past, and of Tom Reynolds' part in it. She owed her that much. Taking a deep breath, she said quickly, 'I knew him before ever I came to live in Blackburn.' She was afraid that otherwise her courage might falter and she would be obliged to postpone the frank talk she had promised Cissie.

Beth's admission that she had known that dreadful man was shocking to the girl, and yet, when she responded, it was with the same quiet dignity. 'How could you come to know Luther Reynolds' son?'

'When I knew him, I had no idea who he was. Even when I married David and met Luther, there was no reason for me to know.' Her dark eyes met the girl's curious stare. 'The man who came here today was my father's clerk. He was never a well-liked man, being too arrogant and devious, always causing mischief.'

'Why didn't your dad get rid of him then?'

'Because he was exceptionally good at his work.' She smiled wryly. 'Too good, I think.'

'He wants you, don't he, Beth?' When she nodded, quietly surprised at Cissie's forthright remark, the girl went on, 'He knows you don't fancy him, and he still wants you, don't he?'

'Tom Reynolds doesn't matter any more, Cissie,' Beth told her. 'What matters is that we have to find somewhere to live before the four weeks are up.'

'It won't be easy.'

'I know that.'

Cissie thought a while, her neck stiff with indignation and her eyes never leaving Beth's troubled face. 'We should tell the authorities what he did to you,' she said at length. 'Happen they'll lock the bugger up and we can stay in this house for ever!'

In spite of everything that had happened, Beth was amused by the girl's unlikely solution. 'Oh, Cissie! Cissie!' she laughed. 'I reckon they'd lock *us* up first.' They were quiet for a while, Beth watching the swirling bubbles in her evening drink and thinking how life took so many cruel twists and turns; Cissie remaining silent, her gaze intent, her love made stronger by Beth's troubled mood.

When it seemed as though she was too steeped in memories to go on, Cissie prompted her by saying, 'You don't have to talk about your family if you don't want to, Beth.'

'Oh, I do want to.' Though she desperately needed to share her past with Cissie, Beth was finding it difficult to talk about those things which she had kept bottled up for so long. 'I don't really know where to begin,' she admitted, with a whimsical smile.

'Tell me about your dad,' Cissie urged.

Beth looked away, the memories flooding back to fill her heart with pain. How could she begin to tell this girl who looked up to her that she had almost killed her own father? A father she adored, and who had disowned her? How could she excuse the shame she had lain at his door? Taking a deep breath, Beth described her childhood and the mother who disliked her so intensely that she would shut her daughter away at every opportunity. She spoke about her father, 'a good, kind man' who was driven by her shame to turn her away. She went on at great length about her first and only true love – Tyler. When she described him, his tall lithe figure, the rich black hair and his handsome face with those beautiful ebony-fringed green eyes, he came alive in her heart and the pain was tenfold.

'He's Richard's daddy, ain't he?' asked Cissie. She was fascinated, hanging on Beth's every word. She was not shocked, only sad that Beth was parted from her love.

'Yes, Cissie,' Beth said softly. 'Tyler is Richard's daddy.'

'Where is he now?'

'I don't know. All I know is that he let me down when I needed him.' She went on, telling Cissie what happened that night when her father had thrown her out and she had gone to Tyler's lodgings. 'He was never faithful to me, Cissie. The landlady's daughter proved that. She showed me that I had never really known him. The picture she painted was a sordid one.'

'She could have been lying.'

'No.' Beth shook her head and leaned back in the chair. She felt strange, ill, yet not ill. The niggling discomfort deep down in her back persisted. 'Oh, Cissie, if only I could believe that!' she cried. 'But she was speaking the truth. You see, he gave her one of my brooches and . . .' She paused, reluctant to remember. 'The girl was with child. Tyler's child.'

'Have you not seen him since?' Cissie was subdued by the awful things which had been revealed. While Beth had been talking, the girl had watched her expression change, and had sensed the awful loneliness within. When Beth shook her head in answer to Cissie's question, she went on, 'Find him, Beth. Make him tell you the truth.'

'Even if I knew where he was, I would never go to him, Cissie.' Beth's voice betrayed her bitterness. 'If he'd wanted me, he could have found me easily enough.' She sighed, a deep sigh that calmed the raging emotions inside her. 'He never wanted me, you see. He only wanted to marry into money, he only wanted to further his own ambitions.' She gave a small laugh. 'Besides, he's married to someone else now, and, from what I understand, achieved his ambition to marry into money, because he's riding in fancy carriages and buying up land from one end of the country to the other. Tom Reynolds took great delight in giving me that particular piece of news.'

'Why don't you write to your dad, Beth?' Cissie wanted to know. 'When he finds out he's got a grandson, he'll forgive you, won't he?'

'No. I shamed him, Cissie. He will never forgive that.'

'What about your mammy? If she knew you were being thrown on to the streets, surely she'd help?'

'Don't confuse my mother with darling Maisie,' Beth warned. 'No two women could be so different. There is no love between us. There never was. In fact, she would be only too pleased to know that I was desperate.'

Cissie snorted. Folding her arms and falling back into the chair, she wrinkled her nose in disgust. 'I don't blame you for running away.'

'I didn't run away,' Beth corrected her. 'I was given no choice.'

'Well, I would have run away!' Cissie retorted. But then she came to kneel before Beth, her bright blue eyes looking up and her voice trembling with emotion. 'We'll always love you,' she said tenderly. 'Me and Richard.'

'I know that, sweetheart,' Beth said, stroking the girl's hair. Then, as though reading Cissie's thoughts, she added with conviction, 'You're not to worry about anything. We'll be all right, you'll see. We'll find somewhere to live.'

Some short time later, Beth made the rear of the house secure while Cissie went and bolted the front door – it was a pattern they had followed these past weeks. Since David's death, Beth's responsibilities had increased tenfold. 'We'll get a good night's sleep,' she told Cissie as they mounted the stairs together. 'Tomorrow, we'll see things in a new light.'

'But four weeks ain't long, Beth,' Cissie pointed out. 'If we can't find nowhere else to live, what will we do when he comes back?'

'We won't be here, I promise you that.'

'But where will we go?'

Realising how concerned the girl was, Beth paused on the landing. Raising the oil lamp in her hand, so that the halo of yellowish light fell on Cissie's anxious face, she replied softly, 'Why don't you let me worry about that.' She gave Cissie a hug. 'Goodnight, sweetheart.'

'Goodnight, Beth.' Cissie had been reassured by her words. She went into her room and closed the door.

For a long poignant moment, Beth remained where she was, her mind turning over the events of the day. She had deliberately made Cissie believe that she had some sort of plan, when in fact she had none at all. Suddenly, she remembered the small bag of coins beneath the floorboards in her room. A smile came to her lovely face. Resolutely, she made her way along the landing towards her son's room. Once there, she went in on tiptoe, to gaze down on that small sleeping figure that touched her so deeply. Even in slumber, the boy was a miniature duplicate of his father. Now, when Tyler threatened to creep into her thoughts, she thrust him away. He had not been there to help before. He was not there now. She was alone. There was no one else to help her through this crisis.

In the privacy of her own room, Beth retrieved the bag of coins from its hiding-place. Spilling them on to the dresser, she counted the silver shillings one by one, making them up into piles of guineas. There were four guineas in total. Not a fortune by any means, and it wouldn't last long, but at least they were not altogether destitute. She glanced around the room, at the painted landscapes hanging on the wall, the princely ornaments and many delicate porcelain pieces on the mantelpiece. They had all belonged to Luther's last wife, David's mother. For one weak moment, Beth was tempted to take some of these precious things with her, for she was sure that David would have wanted her to. But then she recoiled from the idea. Luther had left this house and everything in it to his prodigal son, a man who would not easily turn a blind eye while part of his heritage was stolen. Beth shrugged off the temptation. She had done many wrong things in her life, but she had never taken that which did not belong to her. Nor would she give Tom Reynolds the satisfaction of hunting her down as a common thief.

Scooping the coins up, she replaced them in the bag, then, leaning forward on her elbows, she closed her eyes and covered her face with the palms of her hands. She was so tired. So very tired. Every bone in her body felt as though it had been stretched on the rack, and the child inside her was unusually restless – almost as though it could sense her despair.

At length, Beth raised her face. She was shocked at the image in the mirror. Looking back at her was a shadow, large dark eyes like fathomless black pools in the thin gaunt features. Her hair was lifeless, its shine gone, wisps of stray locks framing her face, and a haunted look about her that bespoke the torment in her heart. The tragic and surprising turns of these past weeks, the loss of a good man, and that shocking incident this morning, had all taken their toll.

Amidst all the awful uncertainty, Beth was sure of only one thing, and it was this – when Tom Reynolds returned to this house, thinking to have her at his mercy, he would be sadly disappointed. By that time, she and the children would be long gone. She recalled what Cissie had said just now. 'Where will we go, Beth?' She had not been able to put the girl's mind at rest at that moment, but the answer had come to her in these last few minutes. Her eyes sparkled as she leaned towards the mirror. 'I'll tell you where we're going, Cissie Armstrong,' she whispered with a smile. 'We're going home. That's where we're going!' Luther had done nothing to make her life easier while she was in this house. How he would turn in his grave to know that, in his wicked intent to punish Matthew by leaving him part of Larkhill, he had inadvertently helped her and the children.

Unbeknown to anyone, Beth had paid a visit to that street where she had been so happy with Maisie. The fire had indeed caused a deal of devastation, and many houses were in a dangerous condition. But Beth realised now that it just might be possible to make some kind of safe secure home from one of the least damaged dwellings. It was not something she would have attempted under normal circumstances, but Luther, and his son after him, had given her no choice. First thing in the morning, she would outline her plan to Cissie. But for now, she must get some sleep, for the baby's sake as well as her own.

Chapter Eleven

'But why?' Esther faced the other woman with a puzzled expression on her stern face. 'There is really no need for you to leave my service, Miss Mulliver,' she went on, at the same time rising from her chair and smiling sweetly. 'My husband may be departing this house, but my son and I most certainly are not. I have need of a capable person to oversee the domestic arrangements as before, and since you have always conducted your duties to my utmost satisfaction, I do feel you should reconsider your decision to leave.' Her smile broadened and, to the watching woman, it was a rare and unpleasant sight. 'I might even be tempted to make a small increase in your wages,' she added reluctantly, her beady eyes fixed on Tilly's face as she waited for her answer.

Deriving a great deal of satisfaction from this interview, Tilly took her time over replying. She had been sad to see the decline of Richard Ward's authority in this household, and the fact that he had been forced by his wife's underhand tricks to leave his own home had deeply angered her. The very idea that she should want to stay in the employ of Esther Ward was unthinkable. 'I'm surprised that you should want me to stay,' she said at length, 'and I'm even more surprised that you've been satisfied with my work here . . . especially when you have gone to great pains, day after day, to tell me how sloppy I am in my duties. You call me your "housekeeper" when in fact I'm nothing short of a dogsbody. You're too mean to employ further help, using me as parlourmaid, scullery-girl, cook, waitress, and everything else required in a house this size. And I, for reasons you would never understand, have been obliged to put up with it.' The astonished look on the other woman's face was a joy to see. Encouraged, she went on, 'As for remaining in your employ, Mrs Ward, it is out of the question. Mr Ward has always treated me with respect and consideration, while you and your son have looked on me as part of the furniture.' She shook her head. 'No. You have my notice and, as in the terms you dictated when you first set me on, I shall be leaving one month from today, on November the first.'

Incensed by the servant's cool, dignified outburst, Esther could not speak for a moment. Trembling with rage, she spread her hands on the desk. Leaning forward, she said in a harsh voice, 'So, you will leave one month from now, will you?' She gave a small laugh, shaking her head from side to side. 'Oh, no, Miss Mulliver. You will leave my house now. Right now!'

'As you wish.' Miss Mulliver was delighted. 'As soon as I've received my due wages.'

Straightening her stiff body, Esther stared at the woman, her fists clenched and the muscles in her face twitching. 'You have ten minutes to get your things together,' she warned. 'There will be no wages. In fact, you can consider yourself fortunate that I haven't called the authorities to have you physically ousted. They would be most interested to hear of the shocking manner in which you have dared to address me, your employer, a prominent member of society. As a matter of fact, it might be wise for me to have you and your belongings thoroughly searched, for who knows what you might have stolen.' Her meaning was unmistakable. Her voice rose as she added viciously, 'Ten minutes, or face the consequences.'

Miss Mulliver smiled. She was thoroughly enjoying this confrontation. 'Ah! I wondered when you might threaten me with the authorities. Well now, I wonder whether they might also be interested in a tale or two that I could tell them? Your son is a dreadful embarrassment to you, isn't he, Mrs Ward?'

'What do you mean?' Esther's hand rose to her throat, nervously clasping the pearl brooch there.

'Oh, I think you know well enough what I mean. Drinking and gambling, coming home in the small hours, often with a painted street-girl hanging on his arm. Oh, and of course, there's the other company he keeps. People of the night, crooks and gamblers, men who would stop at nothing to protect their own underhand activities. Happen the "authorities" might be very interested to know the identity of these villains, and happen they would like to question your son on that very matter.' She could see Esther was shocked by her words, how she seemed to shrink before them. 'But, of course, you must call in the authorities if it pleases you. Though you know as well as I do, Mrs Ward, they will find nothing in my belongings that isn't mine. Unless, of course, you intend deliberately to incriminate me. And I can promise you, that would not be very wise.'

Without saying a word, Esther yanked open the top drawer of her desk, snatching from it a small cash-box. Taking hold of the silver chain around her throat, she tugged on it until the whole length was drawn from within the neck of her dress. Then, with the tiny brass key hanging there, she unlocked the cash-box and angrily counted out a number of coins. These she threw into a buff-coloured envelope which she slid across the desk. 'Ten minutes,' she repeated in a rasping whisper. 'After that I never want to see your face again.'

Collecting the envelope, Miss Mulliver simply smiled. It was good to see this woman experiencing frustration

415

and helplessness, especially when she had taken such delight in treating her husband the same way. One long withering glance at Esther's face, then she turned away.

Her portmanteau was almost packed. Soon she would be gone from this house, never to return. She had waited for this day for a very long time.

'May I come in?' Richard tapped gently on the door and was now peeping in. 'It was open,' he apologised.

'Please, yes. Come in, sir.' As usual when she was in his company, Tilly Mulliver blushed a soft shade of pink.

'I understand you're leaving?' he said. 'I've just seen Mrs Ward, and she appears to be very agitated . . . upset because she couldn't persuade you to stay, I shouldn't wonder,' he said innocently. 'I must say, though, I'm not really surprised. All the same, I thought you might be staying after I was gone.' He glanced at the bulging portmanteau lying on the bed. 'You weren't influenced by my leaving, were you?' he asked, a curious expression on his face.

'Oh, no!' she assured him. 'I've been meaning to hand in my notice for some time now. A personal matter, you see.' She wondered what he would say if she suddenly blurted out the truth . . . that she had stayed at the express wish of Elizabeth, the woman he had wronged all those years ago. What would his reaction be, she wondered, if she were to tell him how Elizabeth had long forgiven him, though she had never stopped loving him? For one dreadful moment, she was tempted to reveal the real reason for her having stayed so long in the employ of a woman as demanding and impossible as Esther Ward, the woman he had chosen above the mother of his child. Instead, she looked into those unhappy hazel eyes and knew he had suffered enough. She gave a small laugh. 'I'm afraid I spoke a few home-truths to your wife,' she said. 'That's why she's so agitated.'

He said nothing for a while, biting his bottom lip as though to stem laughter at her remark. 'I guessed as much,' he said, rolling his eyes heavenward. 'No wonder she has a face as black as thunder. You did right to speak your mind. She hasn't treated you well, I know.'

'She hasn't treated you well either.'

'Ah, but maybe I deserved it.' His reply confused her for a moment, until she realised what he meant. Of course. For over twenty-seven years, ever since the birth of his daughter, Esther must have made his life a living hell. Again, the temptation was strong to tell him everything. Esther might not want or love him, but Elizabeth adored him. He was desperately in need of someone to love him. Surely it would not be so wrong to bring the two of them together? But no! Elizabeth would never forgive her for going against her express instructions. 'I really should be going,' Tilly said now. 'Your wife warned me that if I was not out of this house in ten minutes, she would bring the authorities down on my head.' Turning to the portmanteau, she began squashing the lid down on the pile of belongings inside.

'Here. Let me do that,' he urged, coming to her side and taking over the task when she murmured her thanks and stepped away. 'I'm sorry,' he said, glancing up at her as he pushed his weight on to the lid, 'but the house is hers now. You know, of course, that we're parting company?' She nodded, and so he went on quietly, 'Everything I built up over the years . . . it's almost all gone. Esther has taken the lion's share of what's left. Oh, I have just enough to give me a fresh start, but it won't be easy. Besides, I'm not a young man any more.' He laughed, but it was not a happy sound. 'The truth is, she could afford a better solicitor than me.'

'I'm sorry.' She wanted to say much more.

'Don't be,' he told her, clicking the lid down and smiling at her. 'There, all secure,' he said, sliding the portmanteau to the floor. Suddenly his voice was quieter, more intimate. 'I don't suppose I'll ever see you again.' He looked at her, his expression oddly apprehensive. 'Will I?'

'I . . . really don't know, sir.' He had flustered her.

'Please . . . don't call me sir,' he said softly, bending his head to look into her face which had coloured up at his words. 'May I call you Tilly?' She looked away, unsure of what to say. Thoughts of Elizabeth clouded her mind, making her feel guilty.

'I must go.' She moved away, but he stopped her.

'Will you come with me, Tilly?' he asked now. 'I've arranged to lease a house in Russell Square. It's not a big place but, well, I'll be lost there all on my own, and you must know how useless I am about the house.' Angry with himself for not having handled the situation as he had planned, he was quick to assure her, 'Please don't think I'm proposing anything immoral.' When she looked up with amusement on her face, his whole manner relaxed. 'Though I wouldn't want you to believe it was altogether impossible for me to think of you in that way. You really are a very attractive woman, Tilly.' He gazed at her now, his thoughts a million years away, and was reminded of someone he had known and loved long ago. Elizabeth also had been a gentle soul. 'I would be very happy if you would agree to come to Russell Square with me, Tilly . . . as my housekeeper. And of course I wouldn't expect you to look after the place without help.'

'Much as I would like to, sir,' she remembered what he had said about calling him 'sir' and quickly corrected herself, 'Mr Ward, I'm not able to take you up on your offer.' If the situation was different, she would have jumped at the chance to go with him. 'It has nothing to do with you,' she promised him. 'Like I said . . . it's a personal matter.'

'You're not in any trouble, are you? Is there something I can do?'

'No, no. It's nothing like that.' How much could she tell him without revealing the truth? 'It's just that I have a dear friend who is ill, and I want to be with her.' That was the whole truth, for Elizabeth had grown weaker in health and, against that dear woman's wishes, Tilly had insisted on leaving the Ward household and going home, where she could keep a closer eye on her beloved mistress. It was only after her decision was made that she learned Richard was also leaving, although she had long been aware of the fraught situation which had developed between him and Esther.

Dipping his two fingers into his waistcoat pocket, he drew out a folded piece of paper on which, only moments before, he had hastily written his new address. 'Take this,' he said. 'If ever you should change your mind,' he appeared embarrassed when she raised her eyes to gaze on him, 'well, you'll know where to find me.' How different from his wife she was, he thought. So caring and good. For a long time now he had seen her as she really was, and he had come to like her a great deal. Even to love her a little.

'Thank you,' she said. 'I'll remember.' She didn't want to leave him, but Elizabeth exerted a far stronger pull on her loyalties. They stood for a moment, he looking down at her and she wishing he would leave her now. But he was not ready to go. Bringing his hands up, he cupped her face and without warning placed his mouth over hers and kissed her tenderly. Then, with a lingering look, he murmured, 'Whenever you need me, Tilly, I'll be waiting.' He dropped his hands to his sides and went from her, out of the room and out of her life.

Trembling from head to toe, she sat on the bed, her mind in a whirl. He had kissed her. *Richard Ward had actually kissed her!* Her joy knew no bounds. Until she remembered. 'Oh, Elizabeth,' she murmured. 'Forgive me.' She hurriedly gathered her things together then went quickly out of that house where she had come to know and love a man who was forbidden to her. She could not believe that he might love her too. But he had kissed her. He had kissed her, and her life would never be the same.

Chapter Twelve

Tying the silk scarf loosely about his neck, Tyler flung open the door of his splendid house in Kensington, shivering when the blast of cold air rushed in from outside. Turning up the collar of his overcoat, he took his hat from the hall-stand and clapped it over his thick black hair. As he prepared to go out into the night, a woman's voice caused him to pause. From the depths of the house, she called out to ask whether she should keep supper for him. 'No,' he answered without hesitation, 'I'm going into town and won't be back until late.' He lingered a second, but there was no acknowledgement. Shrugging his shoulders, he stepped out of the house, closed the door, and went into the darkness, his head bent against the wind and the cold breeze slicing into him without mercy. These past months had gone all too quickly and winter had come with a vengeance. He thought he must be crazy to be out on a night like this. But, if he stayed indoors, he would be haunted by thoughts of Beth, and that would never do. Lately, he had come to realise that he would probably never see her again. It was a hard and painful thing to accept.

'Evening, sir.' The constable raised his hand in greeting. He knew this gentleman by sight, as he was often to be seen walking out of an evening, always deep in thought, always pleasant to talk to. 'Bit nippy tonight, wouldn't you say?' He smiled, his face a vague round shape in the rising night fog.

'Evening, officer,' Tyler called back. 'It's certainly bitter tonight. I don't envy you your duty, and that's a fact.'

'Just a job, sir,' the constable replied, giving a slight cough as though to convey how the damp creeping fog had already got on his lungs. 'Goodnight then, sir.'

'Goodnight, officer.' Soon the sturdy figure of the constable had gone from Tyler's sight, melting into the swirling grey vapour, the sound of his coughing growing fainter in the distance.

Emerging from the gloom, the noise of a horse's hooves attracted Tyler's attention; soon he could see the small lamps of an oncoming carriage. Quickly, before it passed him by, he stepped out, his eyes peering towards the approaching lights and his arm outstretched to flag down the vehicle. Seeing a prospective passenger, the driver pulled on the reins. 'Woah, yer old bugger,' he told the tired horse up front. 'Yer day's work ain't done yet.' Drawing the Hansom into the kerb, the old fellow acknowledged instructions to take the gentleman to a certain club in the West End of London, and in no time at all they were on their way.

Seated in the cab, Tyler clung on to the leather strap hanging from the door, his fine eyes downcast and his thoughts quietly assessing the way of his life. He had many regrets. Too many! There were times when he would have given anything to escape from the prison which he had created for himself; a prison built on material possessions and forced ambitions; a prison where there was no love, only a terrible loneliness that grew more unbearable with every day. Memories, that was all he had. No more than that. Just memories of his time with Beth. All the money and power in the world were nothing compared to the joy which she had brought him. But the joy had been too short-lived, a treasure that had once been his and was now snatched from him for ever. And though he knew it was wrong and futile to keep those memories alive in his heart, nothing else in life mattered to him.

Raising his eyes to the window he stared up at the night sky, trying desperately to shut her out, but it was impossible. Wherever he looked, she was there, her golden-brown hair spilling over her shoulders, and those dark laughing eyes that could turn his heart over with one glance. She was here with him now, in the carriage. In the hazy evening sky that merged with the gloomy night and stretched like a silver ocean as far as the eye could see, she was there. In the daytime when he went about his business in the City she walked beside him, and when he went to his bed of an evening it was Beth who lay in his arms. It would always be that way. As long as he lived, he would live only for her.

The quiet streets soon gave way to the busier byways of the heart of London Town. 'Here you are then, Guv.' The driver brought the cab to an abrupt halt and waited patiently until Tyler had disembarked and found the necessary coins with which to pay him.

Once inside the club, it took only a moment for Tyler to deposit his overcoat and hat at the desk. Afterwards he went straight to the bar.

'Go right in, sir.' The man on duty knew Tyler by sight. Pushing open the green baize door, he held it aside while Tyler passed through.

The outer foyer was quiet, a haven from the noise and chaos inside. The din emerged now: music that was harsh to the ear, outbursts of laughter, low mutterings, and the clinking of glasses. The odour of smoke and pipe tobacco rose like a choking cloud. Pressing a silver coin into the man's hand, Tyler went in. The door swung to behind him.

He remained standing a while, taking a long slim case from his pocket and plucking out a cigarette. He held it in his fingers, rolling it round, not attempting to light it while his ebony-fringed green eyes took in the scene before him. The smoky atmosphere was unpleasant, yet comforting to a man wanting to hide. A whimsical smile played at the corners of his mouth. Wasn't that exactly what he was? A man wanting to hide? Impatient, he replaced the cigarette, snapped the case shut and slipped it back into his pocket. The club was crowded tonight. Almost every table was filled and the bar was lined with men from one end to the other. Waiters flitted between the tables, trays held aloft and every move practised to a fine art.

Realising he would have a long wait at the bar, Tyler surveyed the far end of the room. 'Is it a table you're wanting, sir?' The club's manager appeared from nowhere, a small, moustachioed man, immaculate in his dark suit.

'Is there one vacant?' He had no appetite for company. A table out of the way would suit his mood.

'I think we can accommodate you.' The little man's smile might have been painted on; but then he was obliged to smile so many times at so many people, it was no longer a smile but an empty facial expression, part of his uniform, like the dark stiff suit he wore, or the shiny patent shoes that pinched his toes unmercifully. 'If you would please follow me, sir.' Without waiting, he began threading his way through the milling madness. Tyler was only a few steps behind. 'Will this suit you, sir?' the manager asked, standing beside the small circular table for two. It was only an arm's length from the bar, but the two were separated by a high open trellis covered with creeping vine.

'Fine.' Situated in a shadowy corner away from the hubbub, it suited Tyler's quiet melancholy mood. 'That's just fine,' he said. His order was soon taken and he settled back into the surprisingly comfortable red velvet chair. This time when he took out a cigarette, he collected the dainty club matches from the table. Lighting the cigarette, he drew on it with great deliberation, his eyes drawn by the tinkling laughter of a woman seated at a table not too far away; though he could easily see the slim heavily painted female and her companion, they could not see him. The companion was a disgusting lump of a man twice the woman's age, his fat fingers roving her thighs, and his balding head buried in the nape of her neck, while she wriggled deliciously, pretending to enjoy his advances. The man could not see her face, otherwise he would have been in no doubt as to her true revulsion. Tyler looked away. It was sad when a woman was reduced to selling herself in that way.

Suddenly, he was alerted by the sound of a man's voice. It came from nearby, a grating whisper that was familiar to him. Intrigued, he listened, bending his body towards the sound. 'Don't be a fool! Think of what I'm offering you.' Yes, he knew the voice, but for the life of him couldn't place it. Shifting in his seat, he drew aside the foliage and peered through the trellis. When the man at the bar turned suddenly, Tyler shrank back, his eyes wide with astonishment. It was none other than Thomas Reynolds, and the fellow with him was Beth's brother, Ben. Tyler's thoughts were racing. What in God's name was Ben doing with Reynolds? Those two had nothing in common; in fact, when he was working for the Ward Development Company, Tyler had received the distinct impression that Ben had no liking for his father's clerk. And what in God's name could the obnoxious little man offer Ben that he would be 'a fool' to refuse?

His curiosity aroused, and his instincts telling him that all was not well here, Tyler kept a close watch on the pair. In earnest conversation, they kept their heads bent, their low intense muttering too garbled for Tyler to distinguish. Now and then odd words and phrases would drift towards him. 'Trust me,' Tom Reynolds was saying. But why? What the devil was he up to? One thing was certain – the whole time they were talking, the evil little man was constantly topping up Ben's drinking glass.

If only Tyler had known the subject of their conversation, he would have intervened without hesitation. A murder was being planned, and Ben was being set up to commit the deed.

'Think of it, Ben . . . enough money to settle your debts and take you anywhere in the world you want to go. You'll be able to make a fresh start. Think of it, man!'

Reynolds picked up the whisky bottle and poured a measure into Ben's tumbler; only the smallest measure, though, because he wanted the other fellow sober enough to do the job, while at the same time he knew Ben's courage could come only from the bottom of a glass. 'I've given you his name, and I've told you where to find him,' he murmured. 'But it has to be tonight . . . within the hour or he'll be gone, and Christ only knows when there'll be another opportunity. It took me enough time and effort to track him down this time!'

'I'm not sure, Reynolds.' Ben shook his head, the thoughts inside too horrific to contemplate. 'Killing a man . . . I'm not sure.'

'Shut up, you bloody fool!' Reynolds swung round, his sly glance going from one end of the room to the other. 'Do you want to get us both hung?' he hissed. Seeing that the other man was weakening, he reminded him, 'You're into the club for a tidy sum, aren't you?'

'You know bloody well I am,'

'And there are others who have their henchmen out looking for you, isn't that right?' When Ben reluctantly nodded, he went on, 'You've got yourself mixed up with a real bad lot, Ben, and there's no way out, you know that, don't you? And what would your mother do, I wonder . . . if she knew the extent of your debts? She's in dire straits herself, so I'm told. Well, now, she can't help you no more, can she, eh? She might even throw you to the dogs, and who could blame her?'

At this Ben lashed out, causing the little man to lose his balance. 'Leave my mother out of this, you bastard!' he cried, swiping his fist at Reynolds' face, then bending his head to the bar and making broken sounds when Reynolds skilfully dodged the badly aimed blow.

'It might be a good idea if you were to take him home,' the bartender suggested.

'No need for that,' Reynolds told him, 'he'll be all right.' He glared round anxiously. Ben's outburst had brought a few curious glances.

The bartender was not convinced. 'I'm afraid I can't serve him any more drinks,' he warned.

'I'm all right.' Ben straightened himself up and looked at the bartender through bleary eyes; yet there was also a look of determination there. 'I'll be leaving soon anyway.' Not quite satisfied, but not wanting to cause a scene unnecessarily, the bartender moved away; at the same time shaking his head meaningfully to the two burly men who had already started to move in. Seeing his signal, they retreated.

'Good man!' Reynolds patted his colleague on the back. 'I knew you'd see the sense of it.' He ignored the accusing stare that greeted his words. Slyly dipping into his waistcoat pocket, he wrapped his fist round the hard object there. 'Take this,' he whispered. 'You'll need it.' He lowered his fist and surreptitiously slid the object into Ben's hand. Ben shivered. Even through the rag that was wrapped round it, there was no mistaking the long pointed knife inside. 'Go straight there,' Reynolds said, nervously glancing about the room. 'You know where to find him. Don't forget the seaman's name . . . Matthew Armstrong.'

He shook the other man gently. 'Straight there, mind. Do it quick and clean like I told you, then get out of there as fast as you can. If you do exactly as I've said, there'll be no complications.' When Ben looked away, he prodded him angrily. 'You'll never want again. The money's here, waiting for you.' He turned, wrapping his knuckles round the edge of his waistcoat and opening it just far enough for the other man to see the wad of notes secreted there. 'It's yours, I tell you . . . enough to set you up for the rest of your life. Go on, man. Do it! DO IT NOW.'

Ben's mind was made up. What did it matter? A man's life, a stranger who, according to Reynolds, was a villain of the worst order . . . what was that against his own skin? He was in a desperate situation, and Reynolds knew it. But here was his chance to get out from under. He might never be given such an opportunity again. Then there was his mother. Here, his guilt was tenfold, because he blamed himself for what had happened between his parents. He would take her away from London. They could make a fresh start somewhere in the country, perhaps even abroad. The idea felt good. Yes, she'd like that, he thought. 'Where will you be?' he asked, warning 'Don't try anything, Reynolds, or I swear I'll do for you as well.' He had a dark mood on him now. A mood for killing.

'What kind of talk is that?' Reynolds demanded with feigned indignation. 'You know what we arranged.' He looked at the clock above the bar. It was ten minutes past eight. 'I'll be waiting with the money. Midnight. Your father's old offices.' He locked his beady stare on the other man's face; there was fear there. 'Do it quick and clean,' he said in a low threatening voice. 'We don't want no comeback now, do we, eh?'

'Don't worry,' Ben told him in a strangely sober voice, 'I know what's at stake.'

Unaware that Tyler Blacklock had watched their every move, Reynolds kept his beady eyes on his accomplice until he had departed the room and the doors had closed on him. Smiling to himself, he called the bartender and ordered another drink. He was no fool. There was murder to be done this night but he would know nothing at all about it, would he? After all, he was here in a club packed with witnesses.

Assuring himself that Reynolds could not see him, Tyler skirted the perimeter of the room on his way out. 'Don't you want your coat, sir?' the girl called from her desk in the foyer. She recognised Tyler straightaway. She thought him to be unusually handsome, and a real man into the bargain. Not like the creepy smarmy creatures that could often be seen attending the club.

'I'll be back in a minute,' he told her, rushing after Ben, and finding him already getting into a cab some way down the street. 'Ward!' he yelled. 'Ben Ward!' Running forward, he clapped his hands on the open carriage door, catching his breath and smiling at the alarmed man inside, 'Thought I'd missed you,' he said.

'Blacklock!' Ben was visibly shocked to see Beth's old suitor. As always, it was his guilt and jealousy that plagued him. 'What d'you want?' he snapped. 'I'm in a hurry.'

Realising that Ben had no intention of either coming down to talk with him or inviting him to sit a while inside the carriage, Tyler took it upon himself to climb in, telling the driver, 'Hang on a minute, will you?'

'Hey! I don't want you in here. Get out, I tell you. GET OUT.' Ben had only one thought in his head at that moment, and it was to do with a man by the name of Matthew Armstrong. He had nerved himself up to do the deed, and the sooner it was done, the better.

'I'll go when I've said my piece, Ben, and not before.' Tyler settled himself on the edge of the seat opposite. 'I

saw you just now . . . you and Reynolds.' He stared at
Ben through narrow, suspicious eyes. 'He's a rum sort to
be drinking with. He's up to something, isn't he? What
were you talking about?'

'What the hell has it got to do with you what we
were talking about?' Tyler Blacklock always made Ben
nervous. 'Get out of here, or I'll have you thrown out!'
he shouted. He could feel the knife in his pocket. His
fist closed round it. If he had to, he would use it now.

'He was putting you up to something, wasn't he?'
Tyler insisted, 'Why would he think you should "trust"
him? And what could he offer you that you'd be "a
fool to refuse"?' He saw the strain in Ben's face, and
he knew he was close to the truth. 'What has he got you
into, Ben. Look, man, I only want to help you. I can't,
though, if you don't tell me the truth.'

'There's nothing to tell.' Ben's mind was frantically
searching for a way out, but it was fuddled with booze.
'It's a business venture . . . him and me . . . I came
here tonight to check it out.' He was delighted at the
ease with which he could lie. 'Reynolds has the word on
a small piece of land going cheap. He wanted Mother to
go in with him, but I've talked him out of that one.' He
sniggered. 'It's time I stood on my own two feet, don't
you think, Blacklock?'

'If that were true, Ben, nobody would be more
delighted than me. If that were only true, you would
have my best wishes.' It would be a grand thing if Beth's
brother could mend his wasteful ways.

'It's true all right.' Ben felt the worst was over. 'If you
don't believe me, go and ask Reynolds. Go on, ask him
. . . though I wouldn't blame him if he told you to mind
your own bloody business.'

Tyler continued to study the other man. He wanted
to believe him. In fact, he was tempted to believe him.
After all, he had heard Ben tell Reynolds to: 'Leave

my mother out of it!' And it was feasible that when Reynolds told Ben to 'trust me', Ben might have been questioning his sincerity. Also, if Reynolds believed he had found a bargain and was keen to persuade Ben of the same, he might be forced to make the comment that Ben would be a fool to refuse. It all fitted. And yet, there was something here that made Tyler's instincts bristle. Was it his dislike of Tom Reynolds that made him suspicious? But had he really the authority to interfere? 'You're right,' he said at length. 'It's none of my business. But I worry about you, Ben. I would hate to see you get into something with Reynolds . . . something bad, that you couldn't easily get out of.'

Ben laughed, and it was a convincing sound. 'I can take care of myself, Blacklock. Like I said, it was just a small matter of business between me and Reynolds. It was the booze that made me get heated. Just the booze. It's a good deal he's offering.' Suddenly he was afraid that Tyler might question him further. 'But of course, I can't tell you. You might snatch the land from under our noses.'

Tyler shook his head. 'Do you really think that?' he asked.

'Maybe not.'

'You're not in any trouble then? Reynolds doesn't have any sort of a hold over you?'

'I've already told you!'

'Fair enough.' Tyler prepared to leave, 'But you can't blame me if I watch out for you.' He paused before saying in a softer voice, 'I owe that much to Beth.'

'You owe her nothing.' The mention of Beth had touched something half-decent in Ben and his instantaneous reaction against it made him want to lash out. 'You don't owe me anything either, so I'll thank you to get out.' He lurched forward to open the door, but the effects of his drinking were still on him, and he slithered to the floor. When Tyler grabbed hold of him and sat him back in the seat, he silently glowered.

'As you say, Ben, I don't owe you anything. But I reckon you'd do well to get home and sleep it off.' He got out of the carriage and could be heard giving the driver the address of Esther Ward's house. Once the carriage was underway, he returned to the club. There was no use his going home. He might as well stay here and see the evening out.

'What's that, Guv?' Ben's driver strained his ears above the sound of the horse's hooves against the cobbles.

Hanging further out of the window, he shouted his instructions. 'The docks, you bloody fool!' he yelled louder. 'The Mariner alehouse on the docks!' When he was sure that the driver was changing direction, Ben sank back into the seat, hanging on as he was thrown roughly from one side to the other, and repeating Reynolds' words. 'Do it. DO IT NOW!' Murder a villain. It wasn't too high a price to pay for his own safety. Afterwards, he wouldn't let his conscience bother him. Not when he was free from everything that had plagued him these past years. As they came in sight of the London Dockside, Ben Ward was actually smiling. No, it was not too high a price to pay at all.

The sailor was in a hurry. His ship was not long docked and the smell of booze and women was irresistible. 'What's that you say, matey?' Pausing in his stride, he glanced at the figure in the shadows. He couldn't see his face. It unnerved him when he couldn't see a man's face. He came closer, but the man receded deeper into the gloom.

'I'm looking for an old pal o' mine,' the man said in clipped tones. His forced accent was not familiar. The sailor deduced that he was not from these parts, happen a foreigner come in on one o' them Dutch ships. The thought made him relax. A foreigner, eh? All the same, there was no need to hide in the shadows.

'This pal o' yourn, matey,' the sailor asked. 'What name does he go by?'

'Armstrong. Matthew Armstrong.'

The sailor let out a great roar that frightened the man deeper into the shadows. 'Well, I'm buggered! Matthew Armstrong, eh? Why! He only happens to be off the very same ship as meself,' he laughed. 'I do believe he's in the alehouse this very minute. Come on,' he invited. 'Come inside wi' me . . . happen I can persuade yer to dip yer hand in yer pocket and buy us a jug, eh?' A thought suddenly occurred to him. 'Or have yer only got a pocket full o' them foreign coins, eh? Never mind. It ain't no matter, 'cause I've got a fistful o' silver shillings just waiting to be spent.'

'No. Send him out, will you do that?'

'If that's what yer want, matey.'

'Matthew Armstrong. Send him out.'

'Aye, I will that. Happen he'll be able to persuade yer to join us.' Stretching his head forward into the darkness, he saw only the silhouette of a man, a young one judging by the straightness of his limbs. But then he would be young, wouldn't he, if he were a pal o' Matt Armstrong. After all, the lad himself were still a bit wet behind the ears. 'I'll tell him,' he said, swinging away and going at a smart pace into the Mariner alehouse. A swell of noise greeted him as he entered. 'Garn, yer bleedin' old soaks!' he shouted jovially. 'The lot on yer are already six sheets to the wind.'

Inside the alehouse, the sailor went in search of Matt. He found him seated at a table, a sheet of paper before him as he penned a letter. 'Hello, matey,' the sailor's voice caused Matthew to look up. Quickly, he put his half-written letter away. He had learned not to give these old sailors any excuse for ribbing him. 'There's a bloke outside. An old pal o' yourn, I reckon.' The sailor laughed aloud when two females came up to latch on to him. 'Huh! Desperate for me company are yer, gals?' he asked, adding with a wink at Matthew, 'Like 'em in pairs, I do.' He pretended to struggle when the giggling girls tried to pull him away. 'What yer gonna do with me, yer randy buggers?' he asked, his face a picture of delight as he gave in and let them drag him on up the stairs. 'The feller's waiting outside,' he shouted. 'Shy he is . . . I reckon he's a foreigner. Fetch him in, Matt.' He would have said more, but was too quickly whisked away.

Matthew remained seated, racking his brain to try and fathom who it might be that was waiting outside. He didn't have any real pals, and he certainly didn't know any foreigners. For a moment he was tempted to finish his letter to Beth. On the high sea, he had had time to reflect on things. It had taken him a long time to pluck up the courage to write to her, and now that he had, he would rather get the letter finished and away. He even got it out of his pocket with the intention of completing it. But his curiosity was aroused. Obviously the fellow outside must know him, or he wouldn't have been able to ask for him by name. Folding the letter back into his pocket, he pushed back the bench and stood upright. He had grown a good deal these past months, but was still painfully young compared to the old salts that frequented the alehouse.

From his vantage point in the alley, Ben watched and waited. In a short while his patience was rewarded. A tall slim figure appeared silhouetted in the doorway. 'Over here, Matthew,' he called. 'I'm here, in the alley.'

Though intrigued, Matthew paused a while. He had not recognised the voice, nor did he relish the idea of going into that dark alley. 'Who's there?' he asked. He came forward and the light fell on his face. He looked incredibly young and frightened. 'Who is it?' he repeated, coming forward hesitantly. Suddenly, the dark shape sprang forward, wrapping its hand over his mouth. In an instant, he was dragged into the shadows. No one saw. There was no one there but himself, and the stranger that came at him out of nowhere.

It was five minutes to eleven when the carriage halted outside the club and Ben climbed out. He was like a man haunted, his eyes furtive, his manner calculating, and his face set like stone. He knew he was a fool to come back here, but he was driven by a blind unreasoning fury, a sense of revulsion that made him want to seek out Tom Reynolds. And if he was caught in the act it didn't seem to matter any more. The events of the night had sobered him and he desperately needed a drink. They had business between them, he and Tom Reynolds, business that would not wait. As he strode through the foyer, he did not see Tyler Blacklock collecting his hat and coat from the desk; and Tyler did not see him. 'Thank you.' The girl smiled gratefully when Tyler put the two coins into her hand. 'Goodnight, sir.'

'Goodnight,' Tyler replied. He was undecided as to whether he should walk part of the way home. A brisk stroll would clear his mind; but, on the other hand, the streets of London were crawling with all manner of undesirables at such a late hour.

Outside, he remained in the doorway a moment before deciding that he would walk a way after all. The night was cold, but the fog was beginning to clear and he was in no hurry to return to the house in Kensington.

Tyler had barely gone a hundred yards along the street when all hell broke loose; screams of 'Murder!' echoed into the night and frantic shouts, then the unmistakable sound of a constable's whistle shattering the night, and running footsteps coming from all directions, all rushing towards the club. When two officers came bounding along the street, Tyler flattened himself against the wall or they would likely have run straight over him.

Retracing his steps to the club, he was astonished to see four constables emerge, grappling with a man who seemed hellbent on breaking loose from their iron grip. Tyler stared at the man, horror written on his face as the officers dragged him away. It was Ben! In that moment, he raised his head and looked directly into Tyler's disbelieving eyes. 'Help me,' he said, 'I've done for him, the bastard. For God's sake, Tyler . . . help me!' In a moment he was gone, bundled into the waggon that had almost mounted the pavement as it careered to a halt.

The excited crowd took a while to disperse. Only Tyler remained. But then he too was gone. In the wake of pandemonium, the sound of Ben's cry echoed along the street: 'Help me. For God's sake, Tyler, help me!'

Chapter Thirteen

Miss Mulliver had been home only a short while, but in that time Elizabeth had failed before her eyes. The doctor had spoken in serious terms to Elizabeth's devoted companion. 'I'm sorry,' he had whispered, 'she may have six months, perhaps a year at the most.' Time went so quickly, and every passing day was beginning to show. The eyes that had shone like dark coals were now much dimmer, and the beautiful slender hands were never still; always nervously fidgeting as though they wanted to quiet the swirling thoughts that constantly troubled her. From her armchair in the grand drawing room, where she was sewing the hem of one of Elizabeth's nightgowns, Tilly sneaked a glance at the other woman. 'What is it, Elizabeth?' she asked now. 'Are you uncomfortable?' Anxious, she began rising from her chair.

'No, Tilly,' Elizabeth put up her hand in protest. 'Stay where you are. I'm fine, really.' When Tilly sat down again, she added softly, 'I was just thinking, that's all.'

'What were you thinking about?'

'Oh, many things.' A far-off look came into her eyes. 'So many things, Tilly.'

'Oh?' She was delighted when Elizabeth seemed to want to talk, because all too often these days she was withdrawn and unwilling to engage in conversation.

'Oh, Tilly, you should have seen him as a young man.' Her hands went to her face, and her eyes were raised in a beautiful smile, as though she had suddenly seen something wonderful.

'You mean. . .Richard?' She loved and missed him too.

Elizabeth nodded. 'So tall and handsome he was,' she said, turning her face to her companion, and staring yet not seeing. 'I loved him from the moment I saw him.' Sadness clouded her eyes. 'I knew he was married; after all, his wife, Esther, was my own sister. But they were never happy, you know.'

'I know.' Tilly knew it all, because hadn't Elizabeth told her the whole story so many times; how Richard had not been happy with Esther, how she made his life a misery, and how he turned to Elizabeth one particular night when Esther was visiting friends? That was the night when Beth was conceived; when Richard and Elizabeth had found such joy and happiness in each other's arms. When she found that she was carrying his child, Elizabeth was beside herself with worry and shame. The scandal would ruin Richard, she knew, and how could she face the world once they realised she was carrying a child out of wedlock? Worse, how could she bear people to know that her own sister's husband had fathered the child? Frantic, she had gone to Esther and confessed her shame. Furious, Esther played mercilessly on her sister's guilt. Yet all the time she had been desperately concerned that Richard would leave her for Elizabeth. He was a man of consequence, a clever and talented man with a strong ambition which Esther knew would take them right to the top. She was not prepared to sacrifice all of that. Instead, she devised a plan: Elizabeth was to say nothing to Richard about her condition, and was never to see him again. In return, Esther would arrange for the child to be born in a secret place out in the country where no one would know. Afterwards, it was to be found a good home. Distraught and alone, Elizabeth had no choice but to agree.

That night she was sent away, and Esther confronted her husband about his affair with Elizabeth. He did not deny it. But when Esther pointed out how his career would be ruined if it became known – and that she herself would make quite certain that it became known – he conceded to her plan. But with one promise. The child would not be offered to strangers. Instead, with Elizabeth's consent, it was to be brought up as one of his own. Esther fought long and hard on that particular issue. In the end she, like her sister, had no choice but to agree.

These past weeks, Elizabeth had lived and relived her memories so often that they were becoming very real to her. Confused and regretful, she had lost all sense of time and the past began to merge with the present. 'I've missed him,' she said now. 'Oh, Tilly, how I've missed him. And the baby, my beautiful baby girl.' She smiled. 'The nurses said she looked just like me, and she did, you know . . . same hair colour . . . same dark eyes. And from what you tell me, she's grown into a lovely young woman.' Her attention was suddenly drawn by the tap on the door when the nurse came in to tell her, 'It's time for your afternoon nap now.'

'But I'm not tired,' she protested, looking to her companion to confirm it.

'Best do as the nurse says,' Tilly said gently.

'But . . . I want to tell you . . .'

'I know, but we can talk later, when you're refreshed.'

'You'll stay here with me?'

Tilly nodded. 'I'll stay right here,' she promised. She remained in her seat while the nurse plumped the cushions on the settee, and rearranged the blankets until she was satisfied that her patient was comfortable. All the while she chatted and kept the two women entertained with snippets of gossip which she had collected during the day. It was when she spoke about Richard Ward's son that the two women became instantly alert; Miss Mulliver because she had deliberately kept all knowledge of Ben's arrest from Elizabeth.

'What was that you said, dear?' Elizabeth demanded to know. When Tilly began to interrupt, she stayed her by raising the palm of her hand and insisting, 'Nurse . . . what did you say about Richard Ward's son?'

'Why, only that things are looking bad for him.' She sensed the atmosphere and was confused. Glancing towards Miss Mulliver, she saw the look on her face, a look that warned her to say no more. Realising that something was amiss, she quickly assured Elizabeth, 'Oh, but you don't want to know about things like that.'

'Leave me.' Elizabeth was clearly agitated. 'I want to talk with Miss Mulliver,' she said in a firm voice that surprised the nurse who looked again at Tilly.

'It's all right,' Tilly told her. 'Give us ten minutes together.'

'Very well. But only ten minutes, mind.' With one last glance at her patient, she departed.

The ensuing silence was ominous. Then Elizabeth spoke. 'I never thought you would deliberately keep things from me.'

Tilly came to sit on the edge of the settee. 'I'm sorry,' she said, taking the other woman's pale hand into hers, and feeling relieved when it was not snatched away. She knew now that what she had done was wrong. Elizabeth had a right to know everything. 'I should have told you,' she said. 'But I love you, and I only want to do what I think is best for you.'

'I want to know about Richard's son.' The dark eyes flashed angrily, alive again. 'Tell me everything, Tilly,' she warned.

And so Tilly told her everything. She explained how

Ben Ward was in jail, charged with murder, and how it was rumoured that he would be hanged for a dreadful crime to which he had already confessed. She was urged to describe how Esther and Richard had parted on bad terms, and how the business had now folded. She was even made to confess how Beth had been disowned by her father when it was discovered that she was carrying Tyler Blacklock's child; it was this news above all else which made Elizabeth gasp and brought tears to her eyes. At the time when it all happened, Tilly had deliberately kept the painful truth from Elizabeth. Now though, she saw how she had been wrong to do that. The truth must be told, and so Tilly went on to describe how Beth was not with Tyler, and that thanks to the devious Esther and Ben Ward, Tyler had never been aware of Beth's plight. Indeed, Beth's whereabouts were not known to anyone; although Tilly assured Elizabeth that with the help of God her daughter's strong forthright character would see her through.

When the tale was told, Elizabeth sat for a moment, her head bent low, her eyes gazing down to the bed-clothes. Presently she spoke, and what she said was astonishing. 'Bring him to me, Tilly.' Her eyes were clear and determined as she looked at the other woman.

'You mean Richard? You want me to bring him here?' Tilly was shocked.

'You must. Oh, and you must turn Heaven and earth upside down to find Beth.' Her voice was trembling, but she was incredibly calm. 'I need to see them both,' she said softly, affectionately squeezing Tilly's hand. 'Don't you see? I must make my peace with them before it's too late.'

Lost for words, Tilly nodded. 'Of course, I understand,' she said at length. There was an impatient tap on the door and when the nurse entered, Tilly explained, 'I have to go out.' Turning, she kissed Elizabeth tenderly on the forehead. 'Don't worry. Sleep now. I'll be back as soon as I can.' They gazed at each other then, a lifetime of love and devotion flowing between them.

When Elizabeth spoke, it was with regret in her voice. 'Oh, Tilly, have I demanded too much of you all this time?' Her voice caught in a sob. 'I had no right to use you in that way. Can you forgive me?'

Reaching out to hold Elizabeth's pale hand in her own, Tilly reminded her of how she would 'never forget the kindness and love you have shown me and the way you welcomed me into your home, when I had nowhere else to go and no one to whom I could turn. I'm only glad that I could bring you at least some contentment by relating the way of things with Richard and your daughter.' She was careful not to reveal her other reason for remaining in that unhappy household; her love for Richard must remain her secret.

For a while, the two women held each other close, each lost in her own dreams. After a time, Tilly prepared to do as Eizabeth had asked. She would bring Richard here to this house, and she hoped above all else that when he knew the truth and her part in the deception, he would find it in his heart to forgive her.

Richard was devastated by the news which Tilly had brought. Little by little, the story unfolded of how she and Elizabeth lived only a short distance away, and how Tilly had been Elizabeth's eyes and ears all the time she had been employed in the Ward household. 'You see, she had no life of her own, Richard,' Tilly explained now. 'She only lived through you and Beth. It was not a situation I particularly enjoyed, but I could not refuse her.'

'I don't blame you,' he said. 'You're such a kind woman, I'm only glad that she had you to love her.' His guilt about his treatment of Elizabeth had never diminished, and now his life was shattered. With his beloved Beth gone, and his son facing the hangman's rope, his heart was heavy. This evening, when Tilly had knocked on his door, he had hoped that she might have come to stay with him. He loved her, and he had lost her also. But the news she brought had been a great shock. Even now, though they were discussing the part Elizabeth had played in his life as though it were only yesterday, he still could not come to terms with what he had learned.

'Will you come with me?' Tilly asked now. She had broken the news as gently as she could, but it was obvious that Richard was a haunted man. The trauma of the past weeks was telling on him. It was evident in his sad brown eyes and in a face which was devoid of colour. Her heart went out to him.

'You know I love you, Tilly,' he said quietly, making no effort to come nearer.

'I know.'

'Dare I ask if you love me?'

She gave no answer for a moment, but then she told him softly, 'I have always loved you.' But when he made a move towards her, she told him, 'No, Richard.'

'Elizabeth?' he murmured. Her eyes gave him the answer. She, too, was thinking of Elizabeth. 'I'll get my coat,' he said. She did not look at him as he brushed by. She dared not.

A few moments later they left the house, both reliving their last few moments together and both experiencing their own painful regrets. As he locked the door of his house, Richard thought of Elizabeth, the mother of his daughter, and the years between their last meeting and now, were as nothing.

Part Four

1892

LOVERS

Chapter Fourteen

'Why don't you speak up, man? If you insist on remaining silent, you'll only succeed in putting the noose round your own neck, dammit!' Tyler's face was set like stone as he faced Ben across the long well-scrubbed table in the centre of that small forbidding room. Close by, a prison officer watched with suspicious eyes, every muscle in his body alert. He must be ready for every eventuality, not least because this prisoner was suspected of a singularly vicious murder.

'I killed Tom Reynolds. Nothing can change that. I'm guilty, and it's only right that I should hang for it.' Ben's voice was flat, his eyes staring into Tyler's face, and his two hands stretched before him on the table top, according to instructions. He had put a knife through a man's heart. There were no greater depths to which he could sink. Hanging would be a merciful release from his own weaknesses.

'For God's sake!' Tyler gripped the table edge until his knuckles drained white. 'If you won't think about yourself, then think about your father . . . surely you know how all this is tearing him apart? And what about your mother? Have you thought what you're doing to her? She idolises you, Ben, and you won't even let her visit you! She's almost insane with worry.'

'You've seen her?' Of all the things Tyler could have said, the mention of Esther was the one thing that had touched Ben's conscience.

'Yes,' Tyler lied. He had not seen her because she would not permit it. She would not see anyone. Esther had locked herself in that big house on Bedford Square, and there wasn't a soul who could persuade her to open the door; not Tyler, not even her own husband. Frantic for her safety, Richard had urged the police to gain admittance to the house. After a long and lengthy campaign, one officer had eventually succeeded. His report had said that she appeared to be 'completely in charge of herself, and gave no cause for concern. It was purely a domestic matter.' He did not know how cunning she was, nor how she could act out a part so convincingly that even a practised eye could not distinguish the real woman beneath. From one end of London to the other, it was rumoured that when Ben was arrested, and then afterwards when he refused to see her in prison, Esther had lost the will to live. There were those who claimed that she had been seen at night, wandering the dark streets, and loitering outside the prison gates where her beloved son was caged.

'I can't let her come here, you know that, don't you?' Ben said now. There were tears in his eyes, and his hands clenched and unclenched as he looked imploringly at Tyler. 'I've caused her so much heartache. How can I let her see me like this?' A sob broke from him and he bowed his head low, his shoulders shaking uncontrollably.

'I think I understand how you feel,' Tyler told him. It was a hard thing even for him to see this young man in such a state. 'But I believe your mother would rather see you, "like this" as you put it, than not see you at all.' He reached out and stilled Ben's trembling hands, but drew his fingers away when the officer stepped forward. 'You mean everything to her,' he went on. 'Won't you at least try to help yourself? Won't you tell the police exactly what was on your mind that night? Won't you tell *me*? Were you provoked? Why, Ben? In heaven's name, *why did you do it?*'

'Does it matter? I killed a man. That's all there is to it.'

'No!' Tyler had seen how the mention of his mother had seemed to loosen Ben's tongue. He had to press on now or lose his chance. 'There had to be a reason. What were you and Tom Reynolds talking about that night at the club? Don't forget I was there, Ben. I saw you! Where did you go that night? Why did you return? And why . . . why did you kill Tom Reynolds?'

'Will you give my mother a message?' Ben had heard every word, but throughout it all had thought only of his mother.

Tyler's immediate instinct was to assure Ben that, yes, of course he would give Esther a message, even if he had to shout it through her letter box. But then it suddenly occurred to him that he could take advantage of Ben's regard for his mother. 'I'll do that for you,' he said quietly, adding in a more serious voice, 'but first I want answers to my questions.'

'It won't do any good.'

'Why don't you let me be the judge of that?' Tyler recalled the name which Tom Reynolds had uttered that night. He spoke it now. 'Who is Matthew Armstrong?' he asked pointedly. 'And why was Tom Reynolds so fired up when he talked of him?' At the mention of the name, Ben smiled, a strange sad smile, but still he said nothing. 'I want to know, Ben,' Tyler persisted. There were other things he wanted to know, but they could wait. 'Are you going to tell me exactly what happened?' He sighed out loud when Ben actually nodded. 'Everything, Ben. Tell me everything.'

'All right. I have to admit that it's all been a terrible burden to me,' he murmured, his gaze dropping to the

449

table. 'Maybe it would be a good thing if I purged myself before I'm called to a higher judgement.'

The words had shaken Tyler, for he had had no idea that beneath the booze and the devil-may-care attitude that was characteristic of Ben, there was also a man of some faith. 'Let's start with Reynolds,' he suggested. 'What were you discussing that night?'

'You'll talk with my mother . . . give her a message from me?' Ben wanted reassurance. When Tyler gave it, he outlined the message he wanted Tyler to take to Esther; a message of love and regret from a son to his mother. Afterwards, he lapsed into a long soul-searching silence before starting: 'I hadn't intended meeting up with Reynolds. It was he who sought me out. He came to the club and, oh, he was in such a strange mood, Tyler . . . thirsting for blood almost.' Here he shook his head as though trying to rid himself of the memory.

'Whose blood?' Tyler wanted to know. 'Was it Matthew Armstrong's blood he was thirsting for?'

Leaning his head back, Ben raised his eyes to the ceiling, and groaned like a man in pain. 'He was just a boy,' he cried. 'Reynolds wanted me to believe that I'd be doing away with a man not worth the air he breathed . . . a "villain of the worst order", he called him.' He looked at Tyler now and there were tears coursing down his face. 'He was just a boy, no more than seventeen or eighteen years old. Frightened out of his mind, he was. I could feel the poor little sod shaking like a leaf. Just a boy . . . and I was only a heartbeat from ending his life.' He paused. There was so much more to tell about how his reason fled with his fury at Reynolds; about how Reynolds had boasted that murder was so easy, and didn't he know better than anybody, because hadn't he murdered his own father? Other things too . . . how he had come into a fortune. And worse . . . much worse . . . how he had caught up with Beth, and was intent on taking her for himself. All of these things Ben intended to reveal now to Tyler. And, while he was at it, he would ease his conscience about his sister.

But the thought of Tyler's learning the truth about Beth put the fear of God into Ben. Tyler should know that she had never married Wilson Ryan. He had every right to be told the truth . . . that Beth had been turned out of the house when it was discovered that she was carrying Tyler's own child. Ben realised how cruel he had been in deceiving Tyler all this time. This was his opportunity to put it right, but he was afraid that Tyler would be tempted to pull the head off his shoulders for the part he had played in turning Beth out of the house that night.

He looked at the man now, a lonely man, a man hardened by what he had lost. Ben's courage almost failed him as he stared into those green eyes. He couldn't easily confess to what he had done. But, if he didn't, then he must go back to that cell and acknowledge himself for the coward he was. Yet how could he tell Tyler where to find Beth when he didn't know himself? Although it was common knowledge that Tom Reynolds had come into a sizeable inheritance left to him by his father in the North of England, and that he had spent some considerable time there, he had not told Ben where he had seen Beth . . . only that she was in dire straits, and he meant to take her for himself.

It was that which had preyed on Ben's mind as he travelled to commit murder; that, and the fact that Reynolds had sent him to slaughter a mere boy. It was Tyler who had set him thinking, in the carriage when he had pointed out what a scoundrel Reynolds really was. It was Tyler who had made Ben stop and take stock. And so he opened his heart to Tyler now, recounting everything that had been said between himself and Reynolds. And as he talked, he felt better; but when he came to explain

451

about Beth, he saw how Tyler was made to suffer, and Ben knew he would never forgive himself for it.

When he had finished, Tyler remained motionless for a while, his hands spread over his face as though he could not bear to look on the other man. To his watching companion, the silence was unbearable. In a way he would rather have had Tyler lunge for his throat across the table. Instead, when he looked up, Tyler's expression was immensely calm, his eyes seeming to see straight inside the man before him. Then, without a word, he departed, his head high but his broad shoulders drooping as though they carried a great weight.

'I only have a moment, Miss Mulliver.' Tyler had been upstairs packing when he was obliged to answer the door to her urgent knocking.

The only other person in the house was Mrs Bates. His housekeeper was a dear lady, but once she was in her bed there could be an earthquake and she would happily sleep through it all. 'Come in, come in,' he urged. The night was bitter and the hall was losing its warmth. When he first opened the door, he had not immediately recognised Tilly Mulliver for he had seen her only once before on a certain night when he had been bold enough to call for Beth.

'I'm so sorry to bother you, Mr Blacklock,' Tilly started, 'But you see . . .' She paused, nervously looking up at him as she went on,' It's just that, well . . . it's Beth. Do you know where she is? I must find her.'

He had been smiling, but now his face was both grim and curious. 'Come through into the sitting room,' he said, pointing the way with his arm and stepping aside so that she could precede him.

Once inside the pleasant room with its strong dark colours and brown leather armchairs, Tyler bade her sit down. 'It's cold out,' he said. 'Can I get you a hot drink?

Or perhaps you might prefer a drop of good brandy?' When she gratefully declined both, he sat in the chair opposite her, a serious expression on his handsome face. 'It's strange that you should come here seeking Beth,' he told her, 'because I was just packing my bag when you knocked on the door. I have a mind to travel North in search of her.'

'You know where she is?' Miss Mulliver sat up straight on the edge of the chair, her eyes sparkling with anticipation.

'No. Not exactly,' he said with regret. 'But there is word of her, and I mean to find her if it's humanly possible.'

'You know then . . . that Beth was never married to Wilson Ryan?' All the way here she had prepared herself to confess how she had been aware for some time that he and Beth were betrayed, and that Beth had been disowned by the family on account of her being with child . . . his child.

His eyes grew dark with anger. 'Yes, I know.'

'How much do you know?'

'Enough to break my heart,' he confessed.

She looked away and for a moment made no reply, but then she informed him, 'I don't think you know it all.'

'What do you mean?'

'Did you know that Beth was not Esther Ward's daughter?'

The effect of her words on him was remarkable. Getting out of the chair, he looked at her long and hard, a stern expression on his face, an expression of disbelief. 'Not Esther's daughter?' He shook his head, and a terrible thought came to him. He recalled how Beth had idolised her father. 'And Richard?' he asked hopefully. 'Is Richard Ward her father?'

'Oh, yes, there's no doubt about that.' She smiled in the knowledge that she had just left Richard with his long-ago sweetheart; but in the smile there was a tinge of sadness. Just as she had feared, he was lost to her now.

'Then how . . . ?' His brain was racing. He had learned so much tonight, and all to do with his darling Beth. He wanted to get out of here, to find her, to keep her safe for ever. As God was his judge, he would not return until he had found her!

'Beth's real mother is Elizabeth Manners . . . Esther's sister.' She paused at the shocked expression on his face. 'It's a long tragic story,' she said. 'All that matters for the moment is that Elizabeth is seriously ill. Beth's father is with her now.' She stood up, her eyes appealing to him. 'Find your Beth,' she pleaded. 'Make it soon. And God go with you.'

Placing his hands on her shoulders, he promised, 'I will find her, Miss Mulliver. It's my only purpose in life. Where will you be?' Quickly he went to the desk and took up a pen. As she gave him the address of Elizabeth's home, he scribbled it down, afterwards thrusting the piece of paper into his pocket. 'Once I've seen you safely home,' he told her, 'I have a message to deliver to Esther. After that, I must get to the docks. There's a certain young man I need to talk to.' He stroked his face with finger and thumb, his eyes downcast and his thoughts returning to what Ben had told him . . . Tom Reynolds had been left a fortune . . . by his estranged father, and he wanted the Armstrong boy murdered. It was an idea, just an idea, but Tyler wondered about Matthew Armstrong. Why did Reynolds want him killed? And was there a chance that the young man might know enough about Reynolds to reveal where he could have met up with Beth?

He bade Tilly Mulliver sit down again while he collected his portmanteau from upstairs. 'Then we'll be on our way.' He delayed a moment. 'I saw Beth myself, some time back . . . in Liverpool.' He remembered how she was . . . smiling and seeming happy with her family . . . her family! 'She was with child when I saw her,' he went on. 'There was a man with her, but I couldn't see his face. And there were children . . . a girl, who could not have belonged to Beth, and a boy.' The realisation ran through him like a hot poker, jarring every nerve in his body. '*A boy!*' He smiled down on the woman's surprised face. 'Oh, Miss Mulliver, do you think that boy could have been my own son?'

'It's likely, but didn't you say she was with child and that there was a man with her?' She regarded him with a degree of sympathy. 'After all this time, Mr Blacklock, you have to be prepared for the possibility that Beth has married and found happiness in a new life . . . a life with someone else.' Cruel words, but they must be said.

He gave a single curt nod, not wanting to acknowledge what she had said, and yet weren't her words the very same with which he'd been tormenting himself? If it was true that Beth had found contentment in a new life, he would not spoil it for her. Instead he would wish her well, and come away to live out his own loneliness, counting the regrets until the day he died. 'We shall only know when we find her,' he said with a half-smile, 'and the sooner I get started, the sooner I can search her out, God willing.'

Chapter Fifteen

The boy's laughter filled Beth's heart with joy. Going to the kitchen window, she looked out into the snow-covered yard, her face wreathed in smiles as she glanced at the newly made snowman by the back gate. Since early light on this Sunday morning, Cissie and Richard had been hard at work, patiently scraping the snow from the flagstones and piling it up into the bulky misshapen thing which Richard had then proudly named after himself. 'Richard Snowman,' he said in a solemn voice, at the same time plonking one of David's old caps on its wonky head. Cissie wanted to know how Richard knew whether it was a boy or a girl 'snowman', to which he promptly replied, 'Because it's wearing a flat cap, silly!' There then followed a fierce snowball fight and much falling about, with the two of them covered in great wet clumps of snow that clung to their ears and hair, until Beth could hardly tell which of the three of them was the original snowman.

'Come on in, you two,' she told them now, going into the yard with a basket of damp washing between her arms. 'It's time to get ready for church.' The washing had been done since yesterday morning but until now there had not been a single break in the weather. Beth had dried the urgently needed clothes in front of the fire, but the parlour was so small and prone to damp at the best of times.

'Aw, Beth, do we have to go today?' Cissie was

having so much fun, neither she nor the boy wanted it to end.

'And, anyway, it's too cold,' he protested.

'Give over, do,' Beth laughed. 'There's sunshine now, and anyway you can wrap yourself up warm and then you won't feel the cold, will you?' She was used to all manner of tricks. 'We're going to church and that's that.' She drew her long brown shawl tighter about her. There wasn't much warmth in the sun and that was a fact.

'Five more minutes then?' Cissie asked.

Beth had to smile. She didn't know who was the worst, her son or Cissie. 'Go on then,' she conceded. 'Five minutes. But that's all, mind!' Maisie had insisted that the whole family go to church at least once a month. And ever since that dear soul was lost to them, Beth had tried to do the same.

As she pegged out the washing on the line, she could hear the squeals and laughter behind her, and occasionally a round fat snowball would come flying past her ear. Hurrying, she thought that Richard was right. It *was* cold! In a matter of minutes, her ears were frozen and her nose had gone numb. Suddenly, she was aware that she was being observed. Both Cissie and the boy were standing by the gate staring at her and seeming hugely amused. 'What's tickling you two?' she asked. 'I can't be that funny a sight, surely?' She was well aware of her swollen figure, but that would soon be gone.

'Give over, Richard. That's not a nice thing to say!' Cissie reproached the boy. She was suddenly stricken with guilt. 'He says you look like Father Christmas,' she explained sheepishly.

'Well, you do, don't you, Mammy?' the boy wanted to know.

'And how's that?' Beth asked, with some curiosity.

'Because you've got a fat belly and a red nose,' came the innocent observation.

At that, Beth was obliged to burst out laughing. Yes, that was exactly what she did look like. Relieved that she had seen the funny side of it, both Cissie and the boy ran to her and hugged her hard. 'Hey!' Shaking them off, she warned, 'We don't want the baby arriving just yet,' adding with a twinkle in her eye, 'at least, not until after we come back from church.' As she expected, her remark brought wails of protest. 'Go on,' she ordered. 'Your five minutes are up. I'll expect you to be ready and waiting by the time I've finished hanging out this washing.' She watched as they ran indoors. What would she do without them? she wondered. Those two were the light of her life.

Less than an hour later, after walking the few hundred yards to the little church where Maisie had been married and was now buried, Beth and the children were seated in a pew, listening to the sermon; it was a moving one on love and friendship, and companionship with our fellow man. Unfortunately, Beth and her children had seen very little of that since moving back into Larkhill. The neighbours had gone out of their way to show contempt for 'that one as wed David Miller', and it was a sad thing for Beth. But she did not let it get her down, for that would only make matters worse. Instead, she showed a certain dignity, which only served to alienate her neighbours further.

These past months had made heavy demands on Beth's savings, and so when they came to pay their respects to those gone before, there was only a small posy of white winter chrysanthemums for Cissie's mammy; these were laid reverently on the cold hard earth beneath the cross which bore her name. Then, all of them chilled to the marrow, the little trio began its way home.

As she went along, with the boy running ahead and Cissie walking quietly beside her, no doubt thinking of her mammy, Beth's thoughts went to David. The flowers which she had brought to Maisie were half of a bunch acquired cheaply from Moll Sutton's shop. The other half she had taken only yesterday to the grander churchyard some two miles away, where David was buried with his stepfather. It seemed a lifetime since the tragedy, when in fact it was only weeks. Both she and Cissie had often spoken about the way things had come about. But now Beth had learned to put the past behind her. That way she had managed to come to terms with all that had happened in her life. One thing she was thankful for, and that was the fact that Tom Reynolds had not put himself out to track them down; although she could hardly believe her good fortune, because he was not a man known to give up easily. She believed also that he was secretly enraged that his father had left part of his inheritance to Matthew.

'Why don't people say hello to us?' Richard asked, when one couple hurried past, their faces deliberately turned away.

''Cause they don't know no better!' Cissie retorted angrily. 'That's why.'

'Now, Cissie,' Beth reprimanded. 'If people don't want to talk to us, that's their right.' She pretended it didn't matter, but it did. Very much. And it wasn't as if she hadn't gone out of her way to make friends, because she had.

The house was bitterly cold when they returned. But then it wasn't so surprising, when part of the outer wall was missing, and a sizeable chunk of the ceiling above the main bedroom was open to the skies. Still, Beth and the children had worked hard to make a home of sorts here and, to a certain extent, they had succeeded. Some of the furniture was still intact in the house, although it needed a deal of repairing and airing before it could possibly be used; however, Beth had grown useful with a needle and thread and, once they had thrown out the rubbish, scrubbed the place until it shone and lit a fire to air everything, the little house actually began to look cosy. Confining themselves to that part of it which was undamaged, they had made good use of the tiny scullery and the front parlour. Having found numerous old blankets, two eiderdowns and an assortment of old rags, Beth had then recruited the children to help by draping them across that part of the wall which let the weather in. Before the recent snowfall it had worked quite well. But only last night, Beth and Cissie had found it necessary to poke at the billowing 'walls' with a broom, in order to expel the snow which had found its way in through the gaping holes and crevices.

The little clock on the mantelpiece chimed eight. Blissfully tired out by his long busy day and the building of 'Richard Snowman', Beth's son made no protest when she took him up to bed: he fell sound asleep as soon as his head touched the pillow. 'Goodnight, sleep tight,' Beth whispered, before tiptoeing out of the back room which the boy was privileged to have to himself. Cissie and Beth shared the other room at the front of the house.

'I think I'll go to bed an' all,' Cissie told her, soon after Beth had come downstairs. 'I'm that tired.' She gave a huge yawn, stretching her arms above her head. 'I've a mind to do a bit o' singing outside o' the Railway Station tomorrow.'

'You'll do no such thing, my girl,' Beth told her. 'We're not that destitute yet.'

'Yes, but there ain't much money left, is there, Beth?' Cissie reminded her. 'And what good is the piffling few pennies I've brought in these past weeks, eh? Fourpence on me best day . . . an' only the dead flowers that's left over on me worst!' Her vivid blue eyes grew depressed. 'What we gonna do when the money's all gone . . . what we gonna do, Beth?'

'We'll cross that bridge when we get to it, shall we?' Coming across the room with the intention of hugging the girl, Beth was seized by a sudden vicious pain that made her cry out. Clinging to the table edge, she bent forward, breathing easy, the way Maisie had taught her when Richard was on his way.

'Is the babby coming, Beth?' Cissie cried, scrambling out of her chair. 'Is it? Is it?'

Deliberately straightening her aching body, Beth made her voice sound matter-of-fact, 'Goodness me, Cissie . . . don't panic,' she smiled, but all the time her body felt like a tram had run over it. In her heart, she had dreaded this moment. What with the neighbours turning their backs on her, and no one else but Cissie to help, Beth knew it was not going to be easy. The last thing she wanted was for the girl to share her fears. 'Yes, Cissie,' she admitted, 'I think the babby's on its way.' She watched those big blue eyes widen with fear and excitement, and knew she would have to coach the girl in a calm organised manner. She prayed it would be an easy birth. 'The second baby is always the easiest, so your mammy always told me,' she said, and was glad when Cissie also remembered Maisie's words.

'Happen it'll be here afore morning then.' Cissie was greatly excited. 'Happen it'll be a girl.' She helped Beth up the stairs, chattering all the while. 'Don't worry,' she said in a voice that made Beth smile, for it was very like Maisie's, 'you'll be all right, Beth. The babby'll be here afore you know it.'

'Well now, aren't I the lucky one to have such a lady of experience looking after me?' she asked, forcing a laugh; but the laughter was choked back when another pain gripped her with particular savagery.

* * *

The night had been long and hard since Beth felt the first pang of labour. Even in these past hours, winter had set in with a new vengeance. The snow had been falling steadily, and the whole of Larkhill was covered in a glittering soft down. Even the houses that were damaged by fire seemed clean and whole beneath their cloak of white. It was four a.m. The snow was still gently tumbling from the skies, covering all traces of human life, hiding the previous day's footprints, and bringing with it a chill that settled over the rooftops and lingered in every doorway. There was no sound save for the hush of snow as it sped its way downwards.

Only one light could be seen in the row of windows that flanked either side of the road; a small flickering light emanating from one of the bedrooms. A solitary shadow moved behind the curtains, slow, then hurrying; now it was frantic, and in a moment it was gone. Suddenly the morning hush was shattered by the sound of a door being thrown back on its hinges. Running feet, noiseless on the carpet of snow beneath, yet urgent as they sped along the street.

'Wake up!' Cissie banged her fists on a door, her frantic eyes staring upward towards the bedroom window. 'Can you help me? Please . . . Beth needs someone to help!'

Almost at once, the window was flung open to reveal a sour-faced man. Leaning out over the sill, he shouted, 'Clear off. There's nobody here as'll help yer!' Like many of the people along Larkhill, he had not forgotten the rumours that if it hadn't been for Maisie Armstrong's lodger, that fire would never have happened, and they wouldn't have had the heart of the street ripped out of it. More than that, there was much resentment at Beth's having married the landlord's son. 'Get away!' he yelled. 'Get back where yer bloody come from, why don't yer?

463

Back ter the landlord's house. Tell him how we're made to live in a rat-infested hovel.' He knew that old man Reynolds had been killed, and knew that David had gone with him, but it made no difference. Folks such as himself still had to cough up an exorbitant rent. One landlord or another, they were all the same. And round here, folks had little truck with them as mixed in such circles. 'Go on,' he shouted, pushing the snow from the sill on to Cissie's small figure. 'Bugger off, I tell yer!'

Desperate and disillusioned, she watched as he closed the window. Wondering what to do next, she went at a run out of the gate, standing there a while and wondering which house to knock up next. The fact was folks believed it was Beth's fault when the fire started and they had to lay the blame at somebody's door, so why not at hers? Beth Ward, the turncoat who had married the landlord. That was the real reason they could not tolerate her, because she had betrayed the working class by throwing her lot in with the very people who held out their hand and took good money from folk as worked blood and sweat for their pitiful wages. Landlords and them as employed ordinary folk; there was nothing to choose between them. And anybody who took their side had to be every bit as bad as them.

Cissie realised there was only one person in Larkhill who just might help. Old Lou Bolton and Maisie Armstrong went back over many years. Cissie remembered how Lou used to come into their front parlour and sit and chat with her mammy until late at night. Once Beth came to live in the house, though, Lou didn't come so often, and soon she didn't come at all. Cissie always wondered whether Maisie's old friend had grown jealous because of her love for Beth. In fact, Cissie had asked her mammy that very thing, and Maisie had told her, 'If folks want to be childish, darlin', there ain't nothing in the world yer mammy can do about it. Lou Bolton knows where I live. If she wants me, she only has to come through that front door.' But Lou never did. Yet, strangely enough, she was the only one who had spoken to Beth on the street since. Only the other day it was, when Beth was coming home from the market. Lou had passed her on the way and said, 'Mornin'.' Just that, but it was a word of greeting, and Beth was cheered by it. Unfortunately, Lou had passed them on several occasions since, but she was either with her husband or with one of the neighbourhood women and, like them, had remained stonily silent until Beth had gone by.

Cissie had no choice. Beth was in deep labour, and she had need of someone who knew what they were doing. Cissie realised how little she knew about these things, but old Lou had birthed and raised twelve strapping lads of her own. If anybody should know what to do, it was her! Lou's house was down at the very far end of Larkhill. Running as though the wind was at her heels, Cissie was soon banging on the door. 'Lou!' Her voice echoed the length and breadth of the street. 'Lou Bolton . . . it's Cissie Armstrong. Open the door . . . please.'

In a minute, a flickering light appeared in the bedroom window; the curtains were shifted to one side and a large sleepy face peered out. The curtains dropped and, afraid that whoever it was had gone back to bed on seeing her, Cissie shouted again. Suddenly the door was inched open and Lou appeared. 'What the devil's going on?' she demanded.

'It's Beth.' Cissie was still breathless from running. 'The babby's coming and Beth's in terrible pain and I don't know what to do and she says I'm to fetch somebody and I can't get nobody to come and . . .'

'Woah! Get yer breath, young 'un, afore yer drops dead on me doorstep with a bloody 'eart attack,' the woman told her, clutching her night-shift about her sizeable form and glancing nervously up the stairs. 'It's lucky fer you that me old feller sleeps through every kind of noise there is,' she whispered. 'Beth's having the babby, yer say?'

Cissie nodded. 'Please, Lou,' she pleaded, 'I've done all Beth told me to, but it ain't no good. Beth said I was to get help.'

The woman shook her head. 'I can't help yer. I'm sorry,' she said, glancing up and down the street, looking to see whether Cissie's yelling had alerted the neighbours. 'Me life wouldn't be worth living.'

Desperate, Cissie turned away, saying, 'I thought you might help us because you know all about birthing, what with having all them lads, but you're all the same! Folks in Larkhill should be ashamed o' theirselves. If my mammy were here, she'd tell you an' all.'

'Wait on, young 'un,' the woman called quietly. Cissie had touched her conscience. This was Maisie's little gal. Somehow, in their blindness, folks had forgotten that. In her time, Maisie had been a good, kind soul to folk up and down this street. 'I've never known a time when your mammy turned anybody away,' she murmured, and Cissie was surprised to see tears glistening in old Lou's eyes. 'Sometimes we're us own worst enemies. Give me a minute, an' I'll get some'at warm over me old bones.' In that moment, a man's voice called down. 'What's going on, Lou?'

'It's Maisie's lass . . . yon Beth's gone into labour.'

'That's none o' your business. Come and get yourself back in this 'ere bed!'

'Well now, I'm *mekking* it my business,' she retorted at the top of her voice, and Cissie was amused to see lights going on all over the street. 'Get back to sleep, yer silly old bugger,' Lou told him. 'I'll be back when I'm ready, an' not afore.' Telling Cissie to run home and assure Beth that help was on the way, old Lou went back indoors to get dressed. 'I'll be after yer soon as ever I can,' she told Cissie, and the girl went on her way at full speed, to tell Beth she wasn't to worry because Lou Bolton was coming.

'Aw, that's good, Cissie, bless your heart.' Beth raised her head from the pillow. The sweat was running down her face, welding her hair to the pale expanse of her forehead and running into her eyes so she was made to blink through a haze at the girl. 'Watch for her, Cissie,' she urged now. 'Go to the door and watch for her, but be careful not to wake Richard.' Exhausted, she fell back on to the bed. Maisie was wrong, she thought wryly . . . the second one didn't come any easier! For some time now, she had felt the baby desperately trying to make its way, but there was something wrong. She was certain there was something wrong.

'No, lass, there's nothing wrong,' Lou assured her. Having made a short examination, she straightened up, smiling at Beth and conveying encouragement. 'It's just that you're small made, that's all. The babby's finding it difficult to make its way out, but it'll be all right, don't you worry none. Old Lou's seen the like afore.' She gave swift instructions to Cissie, who began hurrying back and forth with hot water, and fetching the clean sheets and towels which Beth had prepared in the days prior to going into labour. 'We've some hard work ahead on us,' Lou told them both, 'but there'll be a healthy babby at the end of it all, I promise yer.'

Lou was as good as her promise. Two hours later, the cry of a newborn echoed through the house. Beth had been delivered of a girl-child, a tiny perfect being that was the image of herself, with a small heart-shaped face and melting dark eyes, though these were presently marbled with slivers of blue.

The cry brought Beth's son running and for a while

he simply stood before the bed, his green eyes staring at that tiny bundle in his mammy's arms, and his fascinated gaze going from the babby to her and then to Cissie, who was standing beside Beth, tears in her eyes.

'There y'are then . . . you've got yer little angel,' Lou said with a broad smile. 'Everything's washed and ship-shape, so I'd best be getting home.' She glanced at the little clock by the bedside. 'God love an' bless us . . . it's quarter past nine of a morning!' she declared with horror. 'Me old man'll have me guts fer garters.' With one last look round, and a kind word for Beth, she unrolled her sleeves, took off her soiled pinnie, which she then rolled into a sausage small enough to squash into her skirt pocket, and went quickly from the room. 'Cissie Armstrong,' she called on her way down the stairs, 'keep yer eye on Beth and the young 'un. If yer worried about owt, just you come and fetch me.'

Cissie went to the bottom of the stairs with her. 'I reckon I'll be just fine now, thank you, Lou,' she said with a broad smile. 'Oh, ain't the baby lovely?'

'*All* babbies is lovely,' Lou retorted. 'It's when the buggers grow up they're trouble!' Two of her lads had been a real heartache in their growing up, but they were all right now, thank God. All the same, she regretted dampening the girl's enthusiasm. 'Aye, yer right, lass,' she said laughingly. 'It's a real bonny bundle.' She sighed. 'All the years I longed fer a little lass . . . an' all I ever got were three-legged 'uns.' She went on her way roaring with laughter, leaving Cissie to think about her words at length. It was a few minutes later when she realised what old Lou meant, and she too laughed out loud. 'Yer a bad 'un, Lou Bolton,' she said out loud. 'But I love yer for what you've done, bless yer heart.'

At first Cissie didn't take any notice when the knock came on the front door. She thought it must be Lou come back for something she'd forgotten. But when the knock sounded a second time with more urgency, she instinctively crept to the scullery door from where she peeped down the passageway. In the fire that had taken her mammy, all the windows in the house had exploded from the heat so Beth had arranged for new panes to be fitted into the rooms which they used. The front door had a glass half-moon shape some two-thirds the way up; Cissie had said they should block it in, but Beth thought different. 'It's handy for seeing who's at the door before we open it,' she said. Cissie had argued that it really was a waste of precious money, but now she thought different because what Beth said had been right. Through the half-moon, she could see the top of one man's head and, by the way he was standing to the side, together with the low murmur of voices, she realised there were *two* men. 'God above! Who's after us now?' she murmured, shrinking away from the door.

The knock came a third time, but now a voice called through the letter-box, 'Cissie . . . are you there?'

At first she didn't recognise the voice, it was so grown up, but then her face went all shades of pink and in her great excitement she careered down the passageway and flung open the door. 'Matthew!' She flung herself into his arms and they danced on the step, and laughed and cried, and only when he spun her to a halt did she see the other man: a tall handsome fellow with an abundance of coal black hair and smiling green eyes. Breathless and embarrassed, she waited for Matthew to introduce him. 'This is Tyler Blacklock,' he explained. 'A friend of Beth's.'

Cissie was speechless for a moment. She stared and stared. This was Tyler Blacklock! This man was Beth's sweetheart; the man she had told Cissie about with such love and longing. Richard's father. Everything Beth had told her was true . . . Tyler Blacklock was the most handsome man Cissie ever seen. But why was he here? Straightaway, she was protective. 'Beth ain't disposed to see no one,' she said. For all she knew, he was here to cause Beth even more heartache.

'Cissie!' Matthew pushed her inside the house. Tyler followed. 'There's a lot you should know. Tyler's here because he loves Beth. We've searched high and low for you. We went to Luther Reynolds' old house . . . we didn't know where you were. Nobody knew. It was only instinct that told me you might have come back here. Thank God we found you.' He closed the front door, lowering his voice to a whisper. 'Where is Beth?' he asked with a smile. 'Everything's gonna be all right, Cis. Everything's gonna be just wonderful.'

Cissie shifted her gaze from her brother to Tyler. 'Is that right, Mister?' she wanted to know. 'You ain't here to make Beth unhappy no more?'

'No,' he said softly, shaking his head. 'I'm not here to make her unhappy.' What could this girl know of him and Beth, and their love for each other? Yet she had been a friend to Beth when he was not, and his heart went out to her for that.

Upstairs, Beth had her daughter tucked in one arm, and her son perched on the bed, happily chatting and showing his toy train to his new sister. 'What's the babby's name?' he asked, never taking his eyes from that tiny little wonder.

'We'll have to think about that, sweetheart,' she said, giving him a hug. She was watching the door, for she had heard someone knocking downstairs and Cissie going along the passageway. There had been so much noise after that, and what with Richard chattering, she was uncertain as to who Cissie had let into the house. Thinking it must have been Moll Sutton, or maybe Lou come back, Beth returned her attention to the boy. 'What do you think we should call her?' she asked. She wished Cissie would come up. She wanted to know who had come visiting. When there was a light tap on her own door, Beth glanced down to make sure she was decent, then called, 'It's all right . . . come in.' The handle turned, the door opened, and her heart did a series of somersaults, for there he was . . . the same tall good-looking man she had never stopped loving. His smile was tender as he gazed on her, and his mop of dark hair tumbled over those beautiful green eyes that were hungry for the sight of her lovely face. 'Hello, Beth,' he said; spoken so simply, but with a world of love. 'I've come to take you home, my lovely,' he murmured, coming across the room towards her.

The shock of seeing Tyler here, in her little house, was too much for Beth. Drowned by the tide of emotion that raged through her, she couldn't speak. As he came nearer, the tears spilled from her eyes and she made a small sobbing sound that caught in the back of her throat. Biting her lip to stem the tears that threatened to overwhelm her, she was shaking her head slowly from side to side as though she thought it was all a dream . . . all a dream which could never come true. But then he was holding her, the warmth of his body pressed close to hers, his mouth soft against her face, and his familiar loving voice murmuring in her ear, telling her things she thought she would never hear. 'Oh, Beth . . . I was so sure I'd lost you for ever. I do love you so,' he whispered. She was crying now, warm wet tears flowing down her face and smudged by his kisses. She clung to him as though she would never let him go. At last, at long last, all of her prayers were answered.

Swallowing her tears, she looked up at him. 'You . . . you married,' she whispered. 'Tom Reynolds told . . .'

He put his finger over her lips. 'No,' he said. He could have told her that the only woman in his house lately was the housekeeper. His previous companion had lied when she claimed to have been expecting his child. In the end she realised, as he had always done, that a marriage between them would only be an unhappy one 'There's so much to tell,' he said. 'So much to talk about. But there'll be time enough for that . . . all the time in the world. Right now, all we need to know is that we're together, and nothing must ever part us again.' He spoke with tenderness, yet there was anger too. In her wickedness, Esther Ward had tried to part them and for a while she had succeeded, but he had Beth in his arms now and he would never again let her go. He gazed at her longingly, she looked so tired, so thin and worn. And yet he thought she had never been more beautiful; with her long chestnut-brown hair cascading over her shoulders and those large dark eyes that shimmered with tears, she seemed like a child, lost and alone. But there was a strength in her that astonished him, for she had been through so much. The awful things she had suffered, the things he had learned, only convinced him that Beth was a special breed of woman, and he loved her all the more. And so he held her close, and whispered his plans for the future, and she clung to him, silently listening, her heart soaring to the skies at his nearness. He was right. There was much to talk about, but not now. Not now, when her every nerve-ending was tingling with excitement. Not now, while he was holding her to his heart.

She had not forgotten her other joys, the girl-child clasped in her arm and her son. . .Tyler's son. . . seated beside her, his large green eyes staring up at this man who so clearly loved his mammy. 'This is your son,' she said, drawing the boy closer. For a long poignant moment Tyler gazed down at the face that was so much like his own, and he was thrilled. 'Hello, Richard,' he said. 'Cissie's told me all about you.'

'Are you my daddy?' the boy asked simply.

'I am,' replied Tyler. 'And we're going to have a lot of fun getting to know each other.' He ruffled the boy's hair. He wanted to grab him and hug him tight, but somehow he didn't think Richard was ready for that.

'Are you *my very own* daddy?' He was fascinated.

'Yes, sweetheart,' Beth laughed through her tears. 'He's your *very own* daddy.' She could feel Tyler's arms strong about her, and her world was complete.

'And can you make wooden trains like this one?' the boy asked of Tyler, holding up the train which Moll Sutton had given to him.

He smiled fondly. 'If my son wants me to make a train for him, then I promise I'll do my very best,' he said. The boy was satisfied. Climbing from the bed, he ran out of the room, calling out, 'Cissie! Cissie! I've got my very own daddy, and he's gonna make me a train!'

Laughing, Tyler turned to Beth. Looking into her eyes, his mood became quiet. Placing his fingers beneath her chin he tilted her head back and kissed her full on the mouth, turning her heart over. Afterwards she laid her head on his shoulder and told him how much she had missed him, and they remained that way for a while, quiet in their thoughts, and so very much in love.

He looked down at the newborn, gently drawing the shawl from those tiny features. 'She's beautiful,' he whispered. 'And, oh, Beth . . . she's so like you.'

'You don't mind her?'

His answer was to take the baby in his arms. 'She'll be ours,' he said softly. 'How could I not love her?' And Beth's happiness spilled over. She looked up, and there at the door was Cissie, the tears coursing down her face and her features so crumpled she looked as though she was in awful pain. 'Oh, Beth!' she cried, wringing her hands together in wonderful anguish, her voice all broken and laughing. 'Oh, Beth . . . it's just like one o' them wonderful fairy-tales that you think won't ever come true.' She burst into a fit of sobbing and, running across the room, she grabbed Beth into her arms. 'Oh, it's grand!' she laughed. 'It's right grand!' Matthew appeared at the door, and when he quietly asked of Beth, 'Can you forgive me?' she opened her arms to him, and he went to her. Soon they were all laughing and chattering, and the excitement was all too much for Cissie, who skipped round the room with Richard at her heels. Their hearts full, Tyler and Beth laughed at her antics, and Matthew cradled the baby, and they were a family at last; the only family Beth ever wanted.

For the next twenty-four hours, until Beth was strong enough to leave, the little house blossomed with happiness, and even the neighbours came to visit. 'We've been wrong,' said one. 'Right bloody cantankerous,' said another. And all was forgiven. When the carriage went away, carrying Beth and Tyler, Cissie and Matthew, and the two children, the neighbours were there to wave them off. 'God bless yer,' called Moll Sutton as they trundled out of sight. 'And don't forget ter send us invitations ter the wedding, lass.'

Less than two months later, on the last day in December, Beth and her family were dealt a sad blow, when Ben was made to pay the full penalty for the murder of Tom Reynolds. His mother was inconsolable. Crazed with grief, she became her own executioner. On the stroke of the same hour that her son was taken to the gallows, she went into his bedroom and there asked the Lord for forgiveness before putting the noose round her own neck and ending her miserable life.

Chapter Sixteen

On 4 February 1893, Tyler and Beth were married. Dressed in a simple but lovely gown of blue and white taffeta, Beth was stunningly beautiful. In a quiet voice, she exchanged her vows with the man she loved, and he stood by her side, tall and straight, adoring and proud, occasionally glancing down into her dark smiling eyes and reassuringly squeezing her hand.

They made a handsome couple as they walked between the rows of guests. So many people. With the exception of one particular character by the name of Ruby Dennings, who enjoyed being miserable, all the Larkhill women had turned out in force, some dabbing at their eyes with hankies as the happy couple walked by, some smiling broadly and some nodding their heads in approval. And there were Beth's parents; her father, that big gentle man who had come to Beth with a full and contrite heart. Beth had eagerly received him, and their reconciliation had been both tender and emotional. With a mingling of pride and humility, Richard had then introduced Beth to her mother, and together they had told their own tragic story.

Deeply moved, Beth was drawn to Elizabeth straight-away and they had spent many an hour quietly talking together, for there was so much that Beth needed to know. Elizabeth was a lovely, gentle lady, and Beth was glad that she had come to know her before it was too late. In those first moments when Beth was made to realise that Esther was not her real mother, she was deeply shocked, but then there had risen in her a stronger emotion, a deep inner instinct that somehow, she had always known she did not belong to that cruel vindictive woman. In Elizabeth's gentle company, she felt wanted at last, loved as a daughter should be loved. The feeling was unique and wonderful. At last, she was home.

Now, when Beth met Elizabeth's proud gaze, that same warm pleasure murmured through her. Their smiles intermingled and each knew the other's thoughts. Momentarily pausing, Beth reached out to wrap her fingers over Elizabeth's pale slender hand. Surprised and delighted by the loving gesture, Elizabeth looked up, her eyes sparkling with tears of joy. Beth stooped to kiss her mother's face. 'I love you,' she whispered. And though she gave thanks for Elizabeth having been returned to her, Beth would never know how much those words meant to that dear woman.

Standing protectively beside Elizabeth was Tilly Mulliver, ever devoted to her mistress but in love with Richard Ward, and he with her. Beth had sensed the love between them, yet, like Tilly herself, understood how this precious time must be shared by her parents.

As they emerged into the crisp morning sunlight, Tyler turned to Beth, his arm round her and his head bent to hers. 'Happy, sweetheart?' he asked.

'More than you'll ever know,' she told him in a whisper. And then they were surrounded by many well-wishers; including Matthew with his pretty new lady-friend, who lived in Larkhill. These two were hopeful that they might even get wed themselves and maybe live in one of the new places which Matthew and a local developer were planning to build down Larkhill. Then there was Cissie, who had stood beside Beth at the altar, and who looked extremely fetching in a 'posh' gown which she had insisted on choosing herself, a pink extravaganza of huge bows and endless ribbons, and bright yellow silk daisies along the hem. All of Beth's attempts to persuade her into something quieter were greeted by cries of, 'I ain't never had a chance to be the bride's maid . . . an' I might never get a chance agin, so I'm mekking the best of it!' Realising that it was as much Cissie's day as it was hers, Beth had gone along with her wishes. And, truth be told, the dress really did look as though it was made for her, and everyone said so.

'Don't you worry about the children,' Tilly Mulliver told Beth. 'Richard and little Maisie will be in very good hands with me and their grandparents.'

Richard Ward came forward to kiss Beth on the forehead, a contented smile on his kindly face. 'The young 'uns will be just fine,' he reassured her. 'Between Elizabeth and Tilly, they'll be spoilt for choice. Then there's Cissie and Matthew staying with us. We'll none of us be short of company, sweetheart.' For her own good reasons, Elizabeth had refused him when he'd offered to marry her; perhaps she thought it was too late, or perhaps she knew how he and Tilly felt about each other. Elizabeth never gave her reason. She was content enough just for him to stay at the house, to have him close for as long as possible.

Looking at her father now, Beth wondered if he would ever really get over losing his only son in such a way, though he had told her: 'I lost Ben many years ago. He was always his mother's boy.' As for Beth herself, she had done her grieving and now she must look to the future.

It was time to go. 'Look after your baby sister,' Tyler told his son, bending to clasp his small shoulders. 'A week will go quickly and then Mammy'll be home again.'

'I will,' Richard declared, flinging his arms round

477

Tyler's neck and hugging him tight. Turning his attention to Beth, he clung to her, promising. 'And I'll look after Cissie and all, because she's the one who gets into trouble, Mammy.' Grinning, he glanced at Cissie then ran away, screeching and hollering with delight when she promptly chased after him.

Taking her small daughter in her arms, Beth held the tiny face close to hers. 'Be a good girl, Maisie,' she whispered. There was no other name she could have called the girl-child. Then, handing the tiny bundle back to Tilly, she looked into that dear lady's quiet eyes and in a low murmur, said, 'You're a good woman, Tilly. I know you don't begrudge them this time together. But your turn will come.'

Tilly was surprised at Beth's words, for she truly believed that no one knew of her love for Richard. Smiling gently, she whispered, 'Bless you, Beth . . . you know I love them both.'

'I know,' Beth went to embrace Elizabeth. 'Keep well, darling,' she said.

'God go with you, Beth.' Elizabeth held out her hand for Richard to hold, and he did so with great tenderness, his soft brown eyes looking to Tilly. Knowing how she loved him, he was content to wait. Like Beth, he knew their time would come, and it was right that it should be so.

When the farewells were said and the carriage pulled away, Tyler and Beth strained their necks to wave to the well-wishers, until they were only specks in the distance. 'At last, Mrs Blacklock,' he smiled teasingly, 'I have you all to myself.'

Beth's answer was to reach up, wind her arms round his neck and blatantly kiss him, content afterwards to nestle in his arms, the warm manly smell of him overwhelming her senses. Tyler had rented a cottage in Dorset. It would be Heaven on earth, he told her.

She shifted in his arms and gazed up into his face, such a strong, handsome face. 'Heaven on earth,' he had said. That was exactly how she felt; as though she was in Heaven on earth. From the corner of her eye she peeped out of the carriage window at the quiet sky, and a prayer of gratitude murmured in her joyous heart.

In her mind's eye she saw Maisie, arm in arm with her fellow and her mischievous grin as broad and warm as ever. Beth smiled to herself. It would be nice to think that Maisie, also, had found her own little Heaven.

Chapter One

'I love you more than life itself. You know that, don't you, child?' Jessica's soft brown eyes swam with tears as she gazed at her daughter's face. Then, when the long guarded secrets returned to haunt her, she turned away, her voice falling to the softest whisper. 'But if you only knew . . . I don't think you could find it in your heart to forgive me.' She closed her eyes but still the images persisted, dark disturbing images of her own brother. With all her heart she prayed he had come to be a better man, for there was nowhere else for Phoebe to go.

Phoebe came forward from the foot of the bed, the ready smile on her face belying her anxiety. 'Oh, Mam! What is it? What's troubling you?' She had heard her mother's murmured words; the same words, always the same. Not for one minute did Phoebe believe her capable of committing even the smallest sin, yet there was no denying that Jessica Mulligan was deeply troubled. When her mother gave no answer, but looked at her with pleading eyes, Phoebe told her gently, 'You don't have to tell me how much you love me, sweetheart. *I know* . . . because don't I love you in the very same way?' Her voice trembled with emotion, but she must not be drawn into that long trek down memory lane. There were things there she did not understand. Things that seemed to haunt her mother. Lurking doubts that raised so many questions. Questions that were never answered.

Phoebe had come softly into the room, hoping that at long last her mother might be sleeping. She was both astonished and anxious to see her wide awake. She seated herself on the bed, entwining her long strong fingers around the thin pale hand, willing her own warmth into it. 'Mam, you know what the doctor said,' she gently chided. 'You must rest. How can you expect to get well if you don't do what he tells you?' She shook her head and sighed aloud. 'What will I do with you, eh?' she demanded with a forced smile; her love was plain to see in her brown eyes as they roved that small familiar face and her heart cried out at the injustice. 'Will you rest now, sweetheart,' she implored. 'Please, Mam. For me, eh?'

Sorry that Phoebe had heard her fearful whisper, and choosing not to mind the girl's plea, Jessica told her, 'You've been such a joy to me, child.' She made a small sound that might have been a chuckle but to the watching girl sounded more like a sob.

'Oh, Mam!' Phoebe was remembering the times when she had caused her mother a deal of heartache. 'I'm so sorry.' Her voice broke with emotion as she dipped her head in shame. 'I wish I could have been a better daughter,' she said regretfully.

'No, child.' The woman smiled, a warm loving smile that betrayed her deep love for the girl. Reaching up, she stroked the rich auburn tresses that cascaded over Phoebe's shoulders. 'We might each have our regrets, but thank God, we've always had each other.' She rested her loving gaze on the girl. She wished she could have given so much more, but when Phoebe's father had died, it was often a struggle just to survive. If she'd had the means she would have dressed this lovely child in the finest clothes. Instead Phoebe's wardrobe consisted of two good dresses – one was a pretty cream thing which she'd made for her daughter some time ago, and the other the one she had on now, a brown shapeless shift with a high neck and three-quarter sleeves. It wasn't much but Phoebe never complained. She made the best of what was given her, and her effervescent beautys hone through.

'Look at me, Phoebe,' Jessica said now. When she looked up her mother said, 'I won't deny there have been times when you've driven me to distraction, but I don't blame you, child. And you mustn't blame yourself.'

Jessica fell silent then, looking into those intense brown eyes and remembering how it had been. Her daughter was her reason for living. Oh, it was true that she'd caused a deal of heartache, that she'd drifted from one place to another since leaving school . . . a sweeper in the mill, assistant to the parish clerk, and now this last position behind the counter at the local paper shop. Only two weeks ago she'd been asked to leave because of a dispute with a customer. There were times when Phoebe was difficult. But the fault wasn't hers because she was a good girl at heart, kind and warm, if headstrong and impossible at times. Jessica laid the blame for Phoebe's restless spirit at the door of her late husband. He had provided for them all those years, it was true, but he couldn't forget how Jessica had come to him. And after his sons died, he could never forgive. It seemed like only yesterday that she had fled from Blackburn, from the man she truly loved. Oh, she had also come to love the man she married, but he had been guilty of one unforgivable thing and that was his resentment of Phoebe.

'It isn't you who should be sorry,' Jessica murmured now as she affectionately pressed the girl's hand to her face, 'Believe me, sweetheart, you've nothing to be sorry for.' Shifting her glance to the windows, she whispered, 'Open the curtains, child. Let the sunlight fill the room.' She tightened her two hands over Phoebe's arm and held it in a vice-like grip, her eyes hardening. 'There's something I must tell you,' she said harshly, glancing furtively towards the door as though afraid she might be overheard. 'Something I should have told you long ago.'

Exhausted by the emotion that surged through her, she relaxed her hold on the girl. Suddenly her face was lit with the most wonderful of smiles; at last she would be rid of her burden, rid of this dreadful thing that had haunted her for too long. The smile faded when she reminded herself that she was only passing that burden on to Phoebe. Suddenly she was torn with doubts. Did she have the right to shift her guilt on to this child who had filled her life with delight? She gazed a moment longer on the girl's lovely face, a face that had always been especially beautiful with its small perfect features and bold fiery eyes that were the golden brown colour of autumn. Whenever Jessica thought of Phoebe, she always thought of those handsome laughing eyes. But they were not laughing now. Not now nor at any time during these past weeks.

'Open the curtains, sweetheart,' Jessica urged again. 'So I can see your eyes brightened by the sunshine.' She smiled, and there was so much love there the girl's heart broke to see it. When Phoebe stayed a moment longer, searching her mother's gaze with anxious eyes and wondering with bitterness why things could not have been different, Jessica knew in her heart that she could never tell her. Suddenly she felt her time was close. 'Hurry,' she said, at the same time drawing her hand from Phoebe's and casting her eyes once more towards the window. 'The daylight will be gone so quickly.'

The girl rose from the bed and walked to the window, her mother following her every move. When suddenly the daylight spilled into the room, Jessica sighed deep within herself. She prayed that Phoebe would find her way on the rough road ahead. Yet she dared not hope for too much because only she and the good Lord knew how evil her brother was. 'I love you,' she murmured, her arms reaching out. She felt wonderfully elated, free at last.

A sensation of glory. An eerie silence. And then only the desperate sound of a girl crying for the one she had loved above all others. Yet all her tears could not bring her mother back.

Chapter Two

'Stop tormenting yourself, Phoebe. It won't do no good to let your imagination run away with you.'

The young woman with the plain face and bobbed fair hair shook her head in frustration. After a moment, she stretched her short fat legs and touched the floor with her toes, bringing the wooden rocking-chair to a halt. Widening her eyes until they resembled round blue marbles, she stared hard at Phoebe, but there was genuine affection in her voice when she attempted to allay her friend's fears.

'There was nothing so mysterious about what were playing on yer mam's mind,' she said reassuringly. 'You only have to read the letter to see what were troubling the poor soul.'

Clambering out of the chair, she reached up to the mantelpiece and picked up the long brown envelope which Phoebe had earlier propped against a metal statuette of a prancing horse. Returning to her chair, she perched herself on the edge, keeping her feet firmly on the ground so as to stop the rockers from tipping backwards.

'We'd best read the letter again,' she said, at the same time withdrawing it from the envelope and carefully unfolding it. Holding the opened document at arm's length, she screwed up her eyes so tightly that they almost disappeared in the fleshy folds of her face.

My dearest daughter,

By the time you read this letter I will have left you. That is my greatest regret for I have no fear of dying, only of leaving you behind. But I want you to know that you are not alone in the world. I pray you will forgive me for depriving you of the truth all these years. So many times I have begun to confide in you, and each time my courage has failed me. Even now, I find it so very hard.

I have an older brother, your Uncle Edward. Unfortunately he is not the most generous of men, nor the most understanding. Edward Dickens is formidable but he has a powerful sense of duty and there are those who say he is a man of conscience. I have no choice but to leave you in his charge, and to ask God that you will somehow find contentment.

Enclosed is his recent reply to my letter. In it you will find his address, together with certain instructions. Deliver yourself into his hands as soon as you are able. He will be expecting you.

I hesitate to say this but I must or I will not rest. *Don't let him break you, child.* He will try, I know. But, thank God, you are strong in heart and have a spirit as determined as his.

God go with you, my darling, and have faith. Love is a powerful and wonderful thing, but it can bring its own heartache. No sacrifice is ever too great. Remember that always. And in spite of what you may discover, remember too that my love for you never wavered.

> Your devoted mother,
> Jessica Mulligan

Lowering the letter to her lap, Dora looked across at her friend. Phoebe's head was bowed, her wild auburn hair tumbling over her forehead and hiding sad brown eyes that gazed downwards, tears spilling over and her heart aching as though it would break. As she stared into the empty firegrate, the iron bars there seemed to Phoebe like the bars of a prison.

'And you think that was all?' she asked in a small broken voice. 'You really think that was what my mother meant to confide in me? She just wanted to tell me about the letters? To explain about this man, this Edward Dickens?' She deliberately kept her gaze averted.

'Your uncle,' Dora corrected. 'Well, o'course that were all! Don't you see, Phoebe? You mam were feeling guilty because she never told you about your uncle or his family. Happen she thought you might not forgive such a thing. You told me yourself how your mam asked "Could you ever forgive me?" Like I said, Phoebe, it were playing on her mind. All these years you thought you didn't have another soul in the whole world, and now suddenly you find out you've got an uncle. And who knows? Maybe this uncle of yours has got children too . . . cousins you never knew about. You could have played and grown up with them. When I first came to live in this street, I remember you telling me how lonely you were.'

'But why didn't she tell me?' Phoebe's heart was heavy. 'Not that I ain't forgiven her, Dora, because I have. I know me mam must have had her reasons.' She had tried so hard to understand.

'There might be any number of reasons why she didn't tell you,' Dora said wisely. 'Sometimes a family fall out among themselves and the bitterness stays for years. Sometimes it keeps them apart for ever. Whatever happened all them years ago was between your mam and your Uncle Edward. There's no use worrying over it, is there, eh? Your uncle's accepted you back into the fold, and that at least is something to be thankful for. Your, mam and this brother made their peace before it was too late, and now you're not alone any more. That's all that matters, isn't it?' Dora was eager to reassure her. Although she was a few years older, she had been Phoebe's one and only friend.

None of the other children in the street was allowed to play with Phoebe on account of her father being an assistant at the workhouse mortuary. 'He smells of death,' the parents would say, their two great fears in life being first the workhouse and then the mortuary. And so, until Widow Little came to live next-door with her daughter Dora, Phoebe had never known what it was to have a friend of her own age. Her mother, though, had always been especially close to Phoebe; had adored the girl. Her father was a private, often morose man who rarely spoke and showed neither emotion nor affection.

Phoebe's mother always defended him: 'Your father never got over the loss of his two sons.' One boy was stillborn, and the other was taken by pneumonia when he was only an infant. She never confessed to her daughter how Mr Mulligan would secretly have preferred Phoebe to have died rather than be robbed of his sons. His bitterness was complete when Mrs Mulligan failed to bear him any more children. But he was a good man at heart and had faithfully provided for his family as a man should. His wife understood his sorrow and forgave him. But there was always a distance between them. And an even greater distance between him and Phoebe.

'Oh, Dora, you're such a friend.' Phoebe's brown eyes were bright with tears. Both her parents were gone and but for Dora she had no one. This man who was her uncle was just a stranger. Far from giving her comfort, her mother's letter had only made her uneasy. She had no one to turn to but Dora and thanked God for that kindly creature. Phoebe looked at her friend now, her heart warmed by the sight of that plain homely face and the affection there. 'Whatever would I do without you?' she asked softly, reaching out to hold a plump dimpled hand. She and Dora had grown up together. Through that time they had shared each other's most secret thoughts and Phoebe had come to love her neighbour as she might a sister.

'Away with you!' Dora laughed, slapping her podgy hand over Phoebe's slim fingers before falling backwards in the chair and beginning to rock herself in some agitation. 'You'll do well enough without me, Phoebe Mulligan,' she declared. 'And you'll cope just fine with your new life. What!' She chuckled and winked at Phoebe. That uncle of yours won't know what's hit him. "Formidable" or not, he'll bless the day you came into his house. How could he help but love you, eh?'

Dora sincerely hoped that she was proved right and Phoebe would win her uncle's affection. Lord only knew how desperately the girl had craved the love of her father. But when that love wasn't given, she had grown bold and defiant, pretending it didn't matter. Only Phoebe's mother and Dora suspected how the girl's proud wilful ways disguised deeper, more heartfelt feelings.

Seven years ago when she was only ten years old, her father had been trampled beneath a carriage and four. Now, at the tender age of seventeen, she was an orphan. Dora looked at her, thinking again how beautiful Phoebe was, a slim vibrant creature full of life and brimming with love. Yet for all that she seemed destined to suffer a turbulent life. Like Jessica Dora hoped that Phoebe would find a place in her uncle's household, but knew only too well that if she was in her friend's place she would be suffering nightmares. All the same, knowing that Phoebe was looking to her for reassurance, she felt obliged to hide her real feelings. There was nothing else she could do; nothing else Phoebe could do, except to follow her mother's instructions. She had no other living relative, no money, and soon the men would be here with the cart to empty the house. The landlord would arrive for the house keys and Phoebe would be sent on her way from her familiar and beloved home in Bury to a place that might as well be on the other side of the world. To the faint-hearted Dora, the prospect of living with an unknown relative was daunting and terrifying. She had been secretly frightened by Jessica Mulligan's warning to her daughter: 'Don't let him break you, child . . . for I know he will try.'

Suddenly, and partly to reassure herself as well as Phoebe, Dora blurted out, 'You're not to worry, d'you hear, Phoebe Mulligan? Things will turn out for the best, I'm sure.'

Phoebe raised her face to the ceiling, her white even teeth biting nervously into her bottom lip as she stared trancelike at the dark smoky patches on the wall above the fireplace. After a while she lowered her gaze, her striking brown eyes searching deep into Dora's. She had detected that note of nervousness in her friend's voice and felt compelled to ask, 'Edward Dickens will be expecting to make a lady of me, won't he, Dora? It's no use him trying to make me something I ain't!'

She sighed deep inside herself; there was so much anger in her, so much frustration that often found outlet in wild, wilful behaviour. And judging by Edward Dickens' reply to her mother's letter, he had been told of his niece's lack of self-discipline. Phoebe had been surprised that her mother should have betrayed her in that way but, on reflection, had come to realise that it was done in good faith. It was only right that this man, this stranger, should know what he was letting himself in for. Either he wanted her or he didn't. And if he didn't, then it was best all round if she knew now. However, the fact that he did want her told Phoebe two things . . . firstly, Edward Dickens was indeed 'a man with a powerful sense of duty' who saw his niece as a responsibility he must accept. Secondly, and much worse in Phoebe's thinking, he had a mind to mend her of her rebellious nature, to mould her into the kind of young lady he would permit to reside under his roof. It was this supposition that gave her sleepless nights. More than once in these past two weeks she had thought about running away, but then she realised how futile that would be for she had nowhere to run to, and besides, her uncle sounded like the sort of man who would hunt her down.

'You mustn't talk like that, Phoebe,' Dora reprimanded. 'You're as much a lady as anyone else.' She suddenly laughed, saying, 'All the same, I reckon they won't know what's hit 'em!'

Though Dora believed that Phoebe's good honest character must win her uncle over in time, she reflected again on Edward Dickens' message, a cold unfeeling letter which to her mind, betrayed too much of the man himself. 'I wish it were possible for you to come here and live,' she told her friend. 'There's nothing I'd like better, you know that, don't you? But there's no room, what with Judd having to sleep in the front parlour, and me and our dad taking the only two bedrooms.' She sighed and suddenly looked old though she was not yet twenty-one. 'I have to be on hand for our dad in case he calls out in the night,' she explained. 'So I can't have you here, gal, more's the pity.'

Phoebe was stricken with guilt, quick to assure her, 'You're not to worry about me. I ain't your problem, and besides you've got your hands full what with your dad being bedridden an' all. I'll be all right, you'll see.'

'Don't forget I've got our Judd to help me, although more often than not he's all worked out when he gets home from the mines. By the time he's had his meal and a strip wash, I've already seen to our dad and there's nothing Judd can do anyway . . . apart from spending part of his evening with the old fella, which he allus does,' she said warmly. 'I'm lucky to have such a fine brother.'

She eyed Phoebe curiously. 'Our Judd's allus had a soft spot for you, you know that, don't you?'

When Phoebe went a soft shade of pink and seemed uncomfortable beneath her gaze, Dora laughed. 'Oh, tek no notice! What am I thinking of?' Her mood became serious as she added, 'All the same, Phoebe, if there was a way we could take you in with us, you'd be more than welcome.'

'Bless you for that.' Phoebe knew what a heavy burden Dora suffered; her mam had run off some years before when Dora's dad had been struck down with a crippling affliction. He was a short-tempered, demanding fellow who gave her little peace. And as she had pointed out, although her older brother Judd was a great comfort to her, his main task was providing for the family; a responsibility which he shouldered admirably.

'I'd best be off.' Dora clambered out of the rocking-chair. 'He'll be awake soon and wanting his food.' She hurried across the parlour, pausing just once to tell Phoebe, 'I'll be back soon as ever I can.' When Phoebe nodded she gave a small satisfied grunt and then was gone.

The silence was unbearable. Phoebe leaned back in the chair that had been her father's, her mind filled with memories of her mother: of the way she sang as she went about her work, of the manner in which she would sit opposite Phoebe at the big oak table when they would talk long into the night – women's talk, aimless chatter that was a delight to them both. Never once had Jessica Mulligan revealed the existence of her brother Edward, and all of Phoebe's questions concerning her mother's family were never really answered.

image of Edward Dickens. It was not a pleasant one. The prospect of living in his house, under his regime, filled her with dread.

Replacing the letters in the envelope Phoebe clutched it in her fist. Heaving a deep sigh, she stood before the mantelpiece thoughtfully peering into the mirror above. 'There's no use fighting it,' she told the face looking back at her. 'These are the cards you've been dealt, Phoebe Mulligan. Play them with the courage your mother gave you. And don't ever shame her.'

The strong classic features stared back, proud and determined. For one fleeting moment the almond brown eyes grew darker, still scarred with grief. All around her the house was unbearably empty, curiously still and bitterly cold. She shivered, hugging her slender arms around her and leaning forward to touch her forehead against the mantelpiece.

'Oh, Mam! Mam!' Her voice broke on a sob. She had tried so hard not to cry but she missed the busy familiar figure who had been the heart and soul of her existence. She craved the sound of that gentle voice, and knowing that she would never hear it again was almost more than she could bear. 'I won't let you down, Mam,' she murmured, 'I promise . . . I'll make you proud of me.'

If you would like to find out what lies in store for Phoebe, in her new life with her uncle Edward, the hardback of JESSICA'S GIRL is available from all major bookshops and is priced £15.99.

More Enthralling Fiction from Headline:

JOSEPHINE COX

LET LOOSE THE TIGERS

In the grand tradition of Catherine Cookson

'A classic is born'
LANCASHIRE EVENING TELEGRAPH

Queenie Bedford fled her native Blackburn and the bitter knowledge that she and Rick Marsden, the man she loved, could never marry. But in 1965 she returned north again to stand by her friend Sheila Thorogood, imprisoned for running a brothel with her mother Maisie. Though Rick had vowed to find her, Queenie took care that he should not know of her whereabouts.

The magnificent Edwardian house in Blackpool was sadly neglected – but Queenie moved in with the ailing Maisie, and set about transforming it into a sparklingly clean, highly respectable guesthouse. Meanwhile, on one of her visits to Sheila, Queenie was to meet the frail and confused Hannah Jason, locked away years ago for murder, and desperate for news of her long-lost son.

As Rick continued his dogged search for Queenie, she set out to find Hannah's son. But both their enquiries threatened to unlock the cage where crucial secrets had long been held captive.

Don't miss Josephine Cox's other sagas of North Country life: HER FATHER'S SINS, WHISTLEDOWN WOMAN, ANGELS CRY SOMETIMES, TAKE THIS WOMAN, OUTCAST, ALLEY URCHIN and VAGABONDS all available from Headline.

FICTION/SAGA   0 7472 4078 7

More Enthralling Fiction from Headline:

JOSEPHINE COX

HER FATHER'S SINS

In the grand tradition of Catherine Cookson

'A classic is born'
LANCASHIRE EVENING TELEGRAPH

Queenie seemed born to suffer. Her Mam died giving birth to her, her drunken father George Kenney ignored her unless he was cursing her, and only beloved Auntie Biddy provided an anchor for the little girl. Growing up in post-war Blackburn, life could be tough when Biddy had to take in washing to make ends meet – at a time when the washing machine began to gain popularity. After Auntie Biddy's death there was only Queenie to care for the home and to earn money, and no one to protect her from the father who blamed his daughter for her mother's death.

But Queenie was resilient. And in spite of hardship, she grew up tall and strikingly beautiful with her deep grey eyes and her abundant honey-coloured hair. Love, in the shape of Rick Marsden, might have released her from the burden of the drink-sodden George. But the sins of the fathers would not be easily forgotten...

**Don't miss Josephine Cox's other sagas of North Country life:
LET LOOSE THE TIGERS, WHISTLEDOWN WOMAN, ANGELS
CRY SOMETIMES, TAKE THIS WOMAN, OUTCAST, ALLEY
URCHIN and VAGABONDS all available from Headline.**

FICTION/SAGA   0 7472 4077 9

A selection of bestsellers
from Headline

LONDON'S CHILD	Philip Boast	£5.99 □
THE GIRL FROM COTTON LANE	Harry Bowling	£5.99 □
THE HERRON HERITAGE	Janice Young Brooks	£4.99 □
DANGEROUS LADY	Martina Cole	£4.99 □
VAGABONDS	Josephine Cox	£4.99 □
STAR QUALITY	Pamela Evans	£4.99 □
MARY MADDISON	Sheila Jansen	£4.99 □
CANNONBERRY CHASE	Roberta Latow	£5.99 □
THERE IS A SEASON	Elizabeth Murphy	£4.99 □
THE PALACE AFFAIR	Una-Mary Parker	£4.99 □
BLESSINGS AND SORROWS	Christine Thomas	£4.99 □
WYCHWOOD	E V Thompson	£4.99 □
HALLMARK	Elizabeth Walker	£5.99 □
AN IMPOSSIBLE DREAM	Elizabeth Warne	£5.99 □
POLLY OF PENN'S PLACE	Dee Williams	£4.99 □

All Headline books are available at your local bookshop or newsagent, or can be ordered direct from the publisher. Just tick the titles you want and fill in the form below. Prices and availability subject to change without notice.

Headline Book Publishing PLC, Cash Sales Department, Bookpoint, 39 Milton Park, Abingdon, OXON, OX14 4TD, UK. If you have a credit card you may order by telephone — 0235 831700.

Please enclose a cheque or postal order to the value of the cover price and allow the following for postage and packing:
UK & BFPO: £1.00 for the first book, 50p for the second book and 30p for each additional book ordered up to a maximum charge of £3.00.
OVERSEAS & EIRE: £2.00 for the first book, £1.00 for the second book and 50p for each additional book.

Name ....

Address ....

....

....

If you would prefer to pay by credit card, please complete:
Please debit my Visa/Access/Diner's Card/American Express (delete as applicable) card no:

Signature ....Expiry Date ....